Lady Whistledown Strikes Back

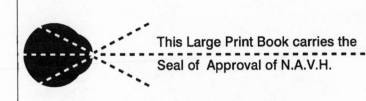

This Large Print Book carries the
Seal of Approval of N.A.V.H.

Lady Whistledown Strikes Back

Julia Quinn,
Suzanne Enoch,
Karen Hawkins,
Mia Ryan

WHEELER PUBLISHING

Published in 2004 by arrangement with Avon Books, an imprint of HarperCollins Publishers, Inc.

Wheeler Large Print Hardcover.

The text of this Large Print edition is unabridged.
Other aspects of the book may vary from the original edition.

Set in 16 pt. Plantin by Minnie B. Raven.

Printed in the United States on permanent paper.

Library of Congress Cataloging-in-Publication Data

Lady Whistledown strikes back / Julia Quinn . . . [et al.].
    Other authors: Quinn, Julia.
        p. cm.
    Published: Waterville, ME : Wheeler Pub., 2004.
    ISBN 1-58724-740-2 (lg. print : hc : alk. paper)
    Subjects: 1. Love stories, American.   2. Historical fiction, American.   3. London (England) — Fiction.
4. Large type books.   I. Title.
PS648.L6L35 2004
    813′.08508—dc22   2004049643

Lady Whistledown *Strikes Back*

National Association for Visually Handicapped
------------------------- serving the partially seeing

As the Founder/CEO of NAVH, the only national health agency solely devoted to those who, although not totally blind, have an eye disease which could lead to serious visual impairment, I am pleased to recognize Thorndike Press★ as one of the leading publishers in the large print field.

Founded in 1954 in San Francisco to prepare large print textbooks for partially seeing children, NAVH became the pioneer and standard setting agency in the preparation of large type.

Today, those publishers who meet our standards carry the prestigious "Seal of Approval" indicating high quality large print. We are delighted that Thorndike Press is one of the publishers whose titles meet these standards. We are also pleased to recognize the significant contribution Thorndike Press is making in this important and growing field.

Lorraine H. Marchi, L.H.D.
Founder/CEO
NAVH

★ Thorndike Press encompasses the following imprints: Thorndike, Wheeler, Walker and Large Print Press.

Contents

*All Lady Whistledown columns written by
Julia Quinn*

The First Kiss

Julia Quinn

For readers everywhere,
who loved Lady W too much to let her go.

And also for Paul,
even though he took it as a personal victory
that I managed to involve Star Wars
in the title of this book.

Chapter 1

This week's most coveted invitation appears to be Lady Neeley's upcoming dinner party, to be held Tuesday evening. The guest list is not long, nor is it remarkably exclusive, but tales have spread of last year's dinner party, or, to be more specific, of the menu, and all London (and most especially those of greater girth) are eager to partake.

This Author was not gifted with an invitation and therefore must suffer at home with a jug of wine, a loaf of bread, and this column, but alas, do not feel pity, Dear Reader. Unlike those attending the upcoming gustatory spectacle, This Author does not have to listen to Lady Neeley!

Lady Whistledown's Society Papers, 27 May 1816

Tillie Howard supposed that the night could get worse, but in all truth, she couldn't imagine how.

She hadn't wanted to attend Lady Neeley's dinner party, but her parents had insisted, and so here she was, trying to ignore the fact that her hostess — the occasionally-feared, occasionally-mocked Lady Neeley — had a voice rather like fingernails on slate.

Tillie was also trying to ignore the rumblings of her stomach, which had expected nourishment at least an hour earlier. The invitation had said seven in the evening, and so Tillie and her parents, the Earl and Countess of Canby, had arrived promptly at half past the hour, with the expectation of being led into supper at eight. But here it was, almost nine, with no sign that Lady Neeley intended to forgo talking for eating anytime soon.

But what Tillie was *most* trying to ignore, what she in fact would have fled the room to avoid, had she been able to figure out a way to do so without causing a scene, was the man standing next to her.

"Jolly fellow, he was," boomed Robert Dunlop, with that joviality that comes from having consumed just a hair more wine than one ought. "Always ready for a spot of fun."

Tillie smiled tightly. He was speaking of her brother Harry, who had died nearly one year earlier, on the battlefield at Waterloo. When she and Mr. Dunlop had been introduced, she'd been excited to meet him. She'd loved Harry desperately and missed him with a fierceness that sometimes took her breath away. And she'd thought that it would be wonderful to hear stories of his last days from one of his comrades in arms.

Except Robert Dunlop was not telling her what she wanted to hear.

"Talked about you all the time," he continued, even though he'd already said as much ten minutes earlier. " 'Cept . . ."

Tillie did nothing but blink, not wanting to encourage further elucidation. This couldn't end well.

Mr. Dunlop squinted at her. " 'Cept he always described you as all elbows and knees and with crooked braids."

Tillie gently touched her hand to her expertly coifed chignon. She couldn't help it. "When Harry left for the Continent, I *did* have crooked braids," she said, deciding that her elbows and knees needed no further discussion.

"He loved you a great deal," Mr. Dunlop said. His voice was surprisingly soft and thoughtful, enough to command Tillie's full attention. Maybe she shouldn't be so quick to judge. Robert Dunlop *meant* well. He was certainly good at heart, and rather handsome, cutting quite a dashing figure in his military uniform. Harry had always written of him with affection, and even now, Tillie was having trouble thinking of him as anything other than "Robbie." Maybe there was a little more to him. Maybe it was the wine. Maybe . . .

13

"Spoke of you glowingly. Glowingly," Robbie repeated, presumably for extra emphasis.

Tillie just nodded. She missed Harry, even if she was coming to realize that he had informed approximately one thousand men that she was a skinny gawk.

Robbie nodded. "Said you were the best of females, if one could look beneath the freckles."

Tillie started scouting the exits, searching for an escape. Surely she could fake a torn hem, or a horrible chest cough.

Robbie leaned in to look at her freckles.

Or death. Her thespian demise would surely end up as the lead story in tomorrow's *Whistledown*, but Tillie was just about ready to give it a go. It had to be better than *this*.

"Told us all he despaired of you ever getting married," Robbie said, nodding in a most friendly manner. "Always reminded us that you had a bang-up dowry."

That was it. Her brother had been using his time on the battlefield to beg men to marry her, using her dowry (as opposed to her looks, or heaven forbid, her heart) as the primary draw.

It was just like Harry to go and die before she could kill him for this.

"I need to go," she blurted out.

Robbie looked around. "Where?"

Anywhere.

"Out," Tillie said, hoping that would be explanation enough.

Robbie's brow knit in a confused manner as he followed her gaze to the door. "Oh," he said. "Well, I suppose. . . . There you are!"

Tillie turned around to see who had managed to pull Robbie's attention off of her. A tall gentleman wearing the same uniform as Robbie was walking toward them. Except, unlike Robbie, he looked . . .

Dangerous.

His hair was dark, honey blond, and his eyes were — well, she couldn't possibly tell what color they were from three yards away, but it didn't really matter because the rest of him was enough to make any young lady weak in the legs. His shoulders were broad, his posture was perfect, and his face looked as if it ought to be carved in marble.

"Thompson," Robbie said. "Dashed good to see you."

Thompson, Tillie thought, mentally nodding. It must be Peter Thompson, Harry's closest friend. Harry had mentioned him in almost every missive, but clearly he'd never actually *described* him, or Tillie would have been prepared for this Greek god standing before her. Of course, if Harry had described him, he would have just shrugged and said something like, "Regular-looking fellow, I suppose."

Men never paid attention to details.

15

"D'you know Lady Mathilda?" Robbie said to Peter.

"Tillie," he murmured, taking her proffered hand and kissing it. "Forgive me. I shouldn't be so familiar, but Harry always called you such."

"It's all right," Tillie said, giving her head the tiniest of shakes. "It's been rather difficult not to call Mr. Dunlop Robbie."

"Oh, you should," Robbie said affably. "Everybody does."

"Harry wrote of us, then?" Peter inquired.

"All the time."

"He was very fond of you," Peter said. "He spoke of you often."

Tillie winced. "Yes, so Robbie has been telling me."

"Didn't want her to think Harry hadn't been thinking of her," Robbie explained. "Oh, look, there's my mother."

Both Tillie and Peter looked at him in surprise at the sudden change of subject.

"I'd better hide," he mumbled, then took up residence behind a potted plant.

"She'll find him," Peter said, a wry smile glancing across his lips.

"Mothers always do," Tillie agreed.

Silence fell across the conversation, and Tillie almost wished that Robbie would come back and fill the gap with his friendly, if slightly inane, chatter. She didn't know what to say to Peter Thompson, what to do in his

16

presence. And she couldn't stop wondering — a pox on her brother's surely laughing soul — if he was thinking of her dowry, and the size thereof, and of the many times Harry had trotted it out as her most shining attribute.

But then he said something completely un-expected.

"I recognized you the moment I walked in."

Tillie blinked in surprise. "You did?"

His eyes, which she now realized were a mesmerizing shade of gray-blue, watched her with an intensity that made her want to squirm. "Harry described you well."

"No crooked braids," she said, unable to keep the tinge of sarcasm out of her voice.

Peter chuckled at that. "Robbie's been telling tales, I see."

"Quite a few, actually."

"Don't pay him any mind. We all talked about our sisters, and I'm quite certain we all described you as you were when you were twelve."

Tillie decided then and there that there was no reason to inform him that Harry's de-scription had fit her to a much later age. While all her friends had been growing and changing, and requiring new, more womanly clothing, Tillie's shape had remained deter-minedly childish until her sixteenth year. Even now, she was boyishly slender, but she did have a few curves, and Tillie was thrilled with each and every one of them.

She was nineteen now, almost twenty, and by God she was no longer "all elbows and knees." And never would be again.

"How did you recognize me?" Tillie ask.

Peter smiled. "Can't you guess?"

The hair. The wretched Howard hair. It didn't matter if her crooked braids had made way for a sleek chignon. She and Harry and their elder brother William all possessed the infamous red Howard hair. It wasn't strawberry blond, and it wasn't titian. It was red, or orange, really, a bright copper that Tillie was quite sure had caused more than one person to squint and look away in the sunlight. Somehow their father had escaped the curse, but it had returned with a vengeance on his children.

"It's more than that," Peter said, not even needing her to say the words to know what she was thinking. "You look a great deal like him. Your mouth, I think. The shape of your face."

And he said it with such quiet intensity, with such a controlled swell of emotion, that Tillie knew that he had loved Harry, too, that he missed him almost as much as she did. And it made her want to cry.

"I —" But she couldn't get it out. Her voice broke, and to her horror, she felt herself sniffle and gasp. It wasn't ladylike, and it

18

wasn't delicate; it was a desperate attempt to keep from sobbing in public.

Peter saw it, too. He took her elbow and expertly maneuvered her so that her back was to the crowd, and then he pulled out his handkerchief and handed it to her.

"Thank you," she said, dabbing at her eyes. "I'm sorry. I don't know what came over me."

Grief, he thought, but he didn't say it. No need to state the obvious. They both missed Harry. Everyone did.

"What brings you to Lady Neeley's?" Peter asked, deciding that a change of subject was in order.

She flashed him a grateful look. "My parents insisted upon it. My father says her chef is the best in London, and he wouldn't allow us to decline. And you?"

"My father knows her," he said. "I suppose she took pity on me, so newly returned to town."

There were a lot of soldiers receiving the same sort of pity, Peter thought wryly. A lot of young men, done with the army, or about to be, at loose ends, wondering what it was they were supposed to do now that they weren't holding rifles and galloping into battle.

Some of his friends had decided to remain in the army. It was a respectable occupation for a man such as him, the younger son of a

19

minor aristocrat. But Peter had had enough of military life, enough of the killing, enough death. His parents were encouraging him to enter the clergy, which was, in truth, the only other acceptable avenue for a gentleman of little means. His brother would inherit the small manor that went with the barony; there was nothing left over for Peter.

But the clergy seemed somehow wrong. Some of his friends had emerged from the battlefield with renewed faith; for Peter it had been the opposite, and he felt supremely unqualified to lead any flock upon the path of righteousness.

What he really wanted, when he allowed himself to dream of it, was to live quietly in the country. A gentleman farmer. It sounded so . . . peaceful. So completely unlike everything his life had represented during the past few years.

But such a life required land, and land required money, which was something Peter had in short supply. He'd have a small sum once he sold his commission and officially retired from the army, but it wouldn't be enough.

Which explained his recent arrival in London. He needed a wife. One with a dowry. Nothing extravagant — no heiress would be allowed to marry the likes of him, anyway. No, he just needed a girl with a modest sum of money. Or better yet, a tract of land. He'd be willing to settle almost anywhere in England as long as it meant independence and peace.

It didn't seem an unattainable goal. There were plenty of men who'd be happy to marry their daughters to the son of a baron, and a decorated soldier to boot. The fathers of the real heiresses, of the girls with *Lady* or *the Honorable* in front of their names, would hold out for something better, but for the rest, he'd be considered quite a decent catch indeed.

He looked over at Tillie Howard — Lady Mathilda, he reminded himself. She was exactly the sort he wouldn't be marrying. Wealthy beyond imagination, the only daughter of an earl. He probably shouldn't even be talking to her. People would call him a fortune hunter, and even though that's exactly what he was, he didn't want the label.

But she was Harry's sister, and he'd made a promise to Harry. And besides, standing there with Tillie . . . it was strange. It should have made him miss Harry more, since she looked so damned like him, right down to the leafy green eyes and the funny little angle at which they held their heads when they were listening.

But instead, he just felt good. Relaxed, even, as if this was where he ought to be, if not with Harry, then with this girl.

He smiled at her, and she smiled back, and

something tightened within him, something odd and good and . . .

"Here he is!" shrilled Lady Neeley.

Peter turned around to see what had precipitated their hostess's louder than normal screech. Tillie stepped to the right — he had been blocking her view — and then let out a little gasp of, "Oh."

A large, green parrot sat perched on Lady Neeley's shoulder, and it was squawking, "Martin! Martin!"

"Who's Martin?" Peter asked Tillie.

"Miss Martin," she corrected. "Her companion."

"Martin! Martin!"

"I'd hide, were I her," Peter murmured.

"I don't think she can," Tillie said. "Lord Easterly was added to the guest list at the last minute, and Lady Neeley pressed Miss Martin into service to even up the numbers." She looked up at him, a mischievous smile crossing her lips. "Unless you decide to flee before dinner, poor Miss Martin is stuck here for the duration."

Peter winced as he watched the parrot launch itself off Lady Neeley's shoulder and flutter across the room to a thin, dark-haired woman who clearly wanted to be anywhere but where she was. She batted at the bird, but the creature would not leave her alone.

"Poor thing," Tillie said. "I hope it doesn't peck her."

"No," Peter said, watching the scene with amazement. "I think it fancies itself in love."

And sure enough, the parrot was nuzzling the poor woman, cooing, "Martin, Martin," as if it had just entered the gates of heaven.

"My lady," Miss Martin pleaded, rubbing her increasingly bloodshot eyes.

But Lady Neeley just laughed. "A hundred pounds I paid for that bird, and all he does is make love to Miss Martin."

Peter looked at Tillie, whose mouth was clamped into an angry line. "This is terrible," she said. "That bird is making the poor woman sick, and Lady Neeley doesn't give a fig about it."

Peter took this to mean that he was supposed to play the knight in shining armor and save Lady Neeley's poor, beleaguered companion, but before he could take a step, Tillie had moved across the room. He followed with interest, watching as she held a finger out and encouraged the bird to leave Miss Martin's shoulder.

"Thank you," Miss Martin said. "I don't know why he's acting this way. He's never paid me any mind before."

"Lady Neeley should put him away," Tillie said sternly.

Miss Martin said nothing. They all knew that that would never happen.

Tillie took the bird back to its owner. "Good evening, Lady Neeley," she said.

"Have you a perch for your bird? Or perhaps we should put him back in his cage."

"Isn't he sweet?" Lady Neeley said.

Tillie just smiled. Peter bit his lip to keep from chuckling.

"His perch is over there," Lady Neeley said, motioning with her head to a spot in the corner. "The footmen filled his dish with seed; he won't go anywhere."

Tillie nodded and brought the parrot over to his perch. Sure enough, it began to peck furiously at its food.

"You must have birds," Peter said.

Tillie shook her head. "No, but I've seen others handle them."

"Lady Mathilda!" called Lady Neeley.

"You've been summoned, I'm afraid," Peter murmured.

Tillie shot him a supremely irritated look. "Yes, well, you seem to have fallen into the position of my escort, so you will have to come along as well. Yes, Lady Neeley?" she finished, her tone instantly transformed into pure sweetness and light.

"Come over here, gel, I want to show you something."

Peter followed Tillie back across the room, maintaining a safe distance when his hostess stuck out her arm.

"D'you like it?" she asked, jingling her bracelet. "It's new."

"It's lovely," Tillie said. "Rubies?"

"Of course. It's red. What else would it be?"

"Er . . ."

Peter smiled as he watched Tillie try to deduce whether or not the question was rhetorical. With Lady Neeley, one never could be sure.

"I've a matching necklace as well," Lady Neeley continued blithely, "but I didn't want to overdo it." She leaned forward and said in a tone that on anyone else would not have been described as quiet, "Not everyone here is as plump in the pocket as we two."

Peter could have sworn she looked at him, but he decided to ignore the affront. One really couldn't take offense at any of Lady Neeley's comments; to do so would ascribe too much importance to her opinion, and besides, one would forever be running around feeling insulted.

"Wore my earbobs, though!"

Tillie leaned in and dutifully admired her hostess's earrings, but then, just as she was straightening her shoulders, Lady Neeley's bracelet, about which she had made such a fuss, slid right off her wrist and landed on the carpet with a delicate thud.

While Lady Neeley shrieked with dismay, Tillie bent down and retrieved the jewels. "It's a lovely piece," Tillie said, admiring the rubies before handing them back to their owner.

"I can't believe that happened," Lady Neeley said. "Perhaps it is too big. My wrists are very delicate, you know."

Peter coughed into his hand.

"May I examine it?" Tillie said, kicking him in the ankle.

"Of course," the older woman said, handing it back to her. "My eyes aren't what they used to be."

A small crowd had gathered, and everyone waited as Tillie squinted and fiddled with the shiny gold mechanism of the clasp.

"I think you will need to have it repaired," Tillie finally said, returning the bracelet to Lady Neeley. "The clasp is faulty. It will surely fall off again."

"Nonsense," Lady Neeley said, thrusting her arm out. "Miss Martin!" she bellowed.

Miss Martin rushed to her side and reaffixed the bracelet.

Lady Neeley let out a "hmmph" and brought her wrist up to her face, examining the bracelet one more time before lowering her arm. "I bought this at Asprey's, and I assure you there is no finer jeweler in London. They would not sell me a bracelet with a faulty clasp."

"I'm sure they didn't mean to," Tillie said, "but —"

She didn't need to finish. Everyone stared down at the spot on the carpet where the bracelet landed for the second time.

"Definitely the clasp," murmured Peter.

"This is an outrage," Lady Neeley announced.

Peter rather agreed, especially since they'd now wasted precious minutes on her shiny bracelet when all anyone wanted at this point was to go into supper and eat. So many bellies were rumbling he couldn't tell whose was whose.

"What am I to do with this now?" Lady Neeley said, after Miss Martin had retrieved the bracelet from the carpet and handed it back to her.

A tall, dark-haired man whom Peter did not recognize produced a small candy dish. "Perhaps this will suffice," he said, holding it out.

"Easterly," Lady Neeley muttered, rather grudgingly, actually, as if she didn't particularly care to acknowledge the gentleman's aid. She set the bracelet in the dish, then placed it on a nearby credenza. "There," she said, arranging the bracelet in a neat circle. "I suppose everyone can still admire it there."

"Perhaps it could serve as a centerpiece on the table while we dine," Peter suggested.

"Hmm, yes, excellent idea, Mr. Thompson. It's nearly time to go in for supper, anyway."

Peter could have sworn he heard someone whisper, *"Nearly?"*

27

"Oh, very well we'll eat now," Lady Neeley said. "Miss Martin!"

Miss Martin, who had somehow managed to put several yards between herself and her employer, returned.

"See to it that everything is ready for supper," Lady Neeley said.

Miss Martin exited, and then, amid multiple sighs of relief, the party moved from the drawing room to the dining room.

To his delight, Peter found that he was seated next to Tillie. Normally he wouldn't find himself next to an earl's daughter, and in truth, he suspected that he was meant to be paired with the woman on his right, but she had Robbie Dunlop on the other side, and he seemed to be keeping her in conversation quite nicely.

The food was, as gossip had promised, exquisite, and Peter was quite happily spooning lobster bisque into his mouth when he heard a movement to his left, and when he turned, Tillie was looking at him, her lips parted as if she were about to say his name.

She was lovely, he realized. Lovely in a way that Harry could never have described, in a way that he, as her brother, could never even have seen. Harry would never have been able to see the woman beyond the girl, would never have realized that the curve of her cheek begged a caress, or that when she opened her mouth to speak, she sometimes

28

paused first, her lips pursing together slightly, as if awaiting a kiss.

Harry would never have seen any of that, but Peter did, and it shook him to the core.

"Did you want to ask me something?" he asked, surprised that his voice came out sounding quite ordinary.

"I did," she said, "although I'm not sure how . . . I don't know . . ."

He waited for her to collect her thoughts.

After a moment, she leaned forward, glanced about the table to ascertain if anyone was looking at them, and asked, "Were you there?"

"Where?" he asked, even though he knew exactly what she meant.

"When he died," she said quietly. "Were you there?"

He nodded. It wasn't a memory he cared to revisit, but he owed her that much honesty.

Her lower lip trembled, and she whispered, "Did he suffer?"

For a moment Peter didn't know what to say. Harry had suffered. He'd spent three days in what had to have been tremendous pain, both his legs broken, the right one so badly that the bone had burst through the skin. He might've survived that, maybe even without too much of a limp — their surgeon was quite adept at setting bones — but then the fever had set in, and it hadn't been long

29

before Peter realized that Harry would not win his battle. Two days later he was dead.

But when he'd slipped from life, he'd been so listless that Peter hadn't been certain whether he'd felt pain or not, especially with the laudanum he'd stolen from his commander and poured down Harry's throat. And so, when he finally answered Tillie's question, he just said, "Some. It wasn't painless, but I think . . . at the end . . . it was peaceful."

She nodded. "Thank you. I've always wondered. I would have always wondered. I'm glad to know."

He turned his attention back to his soup, hoping that a bit of lobster and flour and broth could banish the memory of Harry's death, but then Tillie said, "It's supposed to be easier because he's a hero, but I don't think so."

He looked back at her, his question in his eyes.

"Everyone keeps saying we must be so proud of him," she explained, "because he's a hero, because he died on a battlefield at Waterloo, his bayonet in the body of a French soldier, but I don't think it makes it any easier." Her lips quivered tremulously, the kind of strange, helpless smile one makes when one realizes that some questions have no answers. "We still miss him just as much as we would have done had he fallen off his horse, or caught the measles, or choked on a chicken bone."

Peter felt his lips part as he digested her words. "Harry *was* a hero," he heard himself say, and it was the truth. Harry had proven himself a hero a dozen times over, fighting valiantly, and more than once saving the life of another. But Harry hadn't died a hero, not in the way most people liked to think of it. Harry was already dead by the time they fought the French at Waterloo, his body hopelessly mangled in a stupid accident, trapped for six hours beneath a supply wagon that someone had tried to repair one time too many. The damn thing should have been chopped for firewood weeks earlier, Peter thought savagely, but the army never had enough of anything, including humble supply wagons, and his regiment commander had refused to give it up for dead.

But clearly this wasn't the story Tillie had been told, and probably her parents as well. Someone had tried to soften the blow of Harry's death by painting his last minutes with the deep red colors of the battlefield, in all its horrible glory.

"Harry was a hero," Peter said again, because it was true, and he'd long since learned that those who hadn't experienced war could never understand the truth of it. And if it brought comfort to think that any death could be more noble than another, he wasn't about to pierce the illusion.

"You were a good friend to him," Tillie said. "I'm glad he had you."

"I made a promise to him," he blurted out. He hadn't meant to tell her, but somehow he couldn't help himself. "We both made a promise, actually. It was a few months before he died, and we'd both. . . . Well, the night before had been grisly, and we'd lost many of our regiment."

She leaned forward, her eyes wide and glowing with compassion, and when he looked at her, he saw the rose milkiness of her skin, the light dusting of freckles across her nose — more than anything, he wanted to kiss her.

Good God. Right there at Lady Neeley's dinner party, he wanted to grab Tillie Howard by the shoulders, haul her against him and kiss her for everything he was worth.

Harry would have called him out on the spot.

"What happened?" she asked, and the words should have jolted him back to reality, reminded him that he was telling her something rather important, but all he could do was stare at her lips, which weren't quite pink, but rather a little peachy, and it occurred to him that he'd never, ever bothered to look at a woman's mouth before — at least not like this — before kissing her.

"Mr. Thompson?" she asked. "Peter?"

"Sorry," he said, his fingers fisting beneath the table, as if the pain of his nails against his palms could somehow force him back to the matter at hand. "I made Harry a promise," he continued. "We were talking about home, as we often did when it was particularly difficult, and he mentioned you, and I mentioned my sister — she's fourteen — and we promised each other that if anything should befall us, we would watch out for the other's sister. Keep you safe."

For a moment she did nothing but look at him, and then she said, "That's very kind of you, but don't worry, I absolve you of the vow. I'm no green girl, and I still have a brother in William. Besides, I don't need a replacement for Harry."

Peter opened his mouth to speak, then quickly thought better of it. He wasn't feeling brotherly toward Tillie, and he was quite certain this wasn't what Harry had had in mind when he'd asked him to look out for her.

And the *last* thing he wanted to be was her replacement brother.

But the moment seemed to call for a reply, and indeed Tillie was regarding him quizzically, her head tilted to the side as if she were waiting for him to say something quite meaningful and intelligent or, if not that, something that would allow her to offer a teasing retort.

Which was why, when Lady Neeley's awful voice screeched across the room, Peter didn't mind the sound of it, even if it was to say: "It's gone! My bracelet is gone!"

Chapter 2

The week's most coveted invitation is now the week's most talked about event. If it is possible that you, Dear Reader, have not yet heard the news, This Author shall recount it here: Lady Neeley's hungry guests had not even finished their soup when their hostess's ruby bracelet was discovered to have been stolen.

There is, to be sure, some disagreement over the fate of the precious jewels. A number of guests maintain that the bracelet was simply misplaced, but Lady Neeley claims a crystal clear memory of the evening, and she says that it was burglary, without question.

Apparently, the bracelet (whose clasp was discovered to be faulty by Lady Mathilda Howard) was placed in a candy dish (selected by the elusive Lord Easterly) and set upon a table in Lady Neeley's drawing room. Lady Neeley intended to bring the dish to the dining room, so that her guests might admire its apparent brilliance, but in the rush to reach the food (by this time, This Author is told, the hour had grown so late that the guests, famished all, abandoned decorum and made a mad dash for the dining room), the bracelet was forgotten.

When Lady Neeley remembered the jewels in the next room, she sent a footman to collect them, but he returned with only the candy dish.

This, of course, was when the true excitement began. Lady Neeley attempted to have all of her guests searched, but truly, does anyone think one such as the Earl of Canby would consent to have his person ransacked by a baroness's footman? The suggestion was made that the bracelet was stolen by a servant, but Lady Neeley maintains an admirable loyalty toward her servants (who, quite remarkably, return the sentiment), and she refused to believe that any of her staff, none of whom have been in her employ for less than five years, would have betrayed her in such a manner.

In the end, all of the guests departed in bad humor. And perhaps most tragically, all of the food — save for the soup — went uneaten. One *can only hope that Lady Neeley saw fit to offer the feast to her servants, whom she had so recently defended against attack.*

And one can be sure, Dear Reader, that This Author shall continue to comment upon this latest on-dit. Is it possible that a member of the ton is nothing more than a common thief? Nonsense. One would have to be most uncommon to have spirited away such a valuable piece, right under Lady N's nose.

Lady Whistledown's Society Papers, 29 May 1816

"And then," gushed some elaborately dressed young gentleman, speaking in the tone of one who is quite certain he is always aware of the latest gossip, "she forced Mr. Brooks — her own nephew — to strip off his coat and allow two footmen to search him."

"I heard it was three."

"It was none," Peter drawled, standing at the entrance of the Canby drawing room. "I was there."

Seven gentleman turned to face him. Five looked annoyed, one bored, and one amused. As for Peter, he was profoundly irritated. He wasn't certain what he'd expected when he'd decided to travel to the opulent Canby residence in Mayfair to call upon Tillie, but it hadn't been *this*. The spacious drawing room was overfull with men and flowers, and the small bunch of irises in his hand seemed rather superfluous.

Who knew that Tillie was so popular?

"I'm quite sure," the first gentleman said, "that it was *two* footmen."

Peter shrugged. He didn't much care if the fop had the truth or not. "Lady Mathilda was there as well," he said. "You can ask her if you don't believe me."

"It's true," Tillie said, smiling at him in greeting. "Although Mr. Brooks did remove his coat."

The man who had claimed that three footmen had been searching guests turned to Peter and inquired, somewhat archly, "Did you remove your coat?"

"No."

"The guests revolted after Mr. Brooks was searched," Tillie explained, then changed the subject by asking her assembled beaux, "Are you acquainted with Mr. Thompson?"

Only two were; Peter was still rather new to town, and most of his acquaintances were limited to school friends from Eton and Cambridge. Tillie made the necessary introductions, then Peter was relegated to the eighth-best position in the room, as none of the other gentlemen was willing to relocate and allow another any advantage in courting

38

the lovely — and wealthy — Lady Mathilda.

Peter read *Whistledown*; he knew that Tillie was considered the season's biggest heiress. And he recalled Harry saying — quite often, actually — that he was going to have to beat off the fortune hunters with a stick. But Peter hadn't realized until this moment just how assiduously the young men of London were fighting for her hand.

It was nauseating.

And in truth, he owed it to Harry to ensure that the man she chose (or as was more likely the case, the man her father chose for her) would treat her with the affection and respect she deserved.

And so he turned to the task of inspecting, and then when appropriate, scaring off the lovesick swain surrounding him.

The first gentleman was easy. It took mere minutes to determine that his vocabulary did not reach into the triple digits, and all Peter had to do was mention that Tillie had told him that the activity she enjoyed above all else was reading philosophical tracts. The suitor made haste for the door, and Peter decided that even if Tillie hadn't actually mentioned such a predilection to him the night before, the fact remained that she was certainly intelligent enough to read philosophical tracts if she so chose, and that alone ought to disqualify the match.

The next gentleman was known to Peter by

reputation. An inveterate gambler, all he required to bid his farewells was the mention of an impending horse race in Hyde Park. And, Peter thought with satisfaction, he took three of the others along with him. It was a good thing that the horse race was not fictitious, although the four young men might be a bit disappointed when they realized that Peter had misremembered the time of the event, and indeed, that all bets had been placed some sixty minutes earlier.

Oh, well.

He smiled. He was having considerably more fun than he would have imagined.

"Mr. Thompson," came a dry, feminine voice in his ear, "are you scaring off my daughter's suitors?"

He turned to face Lady Canby, who was regarding him with an amused expression, for which Peter was immensely thankful. Most mothers would have been irate. "Of course not," he replied. "Not the ones you'd want to see her marry, at any rate."

Lady Canby just raised her brows.

"Any man who'd rather throw money on a horse race than remain here in your presence isn't worthy of your daughter."

She laughed, and when she did so, she looked a great deal like Tillie. "Well spoken, Mr. Thompson," she said. "One cannot be too careful when one is the mother of a great heiress."

Peter paused, unsure whether that comment was meant to be more pointed than her tone might imply. If Lady Canby knew who he was, and she did — she'd recognized his name immediately when they'd been introduced the night before — then she also knew he had little more than pennies to his name.

"I promised Harry I would look out for her," he said, his voice stolid and resolute. There could be no mistaking that he meant to fulfill his vow.

"I see," Lady Canby murmured, cocking her head slightly to the side. "And that is why you're here?"

"Of course." And he meant it. At least he told himself he meant it. It didn't matter if he'd spent the last sixteen or so hours fantasizing about kissing Tillie Howard. She wasn't for him.

He watched her conversing with the younger brother of Lord Bridgerton, gritting his teeth when he realized that there wasn't a single objectionable thing about the man. He was tall, strong, clearly intelligent, and of good family and fortune. The Canbys would be thrilled with the match, even if Tillie would be reduced to a mere Mrs.

"We're rather pleased with that one," Lady Canby said, motioning one small, elegant hand toward the gentleman in question. "He's quite a talented artist, and his mother has been my close friend for years."

Peter nodded tightly.

"Alas," Lady Canby said with a shrug, "I fear there is little reason to hold out hope in that quarter. I suspect he is just here to merely placate dear Violet, who has despaired of ever seeing her children married. Mr. Bridgerton doesn't seem ready to settle down, and his mother believes he is secretly besotted with another."

Peter remembered not to smile.

"Tillie, my dear," Lady Canby said, once the annoyingly handsome and personable Mr. Bridgerton kissed her hand and departed, "you have not yet chatted with Mr. Thompson. It is so kind of him to call, and all out of friendship for Harry."

"I wouldn't say *all*," Peter said, his words coming out a little less suave and practiced than he'd intended. "It is always a delight to see you, Lady Mathilda."

"Please," Tillie said, waving good-bye to the last of her lovesick swain, "you must continue to call me Tillie." She turned to her mother. "It's all Harry ever called me, and apparently he spoke of us often while on the Continent."

Lady Canby smiled sadly at the mention of her younger son's name, and she blinked several times. Her eyes took on a hollow expression, and while Peter didn't think she was going to burst into tears, he rather thought she wanted to. He immediately held out his

42

handkerchief, but she shook her head and refused the gesture.

"I believe I shall fetch my husband," she said, rising to her feet. "I know he would like to meet you. He was off somewhere last night when we were introduced, and I — Well, I know he would like to meet you." She hurried out of the room, leaving the door wide open and positioning a footman just across the hall.

"She's off to go cry," Tillie said, not in a way to make Peter feel guilty. It was just an explanation, a sad statement of fact. "She does still, quite a bit."

"I'm sorry," he said.

She shrugged. "There's no avoiding it, it seems. For any of us. I don't think we ever really thought he might die. It seems quite stupid now. It shouldn't have been such a surprise. He went off to war, for heaven's sake. What else should we have expected?"

Peter shook his head. "It isn't stupid at all. We all thought we were a little bit immortal until we actually saw battle." He swallowed, not wanting to feel the memory. But once summoned, it was difficult to hold back. "It's impossible to understand until you see it."

Tillie's lips tightened slightly, and Peter worried that he might have insulted her. "I don't mean to condescend," he said.

"You didn't. It's not that. I was just . . . thinking." She leaned forward, a luminous new light in her eyes. "Let's not talk of Harry," she said. "Do you think we can? I'm just so tired of being sad."

"Very well," he said.

She watched him, waiting for him to say something more. But he didn't. "Er, how was the weather?" she finally asked.

"Bit of a drizzle," he replied, "but nothing out of the ordinary."

She nodded. "Was it warm?"

"Not especially. A bit warmer than last night, though."

"Yes, it was a bit chilly, wasn't it? And here it's May."

"Disappointed?"

"Of course. It ought to be spring."

"Yes."

"Quite."

"Quite."

One-word sentences, Tillie thought. Always the demise of any good conversation. *Surely* they had something in common other than Harry. Peter Thompson was handsome, intelligent, and, when he looked at her with that smoky, heavy-lidded expression of his, it sent a shiver right down her spine.

It wasn't fair that the only thing they ever seemed to talk about made her want to cry.

She smiled at him encouragingly, waiting for him to say something more, but he did not. She smiled again, clearing her throat.

He took the hint. "Do you read?" he asked.

"Do I *read?*" she echoed, incredulous.

"Not *can* you, *do* you?" he clarified.

"Yes, of course. Why?"

He shrugged. "I might have mentioned as much to one of the other gentlemen here."

"Might have?"

"Did."

She felt her teeth clenching. She had no idea *why* she should be irritated with Peter Thompson, only that she should. He'd clearly done something to merit her displeasure, else he wouldn't be sitting there with that cat-with-cream expression, pretending to inspect his fingernails. "Which gentleman?" she finally asked.

He looked up, and Tillie resisted the urge to thank him for finding her more interesting than his manicure.

"I believe his name was Mr. Berbrooke," he said.

Not anyone she wanted to marry. Nigel Berbrooke was a good-hearted fellow, but he was also dumb as a post and would likely be terrified at the thought of an intellectual wife. One might say, if one were feeling particularly generous, that Peter had done her a favor by scaring him away, but still, Tillie did not appreciate his meddling in her affairs. "What did you say I liked to read?" she asked, keeping her voice mild.

"Er, this and that. Perhaps philosophical tracts."

"I see. And you saw fit to mention this to him because? . . ."

"He seemed like the sort who'd be interested," he said with a shrug.

"And — just out of curiosity, mind you — what happened when you told him this?"

Peter didn't even have the grace to look sheepish. "Ran right out the door," he murmured. "Imagine that."

Tillie meant to remain arch and dry. She wanted to eye him ironically under delicately arched brows. But she wasn't nearly as sophisticated as she hoped to be, because she positively glared at him as she said, "And what gave you the idea that I like to read philosophical tracts?"

"Don't you?"

"It doesn't matter," she retorted. "You can't go around frightening off my suitors."

"Is that what you thought I was doing?"

"Please," she scoffed. "After touting my intelligence to Mr. Berbrooke, don't attempt to insult it now."

"Very well," he said, crossing his arms and regarding her with the sort of expression her father and older brother adopted when they meant to scold her. "Do you really wish to pledge your troth to Mr. Berbrooke? Or," he added, "to one of the men who rushed out the door to throw money on a horse race?"

"Of course not, but that doesn't mean I want you scaring them away."

He just looked at her as if she were an idiot. Or a woman. It was Tillie's experience that most men thought they were one and the same.

"The more men who come to call," she explained, somewhat impatiently, "the more men who *will* come to call."

"I beg your pardon?"

"You're sheep. The lot of you. Only interested in a woman if someone else is as well."

"And it is your aim in life to collect a score of gentlemen in your drawing room?"

His tone was patronizing, almost insulting, and Tillie was *this close* to having him booted from the house. Only his friendship with Harry — and the fact that he was acting like such a prig because he thought it was what Harry would have wanted — kept her from summoning the butler right then.

"My aim," she said tightly, "is to find a husband. Not to snare one, not to trap one, not to drag one to the altar, but to find one, preferably one with whom I might share a long and contented life. Being a practical sort of girl, it seemed only sensible to meet as many eligible gentlemen as possible, so that my decision might be based on a broad base of knowledge, and not upon, as so many young women are accused, a flight of fancy."

She sat back, crossed her arms, and leveled a hard stare in his direction. "Do you have any questions?"

He regarded her with a blank expression for a moment, then asked, "Do you want me to go and drag them all back?"

"No! Oh," she added, when she saw his sly smile. "You're teasing."

"Just a bit," he demurred.

If he'd been Harry, she would have tossed a pillow at him. If he'd been Harry, she would have laughed. But if he'd been Harry, her eyes wouldn't have lingered on his mouth when he smiled, and she wouldn't have felt this strange heat in her blood, or this prickling on her skin.

But most of all, if he'd been Harry, she wouldn't feel this *awful* disappointment, because Peter Thompson was not her older brother, and the last thing she wanted was for him to view himself as such.

But apparently, that was exactly how he felt.

He'd promised Harry that he'd look after her, and now she was nothing more than an obligation. Did he even like her? Find her remotely interesting or amusing? Or did he suffer her company only because she was Harry's sister?

It was impossible to know — and a question she could never ask. And what she really wanted was for him to leave, but that would mark her a coward, and she didn't want to be a coward. It was what she owed Harry, she'd come to realize. To live her life with the courage and strength of purpose that he'd exhibited at the end of his.

Facing Peter Thompson seemed a rather pale comparison to Harry's brave deeds as a soldier, but no one was about to send her off to fight for her country, so if she wanted to continue in her quest to face her fears, this was going to have to do.

"You're forgiven this time," she said, crossing her hands in her lap.

"Did I apologize?" he drawled, spearing her once again with that slow, lazy smile.

"No, but you should have done." She smiled back, sweetly . . . too sweetly. "I was raised to be charitable, so I thought I'd grant you the apology you never gave."

"And the acceptance as well?"

"Of course. I'd be churlish, otherwise."

He burst out laughing, a rich, warm sound that took Tillie by surprise, and then made her smile in turn.

"Very well," he said. "You win. You absolutely, positively, indubitably —"

"Indubitably even?" she murmured with delight.

"Even indubitably," he conferred. "You win. I apologize."

She sighed. "Victory has never felt so sweet."

"Nor should it have done," he said with arched brows. "I assure you I don't hand out apologies lightly."

"Or with such good humor?" she queried.

"*Never* with such good humor."

Tillie was smiling, trying to think of something terribly witty to say, when the butler arrived with an unsolicited tea service. Her mother must have requested it, Tillie thought, which meant that she'd be back soon, which meant that her time alone with Peter was drawing to a close.

She should have paid attention to the keen disappointment squeezing in her chest. Or to the fluttering in her belly that amplified every time she looked at him. Because if she had, she wouldn't have been so surprised when she handed him a cup of tea, and their fingers touched, and then she looked at him, and he looked at her, and their eyes met.

And she felt like she was falling.

Falling . . . falling . . . falling. A warm rush of air washing over her, stealing her breath, her pulse, even her heart. And when it was all over — if indeed it was over, and not simply subsided — all she could think was that it was a wonder she hadn't dropped the teacup.

And had he noticed that in that moment, she had been transformed?

She paid careful attention to the fixing of her own cup, splashing in milk before adding the hot tea. If she could just concentrate on the mundane tasks at hand, she wouldn't have to ponder what had just happened to her.

Because she suspected that she had indeed fallen.

In love.

And she suspected that in the end, it would be her downfall. She hadn't much experience with men; her first season in London had been cut short by Harry's untimely death, and she'd spent the past year secluded in the country, in mourning with her family.

But even so, she could tell that Peter didn't think of her as a desirable woman. He thought of her as an obligation, as Harry's little sister.

Maybe even as a child.

To him she was a promise that had to be kept. Nothing more, nothing less. It would have seemed cold and clinical, had she not been so touched by his devotion to her brother.

"Is something wrong?"

Tillie looked up at the sound of Peter's voice and smiled wryly. Was something wrong? More than he would ever know.

"Of course not," she lied. "Why do you ask?"

"You have not drunk your tea."

"I prefer it lukewarm," she improvised, lifting the cup to her lips. She took a sip, faking a gingerly manner. "There," she said brightly. "Much better now."

He watched her curiously, and Tillie almost

sighed at her misfortune. If one was going to develop an unrequited fancy for a gentleman, one would do a great deal better not to choose one of such obvious intelligence. Any more blunders like this one, and he would certainly discern her true feelings.

Which would be hideous.

"Do you plan to attend the Hargreaves Grand Ball on Friday?" she asked, deciding that a change of subject was her best course of action.

He nodded. "I assume you do as well?"

"Of course. It will be quite a crush, I'm sure, and I cannot wait to see Lady Neeley arrive with her bracelet on her wrist."

"She has found it?" he asked with surprise.

"No, but she must, don't you think? I cannot imagine anyone at the party actually stealing it. It probably fell behind the table, and no one has had the shrewdness to look."

"I agree with you that yours is the most likely theory," he said, but his lips pursed slightly when he paused, and he did not look convinced.

"But? . . ." she prompted.

For a moment she did not think he would answer, but then he said, "But you have never known want, Lady Mathilda. You could never understand the desperation that might push a man to steal."

She didn't like that he'd called her Lady Mathilda. It injected a formality into the conversation that she'd thought they'd dispensed with. And his comments seemed to underscore the simple fact that he was a man of the world, and she was a sheltered young lady.

"Of course not," she said, since there was no point in pretending her life had been anything but privileged. "But still, it's difficult to imagine someone having the audacity to steal the bracelet right out from under her nose."

For a moment he did not move, just stared at her in an uncomfortably assessing manner. Tillie got the feeling that he thought her terribly provincial, or at the very least naïve, and she hated that her belief in the general goodness of man was marking her a fool.

It shouldn't be that way. One *ought* to trust one's friends and neighbors. And she certainly shouldn't be ridiculed for doing so.

But he surprised her, and he just said, "You're probably right. I've long since realized that most mysteries have perfectly benign and boring solutions. Lady Neeley shall most probably be eating crow before the week is out."

"You don't think I'm silly for being so trusting?" Tillie asked, nearly kicking herself for doing so. But she couldn't seem to stop asking questions of this man; she couldn't recall anyone else whose opinions *mattered* quite so much.

He smiled. "No. I don't necessarily agree

with you. But it's rather nice to share tea with someone whose faith in humanity has not been irreparably injured."

A somber ache washed over her, and she wondered if Harry, too, had been changed by the war. He must have been, she realized, and she couldn't quite believe that she'd never considered it before. She'd always imagined him the same old Harry, laughing and joking and pulling pranks at every opportunity.

But when she looked at Peter Thompson, she realized that there was a shadow behind his eyes that never quite went away.

Harry had been at Peter's side throughout the war. His eyes had seen the same horrors, and his eyes would have held the same shadows, had he not been buried in Belgium.

"Tillie?"

She looked up quickly. She'd been silent longer than she ought, and Peter was watching her with a curious expression. "Sorry," she said reflexively, "just woolgathering."

But as she sipped her tea, watching him surreptitiously over the rim of her cup, it wasn't Harry she was thinking about. For the first time in a year, finally, *thrillingly*, it wasn't Harry.

It was Peter, and all she could think was that he shouldn't have shadows behind his eyes. And she wanted to be the one to banish them forever.

Chapter 3

. . . and now that This Author has made public the guest list from The Dinner Party That Went Awry, This Author offers to you, as a delicious lagniappe, an analysis of the suspects.

Not much is known of Mr. Peter Thompson, although he is widely recognized as a courageous soldier in the war against Napoleon. Society hates to place a noted war hero on a list of suspects, but This Author would be remiss if it were not pointed out that Mr. Thompson is also recognized as something of a fortune hunter. Since his arrival in town, he has been quite obviously looking for a wife, although as This Author firmly believes in giving credit where credit is due, he has done so in a decidedly understated and unvulgar manner.

But it is well-known that his father, Lord Stoughton, is not among the wealthier of the barons, and furthermore, Mr. Thompson is a second son, *and as his elder brother has already seen fit to procreate, he is a mere fourth in line for the title. And so if Mr. Thompson hopes to live in any manner of style once he departs the army, he will need to marry a woman of some means.*

Or, one could speculate, if one was of a mind to do so, obtain funds in some other manner.

Lady Whistledown's Society Papers,
31 May 1816

If Peter had known the identity of the elusive Lady Whistledown, he would have strangled her on the spot.

Fortune Hunter. He detested the moniker, viewed it more as an epithet, and could not even think the words without nearly spitting in disgust. He'd spent this past month in London behaving with the utmost of care, all to ensure that the label was not applied to him.

There was a difference between a man who sought a woman with a modest dowry and one who seduced for money, and the differential could be summed up in one word.

Honor.

It was what had governed his entire life, from the moment his father had sat him down at the appallingly tender age of five and explained what set apart a true gentleman, and by God, Peter was not going to allow some cowardly gossip columnist to stain his reputation with a single stroke of her pen.

If the bloody woman had an ounce of honor herself, he thought savagely, she would not coyly cloak her identity. Only the craven used anonymity to insult and impugn.

But he didn't know who Lady Whistledown was, and he suspected no one ever would, not in his lifetime, anyway, so he had to content himself with taking out his foul mood on everyone else with whom he came into contact.

Which meant that he was probably going to owe his valet a rather large apology on the morrow.

He tugged at his cravat as he navigated the too-crowded ballroom at the home of Lady Hargreaves. He couldn't refuse this invitation; to do so would have given too much credence to Lady Whistledown's words. Better to brazen it out and laugh it off and take some solace in the fact that he wasn't the only one savaged in this morning's edition; Lady W had devoted a fair bit of space to five guests in total, including the poor beleaguered Miss Martin, whom the *ton* would surely turn upon, as she was merely Lady Neeley's companion and not, as he had already heard someone say, one of their own.

Besides, he'd had to come tonight. He had already accepted the invitation, and furthermore, every eligible young miss in London would be in attendance. He couldn't let himself forget that there was a purpose to his presence in town. He could not afford to finish the season without a betrothal; as it was, he could barely manage to pay the rent on his humble bachelor lodgings north of Oxford Street.

He imagined that the fathers of those marriageable misses might view him a little more carefully tonight, and several would not allow their daughters to associate with him, but hiding at home would, in the eyes of society, be tantamount to admitting guilt, and he would be far better off acting as if nothing had happened.

Even if he wanted rather desperately to put his fist through the wall.

The worst of it was that the one person with whom he absolutely couldn't associate was Tillie. She was universally acknowledged as the season's biggest heiress, and her good looks and vivacious personality had made her quite the catch indeed. It was difficult for *anyone* to pay court to her without being labeled a fortune hunter, and if Peter were seen to be dangling after her, he would never be rid of the stain on his reputation.

But of course Tillie was the one person — the only person — he wanted to see.

She came to him in his thoughts, in his dreams. She was smiling, laughing, then she was serious, and she seemed to *understand* him, to soothe him with her very presence. And he wanted more. He wanted everything; he wanted to know how long her hair was, and he wanted to be the one to release it from the prim little bun at the nape of her neck. He wanted to know the scent of her skin and the exact curve of her hips. He wanted to dance with her more closely than propriety allowed, and he wanted to spirit her away, where no other man could even gaze upon her.

But his dreams were going to have to remain just that. Dreams. There was no way the Earl of Canby would approve of a match between his only daughter and the penniless younger son of a baron. And if he stole Tillie away, if they eloped without her family's permission. . . . Well, she'd be cut off for certain, and Peter would not drag her into a life of genteel poverty.

It wasn't, Peter thought dryly, what Harry had had in mind when he'd asked him to watch out for her.

And so he just stood at the perimeter of the ballroom, pretending to be very interested in his glass of champagne, and rather glad that he couldn't see her. If he knew where Tillie was, then he wouldn't be able to stop himself from watching for her.

And if he did that, then he'd surely catch a glimpse of her.

And once that happened, did he really think he could take his eyes off her?

She'd see him, of course, and their eyes would meet, and then he'd have to go over to offer his greetings, and then she might want to dance. . . .

It occurred to him in a sharp flash of irony that he'd left the war precisely to *avoid* the threat of torture.

He might as well just yank off his finger-nails now.

Peter subtly adjusted his position so that his back was more toward the crowds. Then he gave himself a mental smack when he caught himself glancing over his shoulder.

He'd found a small group of men he knew from the army, all of whom, he was sure, had come to London for the same reason he had, although with the exception of Robbie Dunlop, none of them had had the misfortune of having been invited to Lady Neeley's ill-fated dinner party. And Robbie hadn't been chosen for scrutiny by Lady Whistledown; it seemed that even that wizened old crone knew that Robbie hadn't the guile to concoct — much less carry out — such an audacious theft.

"Bad luck about *Whistledown*," one of the former soldiers commented, shaking his head with honest commiseration.

Peter just grunted and lifted one shoulder in a lopsided shrug. It seemed a good enough answer to him.

"No one will remember by next week," said another. "She'll have some new scandal to report on, and besides, no one really thinks you stole that bracelet."

Peter turned to his friend with dawning horror. It had never even occurred to him that anyone might actually think he was a *thief.* He'd been merely concerned with the bit about being a fortune hunter.

"Er, didn't mean to bring it up," the fellow stammered, stepping back at what must have been a ferocious expression on Peter's face. "I'm certain it will turn out to be that companion. That sort never has two shillings to rub together."

"It wasn't Miss Martin," Peter bit off.

"How d'you know?" asked one of the men. "Do you know her?"

"Does anyone know her?" someone else asked.

"It wasn't Miss Martin," Peter said, his voice hard. "And it is beneath you to speculate with a woman's reputation."

"Yes, but how do you —"

"I was standing right next to her!" Peter snapped. "The poor woman was being mauled by a parrot. She hadn't the opportunity to take the bracelet. Of course," he added caustically, "I don't know who will trust my word on the matter now that I've been labeled as the prime suspect."

The men all rushed to assure him that they still trusted his word on anything, although one was foolish enough to point out that Peter was hardly the *prime* suspect.

Peter just glared at him. Prime or not, it appeared that much of London now thought he might be a thief.

Bloody hell.

"Good evening, Mr. Thompson."

Tillie. The night only needed this.

Peter turned, wishing his blood weren't racing with quite so much energy at the mere sound of her voice. He shouldn't see her. He shouldn't *want* to see her.

"It is good to see you," she said, smiling as if she had a secret.

He was sunk.

"Lady Mathilda," he said, bowing over her proffered hand.

She turned and greeted Robbie, then said to Peter, "Perhaps you might introduce me to the rest of your compatriots?"

He did so, frowning as they all fell under her spell. Or possibly, it occurred to him, the spell of her dowry. Harry hadn't exactly been circumspect when he'd spoken of it on the Continent.

"I could not help but overhear your defense of Miss Martin," Tillie said, once the introductions had been completed. She turned to the rest of the crowd and added, "I was there as well, and I assure you, the thief could not have been she."

"Who do you think stole the bracelet, Lady Mathilda?" someone asked.

Tillie's lips pursed for a fraction of a second — just long enough to inform someone who was watching her very closely that she was irritated. But to anyone else (which consisted of everyone except for Peter) her sunny expression never wavered, especially as she said, "I do not know. I rather think it will be found behind a table."

"Surely Lady Neeley has already searched the room," one of the men drawled.

Tillie waved one of her hands through the air, a blithe gesture that Peter suspected was meant to lull the other gentlemen into thinking she couldn't be bothered to think about such weighty questions. "Nevertheless," she said with a sigh.

And that was that, Peter thought admiringly. No one spoke of it again. One *"nevertheless"* and Tillie had maneuvered the discussion exactly where she wanted it.

Peter tried to ignore the rest of the conversation. It was mostly inanities about the weather, which had been a bit chillier than was normal for this time of year, peppered with the occasional remark about someone's attire. His expression, if he had any control over it, was politely bored; he did not want to appear overly interested in Tillie, and while he did not flatter himself to think that he was the main topic of gossip at the ball, he had already seen more than one old biddy point in his direction and then whisper something behind her hand.

But then all of his good intentions were spoiled when Tillie turned to him and said, "Mr. Thompson, I do believe the music has begun."

There was no misunderstanding that statement, and even as the rest of the gentlemen rushed to fill the subsequent slots on her dance card, he was forced to crook his arm and invite her onto the dance floor.

It was a waltz. It would have to be a waltz.

And as Peter took her hand in his, fighting the urge to entwine their fingers, he had the distinct sensation that he was falling off a cliff.

Or worse, throwing himself over the side.

Because try as he might to convince himself that this was a terrible mistake, that he shouldn't be seen with her — hell, that he shouldn't be *with* her, period — he couldn't quite quash the pure, almost incandescent tingle of joy that rose and swirled within him when he held her in his arms.

And if the gossips wanted to label him the worst of all fortune hunters, then let them.

It would be worth it for this one dance.

★ ★ ★

Tillie had spent her first ten minutes of the Hargreaves' Grand Ball trying to escape her parents' clutches, her second ten looking for Peter Thompson, and her third standing at his side while she chattered about nothing at all with his friends.

She was going to spend the next ten minutes with his complete attention if it killed her.

She was still a little irritated that she'd practically had to beg him to dance with her, *and* in full view of a dozen other gentlemen. But there seemed little point in dwelling upon it now that he was holding her hand and twirling her elegantly around the dance floor.

And why was it, she wondered, that his hand on her back could send such a strange rush of desire straight to the very core of her being? One would think that if she were to feel seduced, it would be from his eyes, which, after ten minutes of studiously ignoring her, burned into hers with an intensity that stole her breath.

But in truth, if she was ready to throw caution to the wind, if she now required every last ounce of her fortitude not to sigh and sink into him and beg him to touch his lips to hers, it was all because of that hand on her back.

Maybe it was the location, at the base of

her spine, just inches through her body to her most intimate place. Maybe it was the way she felt pulled, as if any moment she would lose herself, and her body would be pressed up against his, hot and scandalous, and aching for something she didn't quite understand.

The pressure was relentlessly tender, drawing her toward him, slowly, inexorably . . . and yet when Tillie looked down, the distance between their bodies had not changed.

But the heat within them had exploded.

And she burned.

"Have I done something to displease you?" she asked, desperately trying to shift her thoughts onto anything besides the heady desire that was threatening to overtake her.

"Of course not," he said gruffly. "Why would you think something so absurd?"

She shrugged. "You seemed . . . oh, I don't know . . . a bit distant, I suppose. As if you did not welcome my company."

"That's ridiculous," he grunted, in that way that men did when they knew a woman was right but had no intention of admitting it.

She'd grown up with two brothers, however, and knew better than to push, so instead she said, "You were magnificent when you defended Miss Martin."

His hand tightened around hers, but sadly, only for a second. "Anyone would have defended her," he said.

"No," she said slowly. "I don't think so. I'd say the opposite, actually, and I believe you know I'm right."

She looked up at him, her eyes defiant, waiting for him to contradict her. Smart man that he was, he didn't.

"A gentleman should never wreak havoc with a woman's reputation," he said stiffly, and she realized with a strange little bubble of delight that she loved that little hint of stodginess, loved that he was actually embarrassed by his own strict code of ethics.

Or maybe it wasn't the code as much as the fact that she had caught him in it. It was much more fashionable to be an unfeeling rake, but Peter could never be that cruel.

"A woman shouldn't wreak havoc with a gentleman's reputation, either," Tillie said softly. "I'm sorry about what Lady Whistledown wrote. It wasn't well done of her."

"And do you have the ear of our esteemed gossip columnist?"

"Of course not, but I do approve of her words more often than not. This time, however, I think she may have crossed the line."

"She accused no one." He shrugged as if he didn't care, but his tone could not lie. He was furious — and pained — by that morning's column, and if Tillie had known who Lady Whistledown was, she would have happily trussed her up like a goose.

It was a strange, fierce feeling, this anger that he'd been hurt.

"Lady Mathilda . . . *Tillie*."

She looked up in surprise, unaware that she'd been off in her own thoughts.

He offered her an amused smile and glanced down at their hands.

She followed his gaze, and it was only then that she realized she was gripping his fingers as if they were Lady Whistledown's neck. "Oh!" she let out in surprise, followed by the more mumbly, "Sorry."

"Do you make a habit of amputating your dance partners' fingers?"

"Only when I have to twist their arms to get them to ask me to dance," she shot back.

"And here I thought the war was dangerous," he murmured.

She was surprised that he could joke about it, surprised that he *would*. She wasn't quite certain how to respond, but then the orchestra finished the waltz with a surprisingly lively flourish, and she was saved from having to reply.

"Shall I return you to your parents?" Peter asked, leading her off the dance floor. "Or to your next partner?"

"Actually," she improvised, "I'm rather thirsty. Perhaps the lemonade table?" Which, she had noted, was clear across the room.

"As you wish."

Their progress was slow; Tillie kept her pace uncharacteristically sedate, hoping to stretch their time together by another minute or two.

"Have you been enjoying the ball?" she asked him.

"Bits and pieces," he said, keeping his gaze straight ahead.

But she saw the corner of his mouth curve up.

"Am I a bit or a piece?" she asked daringly.

He actually stopped. "Do you have any idea what you just said?"

Too late, she remembered overhearing her brothers talk about bits of muslin and pieces of . . .

Her face flamed.

And then, God help them, they both laughed.

"Don't tell anyone," she whispered, catching her breath. "My parents will lock me away for a month."

"That would certainly —"

"Lady Mathilda! Lady Mathilda!"

Whatever Peter had meant to say was lost as Mrs. Featherington, a friend of Tillie's mother and one of society's biggest gossips, bustled up next to them, dragging along her daughter Penelope, who was dressed in a rather unfortunate shade of yellow.

"Lady Mathilda," Mrs. Featherington said.

Then she added, in a decidedly frosty voice, "Mr. Thompson."

Tillie had been about to make introductions, but then she remembered that Mrs. Featherington and Penelope had been present at Lady Neeley's dinner party. In fact, Mrs. Featherington was one of the unfortunate five to have been profiled by Lady Whistledown in that morning's column.

"Do your parents know where you are?" Mrs. Featherington asked Tillie.

"I beg your pardon?" Tillie asked, blinking with surprise. She turned to Penelope, whom she had always thought was a rather nice, if quiet, sort.

But if Penelope knew what her mother was about, she gave no indication, other than a pained expression that led Tillie to believe that if a hole had suddenly opened up in the middle of the ballroom floor, Penelope would have gladly jumped into it.

"Do your parents know where you are?" Mrs. Featherington repeated, this time more pointedly.

"We drove over together," Tillie answered slowly, "so yes, I would assume they are aware —"

"I shall return you to their sides," Mrs. Featherington interrupted.

And then Tillie understood. "I assure you," she said icily, "that Mr. Thompson is more than capable of returning me to my parents."

"Mother," Penelope said, actually grasping her mother's sleeve.

But Mrs. Featherington ignored her. "A girl such as you," she told Tillie, "must take care with her reputation."

"If you refer to Lady Whistledown's column," Tillie said, her voice uncharacteristically icy, "then I must remind you that you were mentioned as well, Mrs. Featherington."

Penelope gasped.

"Her words do not concern me," Mrs. Featherington said. "I know that I did not take that bracelet."

"And I know that Mr. Thompson did not, either," Tillie returned.

"I never said he did," Mrs. Featherington said, and then she surprised Tillie by turning to Peter and saying, "I apologize if I gave that indication. I would never call someone a thief without proof."

Peter, who had been standing tensely still at Tillie's side, did nothing but nod at her apology. Tillie rather suspected it was all he could do without losing his temper.

"Mother," Penelope said, her tone almost desperate now, "Prudence is over by the door, and she's waving rather madly."

Tillie could see Penelope's sister Prudence, and she seemed quite happily engaged in conversation with one of her friends. Tillie made a mental note to befriend Penelope Featherington, who was well-known as a wallflower, on the next possible occasion.

"Lady Mathilda," Mrs. Featherington said, ignoring Penelope entirely, "I must —"

"Mother!" Penelope yanked hard on her mother's sleeve.

"Penelope!" Mrs. Featherington turned to her daughter with obvious irritation. "I'm trying to —"

"We must be going," Tillie said, taking advantage of Mrs. Featherington's momentary distraction. "I shall be sure to pass along your greetings to my mother."

And then, before Mrs. Featherington could disentangle herself from Penelope, who had a viselike grip on her arm, Tillie made her escape, practically dragging Peter along behind her.

He hadn't said a word during the interchange. Tillie wasn't quite certain what that meant.

"I'm terribly sorry," she said once they were out of Mrs. Featherington's earshot.

"You did nothing," he said, but his voice was tight.

"No, but, well . . ." She stopped, unsure of how to proceed. She didn't particularly want to take the blame for Mrs. Featherington, but nonetheless, it seemed that someone ought to be apologizing to Peter. "No one should be calling you a thief," she finally said. "It's unacceptable."

He smiled at her humorlessly. "She wasn't

calling me a thief," he said. "She was calling me a fortune hunter."

"She never —"

"Trust me," he said, cutting her off with a tone that made her feel like a foolish girl. How could she have missed such an under-current? Was she really that unaware?

"That's the silliest thing I've ever heard," she muttered, as much to defend herself as anything else.

"Is it?"

"Of course. You're the last person who would marry a woman for her money."

Peter stopped, leveling a hard stare at her face. "And you have reached this conclusion in the three days of our acquaintance?"

Her lips tightened. "No more time was required."

He felt her words like a blow, nearly reeling from the force of her belief in him. She was staring up at him, her chin so determined, her arms like sticks at her sides, and he was seized by a strange need to scare her, to push her away, to remind her that men were, above all else, bounders and fools, and she ought not to trust with such an open heart.

"I came to London," he told her, his words deliberate and sharp, "for the sole purpose of finding a bride."

"There is nothing uncommon in that," she said dismissively. "I am here to find a hus-band."

"I have barely a cent to my name," he stated.

Her eyes widened.

"I am a fortune hunter," he said baldly.

She shook her head. "You are not."

"You can't add two to two and expect it to sum only three."

"And you can't speak in such ridiculous crypticisms and expect me to understand a word you say," she replied.

"Tillie," he said with a sigh, hating that she'd almost made him laugh. It made it prodigiously more difficult to scare her away.

"You might need money," she continued, "but that doesn't mean you'd seduce someone to get it."

"Tillie —"

"You are not a fortune hunter," she said rather forcefully, "and I will say so to anyone who dares to intimate that you are."

And so he had to say it. He had to lay it on the table, make her understand the truth of the situation. "If you seek to repair my reputation," he said slowly, and just a bit wearily as well, "then you will have to depart my company."

Her lips parted in shock.

He shrugged, trying to make light of it. "If you must know, I've spent the last three weeks trying rather desperately to avoid being called a fortune hunter," he said, not quite able to believe that he was telling her all this.

"And I succeeded rather well until this morning's *Whistledown*."

"It will all blow over," she whispered, but her voice lacked conviction, as if she were trying to convince herself of it as well.

"Not if I'm seen to be courting you."

"But that's horrid."

In a nutshell, he thought. But there was no point in saying it.

"And you're not courting me. You're fulfilling a promise to Harry." She paused. "Aren't you?"

"Does it matter?"

"To me it does," she muttered.

"Now that Lady Whistledown has gone and labeled me," he said, trying not to wonder *why* it mattered to her, "I shan't be able to even stand near you without someone speculating that I'm after your fortune."

"You're standing next to me now," she pointed out.

And a damned torture it was. He sighed. "I should return you to your parents."

She nodded. "I'm sorry."

"*Don't* apologize," he snapped. He was angry at himself, and angry with Lady Whistledown, and angry at the whole damned *ton*. But not at her. Never at her. And the last thing he wanted was her pity.

"I'm ruining your reputation," she said, her voice breaking with a helplessly sad laugh. "It's almost funny, that."

He eyed her sardonically.

"We young maidens are the ones who have to watch our every move," she explained. "You lot get to do whatever you want."

"Not quite," he said, moving his gaze over her shoulder, lest it fall to riper areas.

"Whatever the case," she said, waving her hand in that blithe move she'd used so successfully earlier in the evening, "it seems that I am the obstacle in your path. You want a wife, and, well . . ." Her voice lost its breeziness, and when she smiled, there was something missing in it.

No one else would notice, Peter realized. No one would realize that her smile wasn't quite right.

But he did. And it broke his heart.

"Whomever you choose . . ." she continued, bolstering that smile with a hollow little laugh, "you shan't get her with me around, it seems."

But not, he realized, for any of the reasons she thought. If he wouldn't find a wife with Tillie Howard nearby, it would be because he couldn't take his eyes off of her, couldn't even begin to think of another woman when he could sense her presence.

"I should go," she said, and he knew she was right, but he couldn't seem to bring himself to say farewell. He'd avoided her company for precisely this reason.

And now that he had to send her on her

way once and for all, it was even harder than he'd thought.

"You're breaking your promise to Harry," she reminded him.

He shook his head, even though she would never understand just how tightly he was *keeping* his promise. He'd promised Harry that he'd protect her.

From *all* unsuitable men.

She swallowed. "My parents are over there," she said, motioning to her left and behind her.

He nodded and took her arm, turning her so that they could make their way to the earl and countess.

And found themselves face-to-face with Lady Neeley.

Chapter 4

One can only wonder what events will transpire at tonight's Hargreaves' Grand Ball. This Author has it on the best authority that Lady Neeley plans to attend, as do all of the major suspects, with the possible exception of Miss Martin, who received an invitation only at the discretion of Lady Neeley herself.

But Mr. Thompson has RSVP'ed in the affirmative, as have Mr. Brooks, Mrs. Featherington, and Lord Easterly.

This Author finds that she can only say, "Let the games begin!"

Lady Whistledown's Society Papers, 31 May 1816

"Mr. Thompson!" Lady Neeley shrilled. "Just the person I've been looking for!"

"Really?" Tillie asked with surprise, before she could remember that she was actually rather peeved with Lady Neeley and had quite intended to be politely icy when next they met.

"Indeed," the older woman said sharply. "I'm furious over that *Whistledown* column this morning. That infernal woman never gets but half of anything right."

"To which half do you refer?" Peter asked coldly.

"The bit about your being a thief, of course," Lady Neeley said. "We all know you're hunting down a fortune" — she glanced rather obviously at Tillie — "but you're no thief."

"Lady Neeley!" Tillie exclaimed, unable to believe that even she would be so rude.

"And how," Peter said, "did you come to that conclusion?"

"I know your father," Lady Neeley said, "and that is good enough for me."

"The sins of the father in reverse?" he asked dryly.

"Precisely," Lady Neeley replied, completely missing his tone. "Besides, I rather suspect Easterly. He's far too tanned."

"Tanned?" Tillie echoed, trying to figure out how that related to a theft of rubies.

"And," Lady Neeley added, rather officiously, "he cheats at cards."

"Lord Easterly seemed a good sort to me," Tillie felt compelled to put in. She wasn't allowed to gamble, of course, but she'd spent enough time out in society to know that an accusation of cheating was a serious indictment, indeed. More serious, some would say, than an accusation of theft.

Lady Neeley turned to her with a condescending air. "You, dear girl, are far too young to know the story."

Tillie pursed her lips and forced herself not to reply.

"You ought to make certain you have proof before you accuse a man of theft," Peter said, his spine ramrod straight.

"Bah. I'll have all the proof I need when they find my jewels in his apartments."

"Lady Neeley, have you had the room searched?" Tillie cut in, eager to diffuse the conversation.

"His room?"

"No, yours. The drawing room."

"Of course I have," Lady Neeley retorted. "D'you think I'm a fool?"

Tillie declined to comment.

"I had the room searched twice," the older woman stated. "And then I searched it myself for a third time, just to make sure. The bracelet is not in the drawing room. I can say that as a fact."

"I'm certain you're right," Tillie said, still trying to smooth things over. They'd attracted a crowd, and no fewer than a dozen onlookers were leaning in, eager to hear the interchange between Lady Neeley and one of her prime suspects. "But be that as it may —"

"You had better watch your words," Peter cut in sharply, and Tillie gasped, stunned by his tone, and then was relieved when she realized it wasn't directed at her.

"I beg your pardon," Lady Neeley said, drawing her shoulders back at the affront.

"I am not well acquainted with Lord Easterly, so I cannot vouch for his character," Peter said, "but I do know that you have no proof with which to level a charge. You are treading in dangerous waters, my lady, and you would do well not to besmirch a gentleman's good name. Or you may find," he added forcefully, when Lady Neeley opened her mouth in further argument, "that your own name is dragged through the very same mud."

Lady Neeley gasped, Tillie's mouth fell open, and then a strange hush fell over the small crowd.

"This'll be in tomorrow's *Whistledown* for certain!" someone finally said.

"Mr. Thompson, you forget yourself," Lady Neeley said.

"No," Peter said grimly. "That's the one thing I never forget."

There was a moment of silence, and then, just when Tillie was quite certain that Lady Neeley was going to spew venom, she laughed.

Laughed. Right there in the ballroom, leaving all the onlookers gaping with surprise.

"You have pluck, Mr. Thompson," she said. "I will give you that."

He nodded graciously, which Tillie found rather admirable under the circumstances.

"I do not change my opinion of Lord Easterly, mind you," she said. "Even if he didn't take the bracelet, he has behaved appallingly toward dear Sophia. Now then," she said, changing the subject with disconcerting speed, "where is my companion?"

"She's here?" Tillie asked.

"Of course she's here," Lady Neeley said briskly. "If she'd stayed home, everyone would think her a thief." She turned and leveled a shrewd look at Peter. "Rather like you, I expect, Mr. Thompson."

He said nothing, but he did incline his head ever so slightly.

Lady Neeley smiled — a rather frightening stretch of her lips in her face, and then she turned and bellowed, "Miss Martin! Miss Martin!"

And she was off, with swirls of pink silk flouncing behind her, and all Tillie could think was that poor Miss Martin surely deserved a medal.

"You were magnificent!" Tillie said to Peter. "I've never known anyone to stand up to her like that."

"It was nothing," he said under his breath.

"Nonsense," she said. "It was nothing short of —"

"Tillie, stop," he said, clearly uncomfortable with the continued attention from the other partygoers.

"Very well," she acceded, "but I never did get my lemonade. Would you be so kind to escort me?"

He couldn't very well refuse a direct request in front of so many onlookers, and Tillie tried not to smile with delight as he took her arm and led her back to the refreshment table. He looked almost unbearably handsome in his evening attire. She didn't know when or why he'd decided to forgo his military uniform, but he still cut a dashing figure, and it was a heady delight to be on his arm.

"I don't care what you say," she whispered. "You were wonderful, and Lord Easterly owes you a debt of gratitude."

"Anyone would have —"

"Anyone wouldn't have, and you know it," Tillie cut in. "Stop being so ashamed of your own sense of honor. I find it rather fetching myself."

His face flushed, and he looked like he wanted to yank at his cravat. Tillie would have laughed with delight if she hadn't been quite sure that it would just discomfort him further.

And she realized — she'd thought it was true two days before, but now she knew — that she loved him. It was an amazing, stun-

ning feeling, and it had become, quite spec-
tacularly, a part of who she was. Whatever
she'd been before, she was something else
now. She didn't exist for him, and she didn't
exist because of him, but somehow he had
become a little piece of her soul, and she
knew that she would never be the same.

"Let's go outside," she said impulsively,
tugging toward the door.

He resisted her movement, holding his arm
still against the pressure of her hand. "Tillie,
you know that is a bad idea."

"For your reputation or mine?" she teased.

"Both," he replied forcefully, "although I
might remind you that mine would recover."

And so would hers, Tillie thought giddily,
provided he married her. Not that she
wanted to trap him into matrimony, but still,
it was impossible not to think of it, not to
fantasize right here in the middle of the ball
about standing beside him at the front of a
church, all her friends behind her, listening
as she spoke her vows.

"No one will see," she said, pulling his arm
as best as she could without attracting attention. "Besides, look, the party has moved out
to the garden. We shan't be the least bit
alone."

Peter followed her gaze toward the French
doors. Sure enough, there were several couples milling about, enough so that no one's
reputation would suffer stain. "Very well," he

said, "if you insist."

She smiled winningly. "Oh, I do."

The night air was cool but welcome after the humid crush in the ballroom. Peter tried to keep them in full view of the doors, but Tillie kept tugging toward the shadows, and though he should have stood his ground and rooted her to the spot, he found he couldn't.

She led, and he followed, and he knew it was wrong, but there was nothing he could make himself do about it.

"Do you really think someone stole the bracelet?" Tillie asked once they were leaning against the balustrade, staring out at the torchlit garden.

"I don't want to talk about the bracelet."

"Very well," she said. "I don't want to talk about Harry."

He smiled. There was something in her tone that struck him as funny, and she must have heard it, too, because she was grinning at him.

"Have we anything left about which to converse?" she asked.

"The weather?"

She gave him a vaguely scolding expression.

"I *know* you don't want to discuss politics or religion."

"Quite," she said pertly. "Not now, at any rate."

"Very well, then," he said. "It's your turn

to suggest a topic."

"All right," she said. "I'm game. Tell me about your wife."

He choked on what had to be the largest speck of dust in creation. "My wife?" he echoed.

"The one you claim you're looking for," she explained. "You might as well tell me just what it is you're seeking, since clearly I will have to aid you in the search."

"Will you?"

"Indeed. You said I do nothing but make you appear a fortune hunter, and we've just spent the last thirty minutes in each other's company, several of them in full view of the worst gossips in London. According to your arguments, I have set you back a full month." She shrugged, although the motion was obscured by the soft blue wrap she'd pulled tightly around her shoulders. "It's the very least I can do."

He regarded her for a long moment, then lost his inner battle and gave in. "Very well. What do you want to know?"

She smiled with delight at her victory. "Is she intelligent?"

"Of course."

"Very good answer, Mr. Thompson."

He nodded graciously, wishing he was strong enough not to enjoy the moment. But there was no hope for him; he couldn't resist her.

She tapped her index finger against her cheek as she pondered her questions. "Is she compassionate?" she asked.

"I would hope so."

"Kind to animals and small children?"

"Kind to *me*," he said, smiling lazily. "Isn't that all that matters?"

She shot him a peevish expression and he chuckled, leaning a bit more heavily against the balustrade. A strange, sensual lethargy was stealing over him, and he was losing himself in the moment. They might have been guests at a grand London ball, but at that moment, nothing existed but Tillie and her teasing words.

"You may find," Tillie said, glancing down her nose at him in a most superior fashion, "that if she is intelligent — and I do believe you stated that as a requirement?"

He nodded, graciously granting her the point.

"— that her kindness depends upon your own. Do unto others, and all that."

"You may be assured," he murmured, "that I will be very kind to my wife."

"You will?" she whispered. And he realized that she was near. He didn't know how it had happened, if it had been him or her, but the distance between them had been halved.

She was standing close, too close. He could see every freckle on her nose, catch every glint of the flickering torchlights in her hair.

The fiery tresses had been pulled back into an elegant chignon, but a few strands had pulled free of the coiffure and were curling around her face.

Her hair was curly, he realized. He'd not known that. It seemed inconceivable that he wouldn't have known something so basic, but he'd never seen her thus. Her hair was always pulled back to perfection, every strand in its place.

Until now. And he couldn't help but feel fanciful and think that somehow this was for him.

"What does she look like?"

"Who?" he asked distractedly, wondering what would happen if he tugged on one of those curls. It looked like a corkscrew, springy and soft.

"Your wife," she replied, amusement making her voice like music.

"I'm not sure," he said. "I haven't met her yet."

"You haven't?"

He shook his head. He was nearly beyond words.

"But what do you wish for?" Her voice was soft now, and she touched his sleeve with her index finger, ran it along the fabric of his coat from his elbow to his wrist. "Surely you carry some image in your mind."

"Tillie," he said hoarsely, looking about to see if anyone had seen. He had felt her touch through the fabric of his coat. There was no one left on the patio, but that did not mean that they would remain without interruption.

"Dark hair?" she murmured. "Light?"

"Tillie . . ."

"Red?"

And then he could take it no longer. He was a hero of the war, had fought and slain countless French soldiers, risked his life more than once to pull an injured compatriot from the line of fire, and yet he was not proof against this slip of a girl, with her melodious voice and flirtatious words. He had been pushed to his limit and had found no ramparts or walls, no last-ditch defense against his own desire.

He pulled her to him and then in a circle around him, moving until they were obscured by a pillar. "You shouldn't push me, Tillie."

"I can't help it," she said.

Neither could he. His lips found hers, and he kissed her.

He kissed her even though it would never be enough. He kissed her even though he could never have more.

And he kissed her to spoil her for all other men, to leave his mark so that when her father finally married her off to someone else, she'd have the memory of this, and it would haunt her to her dying day.

It was cruel and it was selfish, but he couldn't help himself. Somewhere, deep within him, he knew that she was *his,* and it was a knife in his gut to know that his primitive awareness amounted to nothing in the world of the *ton.*

She sighed against his mouth, a soft mewling sound that moved through him like flame. "Tillie, Tillie," he murmured, sliding his hands to the curve of her bottom. He cupped her, then pressed her against him, hard and tight, branding her through their clothing.

"Peter!" she gasped, but he silenced her with another kiss. She squirmed in his arms, her body responding to his onslaught. With every motion, her body rubbed against his, and his desire grew harder, hotter, more intense, until he was quite certain he would explode.

He should stop. He had to stop. And yet he couldn't.

Somewhere within him, he knew that this might be his only chance, the one kiss he'd ever play across her lips. And he wasn't ready to end it. Not yet, not until he'd had more. Not until she knew more of his touch.

"I want you," he said, his voice husky with need. "Never doubt that, Tillie. I want you like I want water, like I want air. I want you more than all that, and . . ."

His voice failed him. There were no words left. All he could do was look at her, stare deeply into her eyes and shudder when he saw the echo of his own desire. Her breath was passing over her lips in short gasps, and then she touched one finger to his lips and whispered, "What have you done?"

He felt his brows rise up in question.

"To me," she clarified. "What have you done to me?"

He couldn't answer. To do so would be to give voice to all of his frustrated dreams. "Tillie," he managed to say, but that was all.

"Don't tell me this shouldn't have happened," she whispered.

He didn't. He couldn't. He knew it was true, but he couldn't bring himself to regret the kiss. He might later, when he was lying in bed, burning with unfulfilled need, but not now, not when she was so close, her scent on the wind, her heat pulling him near.

"Tillie," he said again, since it seemed to be the only word his lips could form.

She opened her mouth to speak, but then they both heard the sound of someone else approaching, and they realized they were no longer alone on the patio. Peter's protective instincts took over, and he pulled her farther behind the pillar, pressing one finger to his lips to signal for quiet.

It was Lord Easterly, he realized, arguing in hushed voices with his wife, whom, if Peter had the story correctly, he'd abandoned under mysterious circumstances some twelve years earlier. They were quite involved in their own drama, and Peter was optimistic that they would never notice they had company. He stepped back, trying to cloak himself more deeply in the shadows, but then —

"Ow!"

Tillie's foot. Damn.

The viscount and viscountess turned sharply, their eyes widening when they realized they were not alone.

"Good evening," Peter said gamely, since he seemed to have no other choice but to brazen it out.

"Er, fine weather," Easterly said.

"Indeed," Peter replied, at much the same time as Tillie's chirpy, "Oh, yes!"

"Lady Mathilda," Easterly's wife said. She was a tall, blond woman, the sort who looked always elegant, but tonight she appeared nervous.

"Lady Easterly," Tillie returned. "How are you?"

"Very well, thank you. And you?"

"Just fine, thank you. I was just, er, a little overheated." Tillie waved her hand about as if to indicate the cool night air. "I thought a spot of fresh air might revive me."

"Quite," Lady Easterly said. "We felt the exact same way."

Her husband grunted his agreement.

"Er, Easterly," Peter said, finally sparing the two ladies their uncomfortable small talk, "I should warn you of something."

Easterly inclined his head in question.

"Lady Neeley has been publicly accusing you of the theft."

"What?" Lady Easterly demanded.

"Publicly?" Lord Easterly queried, cutting off any further exclamations from his wife.

Peter nodded curtly. "In no uncertain terms, I'm afraid."

"Mr. Thompson defended you," Tillie put in, her eyes alight. "He was magnificent."

"Tillie," Peter muttered, trying to get her to be quiet.

"Thank you for your defense," Lord Easterly said, after a polite nod to Tillie. "I knew that she suspected me. She has made that much abundantly clear. But she had not yet gone so far as to accuse me publicly."

"She has now," Peter said grimly.

Beside him, Tillie nodded. "I'm sorry," she said. She turned to Lady Easterly and added, "She's rather horrid."

Lady Easterly nodded in return. "I would never have accepted her invitation had I not heard so much about the chef."

But her husband was clearly uninterested in the chef's renown. "Thank you for the warning," he said to Peter.

Peter acknowledged the thanks with a single nod, then said, "I must return Lady Mathilda to the party."

"Perhaps my wife would be a better escort," Lord Easterly said, and Peter realized that he was returning the favor. The Easterlys would never mention that they'd found Peter and Tillie quite alone, and furthermore, Lady Easterly's impeccable reputation would ensure that Tillie was not the subject of scurrilous gossip.

"You are more than correct, my lord," Peter said, pulling gently on Tillie's arm and steering her toward Lady Easterly. "I will see you tomorrow," he said to Tillie.

"Will you?" she asked, and he could see in her eyes that she wasn't being coy.

"Yes," he said, and much to his surprise, he realized he meant it.

Chapter 5

As there are no new developments to report in the Mystery of the Disappeared Bracelet, This Author must content herself with her more ordinary subject matter, namely the day-to-day foibles of the ton, as they proceed in their quest for wealth, prestige, and the perfect spouse.

Chief among This Author's topics is Mr. Peter Thompson, who, as anyone with an observant eye will have noted, has been most assiduously courting Lady Mathilda Howard, only daughter of the Earl of Canby, for more than a week. The pair were quite inseparable at the Hargreaves' Grand Ball, and in the week since, Mr. Thompson has been known to call upon Canby House nearly every single morning.

Such activities can only attract attention. Mr. Thompson is known to be a fortune hunter, although to his credit, it must be noted that until

Lady Mathilda, his monetary aspirations had been modest and, by the standards of society, unworthy of reproach.

Lady Mathilda's fortune, however, is quite a prize, and it has long been accepted by society that she would marry none less than an earl. Indeed, This Author has it on the highest authority that the betting book at White's predicts that she will pledge her troth to the Duke of Ashbourne, who, as all know, is the last remaining eligible duke in Britain.

Poor Mr. Thompson.

Lady Whistledown's Society Papers,
10 June 1816

Poor Mr. Thompson, indeed.

Peter had spent the past week alternating between misery and bliss, his mood entirely dependent upon whether he was able to forget that Tillie was one of the richest people in Britain and he was, to be quite blunt about it, not.

Her parents had to know of his interest in her. He'd called at Canby House nearly every day since the Hargreaves ball, and neither had sought to dissuade him, but they also knew of his friendship with Harry. The Canbys would never turn away a friend of their son, and Lady Canby in particular seemed to enjoy his presence. She liked talking to him about Harry, hearing stories of his final days, especially when Peter told her how Harry could make anyone laugh, even while surrounded by the worst degradations of war.

In fact, Peter was quite certain that Lady Canby liked hearing about Harry so much that she would allow him to dangle hopelessly after Tillie, even though he was, as was patently obvious, a most unsuitable prospect for marriage.

Eventually the time would come when the Canbys sat him down and had a little chat, and Peter would be told in no uncertain terms that while he was an admirable, upstanding fellow, and certainly a fine friend for their son, it was quite another thing altogether to make a match with their daughter.

But that time had not yet arrived, and so Peter had decided to make the best of his situation and enjoy what time he was allowed. To that end, he and Tillie had arranged to meet this morning in Hyde Park. They were both avid riders, and as the day was sporting the first patch of sun in a week, they could not resist an outing.

The sentiment appeared to be shared by the rest of the *ton*. The park was a crush, with riders slowed to the most sedate of trots to avoid entanglements, and as Peter waited patiently for Tillie near the Serpentine, he idly watched the crowds, wondering if there were any other lovesick fools in their ranks.

Maybe. But probably none quite as lovesick — or as foolish — as he.

"Mr. Thompson! Mr. Thompson!"

He smiled at the sound of Tillie's voice. She was always careful not to address him by his given name in public, but when they were alone, and especially when he was stealing a kiss, he was always Peter.

He had never before given a thought to his parents' choice of names, but since Tillie had taken to whispering it in the heat of passion, he had come to adore the sound of it, and he'd decided that Peter was a splendid choice, indeed.

He was surprised to see that Tillie was on foot, moving along the path with two servants, one male and one female, following.

Peter immediately dismounted. "Lady Mathilda," he said with a formal nod. There were a great many people nearby, and it was difficult to tell who was within earshot. For all he knew, that wretched Lady Whistledown herself could be lurking behind a tree.

Tillie grimaced. "My mare is favoring a leg," she explained. "I didn't want to take her out. Do you mind if we walk? I brought my groom to tend to your horse."

Peter handed the reins over as Tillie assured him, "John is very good with horses.

Roscoe will be more than safe with him. And besides," she added with a whisper, once they'd moved a few yards away from the servants, "he and my maid are quite sweet on each other. I was hoping they might be easily distracted."

Peter turned to her with an amused smile. "Mathilda Howard, did you plan this?"

She drew back as if affronted, but her lips were twitching. "I wouldn't dream of lying about my mare's injury."

He chuckled.

"She really was favoring a leg," Tillie said.

"Right," he said.

"She was!" she protested. "Truly. I merely decided to take advantage of the situation. You wouldn't have wanted me to cancel our outing, would you?" She glanced over her shoulder, back at her maid and groom, who were standing side by side near a small cluster of trees, chattering happily.

"I don't think they'll notice if we disappear," Tillie said, "provided we don't go far."

Peter quirked a brow. "Disappeared is disappeared. If we're out of their sight, does it really matter how far we venture?"

"Of course it does," Tillie returned. "It's the principle of the matter. I don't want to get them in trouble, after all, especially while they are providing such a thoughtful blind eye."

"Very well," Peter said, deciding there was

little point in following her logic. "Will that tree do?" He pointed to a large elm, halfway between Rotten Row and Serpentine Drive.

"Right between the two main thorough-fares?" she said, scrunching her nose. "That's a terrible idea. Let's go over there, on the other side of the Serpentine."

And so they strolled, just a little bit out of sight of Tillie's servants, but not, much to Peter's simultaneous relief and dismay, out of sight of everyone else.

They walked for several minutes in silence, and then Tillie said, in a rather casual tone, "I heard a rumor about you this morning."

"Not something you read in *Whistledown*, I hope."

"No," she said thoughtfully, "it was men-tioned this morning. By another one of my suitors." And then, when he didn't rise to her bait, she added, "When you didn't call."

"I can hardly call upon you every day," he said. "It would be remarked upon, and be-sides, we had already made arrangements to meet this afternoon."

"Your visits to my home have already been remarked upon. I hardly think one more would attract additional notice."

He felt himself smiling — a slow, lazy grin that warmed him from the inside out. "Why, Tillie Howard, are you jealous?"

"No," she returned, "but aren't you?"

"Should I be?"

"No," she admitted, "but while we're on the subject, why should *I* be jealous?"

"I assure you I haven't a clue. I spent the morning at Tattersall's, gazing upon horses I can't afford."

"That sounds rather frustrating," she commented, "and don't you want to know what the rumor was I heard?"

"Almost as much," he drawled, "as I suspect you wish to tell it to me."

She pulled a face at that, then said, "I'm not one to gossip . . . much, but I heard that you led a somewhat wild existence when you returned to England last year."

"And who told you this?"

"Oh, nobody in particular," she said, "but it does beg the question —"

"It begs a great many questions," he muttered.

"How was it," she continued, ignoring his grunts, "that I never heard of this debauchery?"

"Probably," he said rather starchily, "because it's not fit for your ears."

"It grows more interesting by the second."

"No, it grew *less* interesting by the second," he stated, in a tone meant to quell further discussion. "And that is why I've reformed my ways."

"You make it sound vastly exciting," she said with a smile.

"It wasn't."

"What happened?" Tillie asked, proving once and for all that any attempts he made to cow her into submission would be fruitless.

He stopped walking, unable to think clearly and move at the same time. One would think he'd have mastered the art in battle, but no, it didn't seem to be in evidence. Not here in Hyde Park, anyway.

And not with Tillie.

It was funny — he'd been able to forget Harry for much of the past week. There had been the conversations with Lady Canby, to be sure, and the undeniable pang he felt whenever he saw a soldier in uniform, whenever he recognized the hollow shadow in their eyes.

The same shadow he'd seen so many times in the mirror.

But when he was with Tillie — it was strange, because she was Harry's sister, and so like him in so many ways — but when he was with her, Harry was gone. Not forgotten, precisely, but just not *there,* not hanging over him like a guilty specter, reminding him that he was alive and Harry was not, and such it would be for the rest of his life.

But before he'd met Tillie. . . .

"When I returned to England," he said to her, his voice soft and slow, "it wasn't long after Harry's death. It wasn't long after the death of a lot of men," he added caustically, "but Harry's was the one I felt most deeply."

She nodded, and he tried not to notice that her eyes were glistening.

"I'm not really sure what happened," he continued. "I don't think I planned it, but it seemed so chance that I was alive and he was not, and then one night I went out with some friends, and suddenly I felt as if I had to live for both of us."

He'd been lost for a month. Maybe a little more. He didn't remember it well; he'd been drunk more often than not. He'd gambled money he didn't have, and it was only through sheer luck that he hadn't sent himself to the poorhouse. And there had been women. Not as many as there could have been, but more than there should have been, and now, as he looked at Tillie, at the woman he was quite certain he'd worship until his dying day, he felt rude and unclean, and rather like he'd made a mockery of something that should have been precious and divine.

"Why did you stop?" Tillie asked.

"I don't know," he said with a shrug. And he didn't know. He'd been at a gambling hell one night and, in a moment of rare sobriety, he'd realized that all this "living" wasn't making him happy. He wasn't living for Harry. He wasn't even living for himself. He was simply avoiding his future, pushing back any reason to make a decision and move forward.

He'd walked out that night and never looked back. And he realized that he must have been a bit more circumspect in his dissolution than he'd realized, because until now, no one had brought it up. Not even Lady Whistledown.

"I felt the same way," she said softly, and her eyes held a strange, faraway softness, as if she were somewhere else, some *time* else.

"What do you mean?"

She shrugged. "Well, I didn't go about drinking and gambling, of course, but after we were notified of . . ." She stopped, cleared her throat, and looked away before she continued. "Someone came out to our home, did you know that?"

Peter nodded, even though he hadn't been privy to that information. But Harry was a son of one of England's most noble houses. It stood to reason that the army would inform his family of his demise with a personal messenger.

"It was almost as if I were pretending he was with me," Tillie said. "I suppose I was, actually. Everything I saw, everything I did, I would think to myself — *What would Harry think? Or — Oh, yes, Harry would like this pudding. He'd have eaten double portions and left none for me.*"

"And did you eat more or less?"

She blinked. "I beg your pardon?"

"Of the pudding," Peter explained. "When

you realized Harry would have taken your share, did you eat your portion or leave it?"

"Oh." She stopped, thought about that. "Left it, I think. After a few bites. It didn't seem right to enjoy it so much."

Quite suddenly, he took her hand. "Let's walk some more," he said, his voice strangely insistent.

Tillie smiled at his urgency and sped her pace to match his. He walked with a long-legged stride, and she found herself nearly skipping along to keep up. "Where are we going?"

"Anywhere."

"Anywhere?" she asked bemusedly. "In Hyde Park?"

"Anywhere but here," he clarified, "with eight hundred people about."

"Eight hundred?" She couldn't help but smile. "I see but four."

"Hundred?"

"No, just four."

He stopped, gazing down at her with a vaguely paternal expression.

"Oh, very well," she conceded, "maybe eight, if you're willing to count Lady Bridgerton's dog."

"Are you up to a footrace?"

"With you?" she asked, her eyes widening with surprise. He was acting most odd. But it wasn't worrisome, just amusing, really.

"I'll give you a head start."

"To make up for my shorter limbs?"

"No, for your feeble constitution," he said provokingly.

And it worked. "Now *that* is a lie."

"Do you think?"

"I *know*."

He leaned against a tree, crossing his arms in a most annoyingly condescending manner. "You shall have to prove it to me."

"In front of all eight hundred onlookers?"

He quirked a brow. "I see but four. Five with the dog."

"For a man who doesn't like to attract attention, you're rather pushing the edge just now."

"Nonsense. Everyone is more than wrapped up in their own affairs. And besides, they're all enjoying the sun too much to take notice."

Tillie looked around. He had a point. The other people in the park — and there were considerably more than eight, although not nearly the hundreds he'd bemoaned — were laughing and joking and, all in all, acting in a most indecorous manner. It was the sun, she realized. It had to be. It had been overcast for what had felt like years, but today was one of those perfect blue-sky days, with sunshine so intense that every leaf on every tree seemed drawn more crisply, every flower painted from a more vivid palette. If there were rules to be followed — and Tillie was quite sure there were; they'd certainly been drummed into her since birth — then the *ton* seemed to have forgotten them this afternoon, at least the ones that governed staid behavior on a sunny day.

"All right," she said gamely. "I accept your challenge. Where shall we race to?"

Peter pointed to a cluster of tall trees in the distance. "That tree right there."

"The near one or the far one?"

"The middle one," he said, clearly just to be contrary.

"And how much of a head start do I receive?"

"Five seconds."

"Timed or counted in your head?"

"Good glory, woman, you're a bit of a stickler."

"I've grown up with two brothers," she said with a level stare. "I've had to be."

"Counted in my head," he said. "I haven't a watch with me in any case."

She opened her mouth, but before she could say anything, he interjected, "*Slowly.* Counted *slowly* in my head. I have a brother, too, you know."

"I know, and did he ever let you win?"

"Not even once."

Her eyes narrowed. "Are you going to let me win?"

He smiled, slowly, like a cat. "Maybe."

"Maybe?"

"It depends."

"On what?"

"On the boon I'm to receive if I lose."

"Isn't one meant to receive a boon for winning?"

"Not when one throws the race."

She gasped with outrage, then retorted, "You won't have to throw a thing, Peter Thompson. I'll see you at the finish line!" And then, before he could get his footing, she was off, tearing across the grass with an abandon that would surely come to haunt her the following day, when all of her mother's friends came calling for their daily dose of tea and gossip.

But right then, with the sun shining on her face and the man of her dreams nipping at her heels, Tillie Howard could not bring herself to care.

She was fast; she'd always been fast, and she laughed as she ran, one hand pumping along, the other holding her skirt a few inches off the grass. She could hear Peter behind her, laughing as his footsteps rumbled ever closer. She was going to win; she was quite certain of that. She'd either win it fair and square, or he'd throw the race and hold it over her head for eternity, but she didn't much care.

A win was a win, and right now Tillie felt invincible.

"Catch me if you can!" she taunted,

looking over her shoulder to gauge Peter's progress. "You'll never — Oomph!"

The breath flew from her body with stunning speed, and before Tillie could make another sound, she was sprawled on the grass, tangled up with what was — thank heavens! — another female.

"Charlotte!" she gasped, recognizing her friend Charlotte Birling. "I'm so sorry!"

"What were you *doing?*" Charlotte demanded, righting her bonnet, which had gone drunkenly askew.

"A footrace, actually," Tillie mumbled. "Don't tell my mother."

"I won't have to," Charlotte replied. "If you think she's not going to hear of *this* —"

"I know, I know," Tillie said with a sigh. "I'm hoping she'll chalk it up to sun-induced insanity."

"Or perhaps sun-blindness?" came a masculine voice.

Tillie looked up to see a tall, sandy-haired man she did not know. She looked to Charlotte, who quickly made introductions.

"Lady Mathilda," Charlotte said, rising to her feet with the stranger's help, "this is Earl Matson."

Tillie murmured her greetings just as Peter skidded to a halt beside her. "Tillie, are you all right?" he demanded.

"I'm fine. My dress might be ruined, but the rest of me is no worse for wear." She accepted his helpful hand and stood up. "Are you acquainted with Miss Birling?"

Peter shook his head no, and Tillie made the introductions. But when she turned to introduce him to the earl, he nodded and said, "Matson."

"You already know each other?" Tillie queried.

"From the army," Matson supplied.

"Oh!" Tillie's eyes widened. "Did you know my brother? Harry Howard?"

"He was a fine fellow," Matson said. "We all liked him a great deal."

"Yes," Tillie said, "everyone liked Harry. He was quite special that way."

Matson nodded his agreement. "I'm very sorry for your loss."

"As are we all. I thank you for your regards."

"Were you in the same regiment?" Charlotte asked, looking from the earl to Peter.

"Yes, we were," Matson said, "though Thompson here was lucky enough to remain through the action."

"You weren't at Waterloo?" Tillie asked.

"No. I was called home for family reasons."

"I'm so sorry," Tillie murmured.

"Speaking of Waterloo," Charlotte said, "do you intend to go to next week's reenactment? Lord Matson was just complaining that he missed the fun."

"I'd hardly call it fun," Peter muttered.

"Right," Tillie said brightly, eager to avoid an unpleasant encounter. She knew that Peter despised the glorification of war, and she rather thought he'd not be able to remain polite to someone who was actually sorry he'd missed such a scene of death and destruction. "Prinny's reenactment! I'd quite forgotten about it. It's to be at Vauxhall, is it not?"

"A week from today," Charlotte confirmed. "On the anniversary of Waterloo. I've heard that Prinny is beside himself with excitement. There are to be fireworks."

"Because we want this to be an *accurate* representation of war," Peter bit off.

"Or Prinny's idea of accurate, anyway," Matson said, his tone noticeably cool.

"Perhaps it is meant to mimic gunfire," Tillie said quickly. "Will you go, Mr. Thompson? I should appreciate your escort."

He paused for a moment, and she absolutely *knew* he didn't want to. But even so, she could not quell her selfishness and she said, "Please. I want to see what Harry saw."

"Harry didn't —" He stopped, coughed. "You won't see what Harry saw."

"I know, but still, it's as close as I'm to come. Please say you'll accompany me."

His lips tightened, but he said, "Very well."

She beamed. "Thank you. It's very kind of you, especially since —" She cut herself off. She didn't need to inform Charlotte and the earl that Peter didn't wish to attend. They might have deduced as much on their own, but Tillie didn't need to spell it out.

"Well, we must be going," Charlotte said, "er, before anyone —"

"We need to be on our way," the earl said smoothly.

"Terribly sorry about the footrace," Tillie said, reaching out and squeezing Charlotte's hand.

"Think nothing of it," Charlotte replied, returning the gesture. "Pretend I'm the finish line, and then you've won."

"An excellent idea. I should have thought of it myself."

"I knew you'd find a way to win," Peter murmured once Charlotte and the earl had wandered off.

"Was it ever in doubt?" Tillie teased.

He shook his head slowly, his eyes never leaving her face. He was watching her with an odd intensity, and she suddenly realized that her heart was beating a little too fast, and her skin was tingling, and —

"What is it?" she asked, because if she didn't speak, she was quite certain she would forget to breathe. Something had changed in the last minute; something had changed within Peter, and she had a feeling that whatever it was, it would change her life as well.

"I need to ask you a question," he said.

Her heart soared. *Oh, yes, yes, yes!* This

could only be one thing. The entire week had been leading up to it, and Tillie knew that her feelings for this man were not one-sided. She nodded at him, knowing that her heart was in her eyes.

"I —" He stopped and cleared his throat. "You must know that I care for you a great deal."

She nodded. "I had hoped," she murmured.

"And I believe that you return my feelings?" He said it as a question, which she found absurdly touching. So she nodded again, and then threw caution to the wind and added, "Very much."

"But you also must know that a match between the two of us is not anything that your family, or indeed, anyone, would have expected."

"No," she said cautiously, not certain where he was leading with this. "But I fail to see —"

"Please," he said, cutting her off, "allow me to finish."

She held silent, but it didn't feel right, and her mood, which had been spinning toward the stars, took a brutal tumble back to earth.

"I want you to wait for me," he said.

She blinked, unsure of how to interpret that. "What do you mean?"

"I want to marry you, Tillie," he said, his

voice unbearably solemn. "But I can't. Not now."

"When?" she whispered, hoping for two weeks, or two months, or even two years. Anything, as long as he put a date on it.

But all he said was, "I don't know."

And all she could do was stare at him. And wonder why. And wonder when. And wonder . . . and wonder . . . And . . .

"Tillie?"

She shook her head.

"Tillie, I —"

"No, don't."

"Don't . . . what?"

"I don't know." Her voice was forlorn, and hurt, and it cut through Peter like a knife.

He could tell she didn't understand what he was asking. And the truth was, he wasn't completely certain, either. He'd never intended this to be anything but a stroll in the park; it was simply to be another in this series of engagements that made up his futile courtship of Tillie Howard. Marriage had been the last thing on his mind.

But then something had happened; he didn't know what. He'd been looking at her, and she'd smiled, or maybe she hadn't smiled, or maybe she'd just moved her lips in some bewitching manner, and then it was as if he'd been shot by Cupid, and somehow he was asking her, the words bursting forth from some daring, impractical corner of his soul.

And he couldn't stop himself, even though he knew it was wrong.

But maybe it didn't have to be impossible. Maybe not quite. There was one way he could make it all happen. If he could just make her understand. . . .

"I need some time to establish myself," he tried to explain. "I have very little right now, almost nothing, really, but once I sell my commission, I'll have a small sum to invest."

"What are you talking about?" she asked.

"I need you to wait a few years. Give me some time to make my fortunes more secure before we marry."

"Why would I do that?" she asked.

His heart slammed in his chest. "Because you care for me."

She didn't speak; he didn't breathe.

"Don't you?" he whispered.

"Of course I do. I just told you as much." Her head shook slightly, as if she were trying to jog her thoughts, force them to coalesce into something she could comprehend. "Why would I wait? Why can't we just marry *now?*"

For a moment Peter could do nothing but stare. She didn't know. How could she not know? All this time he'd been in a state of agony, and she'd never even given it a *thought*. "I can't provide for you," he said. "You must know that."

"Don't be silly," she said with a relieved smile. "There's my dowry, and —"

"I'm not going to live off your dowry," he bit off.

"Why not?"

"Because I have some pride," he said stiffly.

"But you came to London to marry for money," she protested. "You told me as much."

His jaw clamped into a resolute line. "I won't marry *you* for money."

"But you wouldn't be marrying me for money," she said softly. "Would you?"

"Of course not. Tillie, you know how much I care for you —"

Her voice grew sharper. "Then don't ask me to wait."

"You deserve more than what I can offer."

"Let me be the judge of that," she hissed, and he realized she was angry. Not annoyed, not irritated, but well and truly furious.

But she was also naïve. Naïve as only someone who had never faced hardship could be. She knew nothing but the complete admiration of the *ton*. She was fêted and adored, admired and loved, and she could not even conceive of a world in which people whispered behind her back or looked down their noses at her.

And it certainly had never occurred to her that her parents might deny her anything she wanted.

But they would deny her this, and more

specifically, they would deny her *him*. Peter was quite certain of that. There was no way they would allow her to marry him, not with his fortunes the way they currently stood.

"Well," she finally said, the silence between them having stretched far too long, "if you won't accept my dowry, then so be it. I don't need much."

"Oh, you don't?" he asked. He hadn't meant to laugh at her, but the words came out vaguely mocking.

"No," she shot back, "I don't. I'd rather be poor and happy than rich and miserable."

"Tillie, you've never been anything but rich and happy, so I doubt you understand how being poor could —"

"*Don't* patronize me," she warned. "You can deny me and you can reject me, but don't you dare patronize me."

"I will not ask you to live on my income," he said, each syllable clipped. "I rather doubt my promise to Harry included forcing you into poverty."

She gasped. "Is that what this is about. *Harry?*"

"What the devil are you —"

"Is that what this has all been about? Some silly deathbed promise to my brother?"

"Tillie, don't —"

"No, now you allow me to finish." Her eyes were flashing, and her shoulders were shaking, and she would have looked magnificent if his heart weren't breaking.

"Don't you ever tell me you care for me," Tillie said. "If you did, if you even began to understand the emotion, then you would care more for my feelings than for Harry's. He's dead, Peter. Dead."

"I know that better than anyone," he said in a low voice.

"I don't think you even know who I am," she said, her entire body trembling with emotion. "I'm just Harry's sister. Harry's silly little sister, who you vowed to look after."

"Tillie —"

"No," she said forcefully. "Don't say my name. Don't even speak to me until you know who I am."

He opened his mouth, but his lips fell silent. For a moment, they did nothing but stare at each other in a strange, noiseless horror. They didn't move, perhaps hoping that this all was a mistake, that if they just remained there one moment longer, it would all just melt away, and they'd be left as they'd been before.

But it didn't, of course, and while Peter just stood there, speechless and impotent, Tillie turned on her heel and left, her gait a painful combination of walk and run.

A few minutes later, Tillie's groom appeared with Peter's horse, wordlessly handing him the reins.

And as Peter took them, he couldn't help

but feel a certain finality in the action, as if he were being told, *Take these and go. Go.*

It was, he realized with surprise, quite the worst moment of his life.

Chapter 6

Poor Mr. Thompson! Poor, poor Mr. Thompson.

It all takes on new meaning, doesn't it?

Lady Whistledown's Society Papers, 17 June 1816

He shouldn't have come.

Peter was quite positive that he did not wish to watch a reenactment of the Battle of Waterloo; the first had been hellish enough, thank you very much. And while he didn't think that Prinny's version — currently raging to his left — was particularly frightening or accurate, it made him rather sick to realize that the scene of so much death and destruction was being turned into entertainment for the good people of London.

Entertainment? Peter shook his head with disgust as he watched Londoners of all walks of life laughing and making merry as they strolled through Vauxhall Gardens. Most weren't even paying attention to the mock battle. Didn't they understand that men had died at Waterloo? Good men. Young men.

Fifteen thousand men. And that didn't even count the enemy.

But despite all of his misgivings, here he was. Peter had paid his two shillings and made his way into the gardens — not to watch this mockery of a battle or remark upon the spectacular gaslighting or even to marvel over the fireworks, which, he was told, were to be the finest ever staged in Britain.

No, he'd come to see Tillie. He was originally to have escorted her, but he rather doubted she'd canceled her plans just because they were no longer speaking to one another. She'd told him that she needed to see the reenactment, if only to finally make her farewells to her brother.

Tillie would be here. Peter was sure of it.

What he was less sure of, however, was whether he'd be able to locate her. Thousands of people had already arrived at the Gardens, and hundreds more were still pouring in. The paths were jammed with revelers, and it occurred to Peter that if there was one thing about this night that was an accurate representation of battle, it was the odor. It was missing the tang of blood and death, but it certainly had that rather distinctive stench of too many people packed too closely together.

Most of whom, Peter thought as he veered

down a lane to avoid a pack of ruffians bounding toward him, hadn't bathed in months.

And who said one had to leave the delights of the army behind upon retirement?

He didn't know what he'd say to Tillie, assuming he was able to find her. He didn't know if he'd say anything. He just wanted to see her, as pathetic as that sounded. She'd rebuffed all of his overtures since their falling out in Hyde Park the week before. He'd called upon her twice, but both times he'd been informed that she was not "at home." His notes had been returned, although not unopened. And finally, she'd sent a letter of her own, simply saying that unless he was prepared to ask her a very specific question, he needn't contact her again.

Trust Tillie not to mince words.

Peter had heard a rumor that most of the *ton* were planning to congregate at the north side of the meadow, where Prinny had set up a viewing area for the battle. He had to skirt the perimeter of the field, and he kept his distance from the soldiers, not trusting that they were all possessed of enough diligence to make sure their guns lacked real bullets.

Peter pushed through the crowds, cursing under his breath as he made his way to the north meadow. He was a man who liked to walk quickly, with a long-legged stride, and the crush at Vauxhall was his version of hell on earth. Someone stepped on his toe, another jabbed him in the shoulder, and as for the third — Peter smacked away a hand he was quite certain was attempting to pick his pocket.

Finally, after nearly half an hour of battling his way through the swarms, Peter broke out into a clearing; Prinny's men had obviously evacuated all but the most noble of guests, giving the prince an unobstructed view of the battle. Which, Peter noted thankfully, appeared to be reaching its finale.

He scanned the crowds, looking for a familiar glimpse of red hair. Nothing. Could she possibly have decided not to attend?

A cannon boomed near his ear. He flinched.

Where the hell was Tillie?

One final explosion, and then . . . Good God, was that Handel?

Peter looked to his left with disgust. Sure enough, a hundred-person orchestra had picked up their instruments and begun to play.

Where was Tillie?

The noise began to grate. The audience was roaring, the soldiers were laughing, and the music — why the hell was there music?

And then, in the midst of it all, he saw her, and he could have sworn that it all went silent.

He saw her, and there was nothing else.

Tillie wished she hadn't come. She hadn't expected to enjoy the reenactment, but she'd thought she might . . . oh, she didn't know . . . perhaps *learn* something. Feel some sense of bond with Harry.

It wasn't every sister who got the chance to see a reenactment of the scene of her brother's death.

But instead she just wished she'd brought cotton for her ears. The battle was loud, and what's more, she'd found herself standing next to Robert Dunlop, who had obviously found it his duty to offer a running commentary of the scene.

And all she could think was, *It should have been Peter.*

It should have been Peter standing next to her, Peter explaining what the battle maneuvers meant, Peter warning her to cover her ears when it grew too loud.

If she'd been with Peter, she might have discreetly held his hand, then squeezed it when the battle grew too intense. With Peter she would have felt comfortable asking him to tell her at what moment Harry had fallen.

But instead she had Robbie. Robbie, who thought this all a grand adventure, who'd actually leaned down and yelled, "Great, good fun? Eh?" Robbie, who, now that the battle was over, was chattering on about waistcoats and horses, and probably something else as well.

It was too hard to listen. The music was loud, and frankly, Robbie was always a bit hard to follow.

And then, just as the music reached a quiet moment, he leaned down and said, "Harry would have liked this."

Would he? Tillie didn't know, and somehow that bothered her. Harry would have been a different person if he'd come home from the war, and it pained her that she would never know the man he'd become in his last days.

But Robbie meant well, and he had a good heart, so Tillie just smiled and nodded.

"Shame about his death," Robbie said.

"Yes," Tillie replied, because really, what else was there to say?

"What a senseless way to go."

At that, she turned and looked at him. It seemed an odd statement for Robbie, who wasn't one for fine points or subtleties. "All war is senseless," Tillie said slowly. "Don't you think?"

"Well, yes, I suppose," Robbie said, "although someone had to go out there and get rid of Boney. I don't think an if-you-please would have done the trick."

It was, Tillie realized, quite the most complex sentence she'd ever heard from Robbie, and she was wondering if there might be a little more to him, when she suddenly . . . *knew*.

It wasn't that she'd heard something, and it wasn't that she'd seen something. Rather, she just knew that he was there, and sure enough, when she tilted her face to the right, she saw him.

Peter. Right next to her. It seemed stunning that she hadn't sensed his presence earlier.

"Mr. Thompson," she said coolly. Or at least she tried for frost. She rather doubted she succeeded; she was just so *relieved* to see him.

She was still furious with him, of course, and she wasn't at all certain that she wanted to speak to him, but the night felt so strange, and the battle had been discomforting, and Peter's solemn face was like a lifeline to sanity.

"We were just talking about Harry," Robbie said jovially.

Peter nodded.

"It's too bad he missed the battle," Robbie continued. "I mean, all that time in the army, and then you miss the battle?" He shook his head. "Bit of a shame, don't you think?"

Tillie stared at him in confusion. "What do you mean, he missed the battle?" She turned to Peter just in time to see him shaking his head frantically at Robbie, who was responding with a loud, "Eh? Eh?"

"What do you mean," Tillie repeated,

loudly this time, "he missed the battle?"

"Tillie," Peter said, "you must understand —"

"They told me he died at Waterloo." She
looked from man to man, searching their
faces. "They came to my *house*. They told
me he died at Waterloo."

Her voice was growing shrill, panicked.
And Peter didn't know what to do. He could
have killed Robbie; did the man have no
sense? "Tillie," he said, saying her name
again, stalling for time.

"How did he die?" she persisted. "I want
you to tell me right now."

He looked at her; she was starting to
shake.

"Tell me how he died."

"Tillie, I —"

"Tell —"

BOOM!

They all three jumped as an explosion of
fireworks took off not twenty yards from their
spot.

"Ripping good show!" Robbie yelled, his
face to the sky.

Peter glanced up at the fireworks; it was
impossible not to look. Pink, blue, green —
starbursts in the heavens, crackling, splin-
tering, raining showers of sparks down on the
gardens.

"Peter," Tillie said, tugging at his sleeve,
"tell me. Tell me *now*."

Peter opened his mouth to speak, knowing he should be giving her his full attention but somehow unable to keep his eyes off the fireworks. He glanced at her, then back up at the sky, then back at —

"Peter!" she nearly yelled.

"It was a cart," Robbie said suddenly, looking down at her during a lull in the pyrotechnics. "Fell on him."

"He was crushed by a cart?"

"A wagon, actually," Robbie said, correcting himself. "He was —"

BOOM!

"Whoa!" Robbie yelled. "Look at that one!"

"Peter," Tillie begged.

"It was stupid," Peter said, finally forcing his eyes off the sky. "It was stupid and horrible and unforgivable. It should have been broken up for firewood weeks earlier."

"What happened?" she whispered.

And he told her. Not everything, not every last detail; this wasn't the time or the place. But he sketched it out, enough so that she understood the truth. Harry was a hero, but he hadn't died a hero's death; at least not in the way England viewed its heroes.

It shouldn't have mattered, of course, but he could tell from her face that it did.

"Why didn't you tell me?" she asked, her voice low and shaking. "You lied to me. How could you lie?"

"Tillie, I —"

"You *lied* to me. You told me he died in battle."

"I never —"

"You let me believe it," she cried out. "How could you?"

"Tillie," he said desperately. "I —"

BOOM!

They both looked up; they couldn't help it.

"I don't know why they lied to you," Peter said once the explosion had trickled down into spiraling green sparks. "I didn't know that you didn't know the truth until Lady Neeley's dinner party. And I didn't know what to say. I didn't —"

"Don't," she said haltingly. "Don't try to explain."

She had just *asked* him to explain. "Tillie —"

"Tomorrow," she choked out. "Talk to me tomorrow. Right now I . . . right now . . ."

BOOM!

And then, as pink sparks rained from above, she took off, skirts in her hands, running blindly through the one clear spot in the crowd, right past Prinny, right past the orchestra.

Right out of his life.

"You idiot!" Peter hissed at Robbie.

"Eh?" Robbie was too busy staring up at the sky.

"Forget it," Peter snapped. He had to find Tillie. He knew she didn't want to see him,

129

and ordinarily he would have respected her wishes, but damn it all, this was Vauxhall Gardens, and there were thousands of people milling about, some to be entertained and some with more malicious intentions.

It was no place for a lady alone, especially one as obviously distraught as Tillie.

He followed her through the clearing, mumbling an apology as he bumped into one of Prinny's guards. Tillie's dress was a pale, pale green, almost ethereal in the gaslight, and once she'd been slowed down by the crowds, she was easy to follow. He couldn't catch up with her, but at least he could see her.

She moved quickly through the throng, at least more quickly than he was able. She was small and could squeeze into spaces through which he could only bludgeon his way. The distance between them grew, but Peter could still see her, thanks to the slight incline they were both trying to make their way down.

And then — "Ah, damn," he sighed. She was heading for the Chinese pagoda. Why the hell would she do that? He had no idea who else was inside, if anyone. Not to mention the fact that there were probably multiple exits. It'd be fiendishly difficult to keep track of her once she ran inside.

"Tillie," he grumbled, redoubling his efforts to close the space between them. He didn't even think she knew he was chasing her, and still she'd chosen the one surefire way to lose him.

BOOM!

Peter flinched. Another firework, for certain, but this one sounded odd, whistling just overhead, as if it had been pointed too low. He looked back up, trying to figure out what had happened, when —

"Oh my God." The words fell unbidden from his lips, low and shaking with terror. The entire east side of the Chinese pagoda had exploded into flames.

"Tillie!" he screamed, and if he'd thought he was trying hard to get through the crowds before, he knew better now. He moved like a madman, knocking people over, trampling feet and elbowing ribs, shoulders, even faces, as he fought to reach the pagoda.

Around him people were laughing, pointing to the fiery pagoda, obviously thinking that it was part of the spectacle.

At last he reached the pagoda, but when he attempted to run up the steps, he was blocked by two burly guards.

"Y'can't go in there," one of them said. "Too dangerous."

"There's a woman in there," Peter snarled, struggling to free himself from their grasp.

"No, there —"

"I saw her," he nearly screamed. "Let me go!"

The two men looked at one another, and

then one of them muttered, "It's yer own head," and let him go.

He burst into the building, holding a handkerchief over his mouth against the smoke. Did Tillie have a handkerchief? Was she even alive?

He searched the bottom floor; it was filling with smoke, but so far the fire seemed to be contained to the upper levels. Tillie was nowhere to be found.

The air was filling with crackles and pops, and beside him a piece of timber fell to the floor. Peter looked up; the ceiling seemed to be disintegrating before his eyes. Another minute and he would be dead. If he was going to save Tillie he was going to have to pray that she was conscious and hanging from an upstairs window, because he didn't think the stairs would hold him for an ascent.

Choking on the acrid smoke, he stumbled out the back door, frantically scanning the upper windows, all the while looking for a route up the west side of the building, which was still entirely intact. "Tillie!" he screamed, one last time, even though he doubted she could hear him over the roar of the flames.

"Peter!"

His heart slammed in his chest as he whirled toward the sound of her voice, only to find her standing outside, struggling against two large men who were trying to keep her from running to him.

"Tillie?" he whispered.

Somehow she broke free, and she ran to him, and it was only then that he emerged from his trance, because he was still too close to the burning building, and in about ten seconds, she would be as well. He scooped her up before she could throw her arms around him, not breaking his stride until they were both a safe distance from the pagoda.

"What were you doing?" she cried out, still clutching his shoulders. "Why were you in the pagoda?"

"Saving you! I saw you run in —"

"But I ran right back out —"

"But I didn't know that!"

They ran out of words, and for a moment no one spoke, and then Tillie whispered, "I almost died when I saw you inside. I saw you through the window."

His eyes were still stinging and watery from the smoke, but somehow, when he looked at her, everything was crystal clear. "I have never been so scared in my entire life as when I saw that rocket hit the pagoda," he said, and he realized it was true. Two years of war, of death, of destruction, and yet nothing had had the power to terrify him like the thought of losing her.

And he knew — right then and there he knew to the tips of his toes that he could not wait a year to marry her. He had no idea how he'd make her parents agree, but he would find a way. And if he didn't . . . Well, a Scottish wedding had been good enough for plenty of couples before them.

But one thing was certain. He couldn't face the thought of a life without her.

"Tillie, I . . ." There were so many things he wanted to say. He didn't know where to start, how to begin. He hoped she could see it in his eyes, because the words just weren't there. The words didn't exist to express what was in his heart.

"I love you," he whispered, and even that didn't seem enough. "I love you, and —"

"Tillie!" someone shrieked, and they both turned to see her mother racing toward them with more speed than anyone — including Lady Canby herself — would have ever dreamed she possessed.

"Tillie Tillie Tillie," the countess kept repeating, once she'd reached their sides and was smothering her daughter with hugs. "Someone told me you were in the pagoda. Someone said —"

"I'm all right, Mama," Tillie assured her. "I'm fine."

Lady Canby stopped, blinked, then turned to Peter, taking in his sooty and disheveled appearance. "Did you save her?" she asked.

"She saved herself," Peter admitted.

"But he tried," Tillie said. "He went in to find me."

"I . . ." The countess looked lost for words and then finally she just said, "Thank you."

"I didn't do anything," Peter said.

"I think you did," Lady Canby replied, yanking a handkerchief from her reticule and dabbing at her eyes. "I . . ." She looked back at Tillie. "I can't lose another one, Tillie. I can't lose you."

"I know, Mama," Tillie said, her voice soothing. "I'm all right. You can see that I am."

"I know, I know, I —" And then something seemed to snap in her, because she lurched back, jammed her hands on Tillie's shoulders, and started to shake. "What did you think you were doing?" she yelled. "Running off by yourself!"

"I didn't know it was going to catch fire," Tillie gasped.

"In Vauxhall Gardens! Do you know what happens to young women in places like these! I'm going to —"

"Lady Canby," Peter said, laying a calm hand on her shoulder. "Perhaps now is not the time . . ."

Lady Canby stopped and nodded, glancing around them to see if anyone had witnessed her loss of composure. Amazingly, they didn't seem to have attracted a crowd; most everyone was still too busy watching the pagoda's grand finale. And indeed, even the three of them were unable to take their eyes off the structure as it finally imploded, collapsing to the ground in a fiery inferno.

"Good God," Peter whispered, sucking in his breath.

"Peter," Tillie said, choking on his name. It was just one word, but he understood perfectly.

"You're going home," Lady Canby said sternly, yanking on Tillie's hand. "Our carriage is just through that gate."

"Mama, I need to speak with Mr. —"

"You can say whatever you need to say tomorrow." Lady Canby gave Peter a sharp look. "Isn't that true, Mr. Thompson?"

"Of course," he said. "But I will escort you to your carriage."

"That is not —"

"It's necessary," Peter stated.

Lady Canby blinked at his firm tone, and then she said, "I suppose it is." Her voice was soft, and just a little bit thoughtful, and Peter wondered if she'd only just realized how deeply he cared for her daughter.

He took them to their carriage, then watched as it rolled from sight, wondering how he would wait until the morrow. It was ludicrous, really. He'd asked Tillie to wait a year for him, maybe even two, and now he couldn't contain himself for fourteen hours.

He turned back to the Gardens, then

sighed. He didn't want to go back in there, even if it meant taking the long way around to where the hackney cabs were queuing for customers.

"Mr. Thompson! Peter!"

He turned to see Tillie's father dashing through the gate. "Lord Canby," he said. "I —"

"Have you seen my wife?" the earl interrupted frantically. "Or Tillie?"

Peter quickly related the events of the evening and assured him of their safety, noting how the older man sagged with relief. "They left not two minutes ago," he told the earl.

Tillie's father smiled wryly. "Completely forgetting about me," he said. "I don't suppose you've a carriage around the corner."

Peter shook his head ruefully. "I came in a hack," he admitted. It revealed his shocking lack of funds, but if the earl wasn't already aware of the state of Peter's purse, he would be soon. No man would consider a marriage proposal for his daughter without investigating the suitor's financial situation.

The earl sighed, shaking his head at the situation. "Well," he said, planting his hands on his hips as he glanced up the street. "I suppose there's nothing for it but to walk."

"Walk, my lord?"

Lord Canby gave him an assessing sort of glance. "Are you up for it?"

"Of course," Peter said quickly. It would be

a hike to Mayfair, where the Canbys lived, and then some to his apartments in Portman Square, but it was nothing compared to what he'd done on the peninsula.

"Good. I'll put you in my carriage once we reach Canby House."

They walked quickly but quietly across the bridge, pausing only to admire the occasional firework still exploding in the sky.

"One would think they'd have shot them all off by now," Lord Canby said, leaning against the side.

"Or stopped altogether," Peter said sharply. "After what happened with the pagoda . . ."

"Indeed."

Peter intended to resume walking — he was quite sure that he did — but somehow, instead, he blurted out, "I want to marry Tillie."

The earl turned and looked him squarely in the eye. "I beg your pardon?"

"I want to marry your daughter." There, he'd said it. Twice, even.

And at the very least, the earl didn't look ready to have him killed. "This isn't a surprise, I must say," the older man murmured.

"And I want you to halve her dowry."

"That, however, is."

"I'm not a fortune hunter," Peter said.

One corner of the earl's lips curved — not exactly a smile, but something at least similar. "If you're so intent to prove it, why not

138

eliminate the dowry altogether?"

"That wouldn't be fair to Tillie," Peter said, standing stiffly. "My pride isn't worth her comfort."

Lord Canby paused for what had to be the longest three seconds in eternity, then asked, "Do you love her?"

"With everything I am."

"Good." The earl nodded approvingly. "She's yours. Provided that you take the entire dowry. *And* that she says yes."

Peter couldn't move. He'd never dreamed it could be this easy. He'd braced for a fight, resigned himself to a possible elopement.

"Don't look so surprised," the earl said with a laugh. "Do you know how many times Harry wrote home of you? For all his rapscallion ways, Harry was a shrewd judge of character, and if he said there was no one he'd rather see married to Tillie, I'm inclined to believe it."

"He wrote that?" Peter whispered. His eyes were stinging, but this time there was no smoke to take the blame. Only the memory of Harry, in one of his rare serious moments. Harry, as he'd asked for Peter's promise to look after Tillie. Peter had never interpreted that to mean marriage, but maybe that was what Harry had had in mind all along.

"Harry loved you, son," Lord Canby said.

"I loved him as well. Like a brother."

The earl smiled. "Well, then. This all

seems rather fitting, don't you think?"

They turned and began to walk again.

"You will call upon Tillie in the morning?" Lord Canby asked as they stepped off the bridge onto the north bank of the Thames.

"First thing," Peter assured him. "The very first thing."

Chapter 7

Last night's reenactment of the Battle of Waterloo was, in Prinny's words, a "splendid success," leading one to wonder if our Regent simply did not notice that a Chinese pagoda (of which we have few in London) burned to the ground.

It is rumored that Lady Mathilda Howard and Mr. Peter Thompson were both trapped inside, although not (rather astonishingly, in This Author's opinion) at the same time.

Neither was injured, and in an intriguing turn of events, Lady Mathilda departed with her mother, and Mr. Thompson left with Lord Canby.

Could they be welcoming him into their fold? This Author does not dare to speculate but instead promises to report only the truth, just as soon as it becomes available.

Lady Whistledown's Society Papers,
19 June 1816

There were many interpretations of "first thing," and Peter had decided to go with the one that meant three in the morning.

He'd accepted Lord Canby's offer of a carriage, and he'd ridden home much earlier, but once there, all he could do was pace restlessly, counting the minutes until he could present himself once again upon the Canby doorstep and formally ask Tillie to marry him.

He wasn't nervous; he knew she would accept. But he was excited — too excited to sleep, too excited to eat, too excited to do anything but wander around his small abode, every now and then thrusting his fist in the air with a triumphant, "Yes!"

It was silly, and it was juvenile, but he couldn't stop himself.

And it was for much the same reason he found himself standing below Tillie's window in the middle of the night, expertly lobbing pebbles at her window.

Thwap. Thwap.

He'd always had good aim.

Thwap. Thunk.

Whoops. That one was probably too large.

Thw— "Ow!"

Ooops. "Tillie?"

"Peter?"

"Did I hit you?"

"Was that a rock?" She was rubbing her shoulder.

"A pebble, really," he clarified.

"What are you doing?"

He grinned. "Courting you."

She looked around, as if someone might suddenly materialize to have him carted off to Bedlam. "Now?"

"So it seems."

"Are you mad?"

He looked around for a trellis, a tree — anything to climb. "Come down and let me in," he said.

"Now I know you're mad."

"Not mad enough to try to scale the wall," he said. "Come to the servants' entrance and let me in."

"Peter, I won't —"

"Til-lie."

"Peter, you need to go home."

He cocked his head to the side. "I do believe I'll stay here until the entire house wakes up."

"You wouldn't."

"I would," he assured her.

Something about his tone must have impressed her, because she paused to consider that. "Very well," she said in a rather schoolteacherish voice. "I'm coming down. But *don't* think you're coming in."

Peter just saluted her before she disappeared into her room, jamming his hands into his pockets and whistling as he ambled over to the servants' door.

Life was good. No, it was more than that. Life was spectacular.

Tillie had almost perished with surprise when she'd seen Peter standing in her back garden. Well, perhaps that was overstating it a bit, but good heavens! What did he think he was doing?

And yet, even as she'd scolded him, even as she'd told him to go home, she hadn't been able to quell the giddy glee she'd felt upon seeing him there. Peter was proper and conventional; he didn't *do* things like this.

Except maybe for her. He did it for her. Could anything have been more perfect?

She pulled on a robe but left her feet bare. She wanted to move as quickly and silently as possible. Most of the servants slept in the upper reaches of the house, but the hall boy was down near the kitchens, and Tillie would have to pass directly by the housekeeper's suite as well.

After a couple minutes of scurrying, she reached the back door and carefully turned the key. Peter was standing just outside.

"Tillie," he said with a smile, and then, before she had the chance to even say his name, he swept her into his arms and captured her mouth with his.

"Peter," she gasped, when he finally let her, "what are you doing here?"

His lips moved to her neck. "Telling you I love you."

Her entire body tingled. He'd said it earlier that evening, but she still thrilled as if it were the first time.

And then he pulled back, his eyes serious as he said, "And hoping you will say the same."

"I love you," she whispered. "I do, I do. But I need to —"

"You need me to explain," he finished for her, "why I didn't tell you about Harry."

It wasn't what she'd been about to say; amazingly, she hadn't been thinking of Harry. She hadn't thought of him all night, not since she'd seen Peter inside the burning pagoda.

"I wish I had a better answer," he said, "but the truth is, I don't know why I never told you. The time was never right, I suppose."

"We can't talk here," she said, suddenly aware that they were still standing in the doorway. Anyone might hear them and wake up. "Come with me," she said, taking his hand and tugging him inside. She couldn't take him to her room — that would never do. But there was a small salon one flight up that was far from anyone's sleeping quarters. No one would ever hear them there.

Once they'd reached their new location, she turned to him and said, "It doesn't matter. I understand about Harry. I overreacted."

"No," he said, taking her hands in his, "you didn't."

"I did. It was the shock of it, I suppose."

He lifted her hands to his lips.

"But I have to ask," she whispered. "Would you have told me?"

He stilled, her hands still in his, hovering between their bodies. "I don't know," he said quietly. "I suppose I would have had to, eventually."

Had to. It wasn't quite the wording she'd thought to hear.

"Fifty years is a long time to keep a secret," he added.

Fifty years? She looked up. He was smiling.

"Peter?" she asked, her voice trembling.

"Will you marry me?"

Her lips parted. She tried to nod, but she couldn't seem to make anything work.

"I already asked your father."

"You —"

Peter tugged her closer. "He said yes."

"People will call you a fortune hunter," she whispered. She had to say it; she knew it was important to him.

"Will *you?*"

She shook her head.

He shrugged. "Then nothing else matters." And then, as if the moment weren't perfect enough, he dropped to one knee, never letting go of her hands. "Tillie Howard," he said, his voice solemn and true, "will you marry me?"

She nodded. Through her tears, she nodded, and somehow she managed to say, "Yes. Oh, yes!"

His hands tightened on hers, and then he stood, and then she was in his arms. "Tillie," he murmured, his lips warm against her ears, "I will make you happy. I promise you, with everything I am, I will make you happy."

"You already do." She smiled, gazing up at his face, wondering how it had become so familiar, so precious. "Kiss me," she said impulsively.

He leaned down, dropping a light kiss on her lips. "I should go," he said.

"No, *kiss* me."

He drew a haggard breath. "You don't know what you ask."

"Kiss me," she said again. "Please."

And he did. He didn't think he should; she saw that in his eyes. But he couldn't help himself. Tillie shivered with a thrill of feminine power as his lips found hers, hungry and possessive, promising love, promising passion.

Promising everything.

There was no turning back now; she knew this. He was like a man possessed, his hands roaming over her with breathtaking intimacy. There was little between her skin and his; she was clad only in her silk nightdress and robe, and every touch brought thrilling pressure and heat.

"Turn me away now," Peter begged. "Turn me away now and make me do the right thing." But his grip tightened as he said it, and his hands found the curve of her bottom and pressed her shockingly against him.

Tillie just shook her head. She wanted this too much. She wanted him. He'd awakened something within her, something powerful and primitive, a need that was impossible to explain or deny.

"Kiss me, Peter," she whispered. "And more."

He did, with a passion that stole her very soul. But when he pulled away, he said, "I won't take you now. Not here. Not like this."

"I don't care," she nearly wailed.

"Not until you're my wife," he vowed.

"Then for God's sake, get a special license *tomorrow*," she snapped.

He pressed one finger to her lips, and when she looked at his face, she realized he was smiling. Quite devilishly. "I won't make love to you," he reiterated, his eyes turning wicked. "But I'll do everything else."

"Peter?" she whispered.

He swept her into his arms and deposited her on the sofa.

"Peter, what are you — ?"

"Nothing you've ever heard of," he said with a chuckle.

"But —" She gasped. "Oh my heavens! What are you doing?"

His lips were on the inside of her knee, and they were moving up.

"Rather what you think, I imagine," he murmured, his mouth hot against her thigh.

"But —"

He looked up suddenly, and the loss of his lips on her skin was devastating. "Will anyone notice if I ruin this gown?"

"My . . . no," she said, too dazed to put together anything more complete.

"Good," he said, and then he gave it a yank, ignoring Tillie's gasp when the left strap separated from the bodice.

"Do you have any idea how long I've been dreaming of this moment?" he murmured, moving his body up along hers until his mouth found her breast.

"I . . . ah . . . ah . . ." She hoped he didn't really expect an answer. His lips had found her nipple, and she had no idea how it was possible, but she swore she felt it between her legs.

Or maybe that was his hand, which was tickling her in the most wicked way possible. "Peter?" she gasped.

He lifted his head, just long enough to look at her face and drawl, "I've been distracted."

"You've . . ."

If she'd meant to say more, it was lost as

he moved back down, his lips replacing his fingers in her most intimate place. Dozens of words flooded her mind, most involving his name and phrases like *You shouldn't, You can't*, but all she could seem to do was moan and mewl and let out the odd "Oh!" of delight.

"Oh!"

"Oh!"

And then once, when his tongue did something particularly wicked, "Oh, Peter!"

He must have heard the squeak in her voice, because he did it again. And then again and again until something very strange happened, and she quite simply exploded beneath him. She gasped, she arched, she saw stars.

And as for Peter, he just lifted himself up and smiled down at her face, licked his lips, and said, "Oh, Tillie."

Epilogue

Triumph!

For This Author, that is.

Was it not hinted right in these pages that a match might be made between Lady Mathilda Howard and Mr. Thompson?

A notice appeared in yesterday's Times, announcing their betrothal. And at last night's Frobisher Ball, Lord and Lady Canby declared themselves delighted with the match. Lady Mathilda was positively radiant, and as for Mr. Thompson — This Author is gleefully pleased to report that he was heard to mutter, "It shall be a short engagement."

Now then, if only This Author could solve the Neeley mystery . . .

Lady Whistledown's Society Papers,
21 June 1816

Julia Quinn

When Julia Quinn created Lady Whistledown in her groundbreaking novel, *The Duke and I*, she never dreamed that the character would take on a life of her own. Readers everywhere were fascinated by the mystery of her identity, and Julia's Korean publisher was even forced to put up an internet bulletin board so that her fans in that country could discuss her books.

The author of twelve novels and four novellas for Avon Books, she is a graduate of Harvard and Radcliffe Colleges and lives with her family in the Pacific Northwest. Her next novel, *When He Was Wicked*, will be published in July 2004.

Please visit her on the web at *www.juliaquinn.com*.

The Last Temptation

Mia Ryan

For my Mamo.
I meant to dedicate one to you
a long time ago, Mams.
Hopefully God lets you take time off
from being the most beautiful angel up there
to get some good reading in.☺

Chapter 1

This Author suspects, however, that if any of Lady Neeley's guests were to point to the true tragedy of yestereve, they would not mention the missing bracelet but rather the uneaten food. (The guests were, rather tragically, torn from their meal during the soup course.) This Author has it on the best authority that the menu was to have included lamb cutlets with cucumbers, veal ragout, curried fowl, and lobster pudding in the first course. The second was to have featured saddle of lamb, roast fowl, boiled capon with white sauce, braised ham, roast veal, and raised pie.

This Author shall not remark upon the desserts, which remained uneaten. It is far too painful a subject to ponder.

Lady Whistledown's Society Papers,
29 May 1816

The entire house smelled of lobster: old, overdone lobster. Not the lovely, enticing smell that had caused Isabella's mouth to water as Lady Neeley had made them wait for dinner the night before. Oh, no, this morning the lobster smell had permeated every thread of every cushion of every sofa and chair, and it absolutely was no longer enticing.

Isabella Martin made her way quietly down the back servants' stairs to the kitchen. She held her breath and carefully stepped over the stair that creaked. She did not want to face Lady Neeley, not yet, at least. And she definitely couldn't deal with Lady Neeley's parrot from hell. That stupid bird had made an awful night nearly unbearable. And the fact that Lady Neeley had done nothing to help Isabella left a very bad taste in her mouth.

After ten years of being her constant companion, Isabella deserved, at the least, to have had the old woman put the pestering pest in the cupboard for an evening. But, no, Isabella had spent the entire night ducking out of the way as the stupid bird had tried to kiss her with its painfully sharp beak.

Bugger the parrot was bugger Lady Neeley, as well, Isabella thought as she finally pushed through the door to the kitchen.

Christophe was busy making some sort of pastry that smelled eerily of lobster. He glanced up as she came in.

"Good morning, Christophe," Bella said with a bright smile.

"Good?" he asked. "You use this word and I do not think I understand it. Maybe, yes, it is good a little bit now that beautiful Bella brightens my kitchen with her smile."

Bella laughed and smiled wider. Ever the charmer, Christophe was. Bella slid onto a stool across the table from the French chef she had found for Lady Neeley about five years before. He was a small man, about five years younger than Bella and a good foot shorter than she, with dark hair and darker eyes. And whenever Bella felt even a little sad, she knew that she could sit in Christophe's warm kitchen surrounded by succulent aromas and receive compliments, one on top of another until her head swam with them.

Christophe shook his head now and blinked his eyes as if fighting back tears. "My dinner ruined!" he cried. "Ruined! For what, I ask you? Some ugly bracelet. Well, I'll tell you, Bella, this household is going to eat lobster soup and lobster biscuits until they turn green."

Bella grinned. "The biscuits or the people?"

Christophe frowned and pounded at his dough. "I am not in the mood for laughing this morning, Bella, *ma chérie*. Is society all abuzz this morning about the artistry that comes out of my kitchen? They should be, *oui? Mais non! Ne pas c'est matin.* No, this morning Lady Whistledown talks about the dinner that never happened and some horrible bracelet."

Christophe sniffed dramatically and shook his head as he viciously pinched off bits of the dough he had finished kneading and placed them onto a greased pan. "I have cried all of my tears, though, so you are fortunate that you will at least not have to see a watery Christophe this morning."

"A watery Christophe sounds terribly unappetizing, I must admit," Bella said.

Christophe paused in his work, a greasy bit of dough suspended between them. Bella frowned at the fishy smell that wafted up from it.

"You seem rather more perky than you ought to be this morning," Christophe said. "Must I remind you that your party was ruined last night? It was my food, *oui,* but you are the one putting all of Lady Neeley's parties together. And as I always do, I will once again remind you that you are a genius."

Bella grinned. "Thank you, dear."

"But you are not at all upset this morning?"

"Well, of course, I am a little sad. But, really, I'm just happy to be away from the parrot."

Christophe grimaced. "What has happened to that devil bird? It was always a really awful thing, spitting at everyone, but all of a sudden it is now trying to make love to you, I do swear. And according to Mrs. Trotter, it now talks incessantly. It will not shut up. It is making the housekeeper mad."

"Yes, well, I was tempted on many occasions last night to leave a window open in hopes that the thing would make an escape," Bella said.

Christophe giggled as only the young Frenchman could. "Perhaps Lady Neeley would follow the dreaded thing."

"Christophe!" Bella frowned at the chef.

He just rolled his eyes and shrugged, and then he shrieked, "My tarts," and ran for the oven. He twirled in a circle, grabbed a quilted pad off the peg on the wall, yanked open the oven, and pulled out a tray laden with beautiful, flaky strawberry tarts.

"I knew I smelled something that was not completely of the lobster variety." Bella sighed and clasped her hands at her breasts. "They're gorgeous!"

"Just wait until you taste them, my beautiful Bella," Christophe said, prancing about the kitchen as he readied a plate for her. "We mustn't forget the pièce de résistance," he said and sprinkled sugar over the whole lot.

Bella could barely contain herself and plunged into the lovely pastry the second

Christophe put the plate in front of her. "Ohhhh," she said around a gooey bite. "You are divine, Christophe."

"Of course I am," he told her. "And before I forget, I need you to tell me what you want to eat for your birthday. Anything your heart desires is yours. Well, in the culinary sense, at least."

"My birthday?" Bella asked, licking at bits of strawberry tart that had clung to her lips.

Christophe batted his lashes at her. "I shall wait until you have swallowed before continuing this conversation, thank you very much."

Bella laughed and swallowed. "It *is* going to be my birthday, isn't it?" she cried. "I had forgotten."

"Of course you have, darling, I shall probably put it completely out of my mind when I turn thirty as well. Thank God that won't happen for five more lovely years, though."

Bella blinked. "Thirty?"

"A traumatic age, *je pense*," Christophe said. "So you just write down exactly what you would like for breakfast, lunch, and dinner, and it is yours, *ma chérie*."

"But I am not turning thirty," Bella said. "It is my twenty-ninth, I'm very sure of it."

"Oh, come, you didn't even remember it was your birthday. And, definitely, it is your thirtieth."

The strawberry tart, which had been light

and sweet and very near perfection, suddenly tasted like dirt in Bella's mouth.

"On June twelfth, eighteen-fifteen, you turned twenty-nine, Isabella Martin. I remember it clearly. You became drunk off the trifle and sang a song to Mrs. Trotter that made Lady Neeley cry."

"You promised you would not repeat that," Bella reminded him.

"And that means that exactly two weeks from today you are going to turn thirty," Christophe announced with a flourish of his hand.

Bella pushed her plate away, her appetite gone. "It is my thirtieth birthday," she said quietly. Thirty. It wasn't the end of the world, of course. But she suddenly realized that she had forgotten the fact of her exact age on purpose.

She remembered thinking last year that something had better happen during the year, something to change her life. Because if her life was the same when she turned thirty years old, there really wasn't much hope it would ever be different.

Because, even though from the time she had first entered Lady Neeley's home ten years before, upon the death of her parents, Bella had been pretty sure that she would probably spend the rest of her life as a spinster in someone else's home, until now she had held fast to a tiny slice of hope in her heart that *something* else might happen.

But, really, after one turned thirty, the chances of anything changing in one's life became very slim. And they hadn't been all that numerous when she was twenty-nine.

"Now then, your menu, Bella?" Christophe stood before her, a feathered quill in hand, a piece of paper on the counter between them.

"Er," Bella said, food being the last thing on her mind.

"There you are, Miss Martin!" shrilled Lady Neeley.

Bella and Christophe turned as the thin, white-haired woman entered the kitchen, the wretched parrot perched upon her shoulder.

Christophe stiffened as the parrot screeched, "Martin, Martin, Martin," and launched himself at Bella.

The bird's talons pierced the material of Bella's dress and scratched her shoulder as his beak pecked mercilessly at her neck and ear. She was going to kill the bird.

"Might I suggest a parrot stew?" Christophe whispered.

"I don't know why he has suddenly found you so appealing, Miss Martin, but it is quite cute, isn't it?" Lady Neeley asked with a laugh.

"Take that bird out of my kitchen," Christophe said.

"Of course, Christophe, of course. Come along, Miss Martin, I have a very big favor to ask of you." Lady Neeley swished her skirts and walked out.

Bella stood, trying to keep the parrot's beak away from her eyeball or anything else that could be permanently damaged, and followed Lady Neeley. Hopefully the woman wasn't going to ask anything too difficult of her. Bella did feel like getting back into bed and pulling the covers over her head.

"Martin, Martin," the parrot screeched again and pecked at her ear. Lovely, she was turning thirty and had only ever been kissed by a bird.

That was utterly pathetic. And in that second, Bella decided that she really ought to do something about it. She had two weeks, after all, before the turning thirty part happened.

Two weeks.

Though her imagination did tend to run away with her, she knew, of course, that her prince in shining armor would probably not show up in the next two weeks. He'd had thirty years, after all, and had not found her.

But perhaps, at least, she could find someone who would kiss her.

The parrot pecked at her again, and Bella shooed him away. Preferably a someone who lacked feathers and a beak for a mouth.

Chapter 2

It is a commonly held belief that the matrons of society are the most mad for marriage (for their progeny, of course, not themselves; far be it from This Author to suggest that any of London's leading ladies secretly dream of bigamy).

However, as there is always an exception to prove a rule, might This Author point a finger in the direction of the Earl of Waverly? The gentleman in question is a most affable sort, but terrifyingly single-minded when it comes to the marital status of his as yet unwed son and heir, Lord Roxbury.

Roxbury, who is, This Author is informed, on the darker side of thirty-five, has yet to show a particular interest in any specific marriageable miss. As a future earl, he is considered a prime catch by persons other than his parents. (This Author assures all Dear Readers that this is not al-

ways the case.) But season in and season out, Roxbury evades the marital noose, and This Author fears that poor Lord Waverly might expire of frustration before his son finally accedes to his wishes and walks someone (anyone) down the aisle.

Lady Whistledown's Society Papers,
29 May 1816

Anthony Doring, Lord Roxbury leaned back against the elegant red silk that covered his favorite chair in his front drawing room and listened as his father, Robert Doring, fourth Earl of Waverly, regaled him with all the reasons Anthony should marry. Anthony nodded and smiled and nodded and smiled some more and then checked his watch and nodded again.

This was actually a common occurrence. Every Wednesday morning, Lord Waverly sat with his son in the front drawing room of Lord Roxbury's town house. And each week the conversation was basically the same. The niceties of weather and health were gotten out of the way early and quickly, and they were always followed by an accounting of any new ladies in town that would make perfect Lady Roxburys. And then, of course, Lord Waverly liked to remind his son of the reasons he must marry.

Lord Roxbury always heartily agreed with everything his father said, for it made the experience much more palatable, and usually shorter.

Today, just as they were coming up to reason number five, a slight knock at the door interrupted them.

Anthony glanced up to see his butler, Herman, at the door. "Beg your pardon, my lord, there is a lady —"

Anthony quickly stopped the man from continuing with a small gesture of his hand. He stood and walked over to the door. "Show her to the green room," he said quietly before the butler could continue. And then turned to smile and nod at his father.

He had not expected Lady Brazleton so early in the day, but the last thing he wanted was his father meeting up with the woman in his hallway. Meeting a married, lone woman in his hallway would surely precipitate a lengthy lecture on the downfalls of debauchery. And, since his father would at least have the decency not to subject him to such a tirade with Lady Brazleton in the house, it would most likely mean an extra visit on top of the usual Wednesday visit, and, really, there was just so much a son could take.

"Now then, Roxbury," his father said. "I've come to a decision."

Anthony nodded, but he didn't smile. His father's decisions were rarely anything one

166

would smile about.

"You, son, are giving a party," his father said.

Anthony nodded and decided to pace rather than sit. He had to contend with a lot of pent-up energy when he listened to his father. Pacing helped. A good round in the ring at Gentleman Jim's was exactly the ticket, actually, and Anthony could usually be found in that establishment every Wednesday afternoon.

"A party, you say?" Anthony asked.

"Yes, sir, a party. You have managed to make yourself persona non grata with most of the eligible young ladies in society, Roxbury. They all believe you to be a rake and a rogue and not husband material at all."

"My job is done."

"I think a party is exactly the thing to put you back in good standing with the mamas trying to marry off their daughters," his father said without acknowledging that Anthony had said anything at all.

"Ah, and that is exactly my highest goal in life."

"No, your goal is marriage."

"Right, but first a party, I presume," Anthony said, stopping for a moment to take in the sight of a very pretty bird in the tree just outside of his window. Spring, finally. Winter had been dreadfully cold, and Anthony was looking forward to a bit of warmth.

Women tended to wear less when it was warm. It made life rather more interesting.

"Lady Neeley gave me the idea, actually," his father continued.

"Ah," Anthony murmured. His father and Lady Neeley had spent ten years courting. Actually, his father had asked Lady Neeley to marry him on many occasions, but the lady was intent on keeping her independence.

It seemed she didn't mind plotting to take his away, though. "I am assuming," he said to his father, "this party Lady Neeley has decided I must have will precede my marriage?" Usually Anthony felt a few steps ahead of his father, but this whole party idea was definitely throwing him a bit of a curve.

"Yes, exactly," Lord Waverly said, thumping the floor with his silver-headed walking stick. "The mothers will see that you are not completely without social graces, and the daughters will see that you have a very lovely home. I think it will help your standing as an eligible bachelor considerably."

"Lovely."

"Lady Neeley, of course, is adept at parties. Her parties are always the best."

"I hear her dinner party last night was not horribly successful. In fact, I think her guests never got fed and were strip-searched to round out the evening."

Lord Waverly pinched his lips in a sour

look. "I don't know what you are talking about, boy. Now, then, Lady Neeley has shared her secret of party success with me, and I am sending her to you."

"Her?" Anthony left the bird to its twittering and continued his pacing in earnest. If he had to spend even a minute alone in the company of Lady Neeley, he would surely go mad.

"You will understand later." Lord Waverly levered himself up with the help of his walking stick. "I will show myself out. I shall expect an invitation to your party within the week, and should like to see the event scheduled before the end of June. 'Tis a good month for a party, is it not?"

Anthony nodded and smiled, and decided that he might just have to take a trip out of town for a few weeks. His father had left pestering behind and had definitely crossed the line into intruding. This was a very bad thing.

As Lord Waverly exited, Anthony let his smile slip into a frown, but then he remembered the tasty morsel awaiting him in the green room, and he smiled again.

Lady Brazleton, just the thing to take his mind off his father and Lady Neeley and parties. Anthony smoothed his waistcoat as he left the front drawing room and crossed the hall toward the green room. He nodded and shushed Herman, who seemed overly eager to explain Lady Brazleton's existence in the green room, and slipped through the half-open doorway.

Lady Brazleton was bent over the table that stood against the opposite wall, obviously intrigued with the ivory inlay. It was a beautiful table, he had to admit.

Although he would argue that his own view at the moment rivaled any other. He stood still for a moment, enjoying the way the soft blue fabric of Lady B's gown clung to the curve of her bottom. She had a bonnet on, of all things, with a huge rim that made it impossible to see any part of her hair or face, but it did show off the nape of her neck.

He had not realized what a lovely neck Lady B had. It was long and slender, and he knew that he must, immediately, press his lips to the soft spot that dipped just where her neck met her back.

Anthony strode forward, placed one hand on the beautiful curve of Lady B's backside, and put his open mouth against her soft nape.

Instead of the sensual sound he was expecting, the woman gave a great yelp of surprise, snapped her head up, and savagely smacked his nose with the back of her damned hard head.

Anthony managed to bite his tongue, and he was pretty sure his nose was broken. He blinked as lights seemed to pop in front of his eyes, and then he saw very large gray eyes staring into his.

Lady Brazleton, if he remembered correctly, had pale blue eyes, he thought hazily as darkness began to edge into his peripheral vision.

For a moment, Isabella could only stare in complete shock at Lord Roxbury. But then she realized that he was bleeding profusely, and he did rather look like he might faint.

"Oh dear," she said. And then she grabbed the handkerchief she could see poking out of a pocket of his jacket and shoved it against his nose. "Pinch your nose," she told him. "It will stop the bleeding."

He blinked and did nothing, so she pinched his nose through the handkerchief and led him over to a settee. "Lie down, put your head back," she ordered.

This time he did exactly what she told him to do. Hopefully that meant his head was clearing. She *had* hit him terribly hard.

She rubbed the back of her head. She was going to have a nasty bump there.

Isabella pressed Lord Roxbury's nose together and bit her lip. She did feel like giggling, and this surely was neither the time nor the place.

"Obviously, you thought I was someone else," she said.

"Obviouswee."

171

She giggled.

Over the handkerchief, dark brown eyes glared at her. "Sorry," she said, trying to subdue her mirth. "You must forgive me, Lord Roxbury, I've never been touched so, and it shocked me. I did not even hear you enter the room."

He didn't answer her this time, but he was still glaring at her like she was some errant child.

That really did not seem fair at all.

"Anyway, I am sorry to disappoint," she said. And then she ruined the apology by letting another laugh slip out.

Lord Roxbury glared a bit more, but then he blinked and seemed more baffled than angry. That was good, at least. She really did not see that he had much of a leg to stand on being angry with her.

He had grabbed her bottom, after all.

And he had kissed her neck.

She suddenly realized that she had been kissed, and her face heated and, probably, turned a few shades of red. Well, goodness, that was fast. She hadn't really been sure how she'd get a man to kiss her before her thirtieth birthday, and here it had happened already.

It had felt very lovely, too. She closed her eyes for a moment and tried to remember the fleeting touch. Lord Roxbury had a reputation as a complete rogue, so he must be a very good kisser. Bella remembered that in the split second before she had reacted, Lord Roxbury's warm lips had felt very soft against her neck.

Bugger it. She really wished she could turn back time. Rather than break the man's nose, she would have turned in his arms and tried to grab a kiss on the lips before he'd realized his mistake.

Bella sighed and opened her eyes.

Lord Roxbury was staring at her.

She blinked, as she had rather forgotten that he was there.

He reached up and put his large, dark hand over hers.

For a long moment, Bella could only stare at the back of Lord Roxbury's hand. In all honesty, she had never in her life been this close to a man before. In fact, she was pretty sure she had never had a man touch her hand, other than her father, of course. But her father had been a small man, with slight hands.

Lord Roxbury was not a small man. She had seen him before, of course, but always at a distance. Now, Bella realized, he had extremely wide shoulders, as he could barely balance on the small settee. And his hands made hers look like those of a porcelain doll.

He raised his dark brows at her, and Bella realized with a jolt that he was holding the handkerchief, and she could pull away. Obviously, he had been waiting for her to pull her hand away for some time.

How embarrassing.

Bella straightened quickly and entwined her fingers together in front of herself.

Lord Roxbury swung his legs around so that he was sitting, and then pulled the handkerchief away from his face carefully. He folded the bloodied thing and stashed it on the table beside him before looking up at her.

"Who are you?" he asked finally.

Bella nearly laughed again, but she managed to keep the impulse checked in the face of Lord Roxbury's rather dour look. "Martin," she said. "I am Isabella Martin. Lady Neeley said that you would be expecting me."

"Lady Neeley," Lord Roxbury said as he shook his head. And then he glanced around. "Shouldn't you have a chaperone?"

Bella did laugh this time. "Oh, I don't usually take a chaperone with me. I'm not anyone . . . that is to say, no one ever takes any notice of me. No one notices that I don't have a chaperone, so I don't think it is necessary."

Lord Roxbury squinted at her and then leaned his head against his hands. "Could you sit down," he said, the words a question, but the tone a command.

Bella quickly sat beside him and then realized that the settee was rather small, but it would be horribly uncomfortable to actually stand and move to another chair. She contemplated the problem for a moment, her eyes on the very small space between her knees and Roxbury's thigh.

"You're Lady Neeley's companion," he said. "I recognize you now."

Bella nodded and said nothing, though a tiny minx within her wanted to ask whom he had been expecting. Who was supposed to be on the receiving end of that dark, soft kiss and the touch of those large hands? Bella shivered and realized that she was once again staring at Lord Roxbury's thigh.

She really couldn't help it, though. He had a muscle running the length of his thigh that one could actually see. Bella didn't think she had ever actually seen a man's muscle through his clothing.

That thought made her giggle. As if she had seen a muscle without clothing. Bella shoved her hand against her lips to try and keep her laugh at bay.

"You find this whole incident rather amusing, don't you?" Roxbury asked darkly.

Bella could only shrug, for if she spoke, she would laugh. She could not seem to keep her mind or her eyes off Lord Roxbury's leg. And once she managed to lift her gaze up to his face, the sight only emphasized the fact that she was very close to an exceptionally good looking man.

He had chocolate brown eyes that seemed to sparkle with hidden amusement, even when he was irritated, like now. He had a long face and a hard jaw, with straight brown hair that, at the moment, at least, tended to hang in his eyes. From her usual vantage point, sitting in the far corners of the ballrooms during the soirees she attended with Lady Neeley, Bella had seen Lord Roxbury. She knew that when he was at a ball, he always had his hair slicked back away from his face.

And she had really never known that Lord Roxbury's very body seemed to hum with an energy that radiated warmth and something else that made her feel extremely jumpy.

"Strange," Lord Roxbury said. "In my experience, young maidens usually yell and scream and cry and have hysterics if something like this happens to them."

Bella smiled. "You mean you've done this to other young maidens?" she asked.

"Well, no, not exactly, but —"

"Anyway, Lord Roxbury, I'm not a young maiden." Bella sat a bit straighter. "I'll have you know that I shall turn thirty exactly two weeks from this very day. And, thanks to you . . ." Bella touched his knee lightly and then pulled her hand away quickly. Honestly, she had not meant to touch him, it had been a reflex.

One she had never had before in her life, but there you go.

Bella curled her fingers in her skirt and cleared her throat.

"Thanks to me?" Roxbury prompted her.

"Thanks to you, I shall at least have been kissed before I turn thirty." Really, that was not what she should have said. Lady Neeley would have dropped dead in her tracks if she'd heard her.

Roxbury blinked. And then he leaned his head back and laughed.

"Sorry," Bella said. "That was forward of me."

"Terribly forward of you," Roxbury nodded. "But if you think that you have been kissed, then, obviously, being forward is not something you are used to."

Bella frowned. "Are you funning me, my lord?"

"Very much so. Now then, Miss Martin, I am going to guess that you are what my father was speaking of when he said Lady Neeley was sending over her secret weapon for a party."

Bella sighed in relief. Finally, a subject she felt in control of. "Yes, I am supposed to help you throw a grand party."

"And why are you going to help me?"

"Because I'm very good at parties, my lord. I organize all of Lady Neeley's. With the exception of last night, Lady Neeley's parties are always wonderful. And last night's debacle was entirely out of my hands."

"Of course it was."

"Now then, Lord Roxbury, I was thinking that we could do something with the Asian theme of the décor in your home. Perhaps a Japanese party?"

"A Japanese party?" Lord Roxbury looked perplexed. "What would a Japanese party be like?"

"I have no idea," Bella said with a laugh. "But we could do some research." Bella stood and turned slowly, taking in the Asian panels Lord Roxbury had hung on his walls. "We could do some wonderful things with the decorations. And you could hire girls to dress up in kimonos and walk around with trays of hors d'oeuvres."

Roxbury didn't say anything, so Bella continued. "Or you could ask the women you invite to wear Japanese garb. People like it when you get them involved in the party theme."

Roxbury stood slowly. "You are the one who organized Lady Neeley's haunted party, aren't you?"

Bella smiled widely. "Yes, I have done all of her parties since I've been with her, but the Haunted Mansion party is the one that I'm most proud of."

"How on earth did you get smoke to billow about on the floor like that?" Roxbury asked.

"I'll never tell," Bella said, holding her

hand up as if she were taking an oath. "So," she asked. "Who did you come as?"

He grinned, and a more wicked grin Bella had never seen before. It really did make her knees feel weak. "Well, we *were* asked to come as our favorite famous person that has passed. . . ."

Bella stopped him by placing her hand on his arm. "Oh, no, I remember!" she cried. "I remember you came as Napoleon. You are so naughty, Lord Roxbury, you were supposed to come as someone who was dead."

"He was, figuratively speaking. I'm just hurt you forgot," he said.

"Only for a moment."

"But I did think I was unforgettable," Lord Roxbury said.

Bella rolled her eyes. "Yes, well, I am sure you are unforgettable to most." She laughed and realized that her hand still rested on Lord Roxbury's arm. Her laugh died away quietly, and she cleared her throat as she pulled her hand back and pressed it against her waist.

She really ought to stop touching Lord Roxbury. He would think she was forward.

"Anyway," she said. "I am sure I will do your party proud, Lord Roxbury."

He nodded, but his expression had turned a bit dark. He turned away from her, paced toward the window, and then turned back. "Yes," he said finally. "I am sure you will, Miss Martin."

"So, I will do a bit of research if you think you would like to continue with the Asian theme?"

"Sounds lovely."

"We must hurry," she told him. "Lady Neeley said you wanted this party to happen quickly?"

"Two weeks, actually," Lord Roxbury said. "Two weeks from today."

"Goodness," Bella said. "That gives us very little time. I shall get right to work. I will write up an outline of what I intend and have it delivered here tomorrow."

"No, I would like you to bring it to me," Lord Roxbury said.

Bella nodded. "Of course," she said.

Lord Roxbury smiled, and again, it was a rather wicked smile. "I shall see you out," he said and put his hand under her elbow.

Bella barely contained the shiver that went through her at his touch. Goodness, she was acting like a ninny. Still, she couldn't help but notice how very tall Lord Roxbury was beside her and how he smelled very nice. He must use a special soap, for the man's scent seemed to intoxicate her senses.

She had always known, of course, that she was a sensual person. She loved good smells and liked to spend any extra money on special oils to put in her bath. And she loved soft clothing and had even made herself a silk-covered pillow for her bed.

She had decided, actually, that if she were ever to live alone, her first purchase would be silk sheets for her bed. And then she would get between her sheets utterly naked.

With that fantasy, Bella let out a decidedly languorous sigh.

Lord Roxbury glanced down at her with a strange look in his eye. Bella blinked up at him, pursed her lips, and turned her gaze forward. All of this was not good for her. She would dream about Lord Roxbury's touch for months, and remember his scent into her dotage, she was sure. And for what?

He was a rake, a scoundrel, a rogue. She didn't want to have anything to do with him.

With that thought, Bella burst out laughing. As if Lord Roxbury wanted to do anything more than have her plan his party. Goodness, but her imagination did tend to run off on its own at times.

"Is something funny?" Lord Roxbury asked.

"Yes," she answered and carefully extracted her arm from his grip as they reached the door. "I shall see you tomorrow then?"

Roxbury nodded.

"Good, then I'm off to read up on everything Japanese."

The small man who had let her in before rushed forward from out of nowhere and opened the door for her.

Bella jumped, and then laughed again.

"Thank you," she said to the butler. He bowed his head, and Bella bounced down the front steps of Lord Roxbury's home and turned left toward Lady Neeley's town house.

Herman stood staring after Miss Martin in the exact same manner that Anthony stood staring after Miss Martin. Anthony let his own gaze settle on his butler for a moment.

"Why are you staring at that young lady, Herman?" Anthony asked.

The man jumped a bit and turned toward him. "I think, my lord, that is the first time anyone has ever thanked me for opening the door for them."

Anthony nodded. "Yes, she's different, isn't she, Herman?"

The butler turned to stare down the street again. "Very," he said.

"There is a bloody handkerchief in the green room, Herman. Have someone attend to it . . . please," Anthony said to his butler.

"Of course, my lord."

"And I'm not using the word as a sobriquet. The handkerchief really is bloody."

"Yes, my lord."

Anthony stood for another minute staring out at the large bonnet that adorned Miss Martin's head. He could still make it out, bobbing along the street. There was something about Miss Martin that had made him decide that he would definitely kiss her before this damned party of hers. He would kiss her for real, so that before she had turned thirty, she would truly have been kissed.

But, suddenly, Anthony realized he could not do that. She wasn't like the jaded married women he usually played with. Miss Martin was unlike anyone he had ever met, really.

She ought to have slapped him and scolded him, yelled at him at the very least for grabbing her like he had. Instead, she had laughed.

With a long sigh, Anthony closed the door. No, he could not take advantage of someone like Miss Martin. He would definitely make sure that he was not home when she returned the next day.

Chapter 3

. . . *And in our list of suspects, one cannot discount the elusive Miss Martin. As Lady Neeley's longtime companion, she would have had, more than any other partygoer, an intimate knowledge of the house and of the bracelet. And, again owing to her position in Lady Neeley's household, it is difficult to imagine that her financial situation would be such that she would not be in need of the funds that such a rubied bauble might bring.*

But This Author would be amiss if it were not pointed out that Lady Neeley refused to entertain even a hint of the notion that one of her servants, and in particular her devoted companion, might have been the thief. And she has declared, quite publicly, that she will not have Miss Martin's rooms searched.

So perhaps the only way one will be able to tell if Miss Martin is indeed an adventuress of the most larcenous

*kind is if the woman in question sud-
denly prances down Bond Street with
coins dripping from her fingertips.*

*Unlikely, but an interesting image
nonetheless.*

Lady Whistledown's Society Papers,
31 May 1816

Anthony tried very hard to pretend that he
didn't notice Miss Martin. If he were in his
right mind, he never would have seen her at
all. She did tend to blend in with the decorations.

Unfortunately he was not in his right mind.
The second he walked in the door of Lady
Hargreaves' Grand Ball, he spotted her. She
was sitting on one of the few chairs available.

She had left the atrocious bonnet at home,
thankfully, and wore a dainty cap pinned
atop her dark hair. With the huge bonnet, he
had not noticed that Miss Martin wore her
hair unfashionably short. There was not a
piece of hair on her head longer than two
inches, if that. And each lock of hair seemed
to have a mind of its own, curling this way
and that.

Anthony had always liked his women to
have long hair that hung about them as they
made love. In that very moment, though, he
decided it just might be interesting to make
love to a woman with a mop of hair that

185

would tickle his nose as she kissed his neck.

He shook his head and looked decidedly away from Miss Isabella Martin. Surely, she was a witch to have him thinking such strange things in the middle of a ballroom. Especially during Lady Hargreaves' Grand Ball. He had never in his life had a lascivious thought at Lady Hargreaves's Annual Grand Ball.

Anthony made his usual rounds kissing the hands of the old, decrepit, married, and debutantes — the hands of as many women as he could so the gossipmongers could not attach him to anyone in particular.

Many thought it was Anthony's way of driving his father mad, but really it was just so the old man would not get his hopes up.

Tonight, Anthony had a devil of a time keeping his mind on whose hand he had kissed and whose he had not. It would be the worst of all crimes if he kissed someone's hand twice. The gossip columns would surely talk of nothing else for at least a week. His father would announce an engagement and order invites.

Anthony decided he had best make his way to the card room. Probably, he should not have come at all, but he had to admit a perverse interest in watching Lady Hargreaves play her grandchildren like toys on a string. Poor sods, all vying for her favor so they would be named in her will. She'd probably outlive them all.

As he maneuvered through the groups of people, all standing because of the deplorable lack of chairs, Anthony spotted Lady Easterly. He caught her eye and winked at her, and Sophia winked back with a smile. Anthony made it a custom always to wink at the statuesque blonde, because she always winked back.

He had tried, actually, to offer particularly warm solace to the woman when her husband had abandoned her twelve years ago, but he'd been politely rebuffed. She had stayed true to her husband, as far as Anthony could tell. A good woman, that one.

And with that thought, Anthony caught sight of Miss Martin once again. The exact opposite of Lady Easterly, Miss Martin: a small, dark girl sitting on a chair in the corner.

Anthony stumbled a bit, something he was not used to in the least. Miss Martin looked over just at that moment and their gazes locked. Even from a distance, Anthony could see the gray of her truly beautiful eyes. The thing that got to him, though, was the way they shone with recognition when she saw him.

And then she stood.

Anthony couldn't help but stop as Miss Martin pushed through the crowd toward him. Plucky thing, seeking him out. He couldn't remember a woman in his lifetime

187

who'd actually approached him at a party. Especially a young single woman like Miss Martin. Actually, she really wasn't all that young. It was just that she seemed so fresh and new. She made him feel like a jaded and terribly sad old man.

She managed, finally, to reach him. "Lord Roxbury!" she said, slightly out of breath. "I had hoped to see you." She leaned toward him and put one of her gloved hands on his forearm.

"Really?" he asked, a bit shaken by the contact. She didn't even notice it. But he did. And he had noticed that she'd touched him when they had first met as well.

He liked it. But he shouldn't.

And, damn it, she should not be this naïve at thirty. Some man was sure to take advantage of her. Why on earth was Lady Neeley not paying this girl more heed?

"I delivered the plans myself, just as you asked, but you weren't at home," she said with a smile. "I realized that we hadn't set a time. I hope that you received them."

"Ah, yes, Herman made sure that I got them."

"Oh good, and what do you think, then?"

She waited for his answer, her small face lifted to his, gray eyes glittering like stars. She really was a fetching little thing: so eager and so damned happy. What did this gel have to be so happy about?

"They seemed fine," he said, though he had not given them a second glance. Which had earned him quite a glare from Herman. Anthony was rather sure his butler was falling in love with the woman.

"Good, good, I shall continue, then. I will need to have accounts opened for me in your name at the places that I listed so that I can order everything. I made a list, of course, of all the amounts that I will spend. I'm quite proud, really. I've managed to whittle it down by making the invitations myself. I've the most wonderful idea for the invitations. They are going to be lovely. I've learned how to make these cranes folded out of paper, and the invitation will be written on the paper."

"Hmm," Anthony said, for he could not truly concentrate on Miss Martin's words. It was all due to the fact that he had just realized that she had a lovely mouth, her lips like those on a perfectly painted doll. Truly, he decided in that moment, he did adore the way her upper lip was shaped like a perfect bow. He was rather sure he would enjoy becoming intimate with this woman's mouth.

She smiled up at him. "Are you happy with it all?"

"Oh yes," he said.

"Good, I am so glad. I have never before worked with anyone but Lady Neeley, and she lets me do whatever I want."

"I've noticed," Anthony said darkly. Honestly, Miss Martin needed a keeper. She was a lovely, innocent woman just waiting for some lecherous rogue to ruin her completely. He glanced around. "Where is Lady Neeley?"

Miss Martin shrugged. "She was speaking with Mr. Thompson and Lady Mathilda, and so I quickly found a seat out of the way. I am not thrilled at how Lady Neeley is dealing with the problem of her missing bracelet, so I try and stay away when she speaks of it."

"I have heard that she is not being subtle about accusing the people who were at her party."

Miss Martin rolled her eyes. "Isn't it horrible?"

"I also noticed that you seem to be a suspect as well."

Miss Martin giggled. "Oh, that is only in Lady Whistledown's column. Lady Neeley would never accuse any of her staff."

Most women would probably have taken to their bed, deathly ill, upon seeing their name linked to thievery in Lady Whistledown's column. Obviously, this was not true of the giggling Miss Martin.

"Can you believe it, Lord Roxbury?" she asked now, her eyes lit from within. "My name graced Lady Whistledown's column. I've never been so thrilled in my life. I have decided that it is because of my birthday. I was a bit put out when I remembered that I was to turn thirty with so many things undone. And here it is, my birthday two weeks away and I've been named in a gossip column and kissed by a lord!"

This last bit earned them a few glances.

"Whoops," Miss Martin said. "I guess I should be a bit less exuberant in public, or I shall grace Lady Whistledown's column again. I'll take my leave then, and send around a copy of the invitation to you tomorrow. Your father has given me a list of attendees, so I shall not need that from you."

That was very bad. "No," Anthony said. "I shall send you a guest list. The one my father gave you can be burned."

"Are you sure?" she asked. And then she laughed and put her hand on his forearm as she leaned into him. "Your father seemed very determined that you should invite the people on his list."

Anthony just nodded. Never in his life had a woman flirted with him so. And the worst part was she didn't even realize that she was flirting.

He could see it in her eyes. She had no idea that when she leaned toward him he caught a whiff of the rose water she used. And that it was making him absolutely randy.

"I must ask you," he said then, "are you a part of Lady Neeley's staff?"

Miss Martin straightened and blinked. "Excuse me?" she asked.

"Well, you said before that Lady Neeley trusted everyone on her staff, and I was wondering if you were hired by her. Somewhere in the back of my mind, I could swear that my father once told me you were related to Lady Neeley."

Miss Martin smiled widely. "Really? You actually remember hearing about me?" She clapped her hands. "How lovely!"

"You are easily amused, I think."

"Too true." She grinned hugely, obviously not at all put out at having a laugh about herself. "But, anyway, I am both. I am a hired relative. Lady Neeley pays me for the work I do as her companion. And she is second cousin to my mother."

"And your mother and father are where?"

Miss Martin cocked her head to the side, her gray eyes dimming a little. "They are both gone."

"Oh, I am sorry."

"It's all right. They were older when I was conceived. I feel blessed that I had a whole twenty years with them."

Anthony glanced away for a moment. Though his mother had died twenty years before, he still had his father. The fact that he had never in his life thought of that fact as a blessing made him feel very much like a wretched toad right now.

As he looked about the room, Anthony realized that there were a few people watching him and the innocent Miss Martin. Damn.

"Why?" she asked him then.

He turned toward her again. "Excuse me?"

"Why do you want to know about my relationship to Lady Neeley? Are you worried about the party? Do you want me to bring you some samples of my work?"

"Oh no, it is not that at all, really," Anthony said. "I was just interested. . . ."

His own words stopped him. He was interested, he'd said. And it was true. He was just plain interested in this strange creature that was Miss Martin.

Truth be told, he did not find many things interesting. Thus, he found it quite alarming that he was interested in the answers Miss Martin was giving him to his questions. On top of this rather strange phenomenon, Anthony realized that he really did want to show Miss Martin that she had not been kissed . . . not really, and not yet.

At the very least, the latter bit was much more true to his character.

Still, Anthony glared at Miss Martin for a moment, trying to figure out why on earth he would want to kiss her most thoroughly, as it could only ever end in some disaster — probably for both of them.

"Have I upset you, my lord?" Miss Martin asked without even a hint of fear. "You look as if you would like to throw something, preferably me."

"No, but I should take my leave. Your reputation is at stake."

Miss Martin leaned forward, her shoulders shaking, and for a split second Anthony believed her to be crying. But then she straightened, her eyes dancing up at him, and he realized that she was laughing.

She kept her hand over her mouth for a moment, obviously trying to control herself. "Oh, Lord Roxbury, I have no reputation." She waved her hand at the people around them. "Most of these people have no idea who I am. I think it is your reputation that you are afraid of ruining." She grinned at him.

"Of course it is not."

Miss Martin laughed. "I was only kidding. But you have already ruined your reputation in my eyes, my lord. You like everyone to believe you are the perfect scoundrel, and really, you are a perfect gentleman."

Now there were two things he felt compelled to dissuade Miss Martin of believing: she had been properly kissed, and he was a gentleman. "I am not a perfect anything, Miss Martin, I assure you."

"Whatever you say, my lord. Now then, I also wanted to let you know that there is a lovely Japanese display at the British Museum. If you were to go and see it, perhaps you might get some ideas for the party. Two heads are always better than just one when it comes to these types of things."

Anthony was still trying to digest the fact that this chit believed him to be a perfect gentleman. He glanced around them again and knew that Miss Martin was completely wrong. He was surely ruining her completely. "Really, Miss Martin, we should not be speaking for so long and so intensely in public."

"Are we speaking intensely?" Miss Martin asked, her eyes widening, her voice lowering to a whisper. She leaned closer to him. "This *is* intense, isn't it, my lord?" She glanced around and then back at him.

He was being teased. It had been quite a long time since anyone had dared tease him, but he realized it was happening now. He rolled his eyes, and Miss Martin giggled again.

Truth be told, Anthony had never liked giggling females. But Miss Martin was different. Her giggles were not high pitched or irritating. And they were definitely not something she was using to try and make herself seem more naïve and innocent. She obviously did not know how to use anything to mean something she was not. Basically, Miss Martin's giggles were pure and soft and infectious. They made him wish to giggle as well.

Giggle, for goodness' sake. He was most definitely going insane.

"I shall put you out of your misery, my

lord," she said then. "I need some punch anyway, my mouth is as dry as the Sahara, I swear. And I will take my leave of you. Though, I may have to do so intensely." She peered about them, looked at him as she dramatically lifted her eyebrows, then turned with a grand sweeping gesture and left him.

In her wake, Anthony caught the faint sound of her laughter.

He shook his head as he watched her for a moment. He wished, actually, that they were alone. He wanted to keep talking with her. He wanted to make her laugh again.

Strange. He had never in his entire lifetime met a woman he'd wanted to be alone with because he'd wished to converse with her.

Anthony closed his eyes and placed the back of his hand against his forehead. Perhaps he had the fever.

Chapter 4

One could not help but note that Lady Neeley's companion was perhaps the only woman not kissed at the Hargreaves' Ball by Lord Roxbury.

Very well, This Author refers only to hands, not lips, but truly, the man needs to be a bit more discriminate.

Lady Whistledown's Society Papers,
3 June 1816

Bella was supposed to be sketching. She stared at the open sketchbook in front of her and then glanced back up at the kimono on display in the museum. She squirmed, trying to find a more comfortable spot on the straight-backed chair Ozzie had found her.

Ozzie came marching up the hall that very second, a small square pillow in his hand. "I thought this might help," he said, offering it to her.

Bella smiled at the young man and stood. "Thank you so much, Ozzie, it is very thoughtful of you."

A dark blush crept up Ozzie's neck. Where most people had dark complexions or light or even yellow, Ozzie's complexion could only be described as red. There was a red cast to his entire visage, which made the freckles that battled for room on his face look distressingly orange. His hair, as well, seemed the color of a ripe orange, though in truth it was a very light blonde.

Bella took the pillow and plopped it onto the seat of the chair, then propped her sketchbook on top of it all. "I do think, though, that I shall walk a little before I continue with my sketches."

Ozzie glanced down at the pad. "You have done a wonderful job. You are very talented."

Bella smiled. "Thank you. Since I am always designing decorations for parties, it helps that I can draw. Still, I am not at all competent at drawing unless I'm copying something else. So, I guess you could say it's a limited talent." She laughed self-deprecatingly as she started walking down the hall.

Ozzie followed along beside her, and she was glad. The boy was lovely company. She had met him the week before when she had come looking for information on anything Japanese. He worked in the bowels of the museum helping to restore and preserve the artifacts on display. And he especially knew a lot about the Japanese artifacts, which had made her job much easier. In fact, it was Ozzie who had taught her how to fold the invitations in a design the Japanese called origami.

"I do wish I could see this party that you are decorating," he said now.

Bella stopped. "You know, I am sure that you can. Would you help me set up the party the day before? That way you can see everything when it is done."

Ozzie's green eyes became glassy as he nodded quickly. "Oh, yes, I would love to."

He did remind her of an overeager puppy. Bella giggled.

"I would know that sound anywhere," a soft male voice said from behind them.

Bella jumped and Ozzie slouched. "Well, my goodness!" Bella said. "'Tis Lord Roxbury, as I live and breathe." She tried very hard to sound nonchalant, which was extremely difficult seeing that every single nerve in her body had started to vibrate, of all things.

Bella pressed her fingers against her chest, wondering if she was about to collapse from apoplexy, with her heart apparently beating much too fast.

"I came to take in the Japanese exhibit you informed me of, Miss Martin," he said, his eye roving slowly over Ozzie until the boy babbled an unintelligible excuse and scuttled away.

Lord Roxbury watched Ozzie fleeing for a minute, and then turned his full attention on Bella. Goodness, being on the receiving end of Lord Roxbury's full attention was quite daunting, Bella decided. No wonder Ozzie had scampered off like a mouse faced with the largest cat in Christendom.

His brown eyes, which she distinctly remembered admiring because they always had a glint of humor in them, had most definitely lost that glint. He seemed to be in a bad mood, actually. And Bella had to curb an intense urge to brush the shock of brown hair off his forehead and ask him what the matter was.

Instead she clasped her hands together tightly in front of her, as a precaution. "Did you get your invitation, my lord?" she asked with a smile.

"Yes, as did my father. He was quite over the moon about the unique design."

Bella smiled. "Oh, lovely, I'm so glad."

"Yes, unfortunately, though, my father was not on my invitation list."

"Ah, well, I took it upon myself to combine your list and your father's list, so that meant he did receive an invitation."

"Really? I'm paying for this party, but my father gets to decide who comes?" Lord Roxbury asked.

"No, not entirely." Bella tightened her hold on her own fingers. "I did notice that each of you had extremes on your lists."

"Extremes?"

"Well, that is to say, I noticed that your father's list was made up of very young unmarried ladies and their mothers, and your list was predominantly made up of men and older married women," Bella said.

"And?"

"And so I cut out the extremes and meshed the middles together. That way you have a much better mix of people."

Lord Roxbury nodded his head but said nothing for a long moment. "Do you not think," he said finally, "that you have rather overstepped your bounds, Miss Martin?"

"Not at all. I am here to make your party a success, and that meant I definitely had to take charge of the invite list. If it bothers you that much, my lord, I shall quit this job."

"I never exactly hired you."

"Exactly," Bella said with a smile. "Your father asked Lady Neeley to allow me to help you. Because of that, I did feel it necessary that I take some notice of his list and not just burn it, as you suggested. But since it is, ultimately, your party, I wanted to invite people on your list as well."

"In other words, you are acting the diplomat to my father and me?" Lord Roxbury asked.

"I was just taking the woman's role when

faced with two stubborn males," she said lightly.

Lord Roxbury blinked.

Lord Roxbury was cute when he was flustered. Though she was sure no one else in society would ever think of cute and Lord Roxbury in the same sentence, it was true.

Even now, he was trying very hard to look angry and pompous, and it was not working in the least. She had realized the day she'd first met him that he was probably one of the nicest men she knew.

She really did like that about him.

"Now then, my lord, did you want to see the Japanese display? It is exquisite, and I must tell you I am actually very glad that I have had this opportunity to study the Japanese. I have learned much about another culture and am thoroughly enjoying myself."

Roxbury just stood there staring at her as if she were a ghost. Or a woman. Obviously, he had never met one who'd actually spoken to him, either that or he'd never listened to any of the women he'd met. Bella bit her bottom lip to keep from laughing. "My lord?" she asked. "Would you like to see the display? Or would you rather keep arguing over something that has already been done?"

Later on Bella realized that she had become so smug by this point in the conversation that she had probably started to sound like a know-it-all, boring schoolteacher. She probably deserved to be taken down a peg, but, really, she did not expect what came next at all . . . though she thoroughly enjoyed it.

Chapter 5

Has anyone noticed that Lord Roxbury seems rather more serious of late? After all that kissing of hands at the Hargreaves' Ball, he's become a veritable monk.

Not a single party attended all week. How very unlike him.

One can only wonder whether his father is rejoicing or sobbing with despair. The lack of merriment might indicate a certain willingness to settle down, but on the other hand, one can't meet an eligible young miss if one never leaves one's house, can one?

Lady Whistledown's Society Papers,
7 June 1816

Anthony was very out of sorts when he sought out Miss Martin. He had been informed by Lady Neeley that her companion was at the museum sketching. That had bothered him on top of everything else. The lady did not care in the least that her young and terribly lovely companion was alone at the museum. Miss Martin needed a chaperone.

As he rode his horse toward the museum, Anthony became even more agitated. He had spent the weekend in a mood that could only be called black. And, as most everyone that knew him understood, Anthony was never anything but happy and easygoing. The last weekend had proved beyond a doubt that he was his father's son.

For he had started sounding just like the man: barking orders to poor Herman and sitting hunched over his desk, his eyes shooting daggers at anyone who'd disturbed him. And, the strangest thing of all, Anthony had not been with a woman since Wednesday.

He'd spent the entire weekend without even the desire to see a woman, much less speak to one or, dread the thought, touch one. Of course, Miss Martin had pervaded his thoughts most unnervingly, and the desire to touch her had almost overwhelmed him.

What on earth was wrong with him?

When he'd found out that his father had received an invitation, Anthony had been immensely relieved because now he could be angry with Miss Martin. That seemed a safer emotion than whatever he'd felt for her before.

But then he saw her walking with some

boy whom he did feel the need to throttle, of all things. She was such a slight thing, slender, with her pixielike hair curled about her head. She wore a plain gray gown that would have looked really horrible on anyone else, but she had added a soft blue sash that accentuated her waist and made her eyes seem like mist. She had also pinned a little bunch of flowers to her collar, and when he stood close, their fragrance went straight to his head.

In truth, every thought in his brain was like those of a besotted schoolboy. And then she laughed at him and spoke to him in that forthright, intelligent manner she had, and Anthony did feel the need to kiss her soundly.

And so he did, finally.

Afterwards, he wasn't really sure what exactly had made him do it, but he did remember feeling like he was either going to hit her or kiss her in that moment, and he would never hit a woman, so he grabbed her arm, pulled her close, and took her mouth.

And then she kissed him back, and he really did lose himself as he had never done before.

He was harsh at first, but she immediately opened to him: Her arms went around his neck, her body molded against his, and her mouth was soft.

He was hard with wanting within seconds,

definitely a besotted schoolboy. He curved an arm around her back and leaned over her, kissing her as he had never kissed a woman. He kissed her with an urgency that was beyond physical.

When he finally came to his senses and realized that they were in a very public place, and that he could ruin her completely in that very second if only one person were to see them, he pulled away from her.

He held her arm for a moment to make sure that she had her balance, but then he let go of her completely and even took a few steps away from her.

She just stared at him, and he really did wish she wouldn't. He was not himself. He could not figure out who he was, or what he was feeling, but it was not normal, that much he knew.

"Do you do that to all the women who aggravate you?" she asked finally.

"No," he said.

"I can now say that I have been kissed, though. Can't I?"

He shook his head, confused.

"You seemed to think it funny that I thought I had been kissed when you kissed my neck. This, though . . ." She waved her hand between them. "This was definitely a kiss, was it not?"

He closed his eyes for a moment. She had no idea how much of a kiss it was. "Yes," he said. "This was a kiss."

She grinned. "Well, that's good then. Now, did you want to see that display?" she asked.

Display? Anthony truly could not remember what she was talking about. He was having a hard enough time remembering where they were or who he was. Truly, he had meant to shock the woman in front of him, and instead he'd put himself into a stupor.

"Uh," he said.

"Come along then," she said, turning and walking off down the hall.

Lovely, he was forever changed by one kiss, and the woman who had inspired it could care less. Anthony stood for a moment staring at the ceiling. Surely this was God's perverse way of getting back at him for his debauchery in days past.

With a shake of his head, Anthony followed the little nymph that was Miss Isabella Martin.

"Isn't this lovely?" she asked when he reached her. She gestured toward the wall with her hand.

Anthony tried to see the display, but instead his gaze stuck on Miss Martin's hand. It was such a lovely hand, slender with perfectly rounded nails. Probably sometime this evening he would sit down and write a bleeding sonnet to Miss Martin's hands. He was that far gone.

Or maybe he just needed to lose himself in another woman? Perhaps that would break this strange spell.

"Miss Martin," he said. "How on earth did you get a name like Isabella?" Just one of the many things that he'd wondered about as he had sat hunched behind his desk over the weekend.

She shook her head, obviously confused by the change of subject, but then smiled. "Ah, it was my mother. I received my imagination from her. She was constantly telling me stories about Spanish princesses and English princes. She named me Isabella after the Spanish Queen."

See, Anthony thought, *nothing so extravagant that it should be pondered to death over an entire weekend.*

"My parents were older when they had me, and they knew they would die when I was relatively young, so they made sure that I had a place to go and someone to take care of me."

"Lady Neeley?" he asked.

"Yes, Lady Neeley offered to take me on as her companion. But my mother always insisted that anything could happen. That I should dream of all sorts of wild and wonderful things, because you never knew, it could happen."

Miss Martin sighed, and her large gray eyes looked sad for the first time since Anthony had known her. "I kept that thought through the years, but it does seem that this is the end."

"Excuse me?" Anthony asked, a bit alarmed.

"I mean, I will be thirty next week. I don't think an English prince rides off with a Spanish princess who is thirty years old."

"But you are not a Spanish princess."

Miss Martin laughed. "Obviously, you don't have much of an imagination, my lord."

That was debatable. He could, in fact, at this very moment, imagine Miss Martin stark naked on his bed.

"All I am saying, Miss Martin, is that a thirty-year-old English miss, perhaps, has more hope than a thirty-year-old Spanish princess."

Miss Martin laughed softly.

He thought, in that moment, that he would not mind hearing that sound every day for the rest of his life, it made him feel that good.

She glanced over at him; her head was at an angle so that her eyes peeked at him from under her long, dark lashes. Oh yes, his imagination was just fine, thank you very much. He could definitely imagine kissing his way down the curve of Miss Martin's neck.

Anthony forced himself to look away from the enticing person beside him and stare at the display of Japanese artifacts. They were lovely — he had always enjoyed the colors and look of Japanese art. It is why he had used so many Japanese pieces when he'd decorated his town house.

He had been thrilled, actually, when he had seen the invitations Miss Martin had made. They were perfect. He had also received the menu and a sample of every food he would be feeding his guests, and they had been exquisite. Miss Martin was doing a magnificent job so far. He could not see this party being anything but a complete success.

He turned toward her suddenly. "Why on earth are you not getting paid for this?" he asked.

She glanced around, and then returned to him. "Excuse me?"

"You are doing an incredible job, and you are working very hard. Why aren't I paying you?"

"Because I am doing it as a favor to your father."

"No one should do my father favors, he has enough money to pay everyone to do everything."

Miss Martin giggled, which made him smile.

"Miss Martin," he said. "You really do have quite a talent for this. Your organizational skills are impeccable, but you also have a wonderful imagination that gives each party you do just that much of a different quality. Guests remember them and enjoy them. Why on earth aren't you doing this for pay? You could be making quite a lot of money, I promise you."

Miss Martin looked rather dumbstruck. She stared at him for a moment, and then turned to stare at the kimono in front of them. "Could I do this?" she asked. But he could tell that she was not asking him.

She turned toward him again, a smile spreading across her face that was the most beautiful thing Anthony had seen in all of his thirty-seven years on the earth.

"You, my lord, have just saved me. You are my English prince, and you have changed my life. It just didn't happen like I thought it would." She clapped her hands together and then grabbed his shoulders, came up on her tiptoes, and gave him a kiss on his cheek. "Thank you!" she said.

Anthony was not exactly sure what was going on, and he was still trying to recover from the feel of her soft lips against his cheek. Since he had had women touch him in ways that made a kiss on the cheek look like child's play, it did strike him as extremely odd that Miss Martin's kiss should paralyze him so. Be that as it may, he was not able to say anything as the girl grabbed up her sketchpad and pencils, fluttered her fingers at him, and took her leave.

All of a sudden, Anthony realized he was alone, and terribly bewildered. Not to mention the fact that he was feeling as randy as a goat, mostly fueled by a kiss on the cheek. Probably he was delusional from that fever that never seemed to show itself.

Old Barney was sitting atop Lady Neeley's sleek coach, waiting for Bella as he always did, and so she clambered aboard. But she could not continue sitting for the entire trip; her heart was beating much too fast to let her body stay still. So she asked Barney to let her off at Mayfair, and she walked home. Charles, one of Lady Neeley's footmen, came running at top speed when Bella had only walked a block.

"Barney sent me," he said as greeting and took up a position about two steps behind her. Usually Bella hated that, and, when Lady Neeley wasn't with her, she cajoled the boys to walk next to her, but today she was happy for the time alone.

Her mind was going at such a fast clip that she was rather sure her mouth would not be able to follow. Here it was: the way her life was going to change. She knew that she would do it. She knew that she could do it. And she was thrilled.

Goodness! Bella's feet ate up the pavement as she nearly ran the rest of the way home. She threw off her coat and hat as she pushed through the front door of Lady Neeley's home. "Is she home?" she asked Mrs. Trotter, who stood waiting for Bella's outer clothing.

"In the back parlor, Miss Martin, but —"

Bella didn't wait. After thirty years of waiting for something to happen, Bella couldn't take even another minute to make her new life a reality.

"Lady Neeley," she said as she nearly ran through the already open doors to the back parlor.

Lady Neeley glanced up, a teacup halfway to her lips, and Lord Roxbury's father, Lord Waverly, sat opposite her, his mouth crammed full of one of Christophe's pastries.

"Miss Martin," Lady Neeley said. "You are back from the museum earlier than I thought you would be."

"Yes," she said and hesitated. She desperately wanted to speak with Lady Neeley about this immediately. Lord Waverly tended to stay forever when he came to take tea with Lady Neeley.

"Good afternoon, dear," Lord Waverly said as soon as he had swallowed most of the pastry. "I received the invitation to my son's party. It was remarkable. You are such an imaginative young lady, I do admire you."

"Thank you, my lord," Bella said with a little bow. "In fact, that is what I need to speak with you about, Lady Neeley. As soon as you have the time."

Lady Neeley put her teacup down without taking a sip, and her white eyebrows lifted in inquiry. "Do take a seat, darling. I am sure you can speak with me now about whatever it is you need."

Bella took a deep breath and glanced at Lord Waverly. It might be a good thing to have the man in attendance. The whole bit about her being imaginative had been a lovely boon.

She sat beside Lady Neeley on the small sofa. "I want to start my own business," she said quickly. It was better just to come straight out with what must be said when speaking with Lady Neeley. One could never be sure how she would react to anything. Sometimes she could be quite a selfish old biddy, but then she would do something that was completely the opposite, like bringing Bella home a beautiful new dress because the color so matched her eyes.

"Really?" Lady Neeley said to this statement. She picked up her teacup again and this time took a small sip.

"What kind of business?" Lord Waverly asked.

"She wants to plan parties," Lady Neeley said. "Am I right?" She looked over at Bella.

Bella nodded.

"You are quite a genius at these things, Miss Martin, I must say," Lord Waverly said.

Definitely, having Lord Waverly in attendance had been a lovely stroke of fortune.

"Yes she is, but it was very nice having her all to myself," Lady Neeley said. "I always knew that my parties would outshine those of anyone else. Except of course for this last one." Lady Neeley's lips thinned as she pressed them together.

The bracelet. Bella folded her hands tightly together in her lap and said a small prayer that God would obliterate that last thought from Lady Neeley's mind. As of late, the second she started talking about the missing bracelet, the woman's mood deteriorated drastically and she started babbling about how tanned Lord Easterly was and how society was going to hell in a handbasket when one could not trust a peer.

"Now, now, my dear, don't bother yourself. I've already told you I will buy you a new bracelet," Lord Waverly said.

"You will do nothing of the sort, Waverly." Lady Neeley glared at the still good-looking Lord Waverly. Lord Waverly had proposed to Lady Neeley at least ten times in as many years, and Lady Neeley had always said no. She had told Bella that she had already been married and raised three sons, and she was ready to live for herself and no one else.

Bella could understand, but she really thought it sounded like a lonely existence, especially since Lord Waverly seemed like a lovely, gentle man. At least he was always like that to her, as well as Lady Neeley, though she *had* heard him yell at his groom once.

"I knew you would finally decide to go off on your own one of these days," Lady Neeley said.

Bella said a little thank you prayer. The bracelet was forgotten temporarily. "I will have to find some investors," Bella said. "And I would appreciate it if you could tell people that I have done your parties."

"Of course, and I shall be your first investor," Lady Neeley said.

Bella clapped her hands in surprise. "Really?" she asked.

"Why on earth are you so surprised, Bella? I will do everything possible to help you succeed. In fact, you can stay here as long as you need, and I will let you take Christophe with you when you leave."

"What?" Lord Waverly cried.

"Truthfully?" Bella asked.

"He is making me fat," Lady Neeley said with a wave of her hand. "All these pastries and tarts are too rich for my old body. I need a bad cook for a while. I want to fit back into my favorite blue silk ball gown before I die."

Lord Waverly looked absolutely forlorn. "I shall miss his strawberry tarts," he said sadly and grabbed another off the tray, as if it might disappear at any moment.

"Every woman should experience independence," Lady Neeley said, patting Bella's knee. "It would be a good thing for our gender. It builds character. Anything you need, just ask, Bella."

Without thinking, Bella leaned across the sofa and put her arms around her companion of ten years.

Lady Neeley was stiff beneath Bella's embrace. "Thank you," Bella said softly and pulled away.

Poor Lady Neeley looked as if she might cry in that moment. But she fluttered her hand between them and said crisply, "Yes, well, I shall have to find a new companion, I guess."

"And a new chef," Lord Waverly reminded her.

She frowned at him. "Is that all I am to you? A place to eat strawberry tarts?"

"I . . . er . . . no . . . um . . ."

Bella stood quickly. "I am off then. Do enjoy your tea." And she made a hasty exit. She could not wait to get started. And she definitely did not want to watch Lord Waverly lose yet another verbal battle with Lady Neeley.

Chapter 6

The secret is out! Lady Neeley's fabulous parties owed nothing to the organization (or imagination) of the hostess and everything to her longtime (long-suffering?) companion, Miss Isabella Martin.

It seems the creative Miss Martin has finally come to appreciate the value of her expertise, because This Author has it on the best authority that she plans to open her own business, and for a fee, any hostess may hire her to plan a party.

It means, of course, that Miss Martin is now in trade, which is, to be sure, a step down. But truly, given her long years of service to Lady Neeley, can anyone blame her?

Lady Whistledown's Society Papers,
10 June 1816

"Come with me, Bella, you are no fun anymore. All you do is work." Lady Neeley stood in the doorway to the kitchen, her dreaded parrot sitting upon her shoulder.

Bella glanced up from the menu she and Christophe were going over just one more time. Lord Roxbury's party was the very next evening, and in the last week Bella had quit sleeping, she was so nervous.

"Go," Christophe said and pushed Bella's shoulder. "Look at the outside! The sun. It is shining I think for the first time since the beginning of time. You are looking like a night owl. Go."

Bella rolled her eyes and sighed. "Thank you, Christophe, you know exactly what to say to flatter a girl."

Christophe shrugged, but he turned away, taking the menu with him. He was just as nervous as Bella. They were going into this business as partners, so Lord Roxbury's party could change his life as well.

"I will go driving in the park with you only if you leave the bird at home," Bella said, pointing to the dreaded bird. At the very least the stupid thing hadn't come squawking over and tried to kiss her.

The older woman tossed her head and stuck her pointy nose in the air. "Such a hoity-toity girl now that you are independent." She turned away. "The bird stays, then."

Bella grinned and went to change. Lady Neeley may tease her about being hoity-toity, but Bella knew that it was exactly that: a tease. Lady Neeley seemed almost as excited about Bella's new venture as Bella herself. The older woman had told her just the other day that she wished she could have done something like Bella planned when she was young.

And she was telling the whole world about Bella's talent and attributing every single successful party to her young companion. No one had come to Bella yet, but Christophe said that he was sure they would flock to Bella of the Ball's doors when Lord Roxbury's party was a hit.

Nothing like a little pressure.

In just one week, Lady Neeley, Christophe, and Bella had found a very cute little building just off Oxford Street. It had a perfect bowfront window with two offices downstairs and a small apartment upstairs. Lord Waverly had put a down payment on the building as an investment, and Lady Neeley had appointed the offices with desks and a painted sign on the front: Bella of the Ball.

Bella was all set to move into the apartment upstairs the day after her thirtieth birthday. She had even hired a maid.

The sun was shining, and it was warm for the first time in what seemed forever. At least it was warmer than it had been lately. Bella was still glad she had worn her wool riding habit, though; there was just enough of a brisk breeze to make her rub her hands together as she and Lady Neeley settled against the leather seats of the older woman's open-topped phaeton. Old Barney kept the horses at a perfect clip so that they hardly bounced at all.

Bella tipped her head back so that she could feel the sun upon her face.

"Can we make a running appointment, dear?" Lady Neeley asked.

Bella glanced over at her companion. "A running appointment?" she asked.

"A drive in the park every Tuesday afternoon, weather permitting. Tea inside when the weather snarls at us?" Lady Neeley looked rather forlorn as she asked this.

Bella impulsively reached over and curled her fingers around Lady Neeley's. "Of course, it is a date. Since I am planning to see you even more often than that, I do hope you do not get bored of me."

"Never," Lady Neeley said succinctly. "Look over there, I think someone is having a footrace, of all things! So unseemly." Lady Neeley made a disgusted sound with her tongue against her teeth, and Bella leaned her head back and closed her eyes again.

She opened them quickly, though, because she could have sworn she'd just seen someone hiding behind a hedge. She craned her neck. Surely she had just seen Lord Easterly skulking in the bushes. She shrugged and didn't mention it, however. The last thing she wanted to do was use Lord Easterly's name in conversation. Where Lord Easterly was concerned, Lady Neeley was bound to go into a tirade about thievery and bracelets, and the entire afternoon would be ruined.

No, she would not bring up Lord Easterly. Bella closed her eyes again.

"Shouldn't you be at my house setting up a party?" a voice said beside her.

Bella jumped and opened her eyes to a knight in shining armor. Or, rather, to Lord Roxbury, tall and dark and gorgeous astride his horse. He trotted beside their open carriage.

Bella put her hand up to shade her eyes.

"Good afternoon, Lord Roxbury," Lady Neeley said. "I am very much looking forward to this party you have decided to hold on my dear Bella's day of birth."

"I am looking forward to it as well, actually," he said.

Bella could not seem to speak at all. She had not seen Lord Roxbury since the day her life had changed. The day he had kissed her like a man was supposed to kiss a woman.

She had pushed the kiss into a small corner of her brain, and it only came out at night. It would trip about her head and run down and beat in her heart a bit, and not let her get any sleep at all.

One night, she had actually played with the

idea of being Lord Roxbury's mistress. He seemed interested. At least she thought he did. And now she had a new life as an independent woman, perhaps she could really, truly be an independent woman?

That idea came back to taunt her now. Roxbury was one of the most beautiful men she had ever seen. And when she talked to him, she did not see the scoundrel that everyone else talked about under their breath.

He had said at the ball that he was interested in her. And she had to admit, she had the same feelings for him. She wished she could ask him questions and have him answer them.

She wanted him to kiss her like he had before.

But she did not want to be his mistress. She did not think she had it in her to be a mistress. She remembered how he had touched her that first day when he hadn't known who she was.

He had thought she was someone else. If she were his mistress, he would touch her like that. But he would touch other women like that too.

No, she could not be a mistress.

She laughed out loud suddenly. As if he had even asked her! As if it were even a possibility. Bella shook her head. Her imagination was seriously outrageous sometimes.

Lady Neeley was used to her sudden bursts

of laughter. But Lord Roxbury wasn't. He blinked and gave her a strange look.

"Is something amusing you, Miss Martin?"

"Yes," she said with a smile. "Don't worry about your party, Lord Roxbury. I have it all under control. I will be on your doorstep bright and early to set everything up. You don't even have to be there," she assured him. He had been avoiding her since their encounter at the museum.

"I think, Lord Roxbury, that your party has already had its desired effect!" Lady Neeley said. "Before it has even happened." She waved to a passing conveyance.

Bella furled her brow and glanced at Lady Neeley. "Desired effect?" she asked.

"Yes, dear, Lord Waverly wanted his son to have a party that would show society he was not just an irresponsible rake. He wants the mothers to understand that, and their daughters to see Lord Roxbury's home and want it for their own. He wants Roxbury married."

"Oh," Bella said. The disparate invitation lists finally made a bit more sense. "Oh!" she said again.

Roxbury was watching her intensely.

"Anyway, Roxbury," Lady Neeley continued. "I overheard a bit of conversation the other day. Mrs. Fitzherbert was mentioning to Lady Reese-Forbes that you have quite settled down lately. Both of those ladies have daughters between the ages of fifteen and twenty, and each of the daughters has a dowry that is quite sizable."

Roxbury looked rather pained. "Did you mention that to my father?"

"Of course!" Lady Neeley cried.

"Lovely."

"See now, look who is coming this way at this very moment. Sit up straight, Roxbury!" Lady Neeley hissed under her breath.

Bella had to bite rather hard on her tongue to keep from laughing out loud at that. Sit up straight indeed.

"Halloooo, Lady Neeley!" a very large woman with an even larger hat bellowed at them. She waved largely as the open carriage she was in came abreast of them.

"Lady Neeley, I should like to introduce you to my daughter. This is Lady Meliscent." She gestured to a poor girl that no one could see. She peeked out from beneath her mother's shadow, and Bella could tell the child was completely terrified of the entire world.

Introductions were made all the way around as Lady Reese-Forbes tried desperately to force her shy daughter to talk to Roxbury.

The poor girl was absolutely making a fool of herself, or, rather, her mother was making a fool of her. The girl couldn't string more than two words together without stuttering horribly.

Bella wanted to save her. She wanted to jump into the carriage and take the girl in her arms.

And then, Roxbury did. Well, he saved her, at least. The man dismounted suddenly and walked around the side of Lady Reese-Forbes's open carriage. "Might I have the pleasure of your company, Lady Meliscent?" he asked.

The chatter between Lady Neeley and Lady Reese-Forbes died completely. Poor Meliscent looked ready to throw up. But her mother finally realized what was happening and threw the girl out of the carriage.

Roxbury smiled warmly and put out his arm, then helped the girl put her hand on his elbow, since she did not move at all.

Lady Reese-Forbes thumped her carriage boy on the head with the handle of a small fan. "Off you go. Follow behind so my daughter keeps her reputation intact, if you please." The carriage boy jumped from his place behind the carriage and followed behind Roxbury and Lady Meliscent.

Roxbury had shrunk. It was like he had pulled in his body: His shoulders were tilted inward, his knees were bent, his head was down. Obviously, he was trying not to be so big and scary to this young girl.

Bella grinned and shook her head. She had told him he was a perfect gentleman. And here he was proving it yet again.

227

A perfect gentleman, with a perfect kiss. She absolutely adored him. She grinned, and then covered her mouth with her hand when she realized what she had just said to herself.

She adored him. She loved him.

Isabella Martin loved Lord Roxbury.

She had a moment of pure happiness followed by complete pain.

And of course, that's how it was with love: pain and happiness on the same footing.

Chapter 7

Can Lord Roxbury be settling down? With Lady Meliscent Reese-Forbes? It seems a most unlikely of pairings, but the two were seen walking arm in arm in Hyde Park yesterday, and Lord Roxbury was leaning down toward the young miss as if he were quite engrossed in their conversation.

This Author dares not speculate further. Perhaps all will be revealed at Lord Roxbury's Japanese ball tonight, which, incidentally, is the debut event for Miss Isabella Martin's new business venture, Bella of the Ball.

Lady Whistledown's Society Papers,
12 June 1816

The party was perfect. As Bella had run about making sure the punch bowls had stayed filled and her geisha girls had their kimonos tied on perfectly, five people had asked her to plan their parties. Lady Neeley told her that at least twenty people had asked for Bella's information.

Bella had made up cards with her information on them, and they were all gone.

The only slight hitch in the night had been when one of the girls in her geisha outfit had tripped over her wooden slippers and fallen on top of Ozzie. The girl was fine, though she had a bruised ankle. And Ozzie seemed no worse for wear. Actually, Ozzie had offered to take the girl home, and Bella had not seen him since. Obviously, Ozzie was more than just fine.

Lord Waverly seemed thrilled with the party. And Roxbury had, of course, acted like the perfect gentleman.

It was over now, finally. And Bella took a moment to sit down on a padded chair in Lord Roxbury's large drawing room. She had sent Christophe home, and she was now overseeing the maids she had hired for the evening. Someday she would have a trustworthy clean-up crew that she could put on staff permanently. Now, though, she was watching every piece of silver and cutlery like a hawk.

But her feet were killing her, and she was dead tired. Ten minutes alone in a dark room would revive her, she decided, enough so that she could finish, at least. She slipped off her shoes and kneaded her toes with her fingers.

A door opened and Roxbury entered.

Bella put her feet on the floor and pushed

her skirts down demurely.

Roxbury came straight over to her as if he had known that she was there.

"Tell me something," he said.

Bella tilted her head and smiled up at him. "Anything," she said.

"What on earth are you so happy about?"

"What do you mean?" she asked in surprise. "What on earth do I have *not* to be happy about? I just planned this beautiful party and it ran perfectly, which bodes well for my business."

Roxbury flopped his hand in front of his face. "Yes, yes, yes," he said. "There is that. But two weeks ago, you were happy too. And you didn't have a successful business. You had a parrot trying to make love to your ear."

Bella laughed. "You are pissed. I am amazed you can even walk straight."

"You have no idea."

Bella sighed and glanced down toward her aching feet. And suddenly, Roxbury was there, kneeling down beside her. His hands reached under her skirt and caught one foot. He rested it in his lap, and then began massaging it with his large hands. Nothing had ever felt better.

"Ohhhh," she said on a long sigh. "Ahhhhh."

"Don't tease me," he said.

She frowned down at him, confused.

"Why," he said. "Tell me why you are happy."

She shrugged and leaned back in her chair. She thought about his question for a moment, and then she said, "This moment will never happen again. This very second is over right now."

"That's achingly profound."

"Don't tease if you want my answer."

"I won't tease."

Bella closed her eyes. "Some moments are easy. They are good and fun and beautiful, and I'm happy. Others aren't so easy. But it is my decision to be happy during the hard times as well as the easy ones. I cannot control most things, but I *can* control my feelings. And I *want* to be happy. So I find something in every moment that I can enjoy."

"So you never cry?" he asked.

"Of course I do. Crying is wonderful. It's like cleaning out the cobwebs. I love to cry." She opened her eyes and grinned down at him.

He stopped rubbing her foot, and she really did feel like crying. Instead she slipped her other foot onto Lord Roxbury's lap. He shook his head and laughed. And then he rubbed her neglected foot.

"I had my party on your birthday for a reason," he said finally.

"Really? And what is that reason?"

"Well, it was because I was going to make

sure you were in my company the day you turned thirty so that I could kiss you and you would know that you had not been kissed yet. But I've already done that."

"And one kiss is all I get?" she asked, hoping with all of her heart that she was wrong.

He just shook his head, which really could mean anything, bugger it.

"But now something is different," he said. He reached into his coat and took out a package. "Happy birthday," he said, handing her the package.

"Thank you," she said, taking it. She held it for a moment, cupped in her palms. "This is my only birthday present."

"Are you enjoying your moment?" he asked with a smile.

She grinned at him. "Always."

"Well, let me have *my* moment when you open it."

Bella pulled open the wrapping and found in her palm a beautiful square silver case. She flipped it around, and engraved on the bottom was Bella of the Ball.

"It's a card case," he said and reached up to flip open the top. Inside was a bunch of beautifully tendered cards for her business. They were much more expensive than the ones she had made for herself.

"I've an entire box of them in my study for you. But they didn't all fit in the case."

"Thank you, Lord Roxbury."

"You are welcome, Miss Martin."

"I have a question for *you* now," Bella said. "Why have you never married?"

"My father is adamant that the title stay in our family, and I don't see the problem. If I just live my life and die, the title goes to my third cousin, Richard Millhouse. Richard is a very good man. He's honest and good, and will probably do a better job with the responsibilities of this title than I ever did."

"Ah."

"I would make a terrible father, and a worse husband. Why should I inflict that upon some poor girl and a child?"

Bella nodded, but anger made her look away for a minute. She wasn't angry very often, but right then it burned in her heart and made her want to thump Lord Roxbury right on his head.

"That's cowardice," she told him.

Roxbury blinked up at her.

Bella pulled her feet from Roxbury's grasp and shoved them in her slippers. "You talk about your title like it's a burden you want to throw away as quickly as you can. How dare you. That's a legacy, a history, a tradition that you have been gifted with. You have a family and you could give this name to your child and they would have those things as well. Right this minute, you can go outside and drive to your father's house and

234

take his hand. You can learn from him. You can talk to him. That is a blessing that you just throw away and don't care about."

Bella shook her head. "I don't understand that at all. I would give away everything I have, every single material item, my business, my very soul, to have a family. I will never give a child a name. I will never gift a person with the memory of my beautiful, imaginative mother and my hardworking, loving father. My history is gone when I die. You have the opportunity to continue a legacy. Instead, you pretend to be a scoundrel and a rake so that no one will marry you." Bella made a sound of pure disgust.

"How on earth can you be so ungrateful?" she asked.

"I don't know. But I know I don't want to be ungrateful anymore. Be my wife Isabella." He stood up quickly and took her hands in his. "I have been an idiot, and I don't want to be one anymore. I want to have children with you. I want to give them my name, and I want them to have your eyes. And I want you to teach them what you have taught me; just make sure it's before they ruin most of their lives being really ungrateful. Please." He smiled widely at her.

Bella felt her mouth go dry. She couldn't speak. The words wouldn't come from her dry throat. "No," she finally said.

"No?" he asked. "Is that a no from shock

or a no, you won't marry me?"

She closed her eyes and shook her head. "I can't. You can't marry me, Roxbury."

"Call me Anthony."

"No, no, no." She pulled her hands from his. "I'm not what you need. I don't have anything to give you. And I'm now a woman in trade. It would be a scandal. Your father would be devastated. We're not from the same place. And, I can't. Especially now!"

"I wouldn't ask you to give up your party planning."

Bella just shook her head. She couldn't believe it. Here was what she had been waiting for, but she couldn't marry Lord Roxbury. He needed someone else. He needed someone with the legacy she had just been talking about. Her father had made shoes, for goodness' sake! She couldn't possibly bring that into Lord Roxbury's family tree.

"I love you enough to say no," she told him and turned and left him.

Chapter 8

As Lord Roxbury paid not a whit of attention to Lady Meliscent Reese-Forbes at his Japanese ball Wednesday eve, This Author must come to the conclusion that the aforementioned walk in Hyde Park on Tuesday was nothing more than an innocent stroll.

Indeed, Lord Roxbury paid no special attention to any lady at his party (much, This Author is sure, to his father's dismay), except for the intrepid Miss Martin, but one cannot read anything into that, as she is quite obviously in his employ.

Not to mention that she is now in trade, and it is difficult to imagine an earl such as Roxbury's father overlooking a detail such as that.

Lady Whistledown's Society Papers,
14 June 1816

Lady Neeley had organized her own little party, and Bella had been invited as if she were one of Lady Neeley's friends instead of an employee. It felt extremely strange, Bella thought as she sat across from Lady Neeley's nephew, Mr. Henry Brooks. They were at a special fete at Vauxhall Gardens that the Regent had organized to commemorate the one-year anniversary of Wellington's victory at Waterloo.

Lady Neeley had hired a private gazebo and, while everyone else in the Gardens was dining on watery punch and the thinnest slices of ham Bella had ever seen, their small party of ten was gorging on roast duck and watercress salad, accompanied by a selection of wines that was making Bella's head feel very fuzzy.

Lady Neeley had borrowed Christophe for this little dinner, since her new chef was terrible and could barely make edible scones. But Lady Neeley was also noticeably thinner, and so she was happy.

That thought made Bella feel like crying. It was like a dagger pushed a bit deeper into her heart each time she thought of happiness now. In the week since her birthday, Bella's life had changed even more dramatically.

She had her own home. She had even purchased silk and made lovely sheets for her bed. It was like sleeping on clouds. She had her diary filled in for an entire year, and with all of the deposits she had required of her clients, Bella of the Ball had already made a profit.

Lord Waverly had been so delighted he'd actually chortled. "My girl," he'd told her just the other day, "I don't think any other business in town has so quickly made a profit. You are a wonder."

Bella had smiled, but she knew that there was something missing. And she also knew exactly what it was. And she suddenly could not seem to find enjoyment in small things as she had before.

As she sat now, sipping at her wine as the moon rose and the dark descended, Bella wondered if it might not have been better if nothing had ever changed.

"My dear girl," a voice boomed from above her. She smiled up at Lord Waverly. "Walk with me," he said.

"Of course, my lord," she said and stood. She pulled her shawl tighter about her shoulders against the cool breeze that had picked up once the sun had gone down, and she placed her fingers on Lord Waverly's arm.

She excused herself from Mr. Brooks, and they left the gazebo and headed through the milling throngs. Bella had never been to Vauxhall before. There were musicians playing constantly and roving magicians and jugglers.

It was amazing, and Bella wished she could just stand still and take it all in. But they walked past the bustle and went down toward the river. "I hear," Lord Waverly said once they had found a quiet walkway, "that you have turned down my son's offer of marriage."

Bella swallowed hard and then started to cough.

"Are you all right, dear?" Lord Waverly asked, pounding her on the back, which in all truth was making it worse.

Bella finally caught her breath. She straightened, her hand resting on her chest.

"Didn't mean to shock," Lord Waverly said.

"Of course not," Bella murmured.

"Do you realize," Lord Waverly continued, "that I have spent the last seventeen years of my son's life visiting him once a week? He never once came to see me. But now, in the last week, he has been at my home every single day."

"Really?"

"S'truth, he's driving me quite mad. I do wish you'd marry the boy and get him out of my hair."

Bella stumbled to a stop. "But —"

Lord Waverly shook his head and didn't let her continue. "I know, I know . . . scandal and all that. A bunch of malarkey." He turned so that they faced each other, and he took her face between his hands. "He's already a bit of a scandal, isn't he? You're not going to taint our name, I promise you that. Grandchildren with your brains'd be a blessing beyond description." He punctuated his statement by kissing her forehead.

"Now then," he said, turning and walking toward the river once more. "I told that boy of mine that I wasn't going to say anything to you at all. I respect a woman's prerogative to say no. Hasn't Lady Neeley been saying no to me for ten years?"

He stopped as if he wanted her to answer, so she did. "Er, yes, my lord."

"Don't be cheeky, girl."

"Sorry."

"But then I was sitting at that table tonight, and I just could not take it. You look like a dog that's lost her favorite bone."

"Lovely."

"No, it's downright disheartening," Lord Waverly said.

The man had obviously never learned the meaning of tact.

"You used to sparkle, girl. When you had absolutely nothing to sparkle about. Now that you do have something to be happy about, you're like a black cloud."

Bella was beginning to feel very unattractive, thanks to Lord Waverly's metaphors.

"Now then, I'd say you need to brighten up and accept my son's proposition. And I don't want any talk of scandals or tarnishing of names. If you'll make my son happy and give me grandchildren, that's all I could ever ask of you."

Bella did not know what to say.

"Here he is now," Lord Waverly said.

Bella glanced up, and there was Lord Roxbury a short distance away. She stopped, her heart thumping hard in her chest as he strode toward them out of the groups of people that stood at the shore waiting for the Regent's show to start.

"Thank you for bringing her to me, Father," Roxbury said.

The man just nodded. "I'll be on my way then. Must let Brooks know you won't be accompanying him to the show, my dear," Lord Waverly said to her.

"Oh dear," Bella said, suddenly remembering poor Mr. Brooks.

She moved to catch Lord Waverly, but Lord Roxbury held her firmly. "Oh no, you don't."

Bella looked up into Roxbury's soft brown eyes. "I can't say yes," she said.

"Yes you can," he said. "Try it, it's easy. You just put your tongue at the roof of your mouth and pull your lips back. . . ." He stopped when Bella rolled her eyes.

"Listen, Bella," he said. She blinked, as he had never said her name before. She rather liked it coming from his lips. "I need to hire you."

"Hire me?"

"Yes, I need to hire you to plan every single party I shall ever have for the rest of my life. And it just seems like it would be ever so much easier if you lived in my house. Don't you think?"

Bella shook her head and laughed.

"That's good, laughing is good," Roxbury said. "Saying no is bad."

"But —"

"Saying *but* is bad, too. You can't say *but*."

Bella giggled.

"That's good, too," Roxbury said.

"Okay, yes, I'll do all of your parties."

"Starting with my wedding party?" he asked. "In which you will be the star attraction as my wife?"

Bella stopped for a moment and just watched Roxbury's face. Such a good face. A good man. She had known he was a good man from the first time they had met. "I know why I love you," she said. "But why do you love me?"

"I don't know," he said.

Bella scowled.

"But I do love you. I have never felt like this before in my life, Bella. The thought of marriage and a family always seemed deadly dull to me, but now, if you will be my wife, it is an adventure I crave. I adore you, Bella. You make me believe I *can* be the perfect gentleman."

Bella smiled.

"So?" he asked.

"So, yes, I'll marry you," she said quickly,

243

before she ran away. She was a little bit afraid of this, but she also knew that she could not live as she had this last week, dreading each day and wishing she could go back and live in the past. She might as well just jump into a very scary, but promising future, rather than stay in a sad present.

Roxbury's eyes glowed, and then they darkened, and his head bent down toward her. "Come with me," he said.

She couldn't help giggling as Roxbury pulled her along, through crowds of people and then out onto a walkway that wasn't lit up at all. It was as dark as pitch, actually.

Bella snuggled closer against Roxbury's body. The glittering excitement of Vauxhall was left behind them, and suddenly they were in a place where bad things could happen.

"Roxbury, I don't like this at all."

"Sh," he said, pulling her deeper into the darkened walkway. And then they were off the path and behind a very large bush.

Roxbury immediately pulled Bella into his arms. "I couldn't continue without having you against me like this."

"Oh," Bella said. "Well, I do like this." She closed her eyes and sank into Roxbury's tall, hard body.

"Tell me again, Bella. Tell me that you will marry me."

"I will marry you, Anthony."

He made a deep rumbling sound in his throat. "Promise me," he said.

"I promise. Could I ask a favor?" she said then.

"Anything."

"I have these brand-new sheets I made for my bed. They're silk. Could we put them on our bed?"

Anthony's body went very still against hers. "First of all, the thought of silk sheets makes it very hard to keep my hands off of you. And second, the way you say 'our bed' makes it very hard to keep my hands off of you."

Bella pushed a little away from him and tilted her head back. "So don't keep your hands off of me."

"Oh, all right," he grinned at her. She could see the whiteness of his teeth in the dark, and then she felt him lean toward her, and his teeth were at the lobe of her ear.

"Oh," she said on a quick intake of breath, and she arched against him.

Where her sound had been light, the sound that came from Anthony was dark. It made Bella shiver right down to her toes.

He trailed his tongue over the lobe of her ear, then just behind it, and Bella felt her legs buckle beneath her. Anthony's arms tightened around her, his mouth moved to cover hers. She gasped again, taking in Anthony's smell and taste completely, and suddenly she needed him more than air or food.

Bella smoothed her hands up Anthony's chest and linked them around his neck as he kissed her lips softly, tasting her as she tasted him. He moaned as she deepened the kiss, and Bella felt a joy she had never known. She felt safe, and she felt loved, but she also felt wanted and needed and excited as never before. It was heady and thrilling.

She leaned her head back so that her lover could take her mouth without hindrance, and he plunged his hand into her hair, holding her against him. She pressed against him, wishing she could climb right inside of him. He was hard against her, his thigh pushed between her legs, and she opened. Her most intimate woman's place pressed against the muscle of Anthony's leg, and she knew that she had just found a new excitement. She could not help the languorous, but heated, sound that escaped her.

Anthony's fingers curled in her hair almost painfully. "God, Bella, I shall come undone," he said against her mouth.

She giggled breathlessly. "I am undone, my love," she said.

"I could only wish it were so," Anthony purred, and Bella felt his words in every nerve ending of her body. Instinct told her exactly what was supposed to happen then, and she needed it, wanted it. She wanted to breathe his air, feel his voice instead of hear it. And she needed more. She needed him to be one with her.

She pushed aside his coat, her palm against his slightly damp shirt. His chest was hard and warm, and she wished she could tear every thread of clothing from his body in that very second and take him into her.

And then the bushes around them rustled and people were suddenly in their own private area.

"Oh!" Bella cried.

"So sorry," a deep voice said. Bella could just make out a tall man and a slim, blonde woman with him before they ducked away.

"Was that? . . ."

"That was Easterly and his wife," Anthony said.

"That's what I thought. You know, I could swear I saw them digging holes behind a bush in Hyde Park the other day. They seem to be lurking in strange places lately. I had never imagined Lady Easterly to be the sort of woman to lurk."

"Yes, but you are also lurking, are you not?"

Bella giggled.

"And I don't think I'd ever imagined you to be the sort of person to lurk."

"No, it is completely because of your bad influence, my lord."

"I do try, my lady."

"Oh my," Bella said, her body shaking at the reminder that she was going to be a lady.

It was a very scary thing to be, she thought.

Anthony's arms tightened around her. "We're having a moment, Bella, enjoy it."

She laughed. "I've created a monster."

"You have no idea." He kissed her lips, and she shivered. "Now, where were we?" he asked.

"Our bed and silk sheets," she said.

"Right," and he took her mouth in a kiss that was even better than the one before it. And Bella just closed her eyes and enjoyed the moment. And she knew with all of her heart that she was not going to have much difficulty enjoying the next few million moments of her life.

Mia Ryan

Mia Ryan writes to stay sane. Those around her know that she hasn't been writing enough when she starts slipping into bouts of inane chatter about painting bathrooms, crocheting blankets, and planting a garden. All of these things she has tried, actually, but with tragic results. Fortunately, she is hard at work right now on her next novel. Her latest book, *The Duchess Diaries*, hit the shelves December 2003. Visit *miaryan.com* to learn more about it.

The Best of Both Worlds

Suzanne Enoch

For my uncle, Beal Whitlock,
whose laugh I will miss.
And for my aunt, Kathleen,
to whom I send a basketful
of hugs and kisses.

Chapter 1

. . . but enough talk of Lady Neeley's ill-fated fête. As difficult as it is for much of the ton to believe, there are other subjects worthy of gossip . . . most notably, London's bluest-eyed earl, Lord Matson.

Although not intended for the title (his elder brother died tragically last year), Lord Matson does not seem to be having difficulty assuming the mantle of man-about-town. Since arriving in London earlier this Season, he has been seen with a different eligible female on his arm each day.

And at night, with ladies who would not be considered eligible at all!

Lady Whistledown's Society Papers, 31 May 1816

"But we weren't invited," Charlotte Birling said.

Her mother, seated behind the morning room's oak writing desk, looked up from the new *Whistledown* column. "That doesn't signify, because we wouldn't have attended, anyway. And thank goodness for that. Imagine us standing about chatting, and having Easterly walk in. Infamous."

"Sophia didn't have to imagine it. *She* was invited." Charlotte glanced at the mantel clock. Nearly ten. With a quickening heartbeat, she set aside her embroidery. She needed to get to the window without her mother making note of it.

"Yes. Poor Sophia." Baroness Birling tsked. "Twelve years of trying to forget that man, and just as her life begins to recover, he reappears. Your cousin must have been mortified."

Charlotte wasn't so sure about that, but she made an assenting sound, anyway. The clock's ornate minute hand jerked forward. *What if the clock was slow?* She hadn't considered that. *Or what if he was early?* Unable to help it, she bounced to her feet. "Tea, Mama?" she blurted, nearly tripping over her cat. Beethoven rolled out of the way, batting his paws at the hem of her gown.

"Hm? No, thank you, dear."

"Well, I'll just have some."

Her gaze out the front window, she splashed tea into a cup. The street in front of Birling House boasted a few stray leaves, fooled by the cold weather into thinking it still winter, but nothing else moved. Not even a vendor or a carriage on the way to Hyde Park. Above the sound of paper rustling at the writing desk, the clock ticked again. Charlotte took a sip of tea, barely noting both that it was too hot and that she'd forgotten to add sugar.

And then, she forgot to breathe. Heralded by a jingle of reins, a black horse turned up the lane from High Street. The world, the clock, the clopping of hooves, the beat of her heart seemed to slow as she gazed at the rider.

Hair the color of rich amber played a little in the soft morning breeze. The dark blue beaver hat shadowed his eyes, but she knew they were a faded cobalt, like a lake on an overcast day. His jacket matched the color of his hat, while his close-fitting dun trousers and his polished Hessian boots said as clearly as any gold-embossed calling card that he was a gentleman. His mouth was set in a straight line, relaxed but somber, and she wondered what he might be thinking.

"—lotte? Charlotte! What in the world are you gaping at?"

She jumped, spinning away from the window, but it was already too late. Her mother nudged her sideways, leaning forward to peer through the window at the passing rider.

"Nothing, Mama," Charlotte said, taking another swallow of tea and nearly gagging at the bitter flavor. "I was just think—"

"Lord Matson," the baroness stated, reaching over to yank the curtains closed. "You were staring at Lord Matson. For heaven's sake, Charlotte, what if he'd looked over and seen you?"

Humph. She'd been looking out the window at him for the past five days, and he hadn't turned his head in her direction once. Xavier, Earl Matson. For all he knew, she didn't even exist. "I'm permitted to look out my own front window, Mama," she said, stifling a sigh as the Arabian and its magnificent rider vanished behind green velvet draperies. "If he saw me, I hope he would assume that I was looking out at our fine roses, which I was."

"Ah. And you regularly blush at the sight of roses, then?" Baroness Birling resumed her seat at the desk. "Put that scoundrel out of your mind. You have the Hargreaves' Ball this evening to prepare for."

"It's ten o'clock in the morning, Mama," Charlotte protested. "Putting on a gown and pinning up my hair doesn't take ten hours. It barely takes two."

"I don't mean physical preparations. I'm referring to mental preparations. Don't forget, you'll be dancing with Lord Herbert."

"Oh, bother. The only preparation I'll need for that is a nap."

She hadn't realized she'd spoken aloud

until the baroness swept to her feet again. "Obviously, daughter, you have forgotten the efforts to which your father went in seeking out Lord Herbert Beetly and ascertaining his interest in finding a wife."

"Mama, I didn't —"

"If you require a nap in order to behave in an appropriate manner, then go take one at once." Scowling, the baroness crumpled the *Whistledown* column. "And have a care with that tongue of yours, lest you end up in here as well."

"I never do anything, so I don't see how that could possibly happen."

"Ha. Sophia's only error was in marrying Easterly twelve years ago. And even after not seeing him in all that time, even after living an impeccable life for over a decade, the moment he reappears, *her* name becomes associated with scandal again. Whatever you may think of Lord Herbert, *he* will not cause a scandal. You can hardly say the same for that man you were gawking at. Lord Matson has been in Town for less than three weeks, and he's managed to be noticed by *Whistledown*."

"I wasn't gawk—" Charlotte snapped her mouth closed. At nineteen, she knew all the steps and turns of her mother's tirades. Interfering now would only make things worse. "I'll be in my room, then, napping," she said stiffly, and left.

Besides, in all honesty, she *had* been

gawking at Lord Matson. She didn't see the harm in it. The earl was exceedingly handsome, and gaping at him through a window or passing by him on the way to the refreshment table was the closest she was likely to get. Dashing, unmarried war heroes certainly weren't allowed on the Birling premises. Heavens, one might wink at her and cause a scandal.

It wasn't as if she wanted or expected to marry him, or something. Even without her parents' obsession with respectability and propriety, she knew better than that. The handsome, daring men were for dancing and flirting. Marrying a man who always had an eye toward his next conquest — that seemed a sure path to misery.

But he hadn't flirted with her *or* asked her to dance. Charlotte sighed as she reached her bedchamber, Beethoven on her heels. It would never happen. She could tell herself that her parents would warn off any male with a single blot on his reputation, and so they would, but she wasn't likely to attract any such man's notice, anyway.

Considering she'd only risen two hours earlier, napping didn't hold much appeal, though Beethoven had already curled up on her pillow and was snoring softly. Instead she retrieved the book she'd been reading and sank into the comfortable chair beneath the window. Ordinarily she would have pushed open the glass, but since summer refused to appear and the sky had already begun throwing down yet another drizzle, she pulled a knitted throw over her legs and settled in.

This was how she prepared for her encounters with Lord Herbert Beetly — by pretending to be somewhere else. In her favorite novels princes and knights thrived, and even third sons of minor marquises were either heroic or villainous. And no one in the faerie realms could be said to be dull.

Charlotte lifted her head, gazing at her faint reflection in the rain-streaked window. Heavens, what if that described her, as well? Was she dull? Was that why her father had chosen Lord Herbert as her perfect match? Narrowing her eyes, she intensified her scrutiny.

She wasn't a ravishing beauty, of course; even without the occasional muttered commentary disparaging her height and her less than bountiful bosom, she'd seen herself often enough in the dressing mirror to know. She did like her smile, and her brunette hair with its tint of red. Brown eyes, but she did have two of them, and they were set at the appropriate distance from her nose. No, it wasn't her appearance. It was the way she always felt like a duck, quacking among elegant swans.

So she enjoyed gawking at Xavier, Lord Matson while he rode to his daily boxing appointment at Gentleman Jackson's. And in all fairness she wasn't the only one who liked to look at him — and at least she didn't doodle his name linked with hers at parties, as she'd seen other girls do. She knew better. But it was still nice to daydream, once in a while.

As the hall clock signaled nine in the evening, Xavier, Earl Matson shrugged out of his greatcoat and handed the sopping wet thing over to the care of one of the Hargreaves' footmen. He took his place in the line of nobility awaiting introduction into the main ballroom, welcoming the rush of warm, if highly perfumed, air coming from inside, which didn't quite cover the faint musty smell. He imagined that in a very short time he would find it stifling. The event itself closed off his breathing, made him want to yank off his cravat and flee back into the cool, dark evening.

It still amazed him that an event so closely packed could feel so . . . isolating. He much preferred an intimate game of cards at some club or other, or even a night at the theater, where at least there was something to focus on besides the gossiping mass of humanity — especially when a large share of them seemed to be focused on him.

Yes, he was newly arrived in Town, and yes, he had a sizeable fortune to his name. But for God's sake, he'd spent the last year at Farley, the family estate — his estate — in Devon, and after twelve damned months of paper-shuffling and mourning clothes, whose damned business was it but his own if he cared to spend a few quid wagering and enjoying a good glass of port? And an actress or two? And an accommodating young widow of uncertain reputation, but well equipped with a seductive smile and lovely long legs?

Places like the Hargreaves' Ball, however, were where eligible, marriage-minded young females came to show off their plumage, and tonight he was hunting more respectable prey. So he handed the butler his invitation and strolled into the main room as his name and title were announced in a stentorian bellow.

"Matson," another voice boomed off to his left, and Xavier turned as Viscount Halloren strode up to grab his hand and pump it vigorously. "Came for the show, have you? Looks as though everyone has."

" 'The show?' " Xavier repeated, though he had a good idea what Halloren was talking about. Apparently everyone read *Whistledown*.

"That Neeley bracelet debacle. Seems all the suspects have put in an appearance."

Xavier didn't much care about the missing bracelet, but at least the mystery columnist had something to discuss besides his social calendar. He nodded. "It looks as though everyone in London's put in an appearance."

"Ha. Have to be seen at the Hargreaves' Grand Ball, don't you know. And I told you, this is the place to begin if you're looking for a likely chit to marry. More lively crowd than Almack's, and that's for damned certain." The viscount leaned closer. "Just a word of advice. Don't drink the sherry. And get to the port early."

"My thanks." When Halloren seemed ready to begin a dissertation on alcoholic beverages, Xavier excused himself.

He'd never been to a Hargreaves' Grand Ball before, but the decorations seemed so sparse as to be nonexistent, and it didn't take a mathematician to see that there weren't enough chairs for everyone by half. Apparently this was expected, however, because the majority of the guests avoided the drinks and snacks, and instead stood in clusters discussing who might have stolen Lady Neeley's infamous bracelet. He'd apparently landed in the gossip capital of London. Grateful as he was that he wasn't the topic of conversation, it was just a damned bracelet, for God's sake.

"Mother, just because Lady Neeley decided to accuse Lord Easterly doesn't mean we have to join the flock," a female voice to one side of him said.

"Hush, Charlotte. She's only saying what everyone is already thinking."

"Not *everyone*," the voice returned. "For goodness' sake, it's just a blasted bracelet. Ignorance about its whereabouts hardly seems to balance out against ruining a man's reputation."

Xavier turned his head. It was impossible to figure out which chit had spoken, since a hundred of them in various ages, sizes, and dress colors seemed to be wedged into a solid slice of feminine charms. He wasn't the only one interested in navigating it, however. A ripple inside the wedge opened to reveal a tall, brown-haired gentleman — Lord Roxbury, if his memory served him.

He took a lady's hand, bowing over it and cooing something that made her flutter, then went on to the next, a tall, thin female with dark hair.

"Good evening, Miss Charlotte," Roxbury drawled, kissing her hand.

"And to you, Lord Roxbury." She smiled at the baron.

That was the voice which had caught his attention. The smile she gave the baron was a little crooked, not poised and perfect and practiced for hours in front of a mirror. Genuine, in a sea of *faux* humor and humility. *Charlotte.* With an impatient breath, Xavier waited until a chuckling Roxbury moved away, and then stepped in before the chits closed ranks again.

"Charlotte, I've told you not to encourage such scoundrels," the older woman beside her hissed. She took the young lady's hand and rubbed at it with the corner of her matronly shawl.

"He didn't leave a mark, Mama," Charlotte replied, her brown eyes dancing. "And he's kissing everyone's hand, for heaven's sake."

"That is his error; you don't need to encourage it. Just be thankful Lord Herbert didn't see you showing favor to another gentleman."

"As if he would no—" She looked up, brown eyes meeting Xavier's. The color drained from her face, and her mouth formed a soft O before it clamped shut again.

Something grabbed his insides and wrenched him forward another step. Oddly enough, the sensation wasn't at all unpleasant. "Good evening," he said.

"Good . . . hello," she returned, offering a curtsy. "Lord Matson."

"You have me at a disadvantage," he said quietly, noting that the mother had stiffened into a fair imitation of a board. "You know my name, but I don't know yours."

"Charlotte," she gulped, then with a breath squared her shoulders. "Charlotte Birling. My lord, this is my mother, the baroness Lady Birling."

The name didn't sound the least bit familiar, but then he'd only been in London a few short weeks. "My lady," he said, reaching out to grip the woman's fingers.

"My . . . my lord."

He released her before she could have an apoplexy, turning his attention back to Charlotte. "Miss Charlotte," he said, taking her hand in turn and repeating the manner in which Roxbury had addressed her. Her fingers through her thin lace gloves felt warm, and despite her initial stammering, both her gaze and her grip remained steady. Abruptly he didn't want to release her.

"I'm surprised to see you here tonight." With a sideways glance at her mother she twitched her fingers free.

"And why is that?"

The smile touched her mouth again. "Warm lemonade, watered-down liquor, stale cake, and a barely audible orchestra with no dancing."

Xavier lifted an eyebrow. "It sounds as though no one should be here." With a glance of his own at her white-faced mother, he leaned closer. "So what is the attraction?" he asked in a lower voice. *Besides this unexpected female, of course.*

"Gossip, and morbid curiosity," she answered promptly.

"I've heard the gossip, but explain the rest, if you please."

"Oh, it's simple. Lady Hargreaves is at least a hundred years old, and she has seventy or eighty grandchildren and great-grandchildren. She refuses to choose an heir, so everyone comes by to see who the latest favorite might be."

Realizing something he'd never expected of the evening — that he was enjoying himself — Xavier chuckled. "And who is the current front-runner?"

"Well, it's fairly early in the even—"

"Charlotte, you were going to escort me to the refreshment table," the baroness broke in, stepping between the two of them.

Xavier blinked. He'd all but forgotten anyone else was there — and given the crowd and the noise and his usual fairly keen sense of self-preservation, that was highly unusual. Paying attention to a proper chit was a good way to either get gossiped about, or worse, entangled — and it was far too early in his selection process for that. "Good evening, then."

"It was nice to meet you, my l—"

"Oh, there's your father," Lady Birling interrupted again, grabbing her daughter's arm.

He looked after them for a moment as they made their way through the crush. She'd known who he was, and while that wasn't all that surprising considering the attention the *Whistledown* columns had been paying him, it bothered him that he'd spent nearly a month in London and she'd never caught his eye. Certainly she wasn't a classical beauty, but he would definitely set her on the pretty side of plain. In addition, her smile and her gaze had been . . . compelling.

"There you are, Xavier," a female voice cooed at him, and a slender hand wrapped around his arm.

"Lady Ibsen," he returned, checking his flying thoughts.

"Mm. It was *Jeanette* last night," she breathed, pressing her bosom against him.

"That was in private."

"Ah, I see. And this evening you're otherwise occupied. Well, I've been keeping an eye out, myself. I have several prospective brides in mind for you. Come along."

He gazed down at her oval, upturned face and into her dark eyes, which bespoke her Spanish ancestry. "Brides who wouldn't mind if their husband continued his philandering with a particular female of questionable reputation, I assume?"

She smiled just enough to hint of private seductions. "Of course."

With a breath he gestured her to lead the way. As they pushed into the crowd, however, he couldn't resist a last look over his shoulder at a tall chit with warm fingers and a crooked smile.

Chapter 2

And finally, in more sedate news, Lord Herbert Beetly was seen earlier this week, shopping for a brown hat to match his brown coat and brown trousers, which, to be sure, all match his brown hair and brown eyes.

Which begs the question — Were Lord Herbert to patronize a restaurant, would he choose brown chocolate cake? This Author somehow thinks not. Browned potatoes seem much more to his taste.

Lady Whistledown's Society Papers,
31 May 1818

"I would have thought your cousin's error with Lord Easterly would have been lesson enough for you, Charlotte. Charlotte?"

Charlotte looked up from her plate of marmalade-covered toast, dismayed to realize that she hadn't heard a word her father had spoken. "Yes, Papa," she returned anyway, deciding that would be a safe response.

"Well, obviously it wasn't. Your mother told me that you not only spoke with Lord Matson, but that you encouraged his conversation."

"I was merely being polite," she countered, doing her best to keep her attention on the conversation and not drift back into an Xavier Matson–colored daydream.

"There is a point at which politeness must give way to responsibility," the baron stated. "Thanks to your cousin's error in judgment, this family is once more in a precarious position. Another scandal could —"

"Papa, Sophia married Easterly twelve years ago. I was seven, for heaven's sake. And I fail to see what was so scandalous about it, anyway."

Lord Birling lowered his eyebrows. "As you say, you were seven. You didn't witness the uproar when Easterly simply left England and abandoned Sophia. I did. And no one in this household will ever be the cause of such a stir. Is that clear?"

"Yes, it's clear. Perfectly clear. And don't worry, Papa. I'm certain Lord Matson will never have cause to speak to me again." Especially not after the way her mother had practically gone into hysterics at the sight of him. Charlotte sighed. First the miracle, that he'd looked at her, and spoken with her, then its destruction — if he even thought about her ever again it would be in gratitude that he'd escaped.

"I'm just thankful that Lord Herbert hadn't yet arrived to witness you talking with another man," the baroness contributed from across the table.

This time Charlotte frowned. "So now I'm not allowed to speak with anyone?"

"You know very well what I mean. We're not being cruel, dear, and I hope you realize that. We are doing our utmost to provide you with the best future possible, and I don't think it unreasonable to hope and expect that you will do nothing to actively sabotage what is in your own best interest."

She hated when her parents were right — especially when her best possible future reached as low as Lord Herbert Beetly. "Of course," she said, reaching across to pat her mother's hand. "It's just that excitement seems terribly rare in my life, and when it's so handsome, it's sometimes difficult to ignore."

"Hm." Her father gave a brief smile. "Do try."

"I will."

At that moment, as if the morning had been waiting in the hallway for its cue, the butler opened the breakfast room door.

"My lord, my lady, Miss Charlotte, Lord Herbert Beetly."

Charlotte stifled a sigh, rising from the table as her parents did to greet their guest.

"My lord," she said, curtsying, and wishing for one second that despite her promise to ignore excitement it could be someone dashing like Lord Roxbury or Lord Matson coming to call.

Herbert's dullness wasn't his fault, she supposed; his entire family seemed to suffer from a singular lack of wit and imagination. As he finished greeting her parents and approached her, she had to admit that he was pleasant in appearance — he did dress well. And if his gaze was a little . . . vapid, his countenance was handsome.

"Miss Charlotte," he said, bowing over her sticky marmalade fingers, "your shopping escort has arrived."

He also tended to state the obvious. "So I see. If you'll give me a moment, we can be off."

"My pleasure."

As she excused herself and hurried upstairs for her bonnet and gloves, she heard her father inquire whether Herbert had eaten already or not. Of course he had; this morning he would have shaved, dressed, eaten, and picked out the exact appropriate carriage for their venture because, well, that was what one did before calling on someone.

"Oh, be quiet, Charlotte," she told herself as she collected her things and returned downstairs. "Your life is just as orderly."

With her maid, Alice, accompanying them,

she and Herbert rode to Bond Street in his coach. She would have preferred a curricle so she could look about more freely, but since it was drizzling yet again, the closed coach made more sense.

"I hope you don't mind the coach," Herbert said as they disembarked, "but with the rain I didn't think the curricle appropriate."

Good God, they were even thinking alike. Fighting a swell of panic, Charlotte forced a smile and hurried through the door of the closest shop. She *was* as dull as Herbert. Did her friends, who always had exciting tales to tell even if she didn't quite believe all of them, think her as vapid as she thought him?

Trying to outrun her own dullness, she didn't see the clothing mannequin until she bumped into it. Before she could grab it, the heavy, metal-ribbed behemoth tipped away from her, thunking into the arms of the nearest shopper. "Oh! I'm so sorry! I wasn't looking where . . . Lord Matson."

With a twist of his lips the earl effortlessly shoved the thing upright again. "Charlotte Birling."

Faded cobalt eyes took her in from head to toe, and she wished that she'd elected to wear something less goose-necked despite the weather. For goodness' sake, she looked like a dowdy old spinster. "I apologize, my lord."

"You've already done that. What —"

"Charlotte," Herbert's voice, tight and

272

high-pitched, came from behind her, "why in the world did you come in here? It's not at all proper."

Tearing her gaze from the gray-and-black-clothed rake standing before her, she looked around. And scowled. *Blast it.* In as much of a hurry as she'd been to flee from her own thoughts, she might have chosen somewhere more appropriate than a men's tailor shop. "Drat," she muttered.

"Are you trying to escape that fellow?" the earl murmured, tilting his head to study her expression.

"No, just myself," she returned, then flushed. *What in the world was wrong with her?* To say such a private thing to anyone, much less a near, if handsome, stranger, was completely unlike her.

Something flashed in his eyes, but it was gone before she could begin to guess what it might be. To her surprise, though, he pulled a card case from his pocket and slipped it into her fingers.

"No," he continued in a normal tone, "I wouldn't have known it was missing until I returned home. Thank you, Miss Charlotte. It belonged to my grandfather, you know. And out in the rain, it would have been ruined."

He held out his hand, and she numbly set the case back into his palm. "I'm only glad I noticed you drop it, my lord." She curtsied, struggling to keep her voice steady when she wanted to sing that this was the nicest thing anyone had ever done for her. "If you'll excuse me, then."

Charlotte would have left, but with Herbert crowding up behind her, the only way out would have been to knock over the mannequin again. Gesturing at the man practically climbing her shoulder, she hid her nervous frustration with a smile. "Lord Matson, may I present Lord Herbert Beetly? Herbert, this is Xavier, Lord Matson."

To his credit, Herbert leaned around her to offer his hand. "My lord."

Matson returned the grip. "Beetly."

A clerk emerged from the rear of the shop. "Are you certain there's nothing else I can do for you, my lord?" he asked hopefully, placing a wrapped bundle on the counter.

The earl kept his attention on Herbert. "No, thank you. You'll send me the bill?"

"Of course, my lord." The clerk finally looked in Charlotte's direction. "May I assist you?" he asked, managing to sound officious and look dubious all at the same time.

Hm. She may not have intended to do it, but she could enter a men's shop if she wished. What if she'd been there looking for a gift for her father or something? Still, if Herbert reported to her parents that she'd spoken again with Lord Matson, she'd be in quite enough trouble without adding anything else into the mix. "No thank you," she replied. "We were just leaving."

Matson picked up the bundle and tucked it under his arm. "So was I," he said, gesturing for Charlotte and Herbert to precede him out to the street.

Goodness. Half hoping that the earl meant to accompany them on their shopping excursion, Charlotte stopped beneath the nearest overhanging eave. Reality had certainly gone astray in the last twenty-four hours. After she'd nearly knocked him down in the tailor's, her heart had begun pounding so hard that she thought even the clerk must have heard it.

Since last night her thoughts had lingered on the humor in Lord Matson's eyes and on his cool, confident manner, which didn't care what anyone else might think. Since she'd been seven and her family had decided that Sophia's troubles meant their disgrace, she'd wished she could be cool and uncaring about other people's opinions.

"Thank you again, Miss Charlotte," the earl drawled. Taking her hand, he stroked her fingertips with his thumb and then released her again. "Beetly."

"Matson."

She watched the earl down the street until he vanished into a pastry shop. A moment later she realized that Lord Herbert stood halfway in the rain, water dripping down the brim of his hat, glaring at her. Charlotte cleared her throat. "I need a pair of silver hair ribbons," she offered, and marched across the street without checking to see whether he followed.

Xavier stood in the pastry shop window, watching as Charlotte Birling entered a milliner's, her escort and her maid following. So the chit with the fine eyes did have a beau. Last night he'd thought her mother had invented one in order to escape his conversation.

He'd liked holding her fingers; in the past day he'd reflected on the feel of her warm hand in his several times. Touching her seemed the best damned idea he'd had in weeks.

He had felt physically attracted to females before, so the sensation wasn't that unusual. The odd thing about his surprising interest in Miss Charlotte Birling was his obsession with her mouth. As soon as he'd seen her smile he'd thought of kissing her soft lips, of saying and doing things to please her so he could see her genuine, crooked smile.

It should have been amusing, except that as he watched Lord Herbert Beetly shadowing her, he wasn't amused. He was used to assessing the character of enemies and supposed friends in a heartbeat, and she seemed to be someone trying very hard to be quiet and demure and finding it a difficult prospect. For reasons few people would understand, he could sympathize.

Another pair of females hurried past the window, their flimsy parasols bucking in the stiff breeze. Lady Mary Winter and her mother, Lady Winter. The younger Winter had made it onto his list of potential prospective spouses, though in truth he'd spent more time scratching names on and off of it than actually looking into a union.

He knew marriage made sense; he was Earl Matson now, and an earl needed heirs. If his own family was any example, he would need two. Then the first one could die of pneumonia, and the second could abandon his military career and rush home to take his brother's place as though that had been the plan all along.

"Sir? Is there something you wish to purchase?"

Xavier jumped, reluctantly turning from the window to the pastry clerk eyeing him from behind the food-laden counter. Since he was using the man's view, he supposed he should pay for the privilege. He approached, pointing at a likely pile of tea cakes. "A dozen of those," he said, dumping a few coins onto the counter.

"Very good, sir."

Having paid his window fee, he returned to the view while the clerk wrapped up his purchase. Charlotte and her small entourage were still inside the milliner's, Beetly no doubt making perfectly staid fashion suggestions and Charlotte politely ignoring every one of them. It amused him that he'd decided he could read her character well enough to deduce the points of her conversation. He wondered what she would select, and whether she would wear it out of the shop.

Now that he'd begun his imaginings, though, his mind wasn't content with guessing the color of her hat or her hair ribbons. He was seeing her removing them, her expressive brown eyes watching him as he watched her undress, her skin warm and radiant in dim candlelight. And he was hearing her soft moans and cries of ecstacy as he taught her a few things that a tall, propriety-minded chit who thought Lord Herbert her best prospect wouldn't know.

Xavier swallowed. *Jesus.* He collected his tea cakes and strode back out into the rain. On the alley corner a small group of urchins huddled against a wall, their usual enthusiasm for begging and picking pockets dampened by the weather. Giving a short whistle to get their attention, he tossed them the package of pastries.

Obviously he needed to go home and look over his marriage plans in a more serious light. Sympathizing with an absurdly strait-laced chit who was completely opposite his usual taste was one thing, but this was rapidly beginning to feel like an obsession. And that was extremely troubling.

"I thought we were here for hair ribbons," Herbert said, his face folding into an impatient frown.

Charlotte looked up from the rack of paste jewel necklaces sitting in the corner of the shop. "We are. I was just looking. Don't you think some of these are pretty?"

In particular, she kept fingering the necklace with an intricate silver chain and a dew-drop-shaped emerald in a delicate silver setting. It was only worth a few shillings, and the length was too long to wear with anything she owned, but she liked it.

"It's worthless," Lord Herbert returned. "And a bit tawdry, don't you think? Whatever would you do with it?"

"Mm," a female voice cooed from the doorway. "Tawdry is the point."

Charlotte leaned around a hat stand to see who had spoken. Dark eyes in a face pale and smooth as porcelain gazed back at her. "Lady Ibsen," she said, inwardly cringing.

Speaking with Lord Matson twice in two days would get her in enough trouble. Conversing with Jeanette Alvin, Lady Ibsen, would likely get her locked in her room for a week. The young wife of the late Marquis of Ibsen had once been respectable, Charlotte was sure, but since her husband's death she'd become known for holding wild parties and for keeping company with any number of gentlemen, both single and married. Her latest, according to rumor, was none other than Lord Matson.

"Miss Charlotte," the marchioness replied, shaking water droplets off her shawl and handing her parasol to her maid.

Herbert's face had reddened the moment Jeanette had appeared behind them. "My lady," he blurted, tugging at his cravat.

So even proper gentlemen couldn't quite control themselves in Lady Ibsen's presence. Hm. Herbert never blushed around *her*. It didn't help that on several occasions Charlotte had wished to have the marchioness's reputation — and her popularity with handsome young men. "Why is tawdry the point?" she asked, mainly because she felt contrary.

Lady Ibsen glided to the rack of necklaces and lifted one in long, delicate fingers. "It draws one's eye," she said, lifting a *faux* ruby bauble so that it caught the lantern light.

"So would any real gems," Charlotte returned.

"Ah, yes, but it isn't merely the sparkle." She fastened the clasp behind her neck and drew her hand down the length of the chain. The ruby hung squarely between her breasts, glinting. "It's also the length."

"Oh, my," Lord Herbert whispered, and for

a moment Charlotte was concerned he might faint.

With a low chuckle, Lady Ibsen returned the necklace to the rack. "And see how effective," she murmured, flicking the ruby to send it into a slow, glittering spin.

Charlotte couldn't help a smile. "I see."

She went back to the hair ribbons as Lady Ibsen purchased a surprisingly tasteful blue hat and swept out of the shop. Herbert made quiet clucking sounds of disapproval the entire time, but neither did he remove his gaze from the marchioness's petite, buxom figure.

With a sigh she brought her ribbons to the counter. When Herbert sidled to the window to gaze after the departing Jeanette, Charlotte swiftly leaned over and snatched the emerald necklace. Indicating with a lifted eyebrow that she wished to include it as part of her purchase, she dropped it into her pelisse pocket.

Nodding, the clerk put the ribbons into a small box and handed it over. "Eight shillings, my lady," she said, amusement in her voice.

Charlotte paid for and collected her package, handing it over to Alice. As they left the shop, Herbert sent a frown back in the clerk's direction.

"I say, I don't think you should patronize that shop any longer. Eight shillings for two ribbons is scandalous."

They returned to his coach, and Charlotte couldn't help looking over her shoulder for any sign of Lord Matson. "Scandalous," she repeated softly, fingering the necklace in her pocket.

Chapter 3

Gossip seems to tell that the splendidly wicked Lord Matson might be looking for a wife, but it is difficult to credit these rumors. After all, what marriage-minded man would turn to Lady Ibsen for advice?
Lady Whistledown's Society Papers,
3 June 1816

Viscount Halloren was late. Xavier checked his pocket watch for the third time, then sank back into the edition of *The London Times* he'd supposedly been reading for the past forty minutes.

At half past noon, White's club was crowded. Understandable, then, that the head waiter didn't look overly pleased at holding a table for only a single occupant who'd requested one glass of port and refused to order luncheon.

Xavier, however, wasn't in an accommodating mood, and he wasn't going to budge until he'd had a chat with William Ford,

Lord Halloren. He and William were distant cousins, and although he'd only met the viscount once before his current venture into London, his relation was proving a valuable source of information — particularly since the damned *Whistledown* column seemed obsessed now with the theft of Lady Neeley's bracelet, and was giving minimal space to the parade of eligible females prancing about Town this Season.

And he needed to find a bride. Quickly. This hunting about, clueless, was making him insane. So much so that for the past two nights he'd dreamed of a tall, dark-haired chit with fascinating eyes and an apparently very capable mouth.

"Matson."

Finally. He looked up from the paper, gesturing for his cousin to take a seat. "Halloren. Glad you decided to join me."

"I almost didn't. With this damned muck of weather we're having, nobody's walking anywhere. I swear I've never seen such a crowd of coaches on the streets in my life."

"So this isn't usual?"

"Good God, no. When's the last time you were in London?"

He actually had to think about it. "Six years ago, I believe. Right before I left for Spain."

"Six years in the army. No wonder you're so set on finding a female now that you're back."

"Five years in the army," Xavier corrected. "One year back at home trying to figure out how to be a landowner."

Halloren nodded, his gaze surprisingly sympathetic. "Knew your brother. I don't think Anthony ever let me pay for a meal."

Hm. If that was a hint, he would accept it. He'd invited the viscount for an interrogation, anyway. He might as well feed the man.

They placed their order, and Xavier saw to it that Halloren had a brimming glass of port. It had occurred to him this morning that asking a confirmed bachelor about a list of prospective brides seemed a bit odd, but the viscount remained his best source so far.

"Why is it that you're unmarried?" he asked anyway, deciding that if the answer was too unsettling, he'd skirt the subject and muck on by himself.

Halloren guffawed. "I'm not married because I have no fortune and because, well, look at me. I'm the size of an ox. Frightens off the young chits, I think."

Xavier chuckled. "But you've kept an eye out for a possible wife, anyway."

"Of course. Marrying a chit with money is my only hope." He tilted his glass back, draining half its contents. "Unlike you, you lucky bastard."

Xavier fiddled with his own glass. "It's not luck," he returned. "Not good luck, anyway. I

285

would rather have had my brother than his title and money."

"I meant your hideous appearance, actually. You ain't exactly been lonely since you came into Town."

Yes, apparently everyone knew about himself and Lady Ibsen, again thanks to that damned gossip column. "A fellow does what he must," he said. "But that brings me to my point. I've met . . . several young ladies, and I thought you might give me a more circumspect opinion of them than I've been able to form on my own."

Halloren burst into laughter, attracting the attention of the diners at several neighboring tables. "Oh, I wish I kept a journal," he snorted. "*You* asking *me* for advice on women."

"Not advice," Xavier countered, frowning. "An opinion. You know more about their family backgrounds than I do, and I want to do this right."

Do it right. That particular thought had haunted him from the moment he'd walked through the door of Farley and realized that it had all just become his responsibility — the house, the land, the tenants, the crops, and the title and its future.

"All right, all right. Who's your first prospect, then?"

The name on his lips wasn't that of anyone from his list, and he clenched his jaw against it. For God's sake. "Melinda Edwards," he said instead.

"Ah, she's a diamond, ain't she?" The viscount sighed. "Barely looked once at me. Her family's good enough; her granddad's the Duke of Kenfeld, you know. Her brother's got a weakness for fast horses, but nothing you can't afford, I'd wager. Ha ha. Wager."

"Very amusing. What about Miss Rachel Bakely?"

"You have an eye toward the pretty ones, don't you?"

"I'm exploring all my prospects."

"Well, that one's got her cap set at Lord Foxton." Halloren gazed at him for a moment. "You could probably change her mind."

They went on for another twenty minutes, and without exception he'd apparently picked a set of well-bred, beautiful, amiable females, any one of whom would love to or could easily be persuaded to become the Countess Matson. And he still wanted to ask about Charlotte Birling. It was nothing serious, of course, just curiosity, so what was the harm? She was an unmarried female, and dumped in with the other chits on his list, hardly conspicuous. Xavier took a breath — and a drink of port. "Charlotte Birling?"

"Who?"

"Birling. Charlotte Birling. Lord and Lady Birling's daughter."

"Oh, yes, yes, yes. Tall chit, doesn't say much." Halloren lifted an eyebrow. "Really, Matson?"

Xavier shrugged, doing his best to look uncaring and slightly bored. "Just curious."

"Well, don't bother. She's first cousin to Lady Sophia Throckmorton. You know, the chit who married Easterly twelve or so years ago. He did something dastardly — don't remember what — and left the country. Terrible scandal." The viscount leaned forward. "And the Birlings ain't going to let any such thing happen to their daughter. They're probably glad she ain't a great beauty, because that way she don't attract all the rakes. They'll marry her off to some safe old dullard before long. Anything to avoid another scandal. With Easterly suspected in that Neeley bracelet fiasco now, they're all aflutter, no doubt." He chuckled again. "So it's not as though they'd let the likes of you anywhere near her."

"Beg pardon?"

"Come on, lad. Everybody knows you've got Lady Ibsen smiling. And that's no easy feat."

With a lifted eyebrow, Xavier dug into his plate of baked ham. He wasn't disposed to comment, no matter whose private relations were being discussed. Besides, a few things about Charlotte Birling abruptly made a great deal of sense. No wonder her mother

288

had seemed so skittish when he'd approached them.

He should have been relieved. Though he disagreed with Halloren's appraisal of her looks, she wasn't his usual sort of petite, buxom prey. And with her parents' hysteria over scandal, no wonder the rest of the men could take a glance, call her less than stunning, and dismiss her as too much trouble.

But he wasn't relieved. Not a bit. Her beauty lay deeper than most, but he'd seen it. And somehow the knowledge that she was unattainable made her even more desirable. Yes, he wanted her, wanted to touch her warm skin and wanted to know what she would be like with her concern over propriety removed — along with her conservative gown and proper bonnet and overly-tight hairpins.

"So you've narrowed it down to a half dozen, then?" Halloren was saying.

Xavier shook himself. "Yes."

"Good choices, I have to say," his cousin agreed. "Difficult thing will be to decide on just one."

"No doubt." Except that he had apparently narrowed it down to just one already — and he had no idea how he might win her.

Taking a long swallow of port, he motioned for a refill. He had the abrupt urge to become very, very drunk. Jesus. It was laughable, except that he wasn't laughing.

"Oh, do come with me," Melinda Edwards cajoled the next morning, tugging on Charlotte's hands to pull her toward the door. "It's not raining, and I'll just perish if I don't take a breath of fresh air."

Although she felt the same way, Charlotte hesitated. Her mother had allowed her to visit Melinda, but she'd made it quite clear that she was only to stay for an early luncheon and then return home. Miss Edwards was known to have gentlemen paying visits in the afternoons, and heaven forbid that Charlotte should be there to bask in her friend's reflected glory and meet someone of possibly tarnished reputation.

Still, no one could call on Melinda if she wasn't even home. And they hadn't eaten yet. "Very well," she agreed. "A short walk."

"Yes, yes. Just a street or two."

Lady Edwards looked up from her letter-writing. "Take Anabel with you. And don't stay out-of-doors long. If you catch a fever you'll have to stay home for the rest of the week."

"Yes, Mama."

Once Melinda's maid joined them, they set out at a brisk pace down White Horse Street toward Knightsbridge. It wasn't raining, but it looked as though that might change at any moment. Still, it was nice to be out-of-doors without having to tote a parasol or risk ruining one's bonnet.

Melinda looped her arm around Charlotte's. "You'll never guess who came to call on me yesterday."

"Please tell me," Charlotte said with a smile. "You know I live to hear of your romantic conquests."

"Well, he's not a conquest, precisely. Not yet, anyway. He did seem quite interested, though, and even brought me white roses." Her delicate brows lowered. "He also seemed a bit . . . intoxicated, though I might have been mistaken."

"Tell me, for heaven's sake!"

"Xavier, Lord Matson. Can you believe it? He has the most beautiful eyes, don't you think?"

"Yes, he does," Charlotte said softly, her heart crumbling. As Melinda looked at her, though, she managed a short laugh. He wasn't for her, anyway. Everyone knew that. Not with his mottled reputation and her ridiculously clean one. Simply because he'd spoken to her twice didn't mean anything. "How exciting! Has he spoken with your father?"

"Oh, it's far too soon for that, goose. But he did ask me all about my interests, and my friends — and when I gave him your name, he mentioned that you'd met! You awful girl! Why didn't you tell me?"

For a moment Charlotte couldn't remember how to breathe or to speak, and she nearly forgot how to walk. He'd mentioned her. He'd remembered her. A tingle ran down her spine. Earl Matson had spoken her name, dull or not, destined for Lord Herbert Beetly or not, and acknowledged that they'd met.

She realized that Melinda still gazed at her expectantly. "Oh, he practically ran into me at the Hargreaves' Ball," she managed. "To say that we met — well, I think he was just being polite."

"Very well. You're forgiven, my dear. I thought it must be something like that. And when I said that you were practically engaged to Lord Herbert, he said, 'Yes, they seem quite attached.'"

Well, that made one thing clear. Lord Matson hadn't paid much attention to their two encounters at all if he thought her "quite attached" to Herbert. She could barely tolerate the man, for goodness' sake. And even though she hadn't expected anything more, it still hurt. There could be few things worse, she supposed, than having one's daydreams sink into the mud. Now she couldn't even pretend that he had a secret infatuation with —

"Good morning, Miss Edwards, Miss Charlotte."

At the sound of that low, masculine drawl, Charlotte whipped her head around so fast that she nearly stumbled. "Lord Matson," she squeaked, as he slowed his magnificent black horse beside them. Of course. It was nearly ten o'clock. He was on his way to the boxing club.

Much more collected, Melinda smiled and gave a half-curtsy. "What a pleasant surprise, my lord! I hardly expected to see you this morning."

Charlotte stifled an abrupt frown. Melinda was a terrible liar. She'd absolutely expected to see the earl, which meant that he had more than one female spying on him as he rode to Gentleman Jackson's each weekday morning.

"Yes, I'm on my way to an appointment," he returned. "But since we seem to be heading in the same direction, might I walk with you for a bit?"

"Of course, my lord."

As he swung down from his horse, Melinda detached herself from Charlotte's arm, making a space between the two of them for the earl. *Oh, dear.* Mama was going to kill her. Three days in less than a week, conversing with Xavier Matson. Except that he wasn't joining them to talk to *her*, of course. He was interested in Melinda. And Charlotte could hardly blame him. Her friend was slender, petite, and blonde, with sparkling green eyes and perfect grace. And for the first time in their long friendship, Charlotte hated her.

But even though she knew he wasn't there

because of her, even though he'd joined them so he could walk with Melinda, her breath stopped as he handed his horse over to their maid and offered her one arm, and her friend the other.

He'd taken her hand twice before, but this was the closest they'd been to one another. Even through his caped greatcoat Charlotte could feel the warmth of him, seeping through her own sleeve and glove and into her skin. Lord Matson was tall, but so was she. The top of her head came to his chin, which would have been perfect, she thought, for waltzing. The muscles of his arm played beneath her fingers, making her want to run her palms up along his shoulders.

As he turned to engage Melinda in conversation, Charlotte couldn't help leaning in a little closer to breathe in his scent. Shaving soap and toast and leather — a surprisingly intoxicating combination.

Faded cobalt looked over at her as if he knew she'd been inhaling him. "And what are the two of you doing out here this morning?"

"Walking," Melinda answered before she could.

"So I see. You took a chance, though, coming outside in this weather."

"We're not made of sugar, my lord," Charlotte returned, trying to recover her composure. "Or at least, I'm not."

He chuckled. "No, you seem to be made

up of several more subtle spices." His gaze lingered on her a moment before he turned to Melinda again. "And you, Miss Edwards? What are your ingredients?"

"Oh, heavens, it must be sugar, for I'm certain I would melt in the rain. I'm not nearly as stalwart as Charlotte."

"Don't worry, Melinda," Charlotte said, wishing she could linger on his comment about spices rather than worry that Melinda made her sound like a farm ox. "I would loan you my parasol." She risked a glance up at Matson's face. "And which ingredients are you, my lord?"

"Charlotte!"

"It's a fair question, Miss Edwards," the earl countered, his soft smile deepening. "I suppose, though, that it would depend on who you asked. My brother used to say that I was full of hot air."

Melinda gave her charming, bubbling laugh. "Oh, surely not."

"I prefer to think of myself as merely blood and sinew and bone, though I suppose that sounds rather mundane."

"It sounds truthful," Charlotte said, keeping her face turned away so the other two wouldn't see her blushing. Yes, her mother would send her away to a nunnery, but it would be worth it. She'd never expected to be able to banter with Lord Matson, much less to discover that he had a sense of humor and a quiet intelligence that quite belied his rakish reputation.

They stopped as they reached Brick Street. "We promised my mother to return home," Melinda said, her gaze making it clear that she wished him to agree to escort them the entire way.

"And Lord Matson has an appointment," Charlotte noted, unable to keep the stiff irritation from her voice. Being this close to him and having him pay attention to someone else was unbearable. Fleetingly she wondered what she would do if he did marry Melinda. It was stupid, because she had absolutely no claim on him, but she wasn't certain she could remain friends with Miss Edwards knowing who her husband was.

"So I do. I assume you ladies will be at the theater tomorrow night?"

"Oh, yes," Melinda gushed.

He detached himself and reclaimed his horse, swinging into the saddle with an athletic grace that made Charlotte ache. He tipped his hat at the two of them. "Then perhaps I'll see you there," he said, his eyes meeting hers for a brief moment. A second later he clucked to his mount, and they were off down the street.

"I think I may swoon," Melinda cooed, hugging herself.

Charlotte tore her gaze from the view. "Don't be silly; the ground's all wet."

"Oh, Charlotte, I'm just being romantic." Miss Edwards gripped her hand again. "Come along, now. I'm suddenly starving. Aren't you?"

"Yes," Charlotte answered automatically, though luncheon had become the furthest thing from her mind. No, now she had to find a way to convince her parents to go to the theater tomorrow night. Xavier Matson might very nearly belong to someone else, but at least she could still look.

"I thought you'd stay for more than dinner." Jeanette, Lady Ibsen, toyed with a candle, flicking her fingers to and fro across the flame. Her footmen had left the dining room twenty minutes ago, and Xavier knew he wouldn't see them again tonight. Jeanette had her staff exceedingly well trained.

"Dinner was magnificent, as usual," Xavier returned, setting his napkin on the table, "but I'm going to the theater tonight. I told you I wouldn't be staying."

She sighed. "Yes, I know. One must always hope, however." Leaning across the edge of the table, she licked the curve of his ear. "I am much better than *Hamlet*, Xavier."

"I don't doubt it. The play tonight is *As You Like It*, however, and you're hardly a comedy."

"Yes, but we could play as you like it all evening," she returned, shifting closer to twine her fingers into his hair.

On any previous evening since he'd arrived in London, she wouldn't have had to go to any such lengths to persuade him. Tonight, though, the sensation he was most aware of was vague annoyance. He needed to be somewhere else. "I would like it very much, I'm sure," he returned, shrugging free of her hands as gently as he could, "but I'm expected."

She straightened, the motion doing some very nice things to the front of her low-cut burgundy gown. "Who is she?"

Xavier pushed back in his chair and stood. "Beg pardon?"

"Oh, I'm not jealous," she said, uncurling to her feet with the grace of a feline, "though I am surprised. I thought we were looking for a wife who would have a certain understanding about our relationship. Whoever she is, though, she has your attention. And your interest."

Frowning, he stopped his retreat. "All I said was that I'm expected. I'm sharing a box with Halloren."

"So you haven't found a woman who piques your interest. Someone you're in a hurry to see at the theater tonight."

"No."

"Hm. Perhaps I'll make an appearance, myself. I do love Shakespeare."

Inwardly cursing, he shrugged. Hiding this

obsession of his was difficult enough without Jeanette lurking in the shadows, trying to outguess him. "Suit yourself, my dear."

"I always do, my dear." She held out her hand, and he bowed over it. "I have an idea already, you know, but I won't spoil your fun."

"Jeanette, d—"

"I told you, I'm not jealous. I like you too much to wish you ill." She smiled. "But I'll be here if it should happen that you're not . . . acceptable to her parents. You have acquired a certain reputation, after all, and will be expected to have high standards. And a roving eye."

Yes, he had acquired a reputation, though most of it was nonsense. Jeanette had said she wasn't jealous, and given the way she lived her life, he tended to believe her. "Hypothetically, how would a gentleman of questionable reputation go about winning over the parents of a proper chit?"

Lady Ibsen tucked her arm around his, speculation in her dark eyes. "Hm. How can we make you appear respectable?"

With a snort, Xavier pulled free. "I'm not that bad," he said, heading for the foyer. "I'll manage."

Yes, he'd taken a few mistresses since he'd been in London, and he'd spent time wagering rather large sums and drinking a bit too much, but he'd never claimed to be a saint, for God's sake. And after a year practically trapped in Devon, trying to wade through a tangle of papers and finances left by someone who hadn't expected to be dead at the age of thirty-one, he'd needed a little release and a little more distraction.

"Perhaps remind them that you're a war hero," Jeanette suggested as he collected his hat and coat. "Oh, or perhaps that you're determined to leave your scandalous ways behind you. In all truth, though, I doubt they will believe their daughter to be the one capable of dissuading you from your fun."

"Then you must be thinking of the wrong female," he drawled, motioning her butler to pull open the door. "Just promise that you won't interfere."

She put a long-fingered hand to her breast. "Me? If I didn't like her, perhaps. But I promise. No interference."

Xavier signaled his coach and climbed aboard. None of the chits on his list would put up any objection at all to his suit. Logic told him to simply choose one of them and get on with making an heir and re-rooting his family tree.

Logic, however, seemed woefully inadequate when he looked at Charlotte Birling. Her mere presence aroused him. But it wasn't solely a physical attraction that he could wallow away with either her or someone else. He liked being in her company; since they'd met, he'd spent more time thinking of how alone he'd become since Anthony's death, and how he didn't feel that way when he spoke with Miss Charlotte.

But before this went any further, he needed to spend more than two minutes talking with her, and he needed to know whether she might be interested in someone with a poor reputation, warranted or not.

Chapter 4

As there is no news of the Neeley affair, This Author will once again focus on one of This Column's favorite subjects: Earl Matson.

Earlier rumors that he might be altarbound appear to have more validity than they did earlier this week; indeed, it has been verified that he called upon Miss Melinda Edwards on Monday, and then he was seen squiring about this very same lady (and an unidentified companion) on White Horse Street yesterday. It appeared to be an accidental meeting, but as all Dear Readers know, no meeting between unmarried men and women is ever truly accidental.

Lady Whistledown's Society Papers,
5 June 1816

"Didn't you say this performance has been sold out for weeks?" Lady Birling asked, sitting beside Charlotte in their newly rented theater box.

"It has been," Charlotte affirmed quickly, hoping there was no one in the neighboring boxes to dispute that. "The weather's probably kept some of them away."

Her father shook out his greatcoat and tossed it over the chair at the rear of the box. "I wish it had kept us away," he grumbled, taking the seat behind his wife.

"You like the theater, Papa."

"Ordinarily, yes. With Easterly in Town, however, I prefer that we keep a low profile."

If her profile was any lower, she would completely disappear. "Sophia doesn't seem to mind much that he's returned."

"I believe Sophia wants to have the entire marriage annulled," the baroness countered in a lower voice, looking about as her husband had done. "And with Lady Neeley's accusations, who can blame her?"

With difficulty Charlotte kept her silence, instead lifting her play book so she could peer around the edges at the boxes on the far side of the theater. She could defend Lord Easterly and Sophia until her breath ran out, but her parents had obviously already made up their minds about the entire episode. Truth be told, she barely remembered Lord Easterly, anyway, except that he'd been quite tall and had had a pleasant laugh.

Melinda and her family were in their seats several boxes closer to the stage. Giving her a quick wave, Melinda went back to gazing at the crowd much as Charlotte was. They were, of course, looking for the same man — and at least Melinda had reason to do so. If Lord Matson braved the weather and made an appearance, it would be because he wished to see Miss Edwards.

"Charlotte?" her mother said quietly, patting her hand. "You look sad. Are you feeling well?"

She shook herself. "Yes, I'm fine. I was only thinking of Sophia."

"Hopefully your cousin will be able to put this unpleasantness behind her. She certainly did when Easterly abandoned her before."

Charlotte wasn't so certain that Sophia had put anything behind her, but her cousin had become adept at convincing people that was so. At times Charlotte wished she could look as calm and elegant and composed. She'd never had much luck with that, but at least she did have the advantage of being able to go virtually unnoticed.

Even her parents succumbed to her near invisibility at times, though not as often now that she'd come of age and needed to be introduced to Society and a potential husband. Her older sister, Helen, had married by the end of her first Season, but then she'd been bubbly and giggly and possessed of large brown eyes and a talent for both the pianoforte and the waltz.

All of which left Charlotte with Lord Herbert. She'd attempted to complain about his lack of animation, but to no avail. Her parents wanted her to marry; she wanted to marry. In her dreams, though, it would be to someone who found her interesting and exciting — and to someone to whom she could at least say something humorous and have him laugh. In her parents' eyes, she would settle for Herbert because, well, how could she expect anything more?

"It's a shame we didn't think to ask Lord Herbert to join us," her mother said, sitting back as the curtains slid open. "Is he fond of the theater?"

"I honestly don't know," Charlotte whispered back. She tended to think not, because enjoying the theater required an imagination, and she didn't believe he had one.

She took one last look around her as the play began and abruptly spied Lord Matson. He sat in the shadows toward the back of the box owned by Lord Halloren, which was otherwise crowded with several overdressed females. Demimondaines, her mother would call them. She leaned forward a little to see better. He seemed to be ignoring the rest of the box's occupants, instead gazing toward the stage.

"Charlotte, stop gawking at people," her mother muttered.

"Everyone else is."

"You are not everyone else."

Charlotte sat through the first and second acts, very conscious that the earl sat somewhere back over her shoulder. Fleetingly she wondered whether she should ask for permission to visit Melinda's box at intermission, because Lord Matson would probably be doing the same thing. Oh, she was so blasted obvious.

As the curtains closed she joined in the applause. Now everyone would leave their boxes to mingle and gossip and be seen, and she and her parents would sit where they were so no one could possibly think they were anything but the height of propriety.

"Charlotte, would you have a footman fetch me a glass of Madeira?" her mother asked. "This weather is going to be the death of me."

Blinking, Charlotte stood. "Of course. I'll be just outside the curtain."

Her mother smiled. "I don't expect you to run away. We do trust you, darling. We just wish you had better judgment."

It wasn't her actions they needed to concern themselves with; it was her thoughts. Settling for a nod, she slipped around her father's chair and out through the heavy black curtains. The upstairs hallway was packed with people and light and noise, and she leaned back against the wall for a moment to get her bearings.

"Are you enjoying the play?" a male voice said softly from beside her.

She recognized the voice immediately, and while a low thrill ran through her body she faced Lord Matson, looking up to meet his faded blue gaze. "I am. And you?"

He gave a short smile. "I can barely hear it. Halloren seems to have invited every opera singer in London to join him in his box."

"They are . . . colorful," she offered.

His smile deepened. "You were looking at me."

Drat. "Well, I — You see, I — You said you would attend tonight."

"So I did."

Oh, she could just gaze at him forever. In the chandelier light his amber-colored hair seemed a rich gold, faintly wavy, with a strand across one eye. Realizing she was staring, Charlotte cleared her throat. "I believe Melinda Edwards is in attendance, as well. You should find her in that direction." She gestured up the hallway.

"I know where she is," he answered. "May I ask you a question?"

"Of course."

For the first time in their short acquaintance he looked uncertain. Charlotte could sympathize. When she saw him from a distance, nervousness flooded through her. When they actually spoke, however, she felt . . . heightened, but calm, as though it was the most natural thing in the world.

"Herbert Beetly," the earl continued, his voice even softer. "Are you betrothed?"

She blushed. "No. Not yet, anyway."

"So you expect a proposal from him."

His voice sounded tight, but no doubt he was thinking of his own future proposal to Melinda. Charlotte forced a smile. "Most likely. He has been my only suitor for the past year."

Matson's brow lowered. "Your only suitor?" he repeated. "Why is that?"

"Why . . ." Her blush deepening, she edged in the direction of the nearest footman. She needed to do as her mother asked and get back before her parents came looking for her. "There's no need to be mean, my lord," she said stiffly.

He caught her arm gently, but firmly enough to keep her there. "I merely asked you a question. Is it a family agreement? Have you been promised to one another since birth or something?"

"No. Don't be ridiculous." He didn't seem to be teasing her; in fact, he seemed perfectly serious. Well, he'd asked a question, and she'd never been one for illusions, no matter how painful the truth might be. "I'm . . . not the sort of female that men clamor over." Charlotte shrugged. "My father and Herbert's are acquaintances, and when no one expressed an interest in me, they came to a mutual understanding."

"So Beetly doesn't own your heart," he pursued, still gripping her arm.

Her unowned heart jumped at the serious look in his eyes. "No, he doesn't own my heart. He does make sense, though."

To her surprise, he tugged her a breath closer. "Make sense how?"

"My lord, shouldn't you be chatting with Miss Edwards?" Charlotte ventured, wondering whether he could feel her pulse beneath his fingers.

"I'm chatting with *you*, Charlotte. How does you marrying the dullest clod in London make sense?"

"We're very similar." She'd never confessed aloud how dull and ordinary she seemed to be. Until now, apparently.

"And who in God's name told you that?" he snapped, his voice rising a little. One or two of the closest theatergoers turned to look at them.

Charlotte wished she could be made of stone so she wouldn't blush and couldn't be tempted to sink to the floor and fade away. "I have a mirror, my lord," she said stiffly. "And ears. Now if you'll excuse me, I have an errand."

He started, looking around as though he'd just remembered that they were in a crowded hallway. "Will you be at home in the morning?"

"Why?"

"Because I intend to call on you. Will you be at home?"

She blanched. "You . . . why?"

Brief humor touched his faded blue eyes. "Yes, or no?"

"I suppose . . . yes. But my parents —"

"Leave that to me." He ran his hand down her arm to grasp her fingers. His eyes holding hers, he lifted her hand and brushed her knuckles with his lips. "Until tomorrow."

A thousand questions flooded her mind, but she couldn't think of one she could utter aloud without sounding like a complete idiot. But still . . . "I don't understand," she whispered.

The earl smiled. "You have very fine eyes," he whispered back, and then retreated into the crowd.

She needed to sit down. The world had just spun into an entirely new realm. Xavier, Earl Matson, meant to call on her. On *her*.

If it was a tease, it was the cruelest thing she'd ever heard of. But rakish reputation or not, it didn't seem in his character to be cruel. In their few encounters, she'd certainly never sensed any such thing in him. And if she was good at anything, it was reading people. When no one noticed you, it was easy to study them.

Charlotte concentrated on breathing as she pushed aside the curtains and returned to her chair. Now that she thought about it, when he'd encountered her and Melinda yesterday, he had seemed to spend a majority of the time talking with her. It had been politeness, though — or so she'd thought. *Oh dear, oh dear, oh dear.*

"My dear?" Her mother's voice made her jump. "You're red as a beet. What happened?"

Blast. "I looked everywhere for a footman, but I couldn't catch anyone's attention," she managed, wishing she could escape somewhere to gather her wits.

With a sigh her father climbed to his feet. "I'll see to it," he rumbled, exiting out the back of the box.

"I'm sorry, my dear," the baroness said. "I wasn't going to send you into such a crush, but your father and I worry that we're being too restrictive. You must be aware of how delicate our position is right now."

"I'm aware," Charlotte returned. But perhaps her parents weren't being restrictive enough — if they'd kept her in the box, she wouldn't have encountered Lord Matson, and he wouldn't have been able to inform her that he intended to call on her.

On the other hand, she couldn't ever recall being so excited and nervous and . . . hopeful. Whatever his reasons, if he did call on her tomorrow she meant to be there, and she meant to see him. Charlotte gave a small smile. He thought she had fine eyes. Even if it only lasted for an evening, she actually felt alluring. It was a sensation, she believed, that only a mirror or Lord Matson's failure to appear tomorrow could dispel. And tonight she wasn't going to look in a mirror.

Charlotte couldn't avoid looking in the mirror the next morning as she dressed. Neither could she ignore the high color in her cheeks and the sparkle in her eyes. "He might not make an appearance," she reminded herself sternly. "He probably won't."

Behind her, Alice paused as she pinned up Charlotte's hair. "Beg your pardon, Miss Charlotte?"

"Nothing. I'm just talking to myself."

"If I may say, you seem a bit unsettled this morning. Shall I have Mrs. Rutledge make you up some peppermint tea?"

Alice wouldn't be the only one who noticed her behavior, because since intermission last night she'd been veering between panic and euphoria. Perhaps admitting to a touch of a cold would keep everyone's suspicions away, until Lord Matson arrived. *If* Lord Matson arrived. "Tea would be lovely. I'll have it with breakfast."

Her maid curtsied and hurried from the room. Sighing, Charlotte finished untangling last night's hair ribbon and laid it across her dressing table. If she thought about it logically, it didn't matter whether she had a

312

caller this morning or not. Her parents would never allow her to see him. They would think he must have an ulterior motive; of course he wouldn't come by just to see her.

From her window, mingling with the tap of the rain, she heard a coach turn up the drive. Her heart seized into a tight, pounding ball. He hadn't been teasing.

She wanted to rush to the window to look out. "No, Charlotte," she told herself sternly. "You'll seem like a rabid dog."

Instead she went about finishing her hair, a difficult prospect without Alice to assist her. With one more pin to go, she abruptly stopped.

Why was she so infatuated with Xavier Matson? Yes, he was handsome and confident and athletic, but how much else did she know about him? His schedule: The way he went boxing at ten o'clock every morning when he didn't have Parliament; his preference for luncheon at White's or Boodle's; the afternoon rides in Hyde Park, weather permitting. Other than that, he was a stranger. And that was partially what she liked about him. He could be handsome and romantic and mysterious, and safely unattainable.

But now he was at her front door.

Alice burst back into the bedchamber. "Beg pardon, Miss Charlotte, but you have a caller." She tiptoed closer. "It's a gentleman, miss."

"Oh," Charlotte said noncommitally. "Help

me finish my hair, will you?"

"Right away, miss." Alice swiftly repinned the work Charlotte had done. "Aren't you curious as to who it might be, miss?"

Oops. She'd forgotten; she wasn't supposed to know. "Of course I am, Alice. Where did Boscoe put him?" she asked, though she assumed the butler had shown the earl to the morning room, the usual place guests were asked to wait. Not that she'd ever had any male guests except for Herbert.

"He's in your father's office. Lord Birling didn't look at all pleased. I'm sure I don't know why, because your visitor is very . . . pleasant-looking, but it's none of my business, anyway."

It wasn't, but Charlotte was so grateful for the news that she didn't complain. She needed to hurry; if she couldn't get downstairs quickly, her father might very well send Lord Matson away before she had a chance to see him.

Finally, with Alice still practically hanging off the back of her hair, Charlotte sprinted downstairs to the first floor. The butler stood at his usual post in the foyer, but even stoic Boscoe couldn't quite mask his curiosity at their visitor.

"Boscoe? Alice said I have a caller." Practically vibrating with nervousness, she couldn't resist a glance toward the closed door of her father's office.

314

"Yes, Miss Charlotte. Your father requests that you wait in the morning room with your mother."

Until those last three words, Charlotte had been almost hopeful. Her mother, though, would have questions, and she had no idea what to answer. "Thank you," she said anyway, slipping through the half-open door.

"Did you plan this?" the baroness demanded, not pausing in her swift pacing.

"To have a caller?" Charlotte asked, keeping in mind that she supposedly didn't know who her father had trapped in his office.

"To have Lord Matson call on you."

Thankfully, hearing the name spoken aloud shook her enough that she didn't have to fake her reaction. "N-no. How could I plan such a thing?"

"I'm sure I have no idea. But you did stare at him out the window the other day, and he approached you at the Hargreaves' Ball."

"Mama, you've made it clear that I should concentrate my efforts on Lord Herbert, since no other gentleman has called on me in a year. Why would I think I *could* plan something like this?"

"But why is he here?" her mother persisted.

"He's here to call on Charlotte." Her father stood in the doorway, his expression tight and clearly displeased. "He wishes to court her."

The baroness sank into a chair. *"What? Charlotte?"*

Through the roaring in her ears, Charlotte was asking the exact same questions. Even so, her mother's reaction pained her. Yes, she was quiet and reserved and not vibrant and beautiful like Helen, but it hurt to know that her parents really did think of her as . . . small, that Herbert was the best match for her.

"Yes, Charlotte. So please collect yourself, Vivian, and I'll show him in."

"But —"

"I can't very well throw him out when he came to ask my permission to call on our daughter," the baron interrupted in a lower voice. "And quite respectfully." He turned his assessing gaze to Charlotte. "Do not encourage him. His reputation is less than snowy, and yours can only be harmed."

"Yes, Papa."

Lord Birling vanished, only to reappear a moment later with Lord Matson on his heels. The earl looked as easy as if he'd been sitting about playing whist, and Charlotte could only envy his composure. Of course, it was beginning to seem very likely that Lord Matson was completely insane. She could think of no other explanation as to why he would wish to broach Birling House to see . . . her.

As his gaze found her, however, he smiled.

"Good morning, Miss Charlotte, Lady Birling."

"My lord," the baroness returned with a curtsy, "what in the world brings you here?"

"As I told Lord Birling, I've found myself somewhat at loose ends here in London, not knowing many people and beginning to fall in with the wrong crowd. Your daughter's kind words and obvious decorum caught my attention."

Charlotte blinked. Good heavens, he sounded almost . . . tame. If not for the twinkle deep in his blue eyes, she would have thought a duplicate of dull Lord Herbert had strolled into the room. A duplicate with wits and a sense of humor, of course.

"In light of that," he went on, "I have asked Lord Birling's permission to call on Miss Charlotte. I had thought we might take a ride in my phaeton, since it has a covered top and will protect us from the drizzle."

A *phaeton?* She'd never ridden in such a sporting vehicle in her life. Charlotte practically clapped her hands together before she could stop herself and clasp them demurely behind her back instead.

"And a chaperone?" her mother pursued, her reaction much more skeptical than her daughter's.

"My tiger, Willis, is holding the team for me now. He will accompany us on horseback."

317

The baroness's brow lowered. "Another man? I don't —"

"I've given my permission," her father cut in. "For today. As I said, my lord, she is to be home by noon."

Matson sketched an elegant bow. "She will be." His gaze still on Charlotte, he held out one hand. "Shall we?"

It was a good thing her father had given permission, because she wasn't about to pass up the prospect of riding in a racing phaeton with Lord Matson, no matter the consequences. She nodded, trying to stifle her excited smile. "As you wish, my lord," she managed in a calm voice.

Alice appeared with a warm wrap, and Charlotte shrugged into it. Both parents followed her out the front door like vultures looking over a fresh kill, so she didn't dare take the earl's proffered hand, and instead let her father help her up into the high seat. Lord Matson tucked a blanket around her feet under the close gaze of the baron and baroness, and in a flash they were off down the drive.

Charlotte sighed, her breath fogging a little in the cold air. "You actually came."

"Of course I did. I said I would." He looked at her. "Why do you let them talk about you like that?"

"Like what?"

"Your mother acted as though she couldn't

conceive of why I would come calling on you, and your father seemed to think I meant to escort you somewhere for the sole purpose of abandoning and embarrassing you."

"Oh, dear," she muttered. "It's just . . . well, you've seen how concerned they are about proprie—"

"It wasn't that."

She kept her gaze on the street. "What do you wish me to say, my lord? That they don't understand why someone with your attractive physical appearance and your considerable income and reputation would be interested in courting their daughter? I don't quite understand it, myself."

He lifted an eyebrow. "Why not? What's wrong with you?"

Charlotte flushed. She couldn't help it. "What do you mean, 'What's wrong with me?' You aren't supposed to ask questions like that."

"I'm merely trying to understand why I'm not supposed to be seen in your company." He shifted so he could face her more fully, flicking the reins from his right hand to his left. "Do you squint?"

"No, my lord. Not unless the sun is very bright."

"Not a problem today, then. Stutter?"

"Not generally."

"Missing a finger or a toe?"

Despite her efforts, a smile tugged at her

319

mouth. "Not as of this morning."

"Are your teeth false?"

"No, my lord."

"Two ears, approximately level with one another, one —"

"Do stop teasing."

"I'm not. I'm looking for your defect. There must be one, for them to be so nervous about exposing me to you. One nose," he continued, "slightly upturned at the tip, one mouth, with lips above and below, two eyes, which we discussed yesterday." His gaze flicked the length of her and back again. "It's nothing I'm not currently seeing, is it?"

"For goodness' sake, my lord. That is too much," she protested, not certain whether to be scandalized or terribly amused. "You're looking precisely at part of the problem, I daresay."

"Then it must be that you're wearing a wig. You're bald, aren't you?"

Finally she chuckled. She couldn't help it. "No, my lord. My hair is my own, firmly attached." She drew a breath before he could question her eyelashes or her bosom or something. "I'm not beautiful or ebullient, and you're quite handsome and wealthy, with your choice of any single female in London. That's what they don't understand. And frankly, neither do I."

" 'Not beautiful,' " he repeated, slowly facing front again, just in time to turn them up Bond Street. With a snap of his wrist he turned the horses to the side of the street and yanked on the reins to stop them. When he faced her again his eyes glinted. "Don't you ever say that again," he said in a low, hard voice. "Is that clear?"

Charlotte swallowed at the fierceness in his gaze. "It doesn't make sense to deny anything. If I carried myself as anything but what I am, I would only appear ridiculous."

"The only ridiculous thing about you is that statement. You . . ." He trailed off, slamming a fist into his knee. "At the Hargreaves' Ball," he began again, his voice lower, "you had better reason than most to spread rumors — or to accept the rumors — of Lord Easterly's part in another scandal. But you defended him to your mother because it was the right thing to do."

For a long moment she looked at him, trying to remember the exact conversation and how he might have overheard it. "That was a private discussion," she finally said.

"That doesn't matter. I liked what you said, that one person's accusation wasn't enough to risk ruining a man's reputation. I spoke with several other chits — young ladies — that night, and not one of them voiced anything but the current popular theory. I doubt it would have occurred to them to do otherwise."

"Perhaps they spoke that way because they

believed him guilty," she offered, her pulse skittering. She wasn't an idiot; he was saying that he admired her.

"If I'd said the sky was magenta and green they would have agreed with me." He sat back a little, still gazing at her. "Would you?"

"If the sky had been that color I certainly would have agreed with you."

After a moment he visibly shook himself. "The rain's stopped. What say we do some shopping?"

"You . . . This is very nice, my lord, but it won't help either of us to be seen together." Despite the relatively deserted streets, someone they knew was bound to see them, and then the rumors would start, and people would begin to wonder what was wrong with *him*, to be seen in her company.

"It will help me a great deal. Willis, hold the horses."

The liveried tiger urged his mount up to the front of the team and took hold of the nearest horse's harness. As he did so, Matson took her chin gently between his fingers and turned her back to face him. Before she could gasp or even form the thought to do so, he touched his warm lips to hers. It could only have been a few seconds, a dozen fast heartbeats, but the moment seemed to stretch into forever, the touch of his mouth to hers. Charlotte closed her eyes, trying to memorize the sensation.

"I feel better already," he murmured. "Open your eyes, Charlotte."

She did so, half expecting to see that he was laughing at her. Instead, though, the soft smile that curved his mouth left her wanting to throw herself in his arms, and damn the consequences. "My lord, this is —"

"This is the beginning," he finished for her. "And call me Xavier."

Chapter 5

It has come to This Author's attention that Lord Matson, about whom, as all Dear Readers will recall, certain altar-bound activities were reported, has been paying rather assiduous attention to a particular young lady.

This Author would be pleased to report the lady in question's name (and indeed, This Author is in possession of this name) except that it is so astounding, so completely and utterly unexpected, that This Author fears falsity.

Especially since, by all accounts, Lord Matson's attempts to woo this young lady have been soundly rebuffed.

Good heavens, is the chit mad in the head?

Lady Whistledown's Society Papers, 10 June 1816

Charlotte Birling was about to rebel. Last Thursday Lord Matson — Xavier — had returned her home before noon, just as he'd promised. The two hours previous to that had been the most glorious of her life. She hadn't expected his interest to last, but she'd intended to enjoy it while she could.

But then her parents had bid him good day, and she hadn't seen him again. No, that wasn't quite true; she'd glimpsed him through her rain-streaked window three times, and she'd heard his voice downstairs when he'd sought entrance, but as for conversation, one or the other of them might as well be residing on the moon.

And even after only three accidental meetings and one morning of chatting about nothing in particular, she missed him. She had always felt comfortable and safe around men in general because she didn't expect to be flattered or flirted with, and they seemed to appreciate her lack of vanity. With Xavier, though, it was different. He did feel comfortable, and easy to talk to, but definitely not safe. No man had ever looked at her as he did, and shivers still ran down her spine whenever she recalled him — which was practically every second of the past week.

She could hardly be expected to put him out of her mind, of course, since he'd called every day of the last four. Rebuff after rebuff, lie after lie from her father or her mother, and still he called. She'd never heard him raise his voice, but the brief glimpse she'd had of him as he'd climbed into his coach yesterday had shown tense, straight shoulders and a fist slamming against the window frame.

"Is he going to call this afternoon?" The baroness stood in her open bedchamber door, wearing the same expression of thinly disguised displeasure she'd had since Thursday.

"Beg pardon?" Charlotte asked, quickly placing her tawdry emerald necklace back in her dresser drawer.

"Don't pretend you don't know what I'm talking about, Charlotte. Your father asked you not to encourage him."

"I didn't. I was being myself, Mama. And believe me, I find it as odd as you that he seems to like me."

"People are beginning to talk. Including *Lady Whistledown*."

Charlotte drew a breath. "Herbert has been in *Whistledown*."

"Only in reference to his perfect character. And speaking of Lord Herbert, he attended the Wivens soiree. Did you even notice?"

"I danced with him," Charlotte replied, ignoring the nagging thought that she'd spent more time looking for Lord Matson, and that she *hadn't* given Herbert a thought until he'd coughed and asked her to dance.

"Well, I can only hope that Matson is enough of a gentleman to realize that we've suffered through enough of his nonsense and that we don't want to see him here any longer."

Charlotte almost let her mother leave without comment. After Xavier's angry reaction to their dismissal of her, though, she couldn't do it. "Would it be so terrible if I had two men courting me? I thought the goal was to see me happily married. As for the specifics, Lord Herbert was simply the only one interested — until now."

The baroness stopped. "It's not . . . that isn't . . . Lord Matson is a rake, Charlotte. We have no reason to believe that he is sincere in his so-called pursuit of you."

"But what if I like him?" she asked in a quieter voice, fighting the abrupt urge to cry.

"You need to have more realistic expectations, my dear. Now cheer up. I have it on good authority that Lord Herbert will be visiting this afternoon. He's expressed an interest in trying out my new pianoforte."

"Oh. Splendid."

"I don't know what's going on in your head any longer, Charlotte. He'll be here any moment now. Please wear something suitable."

Her mother closed the door. Something suitable. According to her parents' thinking, that would be a large sack. Absently Charlotte returned to fiddling with the emerald necklace. She'd tried it on once in private, and had to admit that Lady Ibsen had been correct. It made her feel completely scandalous. She wondered whether Lady Ibsen wore a similar bauble for Lord Matson — and whether he still called on the widow.

"What does it matter?" she breathed. "He certainly isn't having any fun calling here."

At that moment sunlight broke through her window. Smiling, she rose to throw open the glass and lean outside. The light and warmth after two months of cold and four straight days of rain felt glorious. She closed her eyes, basking in the glow.

"Charlotte?"

With a start she opened her eyes and looked down. Lord Matson stood on her drive, looking up at her in the window. "Good afternoon," she whispered, blushing.

"It is now. Can you arrange to meet me somewhere?" he said, his voice barely audible.

Good heavens. Now she felt like Juliet. "Where?"

He frowned a moment, then his expression cleared. "It's a lovely day to go walking in Hyde Park, don't you think?"

Yes, it was, if she could convince Lord Herbert to delay his pianoforte recital. Just how much trouble she would be in if her parents discovered what she was up to, she didn't want to think about. This afternoon, a man who stole her breath with his smile wished to see her. And she very much wished to see him. "I'll try," she called back down. "I'll be waiting."

He returned to his carriage and instructed his driver to leave. As he vanished around the corner of the house, she took a deep breath and left her bedchamber. She really should have taken the opportunity to tell him to stop calling on her — but she couldn't be expected to deny one more chance to live a daydream.

To say that Xavier felt frustrated was quite possibly the understatement of the century. He'd put on his most conservative clothes, conversed with the wit of a damned mortician, called on Charlotte every day for nearly a week, and he'd only managed to see her once. Obviously, after the first surprise ambush, her parents had been ready for him — either that, or Charlotte had the most active social calendar in England. Even after seeing her in her window, he was tempted to knock on her door just to see where her parents would say she'd gone today: tea with friends, the lending library, visiting a sick aunt — he'd heard it all. And so, considering the fact that he'd successfully maneuvered against Bonaparte's best during the war, he had to admire Lord and Lady Birlings' skill at subterfuge.

If this had been simple lust after a simple chit, he wouldn't have cared; despite his reputation he had more than enough self-control to turn away from a female if the trouble began to outweigh the reward. This, though, was far more serious. After two hours of conversation with Charlotte, he'd gone home and torn up his list of prospective brides. It was time, then, to do some maneuvering of his own.

And so he had his carriage leave him at the edge of Hyde Park where he would be able to see anyone coming from the direction of Birling House. Who she might bring with her, he had no idea, but he didn't much care. He wanted to see her again. He wanted to hold her, to kiss her, to see her eyes light with passion and excitement at his touch.

He waited in the shade of an elm tree while the park grew more crowded around him. Apparently everyone meant to take advantage of the sunlight today. Good. It would make Charlotte's attendance less suspicious to her parents.

He wondered what his brother would have said, seeing what a muck he'd made out of his hunt for a bride. Probably the first thing Anthony would have done was laugh at him for concocting a list, for thinking that he could make himself into the perfect nobleman and landowner by finding the perfect wife, as if that would resolve all of his frustrations at leaving behind a promising military career and his worries that he could never fill the boots of his new station. But Anthony would have liked Charlotte. Xavier knew that instinctively. His brother had always had a good eye for character.

He shifted, looking for a more comfortable position against the tree. Blast it, if her parents refused to let her go out-of-doors, he was going to resort to kidnaping. Just as he was beginning to formulate a plan, though, she appeared. Her maid trailing behind her, she walked with her hand around the arm of her escort — Lord Herbert Beetly.

"Bastard," Xavier muttered, though he was more angry at her parents. Marrying Charlotte to Beetly would be like chaining a butterfly to a beetle. Despite himself he smiled a little. Beetly the beetle.

So now he had to figure out a way to get her away from the insect for at least a few minutes, because if he couldn't kiss her this afternoon, he was going to explode. They began a stroll along one of the paths, and he shadowed them from the shrubbery. Herbert continued droning on about some sort of allergic reaction he had to grass. After Xavier nearly brained himself on a low-hanging branch, he began contemplating doing the same thing to the beetle.

Luckily for Herbert, however, an open carriage rattled by. "It's Lady Neeley and that companion of hers," Beetly commented, angling to keep them in sight. "I hear she wants to have Bow Street arrest Easterly for the bracelet theft."

"Nonsense," Charlotte replied, pulling her hand free.

Xavier slipped up behind her maid. Covering Alice's mouth, he signaled for her to be silent, then led her directly up behind the couple. He placed Alice's hand on Beetly's arm, and in the same motion grabbed Charlotte and tugged her backward into the bushes.

Charlotte stumbled, and he caught her up against him before she could fall. "Shh," he breathed, leading her further away from her escort. When they'd reached the relative privacy of a small glade, he stopped. She was out of breath, her bonnet fallen back on her shoulders, and she wore a smile of genuine delight. God, she was fascinating.

"This will never wor—"

Xavier took her by the shoulders and leaned down, covering her mouth with his. She stiffened under his grip, then relaxed into him, giving a soft, throaty moan that made him hard. "Now that is a proper greeting," he murmured, kissing her again.

"No, it's an improper greeting," she corrected, her fingers digging into his sleeves.

It would be so easy to ruin her, to lay her down in the grass and make her his. *Patience,* he ordered himself, releasing her reluctantly. She was proper and terribly worried about appearances, and he didn't want to frighten her. This wasn't about an afternoon's satisfaction; it was about a lifetime of it.

"Lord . . . Xavier . . . I'm not . . . I don't play this sort of game well," she stumbled, her gaze still focused on his mouth. "If that's what this is — a game, I mean — I do wish you would tell me."

Sometimes men were such fools. He'd nearly been one himself, looking at faces and popularity and shades of hair as though that mattered a whit. "It's not a game, Charlotte," he said quietly. "But if my character displeases you, or if you have your heart set elsewhere, please let me know so —"

With a small breath she wrapped her fingers around his lapels, leaned up along his body, and kissed him again. Well, that answered that. He slid his arms around her waist, holding her close.

"Let's make the most of our escape, then, shall we?" he murmured, shifting his attention to her jawline.

She frowned. "I do seem to be better protected than the king, don't I?"

He chuckled. "Don't worry. You can tell Beetly you wandered off and thought he was right behind you."

"You're very devious."

"When I need to be."

Charlotte stepped back a little, meeting his gaze with her warm brown eyes. "I have a few questions for you, Xavier."

His heart stammered a little. "Ask them, then."

"Are you courting Melinda Edwards? Because she's my friend, and I don't want to be put in the middle of anything that might hurt her."

He could make up something flip, he knew, but she'd probably see through it. And besides, there was something so . . . forthright about her that he couldn't help wanting to respond to it. "I consulted a friend of my own," he said slowly, "because I hadn't been to London for quite a while and I wanted to know which lady might best suit me."

" 'Suit you?' " she repeated.

Xavier smiled a little. "You *don't* like games, do you?"

"No, I don't." She sighed. "It sounds silly, and I'm really not that delicate, but it's happened several times, that I'll be out somewhere and a man begins to pay attention to me so his friend can speak with Melinda. I don't like being the distraction."

He touched her cheek, running a finger along her smooth skin. "No, you're distract*ing*," he corrected. "And very refreshing. And I'm not playing games. I'm here to find a wife. Yes, Melinda Edwards was originally on that list. She isn't, any longer."

Color fled her cheeks. "But —"

"I was in the army, you know," he interrupted, not wanting to hear her say something ridiculous like he couldn't be seriously considering her, "and I had quite the career. I'd begun as a lieutenant, and after two years I'd been promoted to major. I was quite happy with that being my life. England's always fighting a war somewhere."

"What happened, then?"

"My older brother, Anthony, died last year. I was summoned home and arrived just in time for his funeral. Some sort of influenza." He cleared his throat, wondering if she could hear how angry being abandoned by his closest friend still made him — and how lonely he still felt. "Anthony hadn't married and had no heirs, which left me with the title." He forced a chuckle. "Compared to being an earl, war was easy."

"Why me?"

"Why you?" he repeated, touching her again because he couldn't seem not to. "You defended your cousin-in-law to your mother."

"But —"

"Not only against popular opinion, and not because you knew whether he was innocent or guilty, but because nothing had been proven. That, my dear, takes a great deal of character."

"So you like my character."

"Charlotte, do you like being required to behave as you do? Do you enjoy your time spent with Lord Herbert? Do you expect you'll be perfectly happy saying yes when — and I do mean *when* — he asks you to marry him?"

Her face folded into a frown. "Of course I don't like any of that. I don't like having my behavior scrutinized by my own parents as a result of a supposed scandal that had nothing to do with me and that occurred when I was seven years old. Who would like such a thing?"

"I have no idea. But I do know that I never expected to have this life thrust on me, and that I would have been perfectly happy to have caught the fun at Waterloo and have had Anthony still alive and shouldering all the responsibility. Except for one thing."

"And which thing would that be?"

"You."

Charlotte looked at him. She'd viewed him from a distance, imagining what brave things he'd done in the war, admiring his self-confidence and ease in talking to and with other people. She'd never imagined that he might be unhappy, or lonely, or especially that he would ever look in her direction. But he had looked, and apparently he saw them as kindred spirits, two people not entirely comfortable with where they'd found themselves and trying to make the best of it. The oddest thing was, she could see it, too.

Oh, my. "I need to walk," she blurted, striding off in a direction roughly opposite of where Herbert should be.

In a second he'd caught up to her. "I didn't mean to upset you," he said in his quiet voice.

"I'm not upset. I'm thinking."

"Thinking in a good way, or a bad way?"

An unexpected chuckle escaped her lips. "That's what I'm trying to de—"

Someone smacked into her, and before she could gasp, she lay sprawled on the ground, her nose inches from —

"Charlotte!" her friend Tillie Howard gasped. "I'm so sorry!"

She sat up, grateful to find that at least her skirt hadn't flown up past her waist. So much for her dignity. "What were you *doing?*" she demanded, pulling her bonnet back over her hair.

"A footrace, actually," Tillie muttered, looking embarrassed. "Don't tell my mother."

"I won't have to." With the park this crowded, someone else was bound to have seen. "If you think she's not going to hear of this —"

"I know, I know," Tillie said, sighing. "I'm hoping she'll chalk it up to sun-induced insanity."

"Or perhaps sun-blindness?" Xavier put in, helping Charlotte to her feet. She thought he looked amused, but then he hadn't been the one knocked to the ground.

Still, her mother would have an apoplexy at

her own behavior today, so who was she to judge anyone or anything? "Lady Mathilda, this is Earl Matson."

"Pleased to . . ." Tillie trailed off as a tall, dark-haired man skidded up beside her.

"Tillie, are you all right?" he asked.

Lady Mathilda answered and received help to her feet, but Charlotte's attention was on Xavier. He'd stiffened a little as the other gentleman had appeared, and he'd immediately taken a step closer to her, keeping her hand in his. A thrill ran through her. Was he actually jealous? And on *her* behalf?

Tillie introduced her to Peter Thompson, but before she could introduce Xavier in return, Mr. Thompson interrupted her. "Matson," he said, nodding.

"You already know each other?" Tillie asked, before Charlotte could.

"From the army," Xavier answered.

"Oh!" Tillie exclaimed, her red curls bobbing. "Did you know my brother? Harry Howard?"

The expression in Xavier's eyes changed for just a moment. Charlotte couldn't read it, but something in that faded cobalt made her grip his fingers just a little tighter.

"He was a fine fellow," he answered after a moment. "We all liked him a great deal."

"Yes," Mathilda agreed, "everyone liked Harry. He was quite special that way."

338

The earl nodded. "I'm very sorry for your loss."

"As are we all. I thank you for your regards."

Charlotte glanced at Mr. Thompson, then looked again more closely. He was eyeing Xavier the same way the earl seemed to be sizing him up, like two stallions each protecting a mare from a rival. *Oh, dear.* "Were you in the same regiment?" she asked, trying to distract them.

"Yes, we were," Xavier returned, "though Thompson here was lucky enough to remain through the action."

"You weren't at Waterloo?" Tillie asked.

"No. I was called home for family reasons."

"I'm so sorry," Tillie murmured.

Abruptly Charlotte wished her friend didn't look quite so attractive, with her bosom heaving and her cheeks glowing from the footrace. *Tart.* "Speaking of Waterloo," she broke in, "do you intend to go to next week's reenactment? Lord Matson was just complaining that he missed the fun."

"Charlotte," Xavier murmured, too quietly for the others to hear.

"I'd hardly call it fun," Mr. Thompson muttered.

"Right," Tillie seconded in a too-cheery voice. Obviously she also wished to be elsewhere. "Prinny's reenactment! I'd quite forgotten about it. It's to be at Vauxhall, is it not?"

"A week from today," Charlotte said, nodding, and beginning to wish she'd just kept her mouth shut, as her mother kept telling her to. "On the anniversary of Waterloo. I've heard that Prinny is beside himself with excitement. There are to be fireworks."

Peter didn't look terribly excited at the prospect. "Because we want this to be an *accurate* representation of war."

"Or Prinny's idea of accurate, anyway," the earl added coolly.

"Perhaps it is meant to mimic gunfire," Tillie said tightly. "Will you go, Mr. Thompson? I should appreciate your escort."

Charlotte shifted uncomfortably. Obviously the subject was even more sensitive than she'd realized. She opened her mouth to change the subject as Tillie and Peter continued debating whether they should attend or not, but Xavier tugged on her hand. When she looked up at him, he shook his head slightly, his gaze on Tillie and surprisingly compassionate. "Leave be," he muttered, glancing down at Charlotte.

"But —"

"Very well," Mr. Thompson was saying to Tillie, though his lips tightened.

"Thank you," Mathilda replied with a grin. "It's very kind of you, especially since —"

At her friend's abruptly uncomfortable expression, Charlotte shook herself. "Well, we

340

must be going," she said, "er, before anyone —"

"We need to be on our way," Xavier finished smoothly.

"Terribly sorry about the footrace,"
Mathilda said, reaching out to squeeze Charlotte's other hand.

Smiling, Charlotte squeezed back. They
were still friends, after all. "Think nothing of
it. Pretend I'm the finish line, and then
you've won."

"An excellent idea. I should have thought
of it myself."

When Xavier tugged her backward, Charlotte didn't protest. Herbert was probably
scouring the park for her by now, and whatever row he caused would be her fault.

"You have interesting friends," he said after a
moment, leading her into thicker undergrowth.

"So do you."

"I wouldn't exactly call Thompson a
friend."

As she realized he'd managed to once again
find a glade sheltered from all other occupants of the park, she pulled her hand free.
"I need to get back to Herbert."

"I know." He closed the distance between
them with one long step. "And I hope you
know that while I've been making every attempt to behave myself for your parents'
sake, I have earned my somewhat . . . colorful reputation."

Her heartbeat quickened. She'd begun to find new levels of boldness since their first encounter, herself. "Oh, have you?"

Reaching out, he took both of her shoulders in his hands and yanked her up against him. As his lips found hers, Charlotte felt heat rush from their point of contact down to her toes, with a warm, unexpected, tingling between her thighs. He meant it. He was serious in his interest. As wondrous as it was, a small, logical part of her mind still wanted to know why. Why her? Why not someone lovely and collected and sophisticated like Melinda? Why —

His hands trailed down her arms, brushing the outside of her breasts while his thumbs stroked across her muslin-covered nipples with just enough authority to let her know that he'd done it on purpose, and that kissing her was only the beginning of what he wanted.

"Xavier," she gasped, leaning into him.

"Shh."

"Charlotte!"

She started, her passion-clouded brain taking a moment to register that Herbert's voice was not right behind her but rather was far enough away that he couldn't possibly have seen anything. "Let go, Xavier," she murmured, unable to resist pursuing his mouth for a last rough kiss.

"You need to break with Herbert," the earl

said, his voice harder.

"And what reason would I give?" she asked, equal parts thrilled and frustrated. "I've already mentioned my dissatisfaction with his exciting character to my parents. In response, my father accepted his invitation to escort me to Vauxhall."

"We'll see about that," Xavier replied. "I'll tolerate this sneaking about for a while, but my patience does have a limit, Charlotte." He cupped her face in his hand. "And Lord Herbert will not be escorting you to Vauxhall. *I* will be. You can wager on that."

It would make things worse, and for once Charlotte didn't mind. As Herbert drew closer, Xavier faded back into the shadows. She gave the excuse he'd suggested, that she'd wandered off and been surprised to find him gone. Being a man of no imagination, he believed the tale. And from Alice's amused expression, the maid wasn't going to give anything away, either.

Xavier had said his patience wouldn't last, and she could only wonder what would happen then. One thing, though, was for certain. She was going to Vauxhall next Wednesday.

Chapter 6

Very well, the secret is out. The object of Lord Matson's affections is none other than Miss Charlotte Birling, whose name, This Author must confess, has never before graced the pages of this column.

The pair in question were seen arm in arm yesterday in Hyde Park, looking rather cozy, indeed.

Lady Whistledown's Society Papers, 12 June 1816

Charlotte hummed as she faced the mirror. She'd barely eaten dinner last night, and she'd barely slept, but even so she felt . . . energized, as though electricity ran just under her skin. Along with it, she became aware of the alarming feeling that nothing could go wrong. That should immediately have alerted her that everything was about to go to hell.

At least her parents allowed her to finish her morning toilette and come downstairs to breakfast in blissful ignorance before they pounced. "Good morning," she said, sweeping into the small breakfast room and breathing deeply the scent of fresh-baked bread.

"Good morning," her mother replied, looking up from her perusal of the new *Whistledown* column. "Wait until you hear this."

"I don't care what anyone else is doing or saying." Charlotte selected a peach and a thick slice of bread from the sideboard. "I don't even care if it's probably going to rain again today."

Her father lowered *The London Times* to look at her. "And what is the reason for this new, careless Charlotte?"

Something in his voice caught her attention, but she pretended to ignore it. She'd changed in the past few days; she couldn't expect that they had. But they would, because she needed them to if she meant to have any sort of future with Lord Matson. And she meant to. "You'll laugh at me."

"We won't laugh," her mother returned.

Don't say anything more, the little sensible voice inside her head began urging. This morning, though, the giddy voice, the one that wanted to sing and waltz across the room, was much louder. "I feel like I've been a caterpillar, and now I'm a butterfly."

She took her seat, and it was a moment before she noticed that neither the baron nor the baroness had commented on her metaphor. As she looked up, they were gazing at one another. Something had happened.

"What's wrong?" she asked.

Slowly her mother slid the gossip column over in front of her. "You may think you're a butterfly," she said quietly, "but that would imply that you've become independent, and that your actions —"

"— and that your actions reflect on no one else," her father finished. "I think we can all agree that you are in error."

Swallowing, Charlotte looked at the *Whistledown* column. *Oh, no.* "I —"

"Consider carefully which lie you intend to tell," the baron interrupted again. "You and Herbert have already regaled us with the story of how you two became separated in the park yesterday. Matson's name did not come up in that conversation."

For just a moment Charlotte closed her eyes. Back to caterpillar again in one second. And now she'd never be allowed out of her cocoon. Ever. Unless she forced it open herself. "I like Lord Matson," she said quietly. "I think you would like him, too, if you would give him a chance."

"We didn't make his reputation, Charlotte. He did that on his own. And he must face the consequences of it — on his own."

"What about my reputation?" she protested. "You decided when I was seven that every breath I took could ruin me, and so I

346

haven't had an opportunity to do anything. Yes, I'm in *Lady Whistledown.* But am I ruined? No."

"That remains to be seen. Did you intend to see him in the park, or was it an accident?" Her mother took the column back. Undoubtedly it would go into a box so she could pull it out every time she wanted to make a point about something.

Charlotte lifted her chin. "It was on purpose."

"Charlotte!"

She pushed to her feet. "I'm not beautiful or vibrant, Mama. Believe me, I know that. And when I'm with Lord Herbert, I feel plain, and ordinary, and small. But when Xavier looks at me and talks with me, I feel . . . attractive. Don't expect me to ignore that. He's a good man, trying to take a place in Society when he never expected to have to do so."

"So he tells you flattering lies and now you're ready to let him use our good name to improve his own standing."

"Papa, it's not —"

"It's not like that? Can you think of another reason why he might be courting you?"

So that was it. In their eyes, she truly was ordinary. Why would someone as handsome and wealthy as Xavier Matson want to associate with her, unless there was something tangible in it for him? "Oh," she said quietly, her voice catching.

"Edward, there's no call for that." To Charlotte's surprise, her mother stood and put an arm across her shoulders. "We don't want to hurt you, but you need to consider that not everyone is as good-hearted and honest as you are."

"And that whether you live under our roof or not, your actions reflect on us and our reputations." The baron's mouth pinched.

"I'll keep that in mind, Papa. May I go to my bedchamber now?"

"Lord Herbert will be taking you to luncheon. Until then, yes, I suggest you retire to think about the consequences of your actions."

As Charlotte clomped back upstairs, she wondered how long Xavier would remain interested in her if her parents never allowed them to meet again. In him she'd found a companion spirit, but while hers was still tethered, his was free.

His actions reflected on no one but himself, and being both a man and wealthy, most anything he did would be excused. As for her own actions, her father was correct. She lived under their roof, shared their name, had been presented to Society by them. And she could accept all of that.

What bothered her was that the standards of conduct expected of every proper female in London didn't apply to her. Or rather they did, but threefold. And she didn't have the awe-inspiring beauty or daring to counter the strict walls put up around her.

Xavier hadn't seemed to notice her faults, but she knew that he was frustrated with her situation. And Melinda Edwards, Rachel Bakely, Lady Portia Hollings, and a half dozen other young ladies were all out to catch his eye — while she sat on her bed, grumbling about her fate in solitude.

"Charlotte?" Her mother's knock sounded softly against the closed door.

"Come in."

The baroness entered the room, closing the door behind her, then strolled over to take a seat at Charlotte's dressing table. She didn't look angry, but Charlotte kept silent, anyway. She certainly didn't want to precipitate another confrontation.

"I had a letter from Helen yesterday," her mother said.

"Good. How are she and Fenton and the children?"

"All doing well. She hopes to come to Town next month, though they won't be able to remain long."

"It'll be nice to see her again."

Lady Birling nodded. "She was twelve when Sophia broke with Easterly, you know."

"Yes, I remember."

"But since she and Fenton had been promised to one another since her second birthday, we weren't worried about the scandal damaging her hopes in Society."

"And I wasn't promised to anyone."

"No, you weren't." The baroness smoothed at her skirts. "We didn't mean to make you feel like a caterpillar. We just wanted to take any steps necessary to make certain you could marry well."

Charlotte fiddled with the rich embroidery on her bed covering. "I understand that. But I hope you know me well enough to realize that I would rather not marry than marry someone I hold in no regard."

"You mean Herbert."

"He's nice, I suppose," Charlotte returned, seeking anything that could be considered a compliment. "And neat. And I understand that you consider us to be well matched. I . . . I just don't agree with that."

"How seriously is Lord Matson pursuing you?"

She looked up. Her mother gazed at her in the dressing mirror's reflection, her expression somber. "I'm not entirely certain," she answered slowly. "But I do know that he's not using me to step up the ladder. Heavens, someone with his looks and wealth could do much better than me."

"Don't say that."

"Why not? You always do."

"Charlotte, I'm trying to be sympathetic.

Pray don't throw insults at me."

That surprised her. "Sympathetic? In what way?" She slid off the bed to her feet. "You mean that you might permit Xavier to call on me?"

"Our situation hasn't changed, daughter. I mean that I might speak to your father about discouraging Lord Herbert. If you truly would rather be alone than married to him."

"I truly would," Charlotte said vehemently.

"You understand that you may not have another opportunity to marry. Each year you remain single, your chances will decline a little further. And don't rest your hopes on Lord Matson. Whatever his interest in you, as you said, he has other choices. You won't."

"Mama, don't think I haven't considered everything you said every day for the past year. I know who I am, and I know that I don't take young men's breath away. And Herbert will never see me any differently. If I ever marry, I would hope that it would be to a gentleman who, if he doesn't see me as beautiful, at least doesn't see me as dull."

The baroness rose. "And how does Lord Matson see you? Or do you have no idea of that, either?"

Charlotte smiled. "He says I have fine eyes."

"I'll speak to your father." Lady Birling walked to the door and pulled it open. "If he agrees, Lord Matson may call on you here.

You will not go anywhere with him, and he will not court you in public. Not until this mess with Sophia has blown over, anyway. Is that clear?"

Her heart beat so fast that for a moment Charlotte thought she might faint. "Very clear," she answered, doing her best not to grin. She would at least get to see Xavier again.

By the time Xavier made his daily afternoon call at Birling House, he was revisiting his kidnaping plan. It had been twenty-four hours since he'd spoken with Charlotte, and he felt stretched tighter than a bowstring. By now he'd given up trying to figure out what it was about her that drew him, but he could no more stay away than he could stop breathing. Anthony was probably having a good laugh at his expense right now.

He tapped the knocker against the door. As it opened he held up the bouquet of red roses, ready to hand them and his card over to the butler when he was once again refused entry. Instead, the liveried servant stepped back.

"If you'll wait in the morning room, my lord."

For a moment Xavier thought he'd called on the wrong house. Recovering himself, he followed the old man into a small, comfortable sitting room and watched the door close.

Perhaps Lord Birling meant to lock him away — but no key turned in the door. He gripped the flowers and paced to the fireplace and back. The baron could warn him away again, but he would return. And he would keep returning until Charlotte herself told him to go away.

The door opened again. As he faced it, Charlotte walked into the morning room. He was halfway across the floor before he registered that her maid had entered behind her. Cursing silently, Xavier brought himself to a halt. She was there; he didn't care whether she'd come accompanied by circus performers.

"Good afternoon, my lord," she said with a curtsy.

Inclining his head, he finished closing the distance between them at a more sedate pace and handed her the bouquet. "Good afternoon. I . . . trust you are well?"

"Yes, thank you. Won't you have a seat?" She lowered her face to the rose petals, glancing up at him from beneath dark lashes. "And thank you for the bouquet," she continued, handing them to her maid, who backed to the doorway and passed them off to a footman.

She seated herself on the couch. He wanted to sit beside her and take her hand, but whatever this was, it appeared they were to act with propriety, and so he took the chair directly opposite her. "You're most welcome."

"May I offer you some tea?"

Xavier sat forward a little. "What the devil is going on?"

Her lips twitched. "You are to be permitted to call on me."

His heart flip-flopped. "I am? Then what —"

"But there are rules."

"Rules," he repeated, settling back again. "What rules?"

"I cannot leave the house in your company, and you may not be seen pursuing me in public."

"May I be seen dancing with you in public?"

"No."

"Then I suppose kissing you is out of the question."

Color flooded her cheeks. "Yes, it is."

"Why the change? Not that I'm complaining, of course." Actually he did have a few complaints, but since they now seemed able to converse, he supposed the rest could wait a short time. A very short time.

"We were in *Whistledown*."

He nodded. "I saw, blast that woman — whoever she is. What did you tell your parents?"

"That I'd gone to the park to meet you."

Xavier lifted an eyebrow. Something had

obviously changed for the better, and if he had to guess, he would say it had much to do with the fetching young woman seated across from him. "You simply told them?"

"Yes." She lowered her voice. "They made me a bit angry."

"It seems to have worked to our benefit."

"Partially, at any rate."

"And Lord Herbert?"

Charlotte grimaced for a moment. "He's not to know, either."

This agreement seemed to be even less advantageous than he'd thought. "So I'm not considered a serious suitor. And then once your engagement is announced I simply go away?"

"Xavier, they know I don't wish to marry Herbert, but my father insists that your intentions may not be . . . sincere, and that my chances at matrimony in the meantime shouldn't be ruined."

After he'd won her once and for all, Xavier intended to have a little chat with Lord Birling about underestimating the value of his daughter. Before he could win her, however, he would obviously need to receive permission to at least dance with her in front of other people, damn it all.

"It's a lot of rules," she continued, glancing at him and then away again. "After all, there are other single wom—"

"I can tolerate the rules," he returned

sharply. "I can even tolerate damned Herbert. But I am sincere in my intentions, and I will make your father understand that."

"You are?"

"Of course I am." Relenting a little, he forced a smile. "After all, I learned a great deal about strategy in the military. I don't pursue a campaign unless I have a good expectation of succeeding."

"And all this because I defended Lord Easterly?"

A chuckle escaped his lips. "That turned my head in your direction. My ears and eyes and mouth took care of the rest." As had his heart, he was beginning to realize, but making her aware of how special she was remained a difficult enough prospect without his frightening her to death with declarations. Hell, hearing him say it aloud would give *him* an apoplexy. Xavier the rakehell falling for a quiet, restrained, witty, intelligent female.

Her lips quirking, she glanced at her maid. "I admit I have felt the effect of your mouth, my lord," she said in a low voice.

This looking and not touching was going to kill him. "You haven't begun to feel the effect of my mouth, Charlotte," he murmured. "And you're causing my patience with this nonsense to shorten considerably."

She gazed at him for a moment. "You're completely serious, aren't you?"

"About you? Yes, I am." He knew what she

was asking, and he knew what his answer meant. To his surprise, though, it didn't unsettle him in the least. Rather, he felt . . . complete. And content. Or he would, if he could figure out what in damnation it would take to get her parents to agree to take his suit seriously.

"I apologize if I sound incredulous, Xavier," she continued slowly, "but my father had to go out and find Lord Herbert when they decided I needed to marry. No man has ever pursued me. I —"

"Until now," he interrupted.

Charlotte looked down at her hands for a moment, then gazed at him again. She always looked him in the eye, he realized. He liked that about her — in addition to the other things he was swiftly coming to appreciate about her character.

"My older sister, Helen," she said after a moment, "is stunning. She had suitors practically climbing through windows to court her. And much as I love Helen, I have to say that I noticed things — the way she hated reading, couldn't bear to discuss anything but gossip and fashion, wouldn't attend the theater unless escorted by someone she wished everyone to see accompanying her — she knew how to be popular, and well-liked, and nothing else interested her."

"It's a common theme among young ladies," he returned, reflecting that he'd known dozens like her sister, and no one like her.

"But not for me," she countered, as if reading his thoughts. "None of the things that interested her, interest me. And I think I told myself that my refusing to play those games was the reason I never had any gentleman callers. But I know the truth. I'm not stunning, and I'm not exciting. And I . . . I want to be certain that you aren't in pursuit simply because my parents' suspicion of your motives has made this some sort of challenge to you."

He smiled slowly, unable to resist running a finger along her cheek. "You are a challenge. And please don't blame me because a shipload of very stupid men looked at you once and declared you uninteresting. I looked at you twice, and I saw what you are."

Color crept up her cheeks. "And what is that?"

"Mine."

"Xavier —"

The baron and baroness swept into the room with enough speed that they'd probably witnessed him caressing her. Damnation. Straitlaced, and spies. He couldn't imagine a worse combination.

"Good afternoon, Lord Matson."

He stood, sketching a bow. "Lord and Lady Birling. Thank you for allowing me to converse with Charlotte."

"We remain unconvinced of your intentions," her father said bluntly, "but Charlotte won't come to her senses without proof of your passing interest."

Beside him, she stiffened. At least she seemed to notice now her parents' low opinion of her desirability — and at least now it annoyed her. "Lord Matson knows all about the rules," she said tightly, "and he's agreed to follow them."

No, he hadn't. "I'm afraid that you are going to be disappointed, my lord," Xavier replied, wondering what they would do if he offered for her on the spot. He wouldn't — couldn't — take the risk, however. If they refused him, as he was fairly certain they would, he'd be put in the position of defying them directly. While he had no qualms about that, he knew that Charlotte would.

"Charlotte is practically engaged to Lord Herbert Beetly," her mother put in.

"You've made that clear, my lady. With all respect, she has neither been proposed to, nor has she accepted any such offer. She is therefore available to be courted, and wooed."

The baron actually blinked. "True, I suppose, but if you are sincere, you are also late to the race. I have confidence in Lord Herbert and his impeccable character. I am much less certain about you."

"You won't have any doubts by the time I'm finished." He would have pushed harder, but Charlotte's face had grown pale, and she practically shook with tension. Xavier took her hand and brushed his lips across her knuckles. "I have a few errands to run. I'll call on you tomorrow, Charlotte."

"Xavier."

He could feel her pulse beneath his fingers, hard and fast. That encouraged him, far more than her parents' obvious disapproval could lower his hopes. As he strode past the Birlings and out their front door, he made a silent vow to himself. He would marry Charlotte Birling. And from then on, anyone with an unkind word for her would have to answer to him.

Chapter 7

Lord Matson continues to face resistance in his pursuit of Miss Birling.

But is it Miss Birling who is doing the resisting, or the young lady's parents?

Given Lord Matson's fine form and figure, one can only imagine that it is the elder Birlings who are proving to be anti-romantical. Miss Birling is made of stern stuff, to be sure, but surely not that stern.

Lady Whistledown's Society Papers,
14 June 1816

"I thought we had an agreement." Charlotte paced back and forth in front of her mother's writing desk. "Lord Matson was supposed to be allowed to call on me."

"Charlotte," Lady Birling replied, setting aside her pen, "he has been allowed to do so."

"Then why haven't I seen him?"

"Lord Matson is obviously a man with

many business and social obligations. I told you that we doubted the depth of his commitment to you. And better to discover that now, before the gossips can make it look as though he led you on and then tired of you."

That thought had occurred to her from time to time, especially at night, alone in her bed, but in the daylight her penchant for reality thankfully won out. "How can he tire of me when we never see one another?"

"Perhaps he has done so already." Her mother gave an obviously forced smile. "Now, don't you have a luncheon today with Melinda Edwards? You shouldn't be late."

Charlotte hid a sudden frown. Over the past few days she had been frighteningly in demand. She'd attributed it to her mention in Whistledown, but friends, relations, her mother, all seemed to require her presence for eating or shopping or strolling in between drizzles. Now she abruptly began to wonder whether her parents were attempting to keep her out of the house so that Xavier *couldn't* see her. He'd been given permission to call on her, but no one had said she must be home to see him. *Drat.* "Melinda sent over a note this morning begging off," she lied. "I believe she has the sniffles."

"It's this atrocious weather." Lady Birling stood. "We don't want you coming down with anything. Why don't you go upstairs and get some rest?"

A short time alone to think up a strategy seemed a very good idea. "Yes, Mama."

Not certain whether to be angry at the machinations going on around her or elated that Xavier might not have been avoiding her, Charlotte made her way upstairs to her bedchamber and sat in her reading chair. Beethoven jumped into her lap, but after a glance at the pensive look on her face, changed locations to the windowsill. So that was how her parents meant to deal with Xavier. Give their permission, make her unavailable to him, and then push Herbert into making a proposal without delay.

Her window rattled. With a yowl Beethoven leapt down and scooted under the bed, while Charlotte whipped her head around. Clinging to the window frame, a scattering of flower petals and pollen across his hair and shoulders, was Xavier.

"Let me in, Charlotte, before I break my neck," he muttered, his voice muffled through the glass.

Gasping, she unlatched the window and shoved it open, grabbing an elbow to help haul him through the opening. "What in the world —"

Sprawled on the floor, he pulled her down across his lap and kissed her hard and deep. Charlotte sank into his embrace. Her mother might call it a fantasy, but she was finding it real enough. And so intoxicating that she could hardly bear not being able to see him.

"Hello," he said after a moment, running a thumb across her lower lip.

She blinked, trying to pull herself back into a logical realm. "What are you doing here?"

Now he was stroking her fingers, concentrating on each appendage as though it were something precious. "I called at the front door first," he said in his low drawl, "but your butler said you had an influenza and couldn't be disturbed. You're not ill, are you?"

It was a terrible lie to tell, especially to someone who'd lost a family member to the same illness. "No, I'm not ill."

Relief touched his face. "Good. But why have you been avoiding me, then?"

"How can I avoid you when you're not about?" she returned.

He gazed at her. "I've called on you every day. You're the one who's been elsewhere. Hence my trellis-climbing today."

Charlotte drew a breath. "You've called every day?"

"I told you I would."

"They told me you hadn't been by. And I've been . . . sent out visiting with everyone. Even aunts I barely knew I had."

Slowly Xavier nodded. "It seems some people are so convinced we don't suit that they've been attempting to force reality to match their convictions." Brushing her cheek with gentle fingers, he kissed her again.

"But it didn't work. You climbed up my trellis." Enveloped in his embrace, Charlotte carefully brushed some of the flower refuse out of his tawny hair.

"And nearly broke my neck. It doesn't look as though anyone's used it as a ladder before."

She smiled. "No one has."

"Well, if this nonsense continues, I'm going to bring some carpentry tools with me next time and make some repairs."

Charlotte could imagine it; Xavier slipping into her bedchamber, into her bed, in the middle of the night, while her parents thought they'd successfully thwarted any encounters at all. Warm damp started between her thighs, and she shifted closer to him, sliding her arms around his shoulders. "That would be nice."

"I suggest you not move around like that," he said, his voice more strained. "I'm not here to ravish you. Not this time, anyway."

She had no idea what to say to that. It sounded very wicked, and it sounded as though her parents were going to have to take stronger measures if they wished to keep Lord Matson away from her. Of course first they would have to find out that he'd begun calling on her in a more direct manner — and she had no intention of informing them.

"So your parents gave permission for me to

call, then made certain you wouldn't be here to see me, all the while telling you I must not be interested."

Charlotte drew a breath. "They're not . . . evil or anything, you know. They think I'm becoming too attached to you, and that you don't return the sentiment."

Xavier lifted an eyebrow, realizing that he was perfectly content to sit there on her floor with her for the rest of the day. For the rest of his life. "They're wrong."

She sighed. "And they'll never acknowledge that fact. I'm sure they'll have Herbert proposing by Vauxhall."

Anger tore at him. "No, they won't." Setting her back a little, he touched her cheek, gazing into her soft brown eyes for a long time. "Marry me, Charlotte," he whispered.

She opened her sweet mouth, then closed it again. "I can't. Not without their permission."

Reminding himself that he liked her in part because she was at heart a good, proper chit, he took a breath. "Say for a moment that I had their permission."

"But you don't. And you won't. I love them, aside from their disbelief that I would attract anyone on my own, but they won't agree to something they think could put a blemish on the family, even if it's only in their own imaginations. No matter how much I might want it."

That was what he wanted to hear. "You would say yes, if not for that."

Slowly she nodded. "Yes."

"Then I'll manage the rest."

With an exasperated look, she plucked the last bit of pollen off his jacket. "I know you're probably used to getting what you want, but it won't —"

He stopped her argument with another kiss. Kissing her seemed the very best thing ever invented. Or the second best thing, rather. It occurred to him that if he ruined her, her parents would probably be happy to marry her off to him. But he didn't want to resort to that — though he would keep the option open. Nothing was going to prevent him from having her. He would find a way around this, because he refused to lose her to anyone else. And especially not to damned Herbert Beetly.

They talked for nearly an hour before Alice scratched at her door. With a yelp Charlotte scrambled to her feet. "What is it?"

"Lady Birling wishes to see you, miss."

"I'll be right down."

"I could hide under the bed," Xavier suggested, rising behind her.

"You could, but eventually you'd starve to death." She smiled, feeling giddy despite the poor prospects for the two of them. He'd asked her to marry him, for heaven's sake.

"Promise me something, Charlotte," he said softly, drawing her into his arms again.

"What?"

"Promise me that whatever your parents or Beetly say, you won't give in. I'll make this right."

Because she couldn't help it, she leaned up and kissed him. Could it be enough that her heart soared at this moment? Even when she knew he was bound to fail? Of course there was always the slight chance that he'd actually succeed. "I promise."

He slipped back out the window, cursing at the condition of her trellis as he descended. Charlotte watched him go over the back fence, before she joined her mother downstairs, only to discover that, of all things, her cousin Sophia had invited her to spend the night.

"Am I permitted?" she asked, eyeing the invitation. Despite their age difference she'd always enjoyed chatting with Sophia, but since Easterly's reappearance she'd barely set eyes on her.

Her mother sighed. "Your father and I have been discussing her invitation since yesterday. I don't like it, but she is family. And hopefully no one else will find out about it. But you're not to discuss Matson. That nonsense never happened, as far as we're concerned."

And obviously her mother, at least, had

begun to realize that something more substantial than a luncheon or a shopping excursion would be needed to keep her unavailable to gentlemen callers. Next would probably be a surprise week in Bath with Grandma Birling. Well, she'd be as discreet as she could, but with Sophia she'd always felt like she could discuss anything. And she was desperate for a friendly ear where Xavier was concerned. "Yes, Mama."

All the while she packed her overnight bags she wondered whether Xavier would try to visit her again tonight, and then break his neck on the trellis when no one came to open the window. *Oh, dear.* Unsettled as she was, the only thing she could do about it was pack twelve times and eat the entire plate of pastries Alice had fetched for her to snack on.

Finally she dressed in her favorite blue visiting gown with matching hat and ribbons, and dove into the family coach as soon as it pulled onto the drive. When she arrived at Sophia's twenty minutes later, her cousin was waiting for her in the foyer. Lady Sophia Throckmorton always looked cool and collected and completely in control, and this afternoon Charlotte envied her for it. As aggravating as Charlotte's situation with Xavier was, Sophia had at least as many worries with her husband returning to London just as she'd decided to marry another man.

The footman had barely taken her bags when Sophia came forward and gave her a sound hug. "I'm so glad you could come!" she exclaimed. "I am in dire need of good, logical, feminine conversation. Are you hungry yet? I ordered a light dinner to be served at seven."

Now Charlotte was beginning to regret her pastry snacking. "That's fine," she replied. "I just had tea and couldn't eat another bite."

"Excellent. I'll have it brought to my room. I've been so looking forward to seeing you, but I must tell you that I have set a rule for this visit."

Charlotte lifted her eyebrows. "A rule?"

Unexpectedly Sophia hugged her again. She probably felt the need for a friend herself, Charlotte reflected, feeling guilty that she hadn't been a better cousin. "Yes, a rule," Sophia continued. "We can discuss clothes, hats, gloves, hemlines, jewelry, shoes, carriages, horses, balls, food of all sorts, women we like or don't like, and which of the latest dances we most enjoy, but we are not going to say one word about men."

Damnation. Charlotte forced a smile. "I think I can do that."

"Perfect!" Taking her arm, Sophia led her to the stairs. "Come and see the new gown I just purchased. It is blue with Russian trim, and it's just the loveliest thing. Oh, and I have a pale pink silk gown with delightful red rosettes that I think would be just the thing for you."

It sounded lovely, but abruptly Charlotte wondered whether Xavier would ever see her wearing it, and what he would think. "For me? I couldn't —"

"You can and will. I purchased it on a whim last month, but it is just not for me, and I so hate to waste things."

As they went to look at the gowns and have a nice long coze, Charlotte wondered what it would be like to be able to see a gown, decide she liked it, and just purchase it — without having to worry whether it made her look fast, would draw too much attention from possibly scandalous men. She jumped when the housekeeper scratched at the door to announce dinner was being brought up.

Chatting had been nice, but as they finished eating and Sophia poured tea, she had to admit that it had done nothing to distract her from Lord Matson. She so wanted to talk about him, to know if Sophia would understand how she felt and agree that it would be worth it to risk nearly everything to be with him.

Their conversation trailed off. Charlotte was beginning to debate whether to break Sophia's rule or not when her cousin opened her mouth to speak, then changed her mind.

Charlotte paused with the teacup halfway

to her mouth. "Yes?" she prompted.

"Nothing. I was just — it was nothing."

Blast it. Charlotte went back to sipping her tea. Now she had no distraction at all, and faded cobalt eyes and a warm, soft smile seemed to lurk in every thought. It wasn't fair, that her parents' doubts over her allure and their fear of scandal could ruin her one chance at a happy life. Especially when she knew that if they would take the time to know Xavier, they would realize that he wasn't a rakehell at all — he'd been sad and lonely, and had decided to enjoy himself a little when he'd arrived in Town. It wasn't his fault, and it wasn't hers. And then there he was, stating that he could single-handedly set everything to rights, while Lord Herbert Beetly stood at the ready.

Sophia's cup clinked into her saucer. "What are you thinking about so seriously?"

Charlotte blushed. "I was thinking of —" No, no breaking the rule unless Sophia did it first. "Nothing really. I was just day-dreaming."

"Your parents are at it again, aren't they? Trying to wheedle you into marrying. I vow, I would shake my Aunt Vivian until her teeth rattle."

"Oh, she means well, but —"

"They all mean well, but that doesn't mean they are right. Perhaps I should speak with Aunt Vivian and Uncle Edward about the dangers of being wed too soon. Do they not see my sad state of affairs as a warning? That every woman should wait until she is at least twenty-five to make such a decision?"

Charlotte blinked. "Twenty-five?" She wanted to marry a different man than her parents had chosen, not merely push back the beginning of her misery.

"Or older."

"Older? Than twenty-five? But that would be six years! Surely — I mean, if you met the right person, that is, if you *thought* you'd met the right person, there would be no reason to wait."

While Charlotte tried not to look too pitiful, Sophia gazed at her. "No, I don't suppose there would be any reason to wait if you'd met the right person. The problem is that there are no guarantees. I married for love, you know. Sometimes even that is not easy." She paused. "Perhaps we should suspend our rule and speak frankly about — a man, a particular man, just to give an example."

"No names, though," Charlotte broke in, remembering her mother's warning. "You know how my mother hates me gossiping." This way at least she could keep Xavier's identity a secret and still talk about him — and receive an honest opinion and advice, which she desperately needed.

"Agreed," Sophia stated.

Charlotte grabbed Sophia's hands, so grateful she felt near tears. "How nice to be able to speak frankly!"

"So it is! I believe that is why men manage to dupe us poor women so often; we do not share our feelings about them in an honest and frank manner." Sophia gave her cousin a knowing gaze. "But you know what I mean when I say that *men* are prideful, difficult creatures."

And very arrogant. "Yes, yes, they are."

"All of them." Sophia paused again, obviously choosing her words — and her advice — carefully. "And stubborn men are the worst."

Charlotte nodded. "Especially those who refuse to listen to reason, even when they have to know you've been completely logical."

Sophia's expression became more enthusiastic. "You are so right!"

"I also believe that some men enjoy causing disruptions simply so they can charge in to set things right again. Or think they can."

"That is certainly true. I also hate the way some men are forever trying to get us to —" Sophia blinked, her color deepening. "I'm sorry. Perhaps —"

"No, you're right." Her own cheeks heated, but this was the best chance she was likely to have to discuss Xavier frankly. "They are

374

always stealing kisses. And in the most inappropriate places, too. And all you have is their word that it means anything at all." What if she was just an infatuation for Xavier, after all? What if she managed to turn Herbert away, and then Xavier turned his back a week later, once the game was won?

Her cousin stood, her expression somber. "I'd rather have Lady Neeley's horrid parrot than any man I know."

Oh, now Charlotte was making Sophia feel bad, too. "Or that monkey Liza Pemberley is forever carting about," she said, trying to cheer them both up. "I heard that it bites."

"Does it?"

"I've never seen it do so, but it would be lovely if it did," Charlotte returned with a slight smile. "I can think of at least one person I'd like that monkey to bite." Lord Herbert. Then if nothing else, at least he might change his expression for a moment.

Sophia's lips twitched. "It would be quite handy to have a trained attack monkey at one's command."

"Better than a dog, because no one would see it coming." And perhaps if she owned a monkey, not everyone would think her so dull and ordinary. She sighed. "I daresay the monkey doesn't even really bite. It always seemed quite a docile creature to me."

"Yes, but one never knows with monkeys. Or men."

"So I've noticed." She frowned. "I've often thought that . . . *men* . . . always seem to think they know best."

"Pride. They are swollen with it, like the Thames after a rain."

Something plinked against the window. Charlotte sighed again. Splendid. More rain.

Sophia glanced at the glass, then turned back. "I also hate it when certain men refuse to admit when they are wrong. I —"

Two taps came this time. For a bare moment Charlotte wondered if Xavier had found her, but she quickly shrugged off the thought. He wouldn't risk causing her a scandal by climbing through someone else's window. "Is it raining? What *is* that?"

The sound came again. "That is not rain," Sophia declared. "It sounds more like a fool standing outside my window, throwing rocks."

She didn't seem all that upset about it, but then Sophia was poised to be married as soon as she and Easterly reached an agreement. "Ah, it must be Mr. Riddleton," Charlotte said. "He's quite infatuated with you, isn't he?"

"I don't believe he is as infatuated with me as you might think." Before Sophia could elaborate, a shower of what had to be pebbles hit the window.

"Goodness!" Charlotte exclaimed, frowning at the window. It wasn't Xavier; she was certain of that. And Sophia seemed to have a good idea, anyway. "He sounds a bit deter-mined. I think he is using larger pebbles."

Her cousin sighed. "Perhaps I should see what he wants, before the window —"

The window shattered. The guilty rock rolled up to Sophia's toes.

"Blast it!" Sophia grabbed the rock and made her way through the broken glass to the window, looking as though she meant to hurl the stone back at the perpetrator. "I cannot believe Thomas —" She stopped, leaning out.

"What is it?" Charlotte asked, her breath catching. It wasn't Xavier; it couldn't be.

Sophia, though, seemed to know exactly who it was. Leaning further out the window, she began a low-voiced conversation with the vandal. Charlotte listened for a moment until she realized it must be Easterly himself. Now if her mother found out, she'd never be al-lowed to go anywhere to visit.

But if Lord Easterly had had to resort to breaking Sophia's window in order to get her attention, maybe their situations weren't that different. At least Sophia could decide who and when she wanted to see all on her own. Charlotte *wanted* to see Xavier, wanted to kiss and be kissed by him, wanted things that he'd only hinted about, and everyone told her it was impossible. Everyone but Xavier, but she had much more experience with her par-ents than the earl did.

She fingered one of the rosettes on her new silk gown. He might convince the baron and baroness to let them wed, but she doubted it. The Birlings were wealthy enough that she didn't need to marry for money, and they certainly considered that Lord Herbert would add more respectability to the family than Xavier could.

It shouldn't even have been a question — and she abruptly realized why she refused to give up hope. She loved him. She loved Xavier Matson. Since she'd set eyes on him she'd been infatuated, but since they'd spoken she admired him. And now that she'd come to know him, she loved him.

" 'Ere now! Whot ye doin' throwin' rocks at a lady's winder?"

"Oh, thank you, Officer!" Sophia called.

Charlotte jumped, scrambling to her feet. Peeking over Sophia's shoulder, she could make out Lord Easterly surrounded by three men wearing the uniforms of the watch. Someone was in trouble.

Lord Easterly glared up at them, not looking very pleased. "You tricked me, you —"

" 'Ere now, guvnor! Not in front o' the ladies. Come along. It's to gaol wit' ye."

"Do you know who I am?"

Charlotte smothered a giggle. She didn't think the watch would care who he was, considering. Perhaps she and Xavier were luckier than Sophia and Easterly and Riddleton. At least she and Lord Matson wanted the same thing. Her cousin, though, seemed to want her estranged husband dragged off in chains.

Strange as the thought was, it left her feeling more hopeful. She and Matson wanted the same thing. He meant to do something about it. What could she do, then?

Chapter 8

Lord Herbert Beetly or Earl Matson?
Really, ladies, which would you
choose?
Lady Whistledown's Society Papers,
17 June 1816

Xavier arrived at the Birling House door just as Lord Herbert's coach turned up the drive. For a moment Xavier considered returning later, but he had a few errands to run this afternoon, and he needed to arrive at Vauxhall before Charlotte and her escort. Besides, he had no intention of setting up camp in the middle of enemy territory. He'd already chosen his field of combat.

The butler pulled opened the door, nodding twice to acknowledge both men as Herbert joined them on the front portico. "My lords."

Beetly eyed him. "You're not welcome here, Matson."

"Perhaps not," Xavier returned, lifting his bouquet of roses and handing it to the butler before anyone could tell him that of course Charlotte wasn't home — not for him, anyway, "but my flowers are nicer than yours."

"I didn't bring any flowers."

"No, you didn't, did you?" Xavier tipped his hat. "Good afternoon."

He hated leaving Beetly there; Charlotte had promised she wouldn't do anything hasty, but he knew that in the face of her parents' criticism and Beetly's mediocrity it wouldn't be difficult for her to forget that not only was she better than that but she also *deserved* better than that.

It killed him every time he went to that door, knowing that her parents would have removed her from his grasp. But he went anyway, to make certain the Birlings knew that he wasn't about to give up. She already knew that; he hoped she believed it.

At least he could tell himself that he only had to wait until tonight. From what he'd been able to discover, thousands would be attending Vauxhall, all to witness the reenactment of the Battle of Waterloo on the occasion of the battle's one-year anniversary. Prince George had apparently managed to spend thousands of quid on the event, money he'd had to borrow and would never repay. Considering that he would be able to see Charlotte there, however, Xavier was willing to forgive the extravagance.

"Lord Matson!"

Xavier jumped, slowing his mount as he looked in the direction of the feminine voice. "Good morning, Miss Bakely," he greeted, tipping his hat.

She approached him, two of her female friends clutching hands behind her and audibly giggling. "Good morning. Do you attend Vauxhall tonight?"

"I plan to, yes."

"It's going to be a sad crush, they say. With fireworks and a battle on the lake!"

"So I've heard." Though what an aquatic battle had to do with Waterloo, he wasn't entirely certain. "I assume you mean to attend, as well?"

"Yes, I do."

"Perhaps I'll see you there, then." She was angling for an escort, obviously, but he had other plans. Having to entertain some flighty, tittering chit while he longed to have Charlotte in his arms didn't seem a very pleasant prospect.

"My parents have rented a box on the east side of the rotunda. I'm sure they would love to see you again."

Hm. Showing up there once she'd invited him was a sure way to the parson's mousetrap. And the odd thing was, a few weeks ago he probably would have gone along with it: She'd been on his list, and back then he didn't care whom he married, as long as the process was painless. His feelings had obviously changed. "I'll manage if it I can," he hedged.

Charlotte said that she liked him and enjoyed being in his company. Her only objection to his marriage proposal had been that her parents wouldn't approve. Xavier decided to take her agreement to heart — *if* he could get her parents to go along with the marriage idea. That particular problem continued to bother him. He'd tried being polite and reserved, and they hadn't given an inch of ground. Suave and charming hadn't worked, either. He could elope with Charlotte, he supposed, but he doubted she would willingly go so far against her parents' wishes. What he did know was that touching her, hearing her voice, had become as necessary to him as air.

Cursing under his breath, he turned his gelding south. Whatever happened, he would be ready for it; as long as it entailed Charlotte becoming his.

It took Lord Herbert's carriage twenty minutes to go from the borders of Vauxhall Gardens to the water bridge entrance. Herbert sat back in his deep leather seat looking bored, but Charlotte perched at the coach's small window peering out at the huge mob of citizens. Lords and ladies, merchants, demimondaines, actresses, shopkeepers — everyone who could afford the two-shilling entrance fee milled at the entrance for their chance to cram inside.

"I've never seen so many people all in one place," she exclaimed, telling herself that she was looking to see how many of her friends were present, and not to determine if Lord Matson was there. He'd said he would attend, but that had been days ago. He hadn't even climbed into her window since Friday, and though she'd avoided exile to Bath, her parents had seen to it that she hadn't been home to receive any of his visits.

"The crowd would be more manageable if the proprietors would raise their entrance fee," Herbert commented. "Hold tightly onto your reticule; even pickpockets pay to get into festivities like this."

"I'm certain I don't have anything to fear in your company," she said. If she was stuck with him for tonight, perhaps she could at least pretend he was gallant and dangerous.

"I'm not doing anything foolish because you can't be bothered to look after your own valuables," he replied, stepping down as the carriage stopped and helping her to the ground. "I thought you didn't like those silly games."

"I don't. What's the sense of me having an escort, though, if you don't intend to perform any action on my behalf?"

"I'm escorting you; that's my duty. And it's your duty to stay out of trouble."

Charlotte freed her hand from his as soon as she could. "That doesn't sound gallant at all."

He gazed at her for a moment. "I might feel more gallant if I didn't know you were encouraging Lord Matson behind my back."

So Herbert did have an ounce of intelligence. "I haven't done anything behind your back."

"Hm. Next you'll be trying to buy those idiotic paste necklace baubles."

Ha. If he only knew. She carried her idiotic emerald bauble in her reticule tonight, just because it made her feel a little scandalous and free. "You seemed to admire the one Lady Ibsen wore."

Color stained his cheeks. "Nonsense. But I didn't come here to argue with you. Let's find our box and order dinner. The fireworks are supposed to be spectacular."

"So I've heard."

With Alice close behind them so they wouldn't be separated in the crowd, they pushed into the main clearing at the center of the Garden. If possible, the rotunda and pavilion were even more crowded than the periphery. The one good thing Charlotte could say about the massive crowd was that at least it created a little warmth; the evening was quite cool.

She'd worn the pink gown with the rosettes that Sophia had given her. Of course her parents had disapproved of the low neckline and the eye-drawing material, but she had to admit that she'd never felt more sensual and alive. All she needed to make the evening completely perfect would be to have Xavier by her side instead of Herbert.

"I've got us a prime box," Herbert went on, as though they hadn't been disagreeing about anything. "I daresay we'll have the best seats of anyone at the Gardens."

"How lovely," she returned. "I'm a bit hungry. Shall we take our seats?"

"Of course."

Already the *faux* French and British soldiers were lined up on opposite sides of the field, awaiting their cue to begin the battle. Closer to the rotunda both Prince George and the Duke of Wellington had taken seats, though with the crowd around them she would wager that they wouldn't see much of the fight.

By the time the footmen arrived with platters of their paper-thin slices of cold chicken and ham, it was nightfall. The orchestra in the main rotunda began playing, and she sat back to watch as, with a crash of cymbals, the gas lights hung along the walks and in the trees all went on simultaneously.

Charlotte joined in the applause, still eyeing the huge crowd for a familiar, handsome face. Nothing. Her whole life had felt like this, she realized, accepting mediocrity and all the while waiting for something — someone — exciting to come along and make everything better. Maybe it was time for her to stop waiting.

"Before the battle begins, I need to freshen up," she said, rising.

"Someone will take our box," Herbert complained, scowling.

"Stay here. Alice will accompany me. I'll be right back."

Shortly after she stepped down from the box she heard the flurry of trumpets announcing the commencement of battle. Everyone began surging toward the field, calling encouragement and clapping with excitement.

"We'll miss Waterloo, Miss Charlotte," Alice said, crowding close to her.

She opened her mouth to answer that she didn't care, when she saw him. Wearing black and gray, Xavier stood at the entrance to the darkened Druid's Walk, gazing at her. Her heart sped. He'd come.

"I need a breath of air, Alice," she said. "Why don't you wait right here against the fence, and I'll be back in a moment."

"I can't leave you alone here! Lord and Lady Birling will sack me!"

"They'll never know. I promise. And this way you can watch the battle. I'll be fine. I promise."

"Oh, Miss Charlotte, this is not a good idea."

"It's a wonderful idea. Wait here."

Still looking terribly uneasy, her maid nodded. "Yes, ma'am."

Charlotte received a few curious looks as she crossed the pavilion, but she scarcely noted them. Tonight she didn't feel like herself. Tonight she felt like someone wild and reckless and free, someone who would leave her attendant to go walking along a dark path with a handsome rake.

"You look lovely," Xavier said in a low voice as she reached his side.

"My cousin Sophia gave the gown to me."

"It suits you."

"I feel half naked."

Faded cobalt drifted down her low neckline and back up to her face again. "Not nearly naked enough," he murmured.

My goodness. He had that predatory look in his eyes, the one she'd seen in Hyde Park when his kisses had practically devoured her. Charlotte swallowed. "I'm glad you came."

"I want you to walk with me," he said, his gaze intent on her face. "But I also want to warn you. If you join me, nothing will ever be the same again. So choose carefully, Charlotte. I'm certain Beetly's waiting for you in his box. He's safe. I'm not."

"I've been safe my entire life, Xavier," she returned, then forced a nervous smile as she gazed down the path past his shoulder. "Other than the fact that it's dark, what's so spectacular down that way, anyway?"

His lips curved up in a slow, sensual smile. "Come and find out."

They weren't alone along the Druid's Walk. In several dim alcoves along the path, above the nearby sounds of battle, she could hear whispers and the unmistakable sound of lips touching lips. Her mother would have an apoplexy if she knew her daughter was visiting one of Vauxhall's infamous dark walks, much less in the company of Earl Matson.

They rounded another curve, the gloom lit only by sporadic fireworks signifying cannon fire. "Are you sure you want to miss the reenactment? You weren't there for the original, you said."

"That's the past," he returned, guiding her beyond a low overhang. "I've recently discovered a new hope for the future."

He meant her. If her heart beat any faster, it would fly from her chest. This was where she needed and wanted to be, and he was the man she needed and wanted to be with. "How far are we going?"

His soft chuckle sent a shiver down her arms. "Just here."

They angled off the path to a small glade set off from the rest of the Gardens by artfully hung blankets. He'd been planning. "What if someone sees?"

"I've taken precautions. Wilson?"

"Aye, my lord."

She wasn't surprised to see one of his footmen standing at the edge of the trail, gazing back in the direction they'd come from. "How long have you been planning this?" she asked, hoping her voice sounded less nervous than she felt inside.

"A few days. I've been thinking about it since we met, however." Inside the shelter of the blankets he faced her, drawing her into his arms. "I told you I was a good strategist," he murmured, tilting her face up to kiss her.

Charlotte moaned, let the soft pull of his mouth send her heart soaring. With no one to see, no one to interrupt, they could do as they wanted. She knew what he wanted; her. And she wanted him as well, with a strength and passion that a few weeks ago she would have thought she didn't even possess. Still, if her parents found out. . . .

"Is this wise?" she whispered, shivering as his mouth moved slowly along the line of her jaw.

"No. But I can't help myself. Forget everything outside of this place, Charlotte. Just be with me. If you want to."

"I want to." So badly, it would hurt to walk away. She remembered the bauble in her reticule and pulled it out. "Lady Ibsen recommended this to me," she said unsteadily.

He took it from her fingers. "Jeanette? When?"

"A few days ago. Herbert said it was tawdry, and she said that was the point."

A slow smile curving his sensuous mouth, Xavier fastened it behind her neck, then drew his fingers down along the length of chain to where the emerald rested between her breasts. "Not quite," he whispered, moving behind her.

"What do you —"

Her gown loosened and then slid from her shoulders. Gasping, Charlotte held the front up over her bosom. *What was she doing?* She'd gone insane, obviously. But any thought of flight vanished as he stopped in front of her again for another deep, satisfying kiss. As if of their own accord, her fingers relaxed, and her gown slid to her feet.

From the distant shouting and cheers and explosions, the Waterloo reenactors and audience seemed to be having a fine time, but she doubted it could compare with hers. Herbert would probably begin to wonder where she was, unless the bright lights distracted him, but she didn't care. Not tonight, not now. Not with Xavier.

All that stood between her and the night breeze was her thin shift. She expected to be cold, but as he slipped his fingers under the shoulders and softly peeled the cotton down her arms, she was only aware of heat and excitement and arousal. His kisses grew harder, more demanding, and she swept her arms around his shoulders to pull him closer.

"Xavier," she panted, kissing his throat as he'd kissed hers, "I refuse to be the only naked party in this."

He moaned. "I want you," he breathed, allowing her to push his jacket down his shoulders. His cravat followed, sinking to the ground in a wilted lump. With his gentle tugging her shift crept down her shoulders, exposing her breasts and then her belly and her legs to the dim moonlight and flashes of fireworks. Xavier tapped the emerald bauble again where it hung heavy and cool now against her bare skin. "Now that is how you should always wear it."

His deft fingers brushed across her breasts, and she gasped again, arching toward the pressure. "Good heavens."

Xavier chuckled, rolling her nipples between his thumb and forefinger. "Do you want to sin tonight, Charlotte?"

"That's why I'm here." She drew another unsteady breath. "But please hurry, because I don't want someone to stop us before . . ." She wanted to say *before she could be satisfied*, but that sounded completely wanton and scandalous.

She tugged his shirt free of his trousers and ran her hands up the warm skin of his chest. Smooth, and yet she could feel the steel beneath. His muscles jumped beneath her touch, and she realized that she affected him as much as his touch affected her.

With her help he pulled the shirt off over his head, and then he lowered them both to the blanketed ground. It excited her even more to know that he'd gone to such lengths to be with her. She wanted to ask what would happen tomorrow, after his male lust had been satisfied, but as he shifted her onto her back and then took her left breast into his mouth, she didn't care what might happen after tonight. She felt hot and coiled inside, growing tighter and tighter, waiting for something only he could provide.

His suckling deepened, and she wrapped her fingers into his tawny hair, pulling him harder against her. The faint mewling sounds she made hardly sounded like her, but none of this was like her. With his free hand he undid his trousers and shoved them down, then leaned down along her to kiss her deeply again.

His arousal felt big and hard against her thigh, and she coiled still tighter inside. "Xavier, now," she demanded, shifting uncomfortably.

He nudged her knees apart and settled between her legs. "Say you'll marry me," he demanded, his own voice shaking at the edges.

"But I —"

"I don't care what anyone else thinks, Charlotte," he interrupted, easing forward so that she could feel him pressing intimately between her legs. "Say you'll marry me."

She could barely form a coherent thought, much less a coherent sentence. "Yes," she rasped, lifting her hips.

Slowly he thrust forward, entering her. Charlotte yelped, but he muffled the sound against his own mouth. "Shh. Relax, my sweet. Just relax."

The pain subsided, and he resumed his slow slide deep inside her. Nothing she'd ever felt could compare to this — so . . . satisfying, and yet leaving her wanting so much more. "Xavier."

In a moment he began to move, his slow, steady rhythm drawing her tighter and tighter. With a loud cheer the fireworks exploded into a celebration of faux victory. She moaned in time with his thrusting, while faded cobalt, nearly black in the dimness, gazed closely at her. Fireworks, cheering, heat, sweat, the weight of his warm, muscled body, filled her until with a surprising rush she shattered. "You belong to me," he growled, following her into release. "Me."

For several long moments Xavier didn't want to move. In advance the plan had seemed abysmally stupid and desperate. Actually planning a rendezvous and securing a secluded glade for it. But then she'd appeared, looking for him, and it had worked.

While his breathing and heart slowed to normal and before he became too heavy for her, he buried his face in lavender-scented hair. This was where he was supposed to be; not at Waterloo gaining glory at the expense of thousands of lives, not sitting alone in Farley Park wishing Anthony were there to shoulder the burdens of the estate and title, not sitting in the smoky dark wagering or sinning with someone just so he wouldn't have to face going home alone.

Charlotte brought something into his life, something he'd known he lacked but had never been able to put a name to. In her company, with her in his arms, he felt . . . content. And indescribably happy.

The pavilion's main orchestra began playing Handel's *Music for the Royal Fireworks*, and more multicolored rockets began shooting into the sky. They'd been here too long; Charlotte's escort would be missing her. The problem, Xavier reflected, was that he didn't want to give her back, even temporarily.

"I don't suppose we could live here in Vauxhall Gardens," she said, echoing his thoughts as she slowly ran her hands along his back. "Like Robin Hood and Maid Marian?"

He chuckled as he reluctantly shifted off of her, sitting up to run a hand through his hair. "It's tempting, but it seems a bit extreme."

"I suppose so."

She shivered a little, and he reached over

to grab her shift. "We need to get you back before you freeze to death."

"Being in Herbert's company doesn't precisely warm my heart," she returned.

At the edge of frustration in her voice he leaned in and kissed her, long and deep. "That won't last any longer than tonight," he said. "You made me a promise."

Soft brown eyes met his gaze. "Short of my complete ruin, I don't see how my promise will persuade my parents." Charlotte brushed her lips against his throat. "It probably would have been better if you'd never noticed me."

His heart lurched. The thought bothered him sometimes, that he'd nearly passed her by without a thought. "No. You belong with me, Charlotte. And for that reason I'll be forever grateful to Lady Neeley and her missing bracelet." He helped her on with her gown, unable to resist kissing the nape of her neck as he fastened the back of the dress.

"Oh," she moaned softly, bowing her head.

That was that. He wouldn't be able to stand parting from her. "Charlotte, what would it take, truly, for your parents to stop this idiotic plan with Herbert? Short of my murdering the bastard, of course."

"I don't know. I've run out of logic, Xavier. They don't believe in me. And you can't force faith."

"You can encourage it, though," he stated, pulling the emerald bauble free from her

gown and setting it between her breasts
again. God, she'd bought that because she
wanted to be scandalous, with him. And he
wasn't about to abandon her to mediocrity.
"As far as I'm concerned, you've married me
already."

"Oh, Xavier," she breathed, eyes wide,
"once again there seems to be a huge chasm
between fact and faith."

"I'll bridge it, Charlotte. I'll find a way,"
he returned, shrugging into his trousers. "I
play to win."

"But my parents —"

"I'm not in love with them, Charlotte," he
said quietly, watching as she unhooked her
necklace and dropped it back into her reticule. There she was, the portrait of propriety
again. Except that he knew better. "I'm in
love with you."

"You . . ." She drew a breath, gazing at
him for a long moment. "I'll be at the
Frobisher ball tomorrow night, Xavier. Will
you be there?"

"And what will change between now and
then? We're going to see your parents tonight."

"No. Give me one more chance to reason
with them."

"Charlotte —"

"Have a little faith in me, Xavier," she
said, smiling softly.

If it had only been trust in her, he would

have acquiesced without hesitation. Risky as the delay was, he could see in her eyes how important this was to her; more important than even he probably realized. "I have faith in you, Charlotte. *That* is a fact."

With a last, lingering kiss, he took her hand and guided her back out to the path. His servant would fold up the blankets and remove all traces that anyone had ever been there. As they neared the end of the walk, the glow from the fireworks and the noise of the crowd increased.

"Look, they've set the pagoda on fire," she commented, leaning into his shoulder with an ease that made him want to reconsider relinquishing her to damned Herbert even for a moment.

"At least it's warmed the evening up some. Charlotte, I will take care of this tonight, if you wish."

"I know. But you've done so much for me. Now it's my turn." She leaned up to whisper in his ear. "I'll see you tomorrow night."

"I'll be there."

Chapter 9

Although the burning pagoda attracted the most attention last night (more, This Author is afraid, than did the actual reenactment), This Author could not help but take note of Lord Herbert Beetly, who sat through the entire spectacle alone in his box, with a decidedly angry expression on his visage.

And in a decidedly uncharacteristic display of emotion, Lord Herbert heaved a chair out of his box, smashed it to the ground, and strode away, his grand departure marred only by his unsure footing, which saw him sprawled in the grass, and then, sadly pelted by a meat pie.

This Author is told that the offending pastry was lobbed by a raucous cockney.

Lady Whistledown's Society Papers,
19 June 1816

"Obviously the solution is not to let you go anywhere without one of us as your chaperone," Lord Birling said, handing his greatcoat over to the Frobisher footman. "And getting lost at Vauxhall could have been serious. There are pickpockets and highwaymen everywhere along those paths, you know."

"And that Chinese pagoda burned to the ground! Thank heavens you weren't anywhere near it," her mother put in.

Charlotte closed her eyes for a moment. They'd been chewing this same subject for the entire day. She'd been as direct as she'd dared in her statements that she had no intention of marrying Lord Herbert Beetly, and that someone else had caught her heart. Her mother seemed to understand, but neither of her parents appeared to be able to believe that someone as spectacular as Xavier Matson could return the sentiment.

She felt less sympathetic with their nonsensical panics and doubts now, knowing just how honorable Xavier's intentions were. A man — *the* man, as far as she was concerned — desired her, wanted her in his life, as much as she wanted to be a part of his.

And since logic had obviously run as far as it could before expiring, more drastic measures had become necessary.

Of course, those measures would require Xavier's presence — and in that moment, she saw him. He stood to one side of the crowded room, gazing at her. The deep blue of his jacket brought out the blue in his eyes, and he looked like some long-forgotten Greek god come to the Frobisher ball to walk among the mortals. Her heart pounded. He'd said she belonged to him, but the reverse was true, as well. He belonged to her.

"Charlotte, I am not going to warn you again. Do not gawk at that man."

"Yes, Mama," she said absently, shrugging out of her shawl and starting across the room toward him. She'd said it was her turn to take action, and now was as good a time and opportunity as she was likely to find.

As soon as she moved, he left his post and came toward her. Her parents would never understand that she didn't care about a stupid bracelet, or Sophia's scandal, or anyone else's opinion. She behaved as she did because it was the right thing to do, not because her misbehavior would bring down London Society or the Birling family.

"Hello," she said, slowing as they met in the middle of the ballroom.

"Good evening," he returned, his gaze sweeping her from head to foot. "Any luck?"

"Not a smidge," she returned.

Brief anger and frustration flashed in his gaze. "Then perhaps you should wait here, and your parents and I will have a chat."

Charlotte shook her head. "I have a better idea."

He lifted an eyebrow. "And what might that be?"

"I love you," she whispered, taking a small step closer, her heart pounding so hard she thought it must burst through her chest. *You can do this,* she told herself. She had to. For him, for them, for her.

"I love you," he replied, tilting his head a little, obviously trying to gauge what she had in mind.

Taking a deep, steadying breath, she went up on her tiptoes, splaying her fingers along his shoulders for balance, and kissed him. All around them guests gasped and roared and tittered in a deafening cacophony. She didn't care.

She felt his stiff surprise, and then his immediate response as he deepened the kiss before lifting his head to look down at her with glinting eyes. "You are in so much trouble," he whispered, then smiled. "And so brilliant."

Xavier took her hand, turning her to face her parents. "Lord and Lady Birling, thank you for not making us wait to announce our betrothal," he said in a carrying voice, strolling in their direction, "and thank you again for giving me Charlotte. She is . . ."

His voice actually faltered a little, and Charlotte looked up at him, squeezing his hand. "We're very happy," she put in.

The baron's mouth hung open, and with visible effort he snapped it closed again. "Yes, well, we knew you didn't wish to wait to make an announcement," he stumbled, white-faced.

"Nor do we wish to wait to marry," Xavier put in, a slow grin warming his eyes. "I was at Canterbury this afternoon, securing a special license for us. I would like her to be my wife before the end of the week. I love Charlotte with all my heart. If not for her fondness for you, I think we might have eloped."

Her mother came back to life. "Well, thank heavens you didn't do that. I couldn't imagine the scandal."

Charlotte couldn't help her chuckle. She'd won. Yes, her parents — or her father, at least — would be angry, but she had a feeling that Xavier could be as persuasive with them as he'd been with her. And nothing anyone said could keep them from being together.

"Charlotte," he said softly, while a crowd of well-wishers surrounded them and her parents — who seemed swiftly to be adapting to the situation, "you are remarkable."

"You make me that way," she replied.

Xavier shook his head. "Perhaps I made you see it, but that's all. You excite me, and intrigue me, and I can't imagine being anywhere but with you."

"Just be quiet and kiss me again," she demanded, and with a chuckle he complied.

Suzanne Enoch

A lifelong lover of books, Suzanne Enoch has been writing them since she learned to read. Born and raised in Southern California, she lives a few miles from Disneyland with her collection of *Star Wars* action figures and dogs, Katie and Emma, both named after heroines from her books. The *USA Today* best-selling author is currently at work inventing the wild, wicked hero of her next historical romance.

Suzanne loves to hear from her readers, and may be reached at P.O. Box 17463, Anaheim, CA 92817-7463, or send her an email at suzie@suzanneenoch.com. Visit her website at *www.suzanneenoch.com.*

The Only One for Me

Karen Hawkins

Chapter 1

One cannot help but notice that one of society's most devoted couples of late is Lady Easterly and Mr. Riddleton. This would be a lovely pairing, as both are of fine form and similar mind, except that Lady Easterly is . . . how can This Author put it delicately . . . married.

Or is she?

Very well, of course she is. She married Viscount Easterly nearly a dozen years ago, and such a union is sure to hold up in any church or courthouse. But mere months into the marriage, the viscount abandoned her and fled to the Continent following an extremely nasty scandal involving a card game.

Which left Lady Easterly quite on her own. Her reputation is spotless and her behavior quite unexceptional, but one can only wonder. . . . What if the lady should fall in love? What then?

Lady Whistledown's Society Papers,
23 May 1816

"It shall be murder, then." Lady Sophia Throckmorton Hampton, Viscountess Easterly, glanced around to be sure none of Lady Neeley's other guests had overheard her. Fortunately, almost everyone was on the other side of the room, admiring their hostess's new bracelet. "I will skewer him through the breastbone with the fireplace poker, and then you can roast him over a candle."

Sophia's brother, John Throckmorton, the Earl of Standwick, eyed their victim doubtfully. "How long should I cook him?"

"Not more than a few minutes, I'd think. Lady Neeley's pet isn't very large."

"True. Lord Afton has a parrot twice as big. Pity we can't roast that one instead." John tilted his head to one side. "I wager it will taste just like chicken."

Sophia pressed a hand to her stomach. "I do wish Lady Neeley would take us down to dinner — we've been waiting an hour. If she doesn't do something soon, someone other than us will think to cook her bird, and they won't be funning about it."

"Richard would have done it, and well, too," John said, a wistful note in his voice.

Richard had been their younger brother as well as a scoundrel, a scamp, and a charming reprobate. Last year, while deep in his cups, he'd taken a wild ride on a spirited horse. Frightened at Richard's unsteady handling, the horse had balked at a fence and Richard had taken a horrid fall. He'd died the next day.

Sophia cleared her throat. "Richard was a master of useless knowledge."

John's answering smile was as unsteady as her own. "Though it has been a year, it is difficult to believe he won't be walking through the door at any minute, full of mischief." The smile slipped a notch. "He would be alive today had I kept him from that blasted horse."

Sophia touched her brother's arm. "He would not have listened. He was not always the best of men, but he never failed to be the best of brothers."

John hesitated, his troubled gaze meeting hers. "Except once."

Sophia's chest contracted. Though everyone had been deeply saddened by Richard's death, it had surprised no one. He had been living a dangerous life for years, but it wasn't until his confession on his deathbed that they'd all realized why — he'd been consumed with guilt. Years before, he had cheated at cards and let Sophia's then new husband take the blame.

That one card game had devastated her life. The months following the incident and Max's subsequent departure was a time she preferred not to think about — a horrible, black stretch of endless days, sleepless nights, and painful scandal, all covered with the heavy stench of false pity.

She shook her head. "That was long ago."

"Not long enough. He sold his honor and drove a wedge between you and your husband. I cannot condone such behavior."

"Had Max and I been truly in love, neither Richard nor anyone else could have torn us apart."

"I suppose, though I always thought you and Max —" John shook his head, his mouth thinned. "No matter. It was cowardly of Richard to allow Max to take the blame for cheating."

"At least Richard made a clean breast of it before he died. Come, don't mar the rest of the evening. We're both hungry and beset with ill temper. Let's talk of something more pleasant."

He sighed. "Of course. What shall we discuss? The weather? Lady Neeley's blasted jewels?" He placed a hand on his grumbling stomach and looked around the room. "I wonder if she has any other pets for our roasting plans. A poodle would not be amiss."

"Birds are one thing, but lapdogs are another altogether."

John's blue eyes rested on her face. "Speaking of lapdogs, where is your friend, Mr. Thomas Riddleton? I thought you never went anywhere without him walking alongside to hold your parcels. Rather like a large, cravat-embossed reticule."

"If you must know, he is in the country, visiting his mother."

"No doubt garnering a blessing for his upcoming nuptials."

"Nuptials?"

"Rumor has it that your friend Thomas has decided to marry. In fact, according to the latest *on dit,* he has decided to marry you."

Sophia's heart sank. "You read too much in his attendance. We are merely friends."

John's gaze grew solemn. "You should have a care, Sophia. Though I know your feelings, people are quick to assume more."

"I don't encourage such talk." At least, not intentionally. Sophia bit back a sigh. Perhaps she *had* been spending too much time with Thomas. He was handsome, well informed, and rather awkwardly gallant, not at all threatening in demeanor or action. And lately, she had been so lonely. Still, she would rather be alone than with the wrong person. "I will speak with Mr. Riddleton as soon as he returns."

"Good." John hesitated, then added, "I was afraid you were beginning to care for him."

She raised her brows. "I thought you liked Thomas?"

"Of all the pompous asses I know, he is my favorite." John crossed his long arms and rocked back on his heels, a habit he'd adopted as a youth that had never quite gone away. "All I know is that you had better dismiss Riddleton before Max returns."

"Max will not return."

"You wrote him asking for an annulment. He will not take that kindly."

"He will be relieved to see me go. I want this sham of a marriage over, and I'm certain he feels the same way. He was never the sort of man to waste his time and energies on the impossible."

"He could have changed, Sophia. You have."

"For the better, I hope. And yes, I suppose Max has changed as well. It has been twelve years, after all." She was silent a moment, mulling this over. "I wonder if he still paints. He had true talent and —" What was she doing? Whatever Max did now, it was no longer her concern.

"I've only seen one of his paintings," John mused, "but I hear they are all quite good."

"Saw? Where?"

John blinked. "Oh. I don't know. When you first married, I suppose." Before she could answer, he added, "When will Max receive your letter?"

"Any day now. In another two weeks, we will have his answer and by late summer, I will be a free woman." If, of course, her plan worked. In the years since Max's abrupt departure, she had had ample time to lay awake at night and analyze all the aspects of her missing husband's character. And what drove Maxwell Hampton was not emotion, but pride. Pure, unalloyed pride. It was that pride that would make him agree to her request for an annulment, her letter would see to that. She smiled at the thought.

"Sophia?" John said, his brow lowered. "That smile . . . I don't trust it. What did you do?"

"Nothing really . . . I just told Max that if he did not grant the annulment forthwith, I would publicly auction off his Uncle Theodore's diary."

Startled, John straightened. "Max left the diary with you?"

"He forgot it in his haste to leave town. I've kept it all this time, thinking it might come in handy. And so it has."

"Sophia, no! Do you know what a scandal that will cause? Theodore slept with half the women of the *ton!*"

She smiled smugly. "Let us just say that there is indeed a reason the Earl of Bessington has the Easterly nose."

"Bloody hell, Soph! Max will be furious."

"His pride will be pricked," she agreed far more calmly than she felt.

"Yes, but . . ." John raked a hand through his hair, oblivious of the fact that he was mussing it. "Max never answers your missives."

"No, he doesn't. But this time he will be

forced to. I won't take a note from the solicitor in answer to *this* question." Sad as it was, that was how Sophia and her erstwhile husband communicated: She wrote whenever an issue involving their joint property arose — usually about business matters and the sale of land or the return on some investment and the such — and he never answered. Each and every time she was at the point of taking matters into her own hands, she would receive word from Mr. Prichard saying that the issue, whatever it was, had been seen to.

Sophia's stomach rumbled yet again. "Where is our hostess? I'm famished."

John lifted his head and looked across the room. "Lady Neeley's by the door, speaking to Lady Mathilda. And —" His brows snapped down and he leaned forward, blinking rapidly, as if trying to clear his eyes.

"What is it?" she asked.

His brows slowly climbed to their normal height as he turned a serious look her way. "B'damn, your missive worked, and all too well. He's here, Sophia. Max has returned."

Sophia's mouth opened, then closed, then opened again, though no sound rang out. Everything around her faded into nothing as blood rushed to her head, her heart galloping as if she were running uphill and not standing in a drawing room in the best part of town. She simply could not credit it. Her mind whirled around the thought, skittered toward it, but refused to touch it.

John placed his hands on her shoulders, bending to look into her eyes. "Sophie? Did you hear —"

"Yes," she gasped, placing a trembling hand on her forehead. Max. Here. Good God. "But — how? He w-would have only gotten the letter —"

"I don't know," John said. He looked over her head in the direction he'd seen Max, then gave her shoulders a squeeze before releasing her. "You had better collect yourself. He's coming this way."

Sophia turned and looked — and then forgot about being hungry, forgot that her brother stood at her side, forgot that her new shoes pinched and her feet hurt from standing so long. All she knew was that Max — the man she'd thought she'd loved; the man who had promised never to leave her, but had; the man who had been her husband for two wonderful months and then walked out without a word — Max was across the room, making his way toward her.

He was so tall and broad shouldered, his thick hair still as dark as night, his eyes the same cutting silver that she still saw in her dreams. Emotion flooded through her, clutching her throat painfully.

In all the times she'd imagined this moment, she'd never thought she'd have to deal with such an overwhelming swell of sentiment. *It is just the shock,* she told herself desperately. *Yes, that's what it is — shock. Once I'm able to grasp that he is really here, really walking toward me, I will be able to act correctly.*

John touched her arm. "Are you well?"

Using every ounce of strength she possessed, she wrenched her gaze from Max. "I am fine." She glanced around the room and realized with a sinking heart that she was not the only one who had noticed Max. Several other people had seen him and were now pointing in his direction and whispering. Sophia knew what would come next — all those people would remember that she was also here, and once again she'd have to face a maelstrom of rumors and innuendo. "I wish we could leave."

"We can. No one would fault you for refusing to be in the same room as your husb—"

Sophia sliced a virulent glare at her brother. "Do not call Maxwell Hampton my husband. He was never my husband, though at first, I believed he lov—" Raw emotion clutched her once again, and this time tears dampened her eyes.

Blast it! She had no wish to appear weepy when she spoke to Max, especially not with so many people watching. Anger would protect her from tears. She forced herself to remember all those years ago, when Max had walked out. She remembered the talking, the pitying glances, and the hollow feeling of being alone, sleeping alone, awaking alone, eating breakfast alone, going to church alone. All of the things she'd been forced to do because her husband, in a fit of pique, had walked out of their house and never returned. Warm, familiar anger stirred in her veins.

"Hello, Standwick." Max's deep voice seemed to fill the air and heat it.

John nodded briefly. "Easterly. How are you?"

So polite, so formal. Which was a good thing, as several people had edged closer, hoping to hear their conversation. Everything said would be repeated, discussed, and analyzed. Taking a deep breath, Sophia forced herself to meet Max's gray gaze — and immediately wished she hadn't.

From a distance, he had appeared much the same. But up close, she could see that his face was harder now; the slash of cheekbones more arrogant, if that was possible. Strands of silver were threaded through his hair at the temple, which gave him a slightly saturnine appearance. He was leaner, and somehow larger, at the same time, as if he'd grown in presence somehow. But it was more than that — beneath his urbane gaze was a streak of red-hot anger. It seared through her, heating her skin like a roaring fire.

"Max," she managed to say through suddenly dry lips. "H-How nice to see you."

He nodded once, his gaze traveling slowly over her, touching on her hair, her eyes, her lips. A jolt of recognition flickered through her, a rampant fire that made her shiver and melted her resolve to appear unmoved. She had to fight the impulse to take a step forward, toward the man who had left her so callously, toward the man who would, if she gave him the chance, reject her yet again so swiftly, so certainly, that her heart would finally break.

The realization lit her ire and fanned her irritation back to its normal heights. Damn him. It was all she could do to force her mouth into a false smile and say through lips suddenly stiff, "It has been a long time."

He nodded curtly. "So it has."

Just the sound of his voice sent a tremble through her.

He reached out and took her limp hand from her side. Then he bowed and brushed his lips over the back of her glove. To her utter dismay, a jolt of lust hit her, fanning over her skin, tightening her breasts, her nipples beading as if in anticipation.

She closed her eyes and let the wave channel through her. How could she have forgotten this? There had always been something raw and physical between them. A connection of the basest kind, she realized as she fought to control her traitorous body and searched for some words to smooth over the stretching silence.

Say something! she told herself. *Everyone is looking. Waiting.* But somehow, her body and mind were no longer speaking of their own accord, and instead, her fingers tightened over his, as if to never let go.

And there they stood, looking at one another, hands clasped, neither speaking, equal amounts of anger and lust pulsing between them.

John cleared his throat. "Ah . . . Sophia?"

Heat flushed her cheeks and Sophia yanked her hand back to her side. Good God, how silly that must have looked! She didn't risk a glance at Max; she couldn't stand to see the smirk that must now be on his face. "I — I'm sorry. I was just — I'm afraid — I'm just —"

"Famished," John said smoothly. "As are we all. I wonder when dinner will be served?"

"Soon, I hope," Max replied, his voice deeper than before, as if he, too, was shaken. His gaze remained on Sophia. "You've changed your hair," he said abruptly.

Her hand moved toward her head. Of course. He'd always wanted her to grow her hair long, but she never had, declaring it took too much time to put up. But after he'd left, she'd felt the ridiculousness of those words. "I haven't cut it since —" She caught herself just in time. It was a trick, an attempt for her to lay her heart bare so that he could stomp it into the ground. But she was no fool. "It is rather long." She swallowed. "So. Max. What brings you to London?"

Something in his eyes flared, a flash of tightly controlled anger that was frightening in its intensity. "You know very well what brought me here. We have much to talk about, we two. I will call on you in the morning."

Blast him! Did he have to speak so peremptorily? Sophia lifted her chin and said frostily, "I will not be home in the morning."

His gaze narrowed and he stepped closer, his broad shoulders blocking the light from the candelabra. "I will be there at ten."

"I have visits at ten."

"Then I will come at nine. We can breakfast while we talk." Sophia stiffened in outrage and a humorless smile touched his lips. "Did you expect pleasantries? If you did, you were sadly mistaken. I do not take threats kindly."

"I thought to force a quick answer from you, not a visit. Besides, it wasn't a threat. It was a promise."

"I don't take those kinds of promises well, either."

"Yes, well, it doesn't matter, for you cannot

come tomorrow. I will not be home at nine, either."

He raised his brows. "You are forgetting something."

"What's that?"

"I know you. You do not rise early in the mornings. You like to lay in bed. . . ." His voice feathered to a halt, deep and warm, both threat and promise in the depths.

John cleared his throat again. "Yes . . . well . . . I uhm —" He glanced helplessly at Sophia.

"I . . . I . . ." Damn. What could she say? No matter what, she had to meet Max face-to-face sooner or later. "Very well. I will see you at breakfast. *But* I eat very, very early."

His gaze narrowed. "How early?"

She started to say six but caught herself just in time. Discomforting Max was one thing, but getting up before it was properly light was another. "Eight," she said, temporizing. That was still four entire hours earlier than she normally ate. Her servants would be up in arms.

"Very well. Eight it will be." He recaptured her hand, only this time, the kiss he pressed to her fingers was more substantial, the heat of his mouth burning through the soft material of her glove.

Sophia's breath fluttered, her legs trembled. After all these years, after all the hurt she had so carefully built into a solid wall of anger, the scoundrel still had the ability to turn her legs into water with the most simple of touches. Blast him to hell.

Lady Neeley let out a cry — something about her bracelet's clasp being broken. Max reluctantly released her hand, gave John a respectful bow, then returned to their hostess's side.

As soon as Max was out of earshot, John said, "Sophia, we don't have to stay if you don't wish. I'm certain everyone would understand."

No they wouldn't. Oh, they would *pretend* to understand and offer their support, and all the while they'd laugh behind their fans. Sophia knew exactly what the world thought of a left-behind wife — a horrid concoction of pity and superiority, all of it bitter and none of it palatable. She lifted her chin. "Never let it be said that a mere Hampton had rousted a Throckmorton from the field of battle."

John adjusted his cravat as if it had grown a notch too tight. "Do you think he'll grant the annulment?"

"Not without cost."

John appeared troubled. "What cost?"

"That," Sophia said grimly, "is the question."

Chapter 2

And as if the excitement of the missing bracelet wasn't enough to fill a column, allow This Author to be the first to inform —

Viscount Easterly has returned to London!

Indeed, the prodigal nobleman appeared quite unexpectedly at Lady Neeley's ill-fated supper and surely would have remained the prime source of gossip had Lady N's bracelet not gone so inconveniently missing. By all appearances, Lady Easterly was unaware that her husband planned to attend, and according to several witnesses, the pair were shooting positive daggers at each other throughout the supper — or rather, throughout the soup course, which is all the guests were allowed to eat before the evening fell quite apart.

Indeed, one lady commented (quite callously, in This Author's opinion) that it was too bad the evening was

423

The next morning, Mr. Prichard entered the sparsely furnished antechamber of his office. He halted on seeing a visitor standing beside the window, face tilted down to observe the street below. A high brimmed hat shadowed the man's face, his broad form blocking the early morning light.

"I am sorry," Prichard said, trying not to sound surprised. It was a rare occurrence that anyone reached the office before he did. "May I assist you?"

The man turned his head, the early morning light slanting across his face.

Prichard took a startled step forward. "My lord! How wonderful — when did you arrive — I —" His voice would go no further.

A deep ripple of laughter broke from the viscount, the somber expression dispelled with a peculiarly sweet smile. He removed his hat, the sun lighting the planes of his face and glinting off his black hair. "I am informing you of my return this very instant." He spread his arms wide. "Behold, the prodigal son returneth."

It had been years since the solicitor had visited Viscount Easterly in Italy. The intervening years had changed the man; he had grown broader of shoulder and leaner of appearance. There was a hardness, a straight line of lip and brow that was far more somber than the man's thirty-two years warranted. Of course, that was only natural, considering everything that had transpired. Indignation filled Mr. Prichard's heart. "You should have never been forced to leave. It is a disgrace that —" He faltered to a halt. The viscount had just thrust his hand forward, as if to shake hands.

Mr. Prichard gulped. "I — It would be unseemly if I were to —"

Max took the man's hand and shook it firmly. Living on his own had shown him several things, one of which was the value of a true heart. "Come, Prichard! I've entrusted you with my soul, as it were. The least I can do is shake your hand."

Mr. Prichard's thin face heated. "Your father never would have approved of —"

"My father lost the family fortune by the time I was sixteen. While I esteem his worthy qualities, there were things about him that I have chosen not to repeat." At one time, Max would have cut out his own tongue rather than admit such a home truth about his father. But the time for politeness was long past. "Had you been a lesser man, you might have robbed me blind whilst I was gone. You did not and for that, I thank you."

Prichard gulped a disclaimer before gesturing toward his office.

Max tucked his hat under his arm as he preceded the solicitor into the warmly lit room and found a chair nearest the desk. As he took his seat, his gaze wandered to the window, to the familiar sight of London's soot-covered buildings and the welcome sound of English voices raised in greeting as street vendors lined the cobblestones.

Prichard took his seat behind the desk, curiosity burning brightly in his gaze. "My lord, I am so glad to see you! Have you been to see the viscountess?"

"We dined together last night, after a fashion." And what a shambles that had been. Lady Neeley's blasted bracelet had gone missing and she'd raised such a rude fuss that everyone had left the dinner in high dudgeon. Which was fine, as far as Max was concerned. It had been pure hell sitting in a room so close to Sophia, and yet not being able to even look her way.

He shifted in his seat, restlessness making his knees ache. "She looked well." Better than well. She had appeared radiantly healthy.

"So the viscountess was happy to see you?"

"She did not flee the room. I took that as an encouraging sign." He reached into his pocket, pulled out a folded missive, and handed it to Prichard. "Read this."

The solicitor took a pair of wire spectacles out of his pocket and placed them on his nose, then squinted at the letter. "She has your uncle's diary? The uncle who supposedly had an affair with the queen?"

"Yes. The diary was locked in the vault and I didn't think to take it with me when I left so quickly. Apparently, Sophia found it. If the diary is made open to the public, the parentage of half the *ton* could be called into question."

The solicitor handed the missive back to Max. "Would she do such a thing?"

Max smiled faintly. "She is as pigheaded as I."

"You seemed the perfect couple. I have often wondered if perhaps you'd been a trifle precipitous in deciding to leave the viscountess."

"What else could I have done? Take her with me into exile? Condemn her to the same hell to which she had condemned me? I couldn't —" He clamped his mouth closed. Damn it, it had been twelve years. He should be used to this feeling, the sense of loss, of betrayal. But somehow, he wasn't. "Lady Easterly made her decision and I made mine."

"My lord, I do not blame you for leaving;

you had every right." The solicitor shifted in his chair. "Whatever the circumstances, I must say that you have been more than generous in dispersing funds to her ladyship. I find it curious how you have managed to bring in such sums of money in these uncertain times. You have never explained that to me."

"No," Max replied calmly, "I never have."

Prichard pursed his lips and then said in a slow, cautious manner, "Last month I went to visit Lord Shallowford. His lordship has an extensive art collection."

Max kept his expression perfectly bland. "How pleasant for him."

"He is quite proud of his collection. While I was at his estate, I saw a painting he had recently acquired." Prichard paused meaningfully. "In Italy."

"Many paintings come from Italy."

"Not like this one. It was a pastoral scene, exactly like a painting I once saw in your lodgings almost ten years ago. If I remember correctly, the paint was still wet. In fact, I believe you were debating the placement of a certain tree."

Damn. How clumsy of him.

"Lord Shallowford said the painter went by the name of Bellacorte." Prichard coughed delicately. "Bellacorte is one of your family names, I believe."

"My great-grandmother was Italian. But

then you know that."

"Of course," Prichard said with a deprecating air. "Lord Shallowford mentioned the value of the painting, too. May I say you are certainly coming up in the art world?"

"I am doing well, thank you." Better than well. In every way but one.

The solicitor cleared his throat. "Will you give her ladyship the annulment?"

"No. Not yet, anyway." Max leaned back in the chair and crossed one booted leg over the other. "I have things to discover before I take that step."

"But the diary?"

"While I'm here, there is little danger she'll act. The mere hope that I might cooperate will keep her from doing anything rash. Meanwhile . . ." Max pursed his lips. "What do you know about a fellow by the name of Riddleton?"

Prichard's gaze shadowed. "I know a little. He is well liked by his peers."

"I think he is a portentous windbag. And his spelling is atrocious."

"Spelling? Are you saying Riddleton has written to you?"

"Four long, pompous pages outlining all the reasons I should grant my wife an annulment." Max absently rubbed his chest, where a hollow ache had formed. He'd known the day would come when Sophia would wish to be free. He'd known it the day he'd left. But when and if Sophia found another man, Max would damn well make sure it was someone worthy.

"My lord, if you are concerned that Mr. Riddleton is a fortune hunter, you may rest easy on that score. He is a very wealthy man."

Max's gaze narrowed. "You seem to have already looked into this matter."

Prichard colored faintly. "When I heard he was frequently found in Viscountess Easterly's presence, I made certain inquiries. I thought you'd wish me to do so."

"What did you discover?"

"Not much. In fact . . . he seems devoted to the viscountess."

Of course the fool was taken with her — who wouldn't be? Sophia was an intelligent, vibrant, beautiful woman. Too much of a woman for a man who would take four pages to ask one blasted question. And a question he had no business asking in the first place. The impertinence of it tried Max's patience to the limits. "Damn it, but I am long overdue for this journey." His gaze landed on the clock by Prichard's elbow. "I must go if I'm to meet her ladyship for breakfast." He stood.

The solicitor followed suit. "Of course. I do hope you mean to stay in England."

"That depends on my fair wife," Max answered shortly. If he closed his eyes right this moment, he knew what he would see — the same thing he'd seen last night. The same thing he'd seen the night before, and the night before that: Sophia's face, her luminous eyes fringed with thick brown lashes, her soft lips parted. When he'd met her at Lady Neeley's, it had been all he could do not to sweep her against him and kiss her senseless, tasting those lips, making her lashes tremble on her cheeks as he brought her — brought them both — to the edge of passion and beyond.

That was the way it had always been for him, from the first time he'd seen her, which was why he'd demanded that they marry so quickly. Last night, seeing her made richer by the years, her body delightfully rounded, her chin still held at that ridiculously proud angle . . . in that one moment, Max had faced the truth. He had convinced himself he was returning to England to see if this Riddleton fellow was good enough for Sophia, but that hadn't been Max's purpose at all. He'd returned home to stake a claim. Sophia belonged to him and no one else, and he would be damned if he would stand by and let some buffoon try and take his place.

If he found one sign — just one — that Sophia's feelings for him weren't entirely spent, then he'd alter the course of the earth and win her back. Heart set, he took his leave of the solicitor and set out for Sophia's house.

At fifteen minutes after eight, Sophia was seated at her breakfast table dressed in her best morning gown of blue muslin, her hair done to perfection, her plate piled high with a sampling of every dish that sat steaming on the buffet. She pressed a hand to her stomach; she was too nervous to eat a bite, but she refused to appear anything other than completely at ease when Max finally arrived.

If he arrived. She eyed the clock with a resentful glare. He was already fifteen minutes late. That shouldn't have surprised her, though it was definitely stretching her nerves. Did he think she'd wait forever while he just —

A light scratching sounded at the door. Sophia's heart tripled a beat. She hurriedly filled her fork with ham. "Yes?"

The door opened and the new butler entered, her brother sauntering behind him. "The Earl of Standwick."

Sophia dropped her fork back onto her plate. "Thank you, Jacobs." She barely waited for him to close the door before she whipped a razor-sharp gaze on John. "What are *you* doing here?"

"I came to eat your food." John loped to the buffet and proceeded to lift the silver covers, the gentle clangs filling the air. "There are no kippers."

She refused to be distracted. "I can handle Max quite well on my own."

"Of course you can." He replaced the covers and then turned toward the table, pausing when he caught sight of her plate. His eyes widened an excessive amount. "Good God! Are you going to eat all of that?"

"Every bite."

He dropped into a chair opposite hers. "Believe it or not, I'm too nervous to eat. I didn't even sleep."

"Yes, well, I slept like a rock," Sophia lied, briskly cutting her ham into small bites.

"Wish I had slept, but I kept dreaming of that night. You know, when Max left." John leaned his elbows on the table. "Can't decide what is worse — guilt or anger."

Sophia knew exactly what he meant. Whatever the mix was, it was not pleasant. But she still had no wish to discuss the issue. She needed all of her faculties sharp and ready when Max finally arrived. "Can we speak of something else, please?"

"Of course." John rubbed a hand over his face. "The worst of my dream was that this time, I knew Max was innocent, but I couldn't say anything. It was as if my tongue had been glued to the roof of my mouth and —"

"John. I do not wish to speak about that matter. Not again."

"Oh. Of course." He immediately fell into a brown study, his expression distant.

Silence reigned. Sophia drew a design in her eggs with the tines of her fork, remembering another time she'd waited on Max at a breakfast table much like this one, only he hadn't returned. Her throat constricted. One wouldn't think a memory could hurt, but she knew from long practice that memories could slice one's heart as readily as the sharpest knife.

"Blast it, Sophia!" John leaned back, his chair creaking at the sudden move. "We must talk about this. When I remember events from that night, it makes so much sense. But back then, when Lord Chudrowe threw down the cards and looked at Max as if . . . well, everyone knew who had been winning. We all just assumed it was Max. And he sat there, icy cold, back stiff as a board, not uttering a blasted word. It was as if he was daring someone to say it aloud." John shoved himself to his feet to pace angrily about the room. "Why didn't he speak out?"

"Pride," Sophia said wearily. "It is the beginning and end with him."

"Damn! One word, that's all he had to say. And Richard —" John halted, his mouth thinned.

Sophia replaced her fork beside her plate. "I'm as much at fault as Richard. When Chudrowe called Max a cheat, I had the opportunity to change things. I could have said something, championed Max. Instead, I asked him why. Not if. But *why*. That is what truly damned him."

"Sophia, even if you had championed Max, everyone would have assumed it was only because you were his wife."

"It was because I *was* his wife that what I said had so much effect. I, who should have had more faith, more trust —" To her horror, a tear leaked out.

John was beside her instantly, shoving his handkerchief into her hand.

"Thank you." Sophia wiped at her eyes. She hadn't thought she had any more tears left. "There is no sense in going back over this. What Max and I had is gone, if it ever existed." Over the years, she'd grown to doubt even that. Until yesterday. Their meeting had stirred up . . . something. A vestige of feeling perhaps, a memory of What Had Been. But surely nothing more than that.

John scowled. "Though Max was given a raw treatment, there is no excusing the way he abandoned you. You had to face the scandal alone, too."

Sophia opened her mouth, but there was a knock at the door. The sound seemed to reverberate in the small room.

Jacobs entered, and Sophia hurried to tuck the handkerchief out of sight. "Yes?"

"There is a gentleman demanding to see you who says —" Jacobs frowned. "My lady, he says he is Viscount Easterly."

"Show him in."

Jacobs lifted his brows, but bowed and did as requested. Sophia stood and practically ran to the mirror over the fireplace. She adjusted her hair and pinched her cheeks, adding some color.

"What are you doing?" John asked, amusement in his tone.

"Nothing. You can leave now. I will deal with this."

"Of course you will." John made his way to the buffet. He took a warmed plate and piled it high with ham and eggs. "I shall leave as soon as I eat."

"John," she said, narrowing her eyes. As much as she loved John, he was the most obstinate man of her acquaintance, except for Max. "I do not want —"

The door opened and Max entered, his broad shoulders and muscular physique at distinct odds when compared to John's lanky handsomeness. The room seemed to warm, and Sophia found that she had to gasp to fill her lungs with air. He was dressed for morning visits, and looked even more handsome than he had the night before.

He waited for Jacobs to close the door before turning to face her, his dark brows accentuating the silver of his eyes. "I apologize for being late. There are so many carts and wagons on the road that one can scarcely get about town."

"That is quite all right. I hope you do not mind that we did not wait on you."

Max's silver gaze swept past her to her plate where it sat on the table, piled with food. Humor sparkled in his eyes. "So I see." His gaze flickered back to her. "You used to hate mornings."

"It has been many years since I slept 'til noon," she said loftily, ignoring John's choked laugh. She sent her brother a quelling glance.

"Another change," Max said. "I daresay there are many."

"Lud, yes," John said. "Maxwell, I want to say how sorry we all are about Richard's —"

"There is no need to bring up past history. I never think of it myself."

He appeared at ease, so . . . calm. Sophia wished she could say the same. Her heart was beating a thousand times faster than was normal, her body piqued with awareness. How could she have forgotten how attractive Max was? How masculine and overtly sensual? Especially when humor lurked in his cool gray eyes. That, Sophia decided, was when he was at his most deadly.

"Sophia?" John's voice broke her reverie. "Perhaps we should sit."

"Oh. Yes." She gathered her thoughts, wishing she could fan some of the heat from her cheeks. "Max, would you like some breakfast?"

"No, thank you. I ate some time ago." He waited for her to sit before taking the chair at her left.

John followed them, placing his plate before him and picking up his fork and knife. "You're missing a sumptuous meal. Sophia's cook does wonders with eggs."

"I'm sure she does," Max said quietly, his voice the brush of velvet on damp skin.

Sophia had to fight a shiver.

John spoke up. "You know, Easterly, you're lucky Sophia will even talk to you. You left her and she has every right to be furious. Which is why she wants an annulment."

Sophia kicked John under the table.

"Ow!" He peered under the tablecloth. "What in the hell was that?"

Sophia wished her brother to Hades or some other equally uncomfortable place, like Leeds or Harrowgate. "I daresay you bumped your knee on something."

John rubbed his shin. "Whatever it was, it was pointed and sharp."

"Rather like your head," she returned,

"I see that some things have not changed at all," Max said drily.

"Sophia has always had a devil of a temper," John agreed, returning to his plate.

Max smiled. "You should read some of the

438

missives she sent me. My favorite was when she traced my family roots from myself all the way back to a worm. She used colored ink, too. I had that one framed."

Sophia narrowed her gaze. "You did not."

"Indeed I did," he replied gently. "It hangs on the wall by my desk even now."

She sniffed. "It is possible that some of my first letters might have sounded somewhat irritated —"

"Irate," Max corrected. He crossed his arms and leaned back in his chair. "Angry. Fuming. Enraged —"

"Irritated," she repeated firmly.

John opened his mouth —

"No." Sophia impaled him with a fierce look. "Unless you wish to leave my house with a spoon embedded in your forehead, you will stay out of this conversation."

John smacked his mouth closed, though his eyes danced with humor.

"Thank you." She then eyed Max, who sat regarding them with a faint smile. "Since John brought it up. . . . *Will* you give me the annulment?"

His gaze slid over her face, lingering on her lips. After a moment, he said in a quiet voice, "Perhaps."

Perhaps? What kind of an answer was that? "I have the diary."

"I know. I shouldn't have left it with you, but who knew you'd use it in such a nefarious manner."

"Nefarious!" Her cheeks heated. "I want this farce of a marriage over."

His expression froze. After a moment, he said, "I will give you an answer when I've thought it through."

Sophia tried not to be impatient. And really, she wasn't quite sure why she was. After all, she'd waited twelve years. But somehow, she wanted action now. "I will not wait longer than a week. And then your uncle's diary will go up for auction."

Anger glittered in Max's eyes. "Sophia, do not press me to —"

"Easy, you two." John cut his ham. "Max, perhaps you should know that Sophia wants an annulment because she has a beau."

Sophia clenched her hands about the edge of the table to keep from leaping up and boxing John's ears. What on earth was he doing? John had never been a model of propriety, but this was outside of enough.

"A beau?" A note of accusation colored Max's words. "A little early, isn't it?"

"It has been twelve years," she replied stiffly.

"But only a week since I received your request for an annulment."

"I am not asking for the annulment because I wish to be with someone else. I just wish to be free."

"To marry again?"

Marry again? "Ha! I'd rather be poached like an egg and left to die on the banks of a dry riverbank!"

Max's brow cleared, while John choked, chortled, then clamped his napkin over his mouth. After a moment, he removed his napkin and said in a hoarse voice, "God love you, Sophie. No one has a way with words like you."

"I was just stating a fact," Sophia said a little defensively. Every once in a while, when she least expected it, a blast of anger escaped from somewhere deep in her soul, surprising her as much as it did those around her. It was most disconcerting.

John chuckled, then looked at Max. "So, Easterly! How long will you be with us?"

Max shrugged. "I don't know. Last night's dinner made me realize how little I've missed the *ton*. Lady Neeley made me yearn for the shores of Italy."

"Me too, and I've never been there. She usually has the most exquisite dinners and everyone flocks to them even though she is a rude old bat."

"I cannot believe she had her own nephew searched."

"I know. She seemed determined to prove that someone at the dinner had stolen her silly jewelry. You know, Max, since you have the disadvantage of not knowing Lady Neeley at all, I am rather surprised she didn't accuse you."

"Accuse Max?" Sophia snapped instantly. "She would not *dare!*"

Two pairs of eyes locked on her.

"Sophia!" John said, his brows as high as they would go.

Blast it, she was making a fool of herself. Sophia cleared her throat. "I'm sorry, but the whole thing is preposterous. All the good that John and I managed to do trying to set things right after Richard's death will be undone if Lady Neeley begins such a horrid rumor."

"That's true," John agreed, replacing his fork and knife beside his plate and regarding his empty plate with fond regret.

"You needn't have bothered," Max said. "I don't care for the opinion of others."

"You should care," John said, flickering an irritated glance at Max. "What people think of you, they also think of my sister."

"Balderdash," Sophia said. "I just don't want anyone to think things that are not true. We've suffered enough for such folly."

"Sadly, I agree," John said. He wiped his mouth and placed his napkin on the table, then stood. "Sophia, that was lovely. Wish I could stay, but I'm due at White's."

Max stood as well. "Allow me to walk you out. I have an appointment myself and really should be going."

That was it, Sophia realized with a sudden

sinking feeling. Max had agreed to consider the annulment, more or less. In a way, she had accomplished what she wanted. So why did she feel so lost?

Silently, Sophia rose and followed them to the door, her napkin absently clutched in her hand. "John, do stop by later."

John bent and kissed Sophia's cheek. "I shall. Good day, my dear." He winked once and then left. Sophia heard him asking Jacobs for his coat.

Max followed, but just as he reached the door, he paused and then turned. "There is one more thing I must ask."

To hide her trembling hands, Sophia clasped them behind her back, the napkin crushed between her fingers. "Of course."

Max closed the space between them. He reached up and flicked the tips of his fingers over her cheek, his touch sliding from there to her chin. His gaze deepened.

His touch sent jolts of awareness through her. "Wh-what do you want to ask?" she stammered.

The question hovered in the air for a scant moment, then Max bent down and pressed his lips to hers.

It was a chaste kiss, a simple touch of lips to lips. But it didn't remain simple for long. As it ever had, the moment Max touched her, things began to change. Her skin heated, her breath shortened, her body softened in yearning. It felt so right. So incredibly right. It had been so long since a man had touched her like this, kissed her, made her melt inside. Sophia threw herself into the kiss, committing herself to it body and soul. Her arms crept around his neck, her mouth opening beneath his lips.

Max gave a muffled groan, and then he deepened the kiss. His mouth teased and tormented, his tongue sliding between her lips. His hands cupped her bottom through her dress and held her firm against him.

A low moan grew in Sophia's throat. God, but he was so *good* at this. And how she had missed it, missed him. She pulled him closer, straining to get nearer to him somehow, though there was nothing but clothing between them now. His powerful legs pressed against hers through her skirts, sending delicate flashes of fire through her stomach and lower. . . . Just as Sophia's body began a trembling assent, Max broke the kiss. He loosened his hold, his chest rising and falling, his skin flushed.

Sophia's entire body was afire. Heaven help her, but she wanted him. She pressed a hand to her cheek, aware that she was trembling from head to foot.

Good God, this was not a good thing. Of course, it was *purely* physical. Yes, she told herself desperately, it was just a reaction, like flinching when you touched a hot coal.

She was aware of his gaze and realized that she needed to say something. Find the words to make the moment go away. But she couldn't get her lips to move.

"I believe that has answered my question," he said, his voice velvet rough against her ravished nerves.

"Question? What question? That I still enjoy kisses? It was nothing."

He gave her a burning look. "It was more than nothing and you know it."

"Oh? How can you tell?"

"You dropped your napkin."

Her gaze followed his to the floor. A pool of white lay at her feet. Blast. It must have fallen from her unfeeling fingers. "That proves nothing," she finally said. "My hand just went numb. I — It often does that."

Oh dear, where had that come from? She could tell from his stunned look that she had at least made an impression.

A faint quirk of humor warmed his eyes. "Your hand goes numb? How long has that been happening?"

"Oh . . . weeks," she said airily, determined to stay the course. "In fact, it has happened so often that I scarcely notice it any more."

He chuckled. "You'd cut off your nose rather than admit that I affected you, wouldn't you?"

She tried to collect her thoughts, her mind scattered a thousand different directions.

"I — I hope you don't think that just because you kissed me, that I will give you the diary. I am quite serious in my request, Max. I want an annulment or I will auction the diary to the highest bidder."

His mouth curved in a smile that was arrogant and smug. "Will you be at the Hargreaves' Grand Ball?"

What was this? "Perhaps," she answered cautiously.

"Then I will see you there and we will discuss this more thoroughly." His gaze spilled over her once more, molten silver that burned even as it pleasured. "Until then, Sophia." He gave her one last smile, then turned and walked out.

Sophia was left standing in the middle of the room, one hand on her still-tingling lips, her body shivering, her mind awhirl with the realization that after all these years, after all the hurts, after all was said and done, Max still had the ability to melt her bones into a puddle of desire with nothing more than a touch of his lips.

Her thoughts too chaotic to lend themselves to something as mundane as morning visits, Sophia retired to the solitude of her room.

But once there, she found the quiet ringingly loud. She paced back and forth between the bed and the fireplace, her mind racing. Why had she reacted to Max's kisses in such a way? She'd meant to remain aloof, composed. But all that had fled under the force of his passion.

She pressed her hands to her cheeks. There had always been a physical bond between them. But she'd forgotten the strength of that bond and how it affected her emotions. "It's nothing," she told her reflection as she passed it in her pacing, trying to ignore her kiss-swollen lips and glowing skin. "It will go away and everything will be back the way it was." Just like Max.

She pressed a hand to her chest, where it ached with the fury of her response. Honestly, this was ridiculous. Her heart wasn't still tied to Max's; it couldn't be. She'd just been startled and thus had reacted far more strongly than she'd expected. After all, their previous union had been extremely passionate and exquisitely physical. Added to that, it had been twelve long, lonely years since she'd experienced the wonder of genuine love-making, something she had enjoyed immensely. *Of course* her body had overreacted at Max's touch.

The reasonableness of the explanation soothed her. Sophia brushed her fingertips over her lips, the pressure of his mouth lingering yet. She still missed that portion of their lost relationship — the joy and intimacy of being completely uninhibited with a man. The memories flooded back, fresher and more poignant than before, and she paused in the center of the room, remembering with renewed vigor the breathtaking feel of his hands, the delightful heat of his mouth, the tortuously delicious taste of his bared skin, the —

"No!" She sunk her chin to her chest and began pacing more furiously than before. That was all in the past and there was no gain to be had in such thinking. If she wanted the warmth of a real relationship again, she'd have to find some way to get Max to agree to the annulment. Her future lay somewhere else, with someone who would never leave her. Someone who did not return only because she'd threatened to expose his family to ridicule.

In truth, that part hurt — that she'd been forced to such low tricks. But she was so tired of being tied to a man who did not care. Who did not seem capable of ever caring.

Her mind flew to the kiss, to the deep tenderness she had felt. What had he been trying to prove? That she was still a victim for his sensual spell? Blast it, she hoped she had not shown her weakness. Surely that one kiss wouldn't lead him to make such a hasty conclusion. Sophia plopped down on the edge of her bed, her arms crossed as she made up her mind. Whatever had happened this morning, she would not be so weak again.

When next she met Maxwell Hampton, she would be ready . . . for anything.

Chapter 3

This Author once again proves herself the most intrepid and meticulous journalist in London. Herewith, the guest list from Lady Neeley's failed dinner party:

The Earl and Countess of Canby, with their daughter, Lady Mathilda Howard.

The Earl of Standwick, brother of Lady Easterly.

Lord and Lady Easterly (although all accounts point to their having arrived separately).

Lord and Lady Rowe.

Lord Alberton.

Lady Markland.

The Hon. Mr. Benedict Bridgerton.

The Hon. Mr. Colin Bridgerton.

Mr. Brooks, nephew of the hostess.

Mr. Thompson, of the 52nd Foot Guards, son of Lord Stoughton.

Mr. and Mrs. Dunlop, with their son Mr. Robert Dunlop, also of the 52nd Foot.

Mrs. Featherington, widow, with her daughter Miss Penelope Featherington.

Mrs. Warehorse, widow.

Miss Martin, companion to the hostess.

And, of course, Lady Neeley.

The above names should not be construed as a list of suspects, although of course that is what Lady Neeley insists it is. One would be remiss, however, if one did not point out that Lady Neeley's name is also on the list.

Lady Whistledown's Society Papers,
31 May 1816

Since she wouldn't be seeing Max until Lady Hargreaves' Grand Ball, Sophia had to wait a little longer to prove her indifference. It made perfect sense that one should look one's best while making such an important point, so she dressed in a ravishing gown of cornflower blue overlaid with a white silk netting, her blonde hair twisted onto her head with little tendrils curling before each ear, her feet encased in a gorgeous pair of new beaded white slippers that sparkled with every step. She knew she looked her best when the footman's mouth dropped a little as she walked into the front foyer on her way to the carriage.

She arrived at exactly ten, a long line of coaches filling the street before the house, lights blazing in the darkness. Lady Hargreaves held one and only one ball at the height of the season, a very paltry, frugal attempt to repay the many invitations she received throughout the course of the year. The old woman disliked spending her fortune on anything that smacked of splendor, luxury, or comfort, so she offered little in the way of refreshments or entertainment. Yet still people flocked to her grand ball, some to see how scavengerly the old woman could be; others to guess which of her many grandchildren was currently in favor. Since Lady Hargreaves had a disconcerting habit of taking offense at the slightest imagined wrong, every year a different grandchild could be seen holding the position of favorite. It was said that whoever was in favor when the old lady died would inherit a fortune. All told, it was a rather macabre game of musical chairs.

Sophia arrived in the main ballroom to find that Lady Hargreaves had hired an insufficient orchestra. The talking of the guests overpowered the rather desultory efforts of the musicians, making dancing nearly impossible. The rooms were already warm, and the faint musty odor that permeated the entire ballroom due to the fact that it was only used for this one event a year added to the general discomfort of the many guests, all of whom were standing around, gossiping with fevered determination in an effort to overcome their boredom.

Sophia made her way through the room, nodding to this acquaintance and smiling at that. Her cheeks pinkened when Lord Roxbury walked by, gracing her with a wink. The man was a sad scamp. He'd attempted to begin a flirtation with her on more than one occasion after Max had left, but by that time, Sophia had hardened her heart against all men and she'd sent him on his way. Still, she couldn't help but give him an appreciative glance; he was an attractive man for all that.

She made her way to the far side of the room, near the terrace doors, catching sight of her brother leaning against a wall, looking with some misgiving at the contents of the plate in his hand.

As she made her way to his side, he held out the plate for her inspection. "I've never seen cake this stale."

She lifted on tiptoe to peer at the morsel. "It does look rather dry."

He tapped a fork on it. "Hard as a rock. Dropped a piece on my foot and bruised my small toe."

Sophia shook her head ruefully. "I daresay Lady Hargreaves didn't spend more than twenty pounds on this entire affair. She is invited everywhere on account of her fortune and yet she has not the grace to offer fresh cake for her guests."

"The music is appalling, the rooms stifling, and the food . . ." He glanced around and then surreptitiously pulled a flask from his inner pocket and held it over the cake, dribbling liquid over the entire plate. Once he was done, he took a swig from the flask and then replaced it in his pocket. Sighing happily, he took a bite of the soaked cake. "Mmmm! Rum cake. One of my favorites."

"How can you eat that?"

"Easily," he replied with unimpaired cheer, finishing off the cake with great relish. As soon as he finished, he placed the empty plate on a nearby table, glancing around expectantly. "Have you seen Max? I thought he'd be here."

So had she. But for John's benefit, she shrugged as if she couldn't care less. "I haven't seen him."

"Really? I rather thought —" John pursed his lips.

"You thought what?"

"Nothing. Nothing at all." He pushed his hands into his pockets, his lank form bowing as he leaned against the wall. "Know what I heard in the foyer when I arrived? Lady Neeley was there, telling everyone within hearing that she had thought it through and knew who had stolen her bracelet."

Sophia stilled. Something about the way John was looking at her made his words seem imminently important. "What else did she say?"

"I don't know, for the crowd separated us. But I wouldn't put it past her to indicate Max. Seemed to me she was heading in that direction."

Sophia stiffened, outrage flashing through her. "If Lady Neeley thinks she can spread such vicious rumors, she has another think coming. Max was merely a guest, as were we all, and —"

"Easy, my dear! Don't flash at me! I'm just telling you what I heard."

"Well, she's wrong."

"Of course."

"Max would never do such a thing."

"I can't imagine it either."

"She should be *shot* for making such accusations."

"I will help you load the pistol." He grinned. "You are certainly testy this eve. Missing your lapdog, that Riddleton fellow?"

"Thomas is not my lapdog," she said, a slight tinge of irritation still resting on her shoulders. "He is a friend and a wonderful person."

John pursed his lips in a silent whistle. "Poor bugger. Describing a fellow as 'a wonderful person' is the kiss of death in a courtship."

"It is not a courtship! Besides, what do you know about courtship? You spend all your time dangling after plump women with notoriously good cooks rather than having any serious flirtations."

"I am a member of White's," he said loftily. "I know all about male suffering. I hear it every day."

"You hear a lot of drunken lumps complaining about things they secretly cherish."

"There are no drunken lumps at White's. Drunken peers, yes. But drunken lumps, no. They have a very strict admission process."

"It can't be too strict; they allowed you in."

"You —" John's gaze flickered over her head, into the room beyond. "Welllll . . ."

"Sophia." Max's voice came from behind her. It spilled over her and warmed her head to toe. *Act unaffected,* she told her unruly senses. *Act as if you don't care. As if you never cared. As if you'll never care again.* Pasting a determinedly casual smile on her lips, she turned to face him. He was dressed in very fashionable garb this evening, his black coat perfectly fitted, his hair trimmed. But no matter how Max dressed, there was still an edge of danger to him, as though the civilized clothes hid an untamed heart. "Easterly," she said with a smoothness she did not feel, "how nice to see you."

"And you." He bowed, his gaze flickering to John. "Standwick. How are you?"

"Fine. Just enjoying a touch of rum cake

and talking to m'sister. How are you enjoying this lovely, overly plum event?"

"It is without compare and will be even better once I've had some rum cake and a chance to speak with your sister, as well."

"Well, you're out on the rum cake. I had the last piece. Damned good it was, too." John straightened from the wall. "But if you wish to talk to Sophie, she's yours. I might wander over to the card room and see what's occurring there."

Sophia stared. Blast it, what was John doing? She grabbed his arm and said through a false smile, "The card room! What a wonderful idea! I believe I should accompany you. I'm dying to play piquet."

John removed her hand from his arm. "You hate piquet."

"I *love* piquet."

"No. Heard you say at the Remingtons' soiree that piquet was for imbeciles and those too stupid to engage in a real game of cards. Doesn't sound like 'love' to me."

She was going to kill him; it was her only hope for a normal, pleasant life. But before she could figure out how to do it in so public a place, Max took her arm. "Shall we dance?"

She ignored the heated tingle that raced through her at his touch and instead tilted her head to one side, straining to hear the sounds of the orchestra. None came. "I cannot hear the music."

"Then we'll take a breath of air on the terrace."

Good God, the terrace! She could not be alone with Max. Sophia turned to John and was just in time to see the back of him as he disappeared among the crowd. Blast his carcass! She'd have a strong word to say to him the next time she saw him. Several words, in fact, and none of them pleasant.

Max tucked her hand in the crook of his arm. "Come."

She kept her feet planted. "I have no wish to go on the terrace."

A sliver of humor touched his mouth. "Not even if I promise to talk about the annulment?"

The annulment. It was what she wanted. Perhaps if they did have this one, simple conversation, she could get his agreement and he would be on his way all the sooner. "I suppose —"

"Excellent." He led her to the door and opened it, guiding her outside in one smooth movement.

The noise of the ballroom faded as the door clicked shut, the cool night air wrapping about them. To her relief, Max released her and merely walked at her side.

The fresh scent of the damp gardens cleared her head and calmed her racing heart. She walked to the top of the wide stairs that led down into the garden and viewed the vista lit from the bright glow of the moon. "It's lovely out here."

Max moved to stand beside her, leaning his shoulder against a pillar. "Lovely, indeed," he murmured, and she had the oddest sensation that he wasn't looking at the gardens.

Sophia swallowed, feeling the strangest urge to whisper. It was so quiet out here, almost peaceful. Or it would be if she weren't so painfully aware of the man beside her. She stole a glance at him, a pang of homesickness hitting her. Strange as it was, even standing with him now, she still missed him, missed the way things used to be for those brief shining months.

He caught her gaze, a frown flickering over his face. "What are you thinking?"

She sighed. "I was wondering where we'd be if Richard hadn't lied in that card game all those years ago."

The quiet question hung in the moist air. Max looked down at her. The moonlight caressed the delicate planes of her face, touching the line of her cheek and throat, clearly showing the hint of regret in her eyes. His chest tightened and he turned so that he could face her more completely. "I fear that if it hadn't been for Richard's betrayal, something else would have torn us apart. We were too young, too foolish."

She flicked a glance his way, her eyes shadowed so that he could not read her expression. "You think we made an error in marrying."

"We made an error in marrying so quickly," he amended. "We didn't know one another. Well enough. That was proven by our inability to handle adversity."

"Had we loved one another, we would have been fine. We had passion and nothing else." Her mouth curved, a bitterness to her smile that deepened his ache. "That's what you told me as you packed your bags. I will never forget that."

"I had rather hoped you would. Sophia, I didn't mean what I said that night. I was hurt. Pained that you, the woman I adored, could think so poorly of me as to believe I'd cheat."

She shook her head. "I didn't mean to believe it, it's just that . . . John and I had practically raised Richard. And you wouldn't answer the accusations. It just seemed —" She bit her lip, a quiver passing over her face. "Max, I am sorry for not supporting you. I should have. If I had it to do over, I would do it differently."

"Really? If I had it to do over, I would have done the exact same thing. I do not have to refute the allegations of fools or imbeciles."

"Would you have left me, as well?"

"I could not subject you to the embarrassment of being banished. That was my burden to bear, not yours."

"I disagree. I asked you to take me with you. I — I even begged."

Even in the pale light, he could see the color lifting in her cheeks. "What kind of a man would I have been to have taken you into exile with me? To live without a home, without your family, your friends. I could not do it. Besides . . . you'd made your choice."

She flushed. "I'm sorry for that. I cannot keep saying it. It's just that . . . you do not leave someone if you love them."

"You do when staying would hurt them more. I loved you, Sophia. It was just a pity you didn't feel the same."

It seemed in the uncertain light that she paled before she turned away. "Make no mistake; I did care."

The word "did" tore through his heart, and he realized in that instant how much he still wanted her, still desired her. All these years he had told himself over and over that she was not for him. That he could live without her. That he was fine alone. It was all a lie. And now, standing here on the moon-soaked terrace, with Sophia only an arm's length away, he knew what he really wanted. Her. But was he too late? Could she ever feel for him like she once did? And would that love prove more true? Stronger, just as she was stronger?

He sighed, wishing he knew at least some

of the answers. "I thought you'd eventually write and ask for an annulment."

"I didn't need one. Until now."

"What happened?"

She shrugged, the gesture graceful. "I don't know. Life just seemed to be passing me by."

"What of this Riddleton fellow?"

"He is a friend, no more."

"Good," Max said roughly. "He's not man enough for you."

She took a deep breath, her chest lifting against the thin silk of her gown. "Please do not disparage Thomas. He has been kind to me."

Max didn't answer. He was too busy trying to control his body's heated reaction to the sight of those tempting breasts. . . . He remembered her breasts, and her skin, and the taste of her lips. Every inch of her had been his. Max had to ram his hands into his pockets to keep from reaching for her.

She made an impatient gesture. "Enough of this. We came here to discuss the annulment. And your uncle's diary."

"Auction the diary." Max shrugged. "I don't care."

She almost sputtered. "You don't — you have to care!"

"If I didn't care that people thought me a cheat, why would I care what they thought of my dead uncle?"

"Then . . . why are you here?"

"To prove to myself that we are indeed finished."

"How will you prove that?"

He stepped forward. "Kiss me, Sophia. Show me you don't care."

Sophia had to use every ounce of her will not to throw herself into his arms. It was almost as she'd once dreamed it, Max returning to declare his love. Only . . . he didn't love her. He hadn't once used those words. She stiffened. "No. You cannot come back into my life and then demand that I give what you once threw away. I want my freedom and I will not halt until I have it."

His jaw tightened, his hands spread over her back as he pulled her flush against him. He was as solid as rock, his muscles firm, his manhood pressing against her. His mouth curved into a taunting smile. "Are you afraid to kiss me? Afraid to see what might happen?"

Sophia's heart bounded at the challenge, but her traitorous body was already reacting to him. "I kissed you once. Wasn't that enough?"

He leaned forward, his mouth a scant inch from hers. "I don't know. Is it? Do you think —"

"Ow!" came a soft feminine voice from behind them.

Max instantly released Sophia, and they turned toward the voice. They could just make out Lady Mathilda Howard and Mr. Peter Thompson standing in the dim light.

An awkward silence ensued, broken when Mr. Thompson gamely offered a cheery, "Good evening."

Max took a deep breath. "Er, fine weather."

Sophia had to bite back a surprising giggle at the inane comment. Max *never* made small talk.

"Indeed," Mr. Thompson said at the same time Lady Mathilda popped in with a lively, "Oh yes!"

The poor dears, Sophia thought. It was little wonder they were out here on the terrace. It was deuced hard to get a few moments alone, especially at a crowded ball. And since Lady Hargreaves hadn't the decency to at least provide a suitable orchestra for dancing, the younger set was left without recourse. Sophia smiled kindly at Mathilda. "Lady Mathilda."

The younger girl greeted her in return, a breathless note to her voice. "Lady Easterly. How are you?"

"Very well, thank you. And you?"

"Just fine, thank you. I was just er, a little overheated." The girl waved a hand toward the garden. "I thought a spot of fresh air might revive me."

"Quite," Sophia said, wondering whether Mr. Thompson or the heated ballroom was responsible for the color in the girl's cheeks. "We felt the exact same way."

Max grunted his agreement.

"Er, Easterly," Mr. Thompson said, stepping into the breach. "I should warn you of something."

Max inclined his head in question, his gaze narrowing on the younger man's face.

"Lady Neeley has been publicly accusing you of the theft."

"*What?*" Sophia asked, outrage pouring through her.

Max slanted a sharp glance her way before looking back at Mr. Thompson. "Publicly?"

Thompson nodded curtly. "In no uncertain terms, I'm afraid."

Lady Mathilda added in an eager voice, "Mr. Thompson defended you. He was magnificent."

"Tillie," Mr. Thompson murmured, clearly embarrassed.

"Thank you for your defense," Max said. "I knew that she suspected me. She has made that much abundantly clear. But she had not yet gone so far as to accuse me publicly."

"She has now."

"I'm sorry," Lady Mathilda said. "She's rather horrid."

Horrid didn't begin to describe the woman. Sophia said sourly, "I would never have accepted her invitation had I not heard so much about the chef."

Max flicked a glance at Mr. Thompson. "Thank you for the warning."

Mr. Thompson gave a nod. "I must return Lady Mathilda to the party."

"Perhaps my wife would be a better escort."

Sophia glanced up at Max, shocked to hear the words *my wife* on his lips. It seemed . . . intimate, somehow. She opened her mouth to speak, then realized that she could say nothing in front of the other two. Besides, Max was right about suggesting that she escort Lady Mathilda back into the ballroom. There surely would have been comment had Mr. Thompson attempted to do it himself.

"You are more than correct, my lord," Mr. Thompson said, pulling gently on Lady Mathilda's arm and steering her toward Sophia. He bent toward Mathilda and added in an undertone, "I will see you tomorrow."

Mathilda's eyes shone, and she said in an adorably breathless voice, "Will you?"

"Yes." He gave her a final look, then Sophia took Mathilda's arm and led her toward the terrace doors. As she stood back to allow the younger girl entrance, Sophia glanced back at Max. He was watching her, his eyes shadowed, his face expressionless. It was just like Max to be worried about the propriety of someone else's good name, and yet care nothing that Lady Neeley was somewhere spilling poison over his own.

Well, Max may not care, but Sophia did. And she owed him for her past error. Determination stole through her. By God, this time she wouldn't let Max down. She'd stop Lady Neeley's assault on his reputation, no matter what it took.

In that moment, Sophia knew how she would make up for her transgressions. Make up for them and more. Flushed with renewed purpose, she turned and entered the ballroom, bid a hurried good-bye to Lady Mathilda and then went in search of John.

Chapter 4

And to conclude this column's analysis of the Neeley suspects (or at least of five of them; This Author was unable to provide lengthier descriptions of all twenty-two), one must mention the surprise guest of the evening: Lord Easterly. Not much is known of the viscount, as he has spent the last twelve years on the Continent, specifically Italy. There is, of course, the unsavory scandal in his past, which necessitated his flight abroad, but even though Lord Easterly suffered his disgrace in a card game, there is nothing at present to indicate that he is short of funds.

Indeed, it is difficult to imagine why the gentleman might desire a ruby bracelet. Perhaps to woo back his wife?

Lady Whistledown's Society Papers, 31 May 1816

After an entire night of tossing and turning and trying hard *not* to think about Max, Sophia formulated the beginning of a plan. To the startlement of her servants, she rose with the sun and was dressed and ready for breakfast at the unlikely hour of seven. Her mind full, she made her way to the breakfast room, sublimely unaware that the cook had been hurriedly summoned and was now in the kitchen, tying an apron over her night-gown and muttering vile sentiments about people who rose before the sun was properly fixed in the sky.

Sophia took a seat at the long mahogany table and requested that Jacobs bring paper and pen. The butler did as asked, though it could be noticed that his wig was askew and his cravat rather hastily knotted.

Sophia, however, noticed little. Careful not to drip ink on the crisp paper, she made a list of all twenty-two guests who had graced Lady Neeley's dinner party. Then, nibbling thoughtfully on the end of the pen, Sophia considered each and every name. The list it-self was a tribute to Lady Neeley's wondrous chef, for only culinary wonders of the highest caliber could have drawn such a sparkling company hither.

Sophia dipped the pen into the inkwell. The fact that there had been so many highly placed people present made her job all the easier. All she had to do was mark those who might have had a reason for stealing a bracelet. And that meant people in need of quick funding of some sort. By the time Sophia finished, she had circled five names.

Jacobs knocked and announced that not only was breakfast ready but her brother was standing in the entryway, demanding to be let in. Sophia raised her brows; it was early for John to be up and about. As it turned out, he was actually on his way home. Still dressed in his evening attire, he had passed her house, seen lights flickering in the main rooms, and had boldly concluded that breakfast might be had.

"You are a pig," she told him as he piled his plate high with kippers, eggs, and bacon. "And you are going to get fat."

"Not me. I have an iron constitution. Besides, it's a chance I'm willing to take as there are kippers involved." John sat beside her, his gaze resting on the list at her elbow. "What's that?"

"The guests at Lady Neeley's dinner. I'm marking the ones who had a motive to steal the bracelet. I thought to speak with them — without divulging my suspicions, of course — and see if there are any clues as to who might have taken the silly thing."

"Splendid idea!" he said, salting his eggs. "Where are you off to first?"

Sophia sighed. "I suppose I must start with Lady Neeley, though to what purpose, I'm

470

not sure. She has quite made up her mind to blame Max."

"Perhaps she has some new information."

"She had none to begin with." Sophia examined her list. "After Lady Neeley, I shall visit Lord Rowe." Lord Rowe was a loquacious man, warm and humorous, and a notoriously poor gambler. When other men cut their losses and walked away from possible ruin, he'd been known to foolishly continue on, bringing his family to the brink of the poorhouse on more than one occasion. Luckily, as oft as he lost his fortune, he also re-earned it, that same stubbornness allowing him to ride out a bad streak to which others would have bowed.

"Rubber Rowe, eh?" John finished his eggs and began to work on his kippers. "He's bounced between riches and rags so oft, I never know if I should offer to spot him a guinea or borrow a groat." John chewed thoughtfully, then nodded. "If his fortune is once again on the downward swing, he might make a good suspect."

"Possibly. He's a gambler, not a thief, and a horribly nice man. I truly hope he didn't do it, but I simply could not leave any stone unturned." She stood. "I had best make my calls before it gets too late. I have much to do."

"Go ahead, my dear," John said expansively, gesturing with his fork and knife. "I'll just finish up here. Unless, of course, you need me to accompany you."

"You'd be asleep in the carriage before we reached Lady Neeley's."

"Balderdash," John said in a mild tone. "I've two good hours left before I fall into a stupor."

"Two minutes is more likely. Feel free to make use of the guestroom if you find your bed too far away." She bent and kissed his cheek, then left to call for her carriage.

Her interview with Lady Neeley was as unpleasant as Sophia had expected it to be. The woman was horrid, briskly repeating her accusations without one sign of remorse or thought. Sophia was forced to grit her teeth before replying to such unalleviated twaddle. "Lady Neeley, I cannot believe you'd make such an accusation without proof."

"Proof?" Lady Neeley held out a bit of a tea cracker for her parrot. It squawked and whistled, turning a haughty shoulder on the tidbit. "Poor bird! I just do not know what is wrong with him for he won't eat any of his treats! He hasn't been the same for the last two weeks. Always fluttering about and squawking and stealing my best ribbons."

Sophia, who knew nothing about birds and preferred to keep it that way, merely said, "The weather has affected us all. Lady Neeley, I wish to speak to you about the missing bracelet. Why do you think Lord

Easterly took it?"

"Perhaps he needed the money," Lady Neeley offered.

Sophia thought of the generous allowance Max had provided for her over the years. "No, he does not need the money."

"Oh. Then perhaps he collects ladies' jewelry. I had a cousin once who collected women's chemises. On his death he had over one hundred and fifty of the things in his possession." Lady Neeley leaned forward. "At the funeral, I overheard my aunt say that he'd asked to be buried in one, but that the church wouldn't allow it."

"Lord Easterly does *not* collect other people's jewels. Nor does he collect chemises." Not that she knew of, anyway.

"Then perhaps he took the bracelet merely because he could," Lady Neeley said, obviously uninterested. "Who knows how the criminal mind works?"

Sophia came to her feet. "Lord Easterly does *not* have a criminal mind!"

There was a stunned moment, then the parrot squawked. Lady Neeley managed an uncertain laugh. "My dear, it does you great credit to stand by Easterly —"

"I am not standing by Easterly. I am searching for the truth. Lady Neeley, I will find your bracelet and prove how wrong you are. In the meantime, you have no evidence and should not be spreading such horrid rumors about my husband."

"How can you say that when Easterly all but abandoned you at the altar —"

"My relationship with Lord Easterly is none of your concern." The words were softly spoken, but Sophia's anger had frozen into an icy rock of disdain. She clung to the jagged edges, daring Lady Neeley to step closer.

Lady Neeley flushed a deep red. "Of course I won't say another word. At least, not unless someone asks me about it." That said, she turned her attention back to her parrot.

Though Sophia wished for a more substantial promise, she knew that was all she was going to get. As soon as she could, she excused herself and left for Rowe House.

Sophia stepped out of her carriage into a brisk wind that stirred her skirts. The sunlight was just beginning to peek between the clouds, a fortunate happenstance that lifted Sophia's spirits immensely.

She discovered that both Lord and Lady Rowe were at home, though the house was in horrible disarray. They were in the process of ordering about several stalwart footmen in an effort to arrange a place for a new pianoforte. As Lord Rowe wished a place by the window and Lady Rowe favored a place near her harp, away from the burning afternoon light, the poor footmen were torn between a spate of conflicting orders.

These all came to a halt when the piano-forte itself arrived not ten minutes later. The instrument was a piece of exquisite artistry that effectively answered Sophia's question — the Rowes were indeed on an upward swell, and, judging by the new rugs and other freshly acquired furniture, they had been experiencing good fortune for some time now. Certainly more than a single bracelet could afford.

Sophia made her farewells and went off to locate the next person on her list — Mrs. Warehorse, a widow who stretched her thin income by exchanging dinner invitations for sycophantic utterances. The elderly widow lived with a talkative, distant cousin in a set of lodgings that could only be described as sparse. Sophia tried to make it plain that she was in a hurry, but Mrs. Warehorse's cousin was determined to hold her prisoner, at least through one cup of tepid tea. After much hinting, the cousin finally revealed that Mrs. Warehorse had gone in search of some ribbon to remake a hat.

Sophia ordered her carriage to Bond Street, and she soon spied her quarry coming out of a shop, meager purchases clutched in one hand. Mrs. Warehorse brightened when Sophia hailed her, and the widow agreed with alacrity to walk a way down the street and then enjoy the comfort of Sophia's carriage for the ride home. It was an invitation Sophia would immediately regret, as the older woman could not speak without uttering a flurry of simpering compliments intermingled with deep sighs about her own plight, done in an obvious (and irritating) effort to elicit sympathy and garner favor at one and the same time.

Gritting her teeth at such obvious flummery, Sophia interrupted with a deftly worded question about the night of the fated dinner. The widow immediately poured forth her remembrances. Unfortunately, most of her memories had to do with how lovely Mrs. Warehorse had thought Sophia's gown. Sophia clamped her lips against such asinine utterances, determined to let the information flow unchecked in case something of importance happened to tumble out. Nothing did.

Finally, the endless chatter was more than Sophia could stand. She cut the widow short and suggested they walk back to the carriage as the wind was picking up. The discourse had proven one thing: Mrs. Warehorse was an unlikely suspect. The woman had neither the gall nor the brains for such an endeavor as a bold theft.

Sophia led her companion back down Bond Street, a warming wind ruffling their skirts and tossing the feather on Mrs. Warehorse's bonnet. They had just gotten within sight of the carriage when, out of the corner of her eye, Sophia caught sight of a spanking new curricle led by an amazingly perfect set of bays. She had to admire the rig, and she did. At least, she did until she saw who was handling the reins — Max, attired in a new multicaped greatcoat with brass buttons, an elegant hat resting on the seat beside him. The wind ruffled his dark hair as his gaze met hers, a hint of arrogant surety lurking in his silver eyes.

For one brief, unguarded instant, happiness bubbled through her, lighting her from head to foot with the quickness of a strike of lightning. A wide, welcoming smile almost slipped out. Fortunately, Mrs. Warehorse chose that minute to exclaim, "My dear Lady Easterly! Is that your husband? Oh! Wait. I don't suppose you'd call him a 'husband,' not after he left you all alone all those years. And good thing, too, considering he's nothing more than a thief."

Sophia stiffened, coming to such a sudden halt that the man walking behind her almost ran into her back. She ignored the man's protestations and said to her companion in a frosty voice, "Are you accusing Lord Easterly of theft?"

The widow's smile faded before such an icy wind. "I — I — Everyone knows —"

"All that anyone knows is that Lady Neeley's bracelet is missing and there is no evidence of who took it. *None* at all."

"Oh! Well, y-yes. Of course. I . . . I was just repeating what Lady Neeley — that is, I'm certain I did not mean to imply that —" Mrs. Warehorse's desperate gaze flew over Sophia's shoulder. "Oh dear! There is Lord Easterly now."

Sophia whirled around to see Max attempting to maneuver the curricle through the crowded street toward the curb. The one, brief flare of happiness she'd felt on seeing Max returned in full force, and she clenched her teeth against it. She had no desire to see her recalcitrant husband, not now. Not until she had some evidence that would show Lady Neeley's accusations against Max for what they were.

Sophia didn't know why it was important that she prove herself; perhaps it was just an attempt to pay a long due debt. Yes, that was what it was — an attempt to repay Max for her irresolution all those years ago. And she was determined to be successful.

"My dear Lady Easterly," Mrs. Warehorse said with a vacuous smile, "it looks as if Lord Easterly has found a break in the traffic. Do you think he will come here —"

Sophia grabbed Mrs. Warehorse's arm and stepped up her pace, practically dragging the poor woman down the street. "It cannot be Lord Easterly. It must be someone else."

"It certainly *looked* like him," Mrs. Warehorse said, struggling to keep up, her package dangling from one hand. She allowed Sophia to drag her along, glancing back over her shoulder, her watery blue eyes sharp with curiosity. "Whoever he is, he looks quite put out that we're rushing in the opposite direction."

Sophia increased her pace even when Mrs. Warehorse puffed an exclamation of distress at being dragged down the busy walkway. Sophia gave a sigh of relief when they finally reached the carriage.

"Where to, my lady?" the footman asked, assisting Mrs. Warehorse into her seat.

"Anywhere but here!" Sophia climbed in without allowing the footman time to reach for her, then she lifted the step back into the carriage and slammed the door. "Let us go!"

The snap of her voice jolted the footman into action. "Yes, my lady!" He ran to the front of the carriage, repeated Sophia's instruction to the coachman and with a crack of the whip, they rumbled into the crowded lane of carriages and carts, leaving Max far behind.

After seeing Mrs. Warehorse home, Sophia attempted to interview Lord Alberton. Since he was a sportsman and it was a particularly fine day, he proved a greater challenge to locate than either Lord Rowe or Mrs. Warehorse. Sophia ended up traveling from one location to another, only to find that she was a good ten to twenty minutes behind Alberton everywhere she went. By late afternoon, tired and hungry, Sophia gave up the chase and repaired for home.

She was upstairs in the sitting room, reading through her list and enjoying the reviving properties of tea and cakes, when Jacobs came to the door.

"My lady, Lord Easterly has come to call."

Sophia set her cup down on the plate with a snap. "Pray inform him that I am not at home."

"Yes, my lady." Jacobs bowed and went back downstairs.

There. That is that. She lifted the teacup to her lips, pausing at the sound of the front door opening and then closing as Max left the house, aware that her hand was trembling. A faint sense of relief, tainted by a bitter dash of disappointment, made her set her teacup back on the table beside the much-creased list of suspects.

She hadn't expected Max to take such a rebuff so tamely. At one time he would have risen to the challenge and thrown one of his own. At one time . . . she paused. At one time he had loved her. Or so he'd said.

She sighed, suddenly restless, her gaze landing on the list where it sat beside her cup. Perhaps she should ask John for his help in locating Lord Alberton. If anyone knew where a man addicted to sporting activities may go, it would be John. Sophia stood and turned to the door, then gasped. *"Max!"*

Dark and dangerous, he leaned against the doorframe, his hands deep in his pockets. He quirked a brow. "You look surprised."

"Me? Oh! No! I mean, I didn't know you were there, but I had thought that —" She stammered to a halt. "I suppose I *am* surprised."

"You shouldn't be." His gaze dropped over her, lingering here and there. "How are you today? Tired from your mad dash down Bond Street?"

Though she wore a very proper gown, fashion still permitted some skin to show — her neckline was scooped, her arms practically bare except for light gauzy puffs of sleeves. Under Max's deliberate gaze, every inch of exposed skin tingled and heated, as if he'd dared to touch her. Sophia smoothed her gown nervously. "Bond Street? Whatever do you mean?"

Amusement glinted in his silver eyes. "You know what I mean. I saw you, dragging some poor mousy woman the entire length of the street."

Sophia lifted her chin. "I'm sure I don't know what you are talking about. Not that it signifies. Why are you here, anyway?"

He tilted his head to one side, his lashes dropping to shade his eyes from silver to stormy gray. "I'm not sure. I'll tell you when I reason it out."

Jacobs appeared behind Max, pure shock on his thin face. "My lord! Where did you come from? How did you get inside?"

"Simple," Max said, imperturbable as ever. He dug into his pocket and pulled out a large brass key. It swung gently on his finger, the sunlight sparkling on the filigree.

"The key?" Jacobs looked at Sophia, obviously shocked.

"Where did you get that?" Sophia demanded.

Max smiled, his teeth white against his tanned face. "It was with the papers I signed on purchasing the house."

It must have been a spare key. "You should have returned it."

"I returned the one I had for the house we owned when I left." His gaze narrowed. "A house that was not good enough for you."

Her cheeks heated. "It was good enough for me! I simply could not bear the memories. So I wrote and asked your permission to sell it, and you agreed."

"Yes, I did." He looked around with an appraising eye. "I must give you credit, my dear. This house is much brighter than our last one. Larger, too."

Sophia tried not to look too longingly at the key he held. It was a wretched idea for Max to have access to her house day and night. Especially night.

Max tucked the key back into his pocket.

"So here I am, with a key."

Jacobs stepped forward, outrage in every line of his thin body. "My lady, shall I call the footmen and remove Lord Easterly?"

That was a tempting thought. Sophia caught Max's eye. He grinned, an easy shrug moving his wide shoulders. "They could try," he said softly.

He was right, the footmen *could* try, and they might even succeed. But only for the moment. Max would just come back once the way was clear again. That was Max's way — if he decided on a course of action, he followed it, regardless of the consequences. She sighed and gestured to the chair opposite hers, saying crossly, "Oh very well. You might as well stay."

"Thank you," Max said, a faint smile on his lips.

Jacobs frowned, but he could not disagree with his mistress. He bowed stiffly. "Very well, my lady." Head held high, he sent Max a quelling look, then turned on his heel and left.

It was exactly what Max wanted. Ever since the grand ball, he'd been yearning for another taste of Sophia. A long, lingering taste this time. Once he'd re-memorized the taste of her kiss, he then wanted to see if his other memories were just as true to the mark. The feel of her skin beneath his fingers, the curve of her hips, the warmth of her leg thrown over his while she slept. All things he remembered in painful detail, now within reach. It was agonizing.

He walked forward, noting how she nervously wet her lips. The afternoon sun caught the moisture and glistened appealingly. Good God, what had he been thinking, to leave a woman like this? But then, it hadn't been that simple. With Sophia, it never was.

"Pray have a seat," she said.

Max sat, his long legs brushing against her knees. She jerked as if the faint touch had burned.

"What do you want?" she asked bluntly.

"I came to see what schemes you were hatching."

A delicate flush touched her cheeks and made him yearn to follow it with his lips. "What makes you think I am scheming?"

"You cannot help it; it's in your blood. Like using my uncle's diary against me."

Her cheeks bloomed with more color. "I may have been willing to use that diary to get you to return for the annulment, but for no other reason."

It was difficult to believe it had been twelve long years since he'd allowed himself the pleasure of seeing her. Funny, it didn't seem so long now that she was sitting before him, her skin flushed a becoming pink, her blue eyes sparkling with suspicion, her golden hair pinned onto her head in a profusion of temptingly soft ringlets. Blast it, but she was beautiful. Beautiful and intelligent and something more . . . something that had held him enthralled since the first day they'd met. What was it? he wondered. What made every woman he met fade to insignificance beside Sophia? He saw her gaze drop to the pocket that held the key. "I will not use it without permission."

Her lashes lifted, and she regarded him with suspicion. "Oh?"

"If I really wished to enter this house, I wouldn't need a key. I could break in, or trick the servants into thinking I'm a coal scuttler or some such thing."

"No one would think you were a coal scuttler," she scoffed.

"No, just a thief."

Her lush lips turned down at the corners. Max found that he could not look away from her face, from the transparent emotions that flickered through her eyes.

She grasped her hands in her lap. "Max, I am sorry —"

"Don't. I do not want you to be sorry." He wasn't sure what he wanted, but it wasn't her pity or concern. "It's over and done with and I don't wish to speak of it again. Like Lady Neeley's accusations, it is stupid talk from stupid people, best left unnoticed and unanswered."

That lit her fires. "As if such a thing could go unnoticed and unanswered!" she returned hotly, her eyes flashing daggers. "Everyone is discussing it and condemning you, all without a single scrap of evidence. It is more than I can bear!"

That was it, Max suddenly realized, a sense of wonder filling him. That was what had attracted him to Sophia from their very first meeting — her passion. And not just for him, but for everything she considered right, for everything she valued. There was color to her soul, color and a richness of texture that made his heart sing in response. The ultimate irony was that what had attracted him to Sophia, what had captivated him so completely, had eventually led to the end of their union. Her passionate loyalty had led her to champion her brother Richard at the expense of her own husband. "Ah, Sophia, we are foolish, both of us."

"Balderdash. Speaking of which, we never did resolve the issue of the key. Please return it at once."

He lifted a brow. "The key was delivered to me and I shall keep it."

"Why on earth would you want it?"

"Ah," Max said tightly. "Why do I want a key to the house where you live? Could it be because I am your husband? Isn't that reason enough?"

She crossed her arms over her chest and

leaned forward until their noses almost touched, her chin jutted to a pugnacious angle. "We are married in name only, and you are not allowed the full privileges of a husband. Return that blasted key!"

Moving with deliberate slowness, he pulled the key from his pocket and placed it on the table.

"Thank you." She reached for it, but just as her fingers grazed it, Max placed his large hand over hers and held her there. Sophia could only stare down at her hand, engulfed in his. She noted absently that he had a paint smear along the edge of his thumb. It reminded her of when they'd first been married and she'd had to inspect his hands and shoes for paint splatters before they went anywhere. It had always amused her that Max, usually so neat in person, could be so careless when he painted.

But that was long ago. Heart aching, she tugged on her hand, but he wouldn't allow it, holding her fingers tight. "Stop it," she hissed.

He smiled then, a slow, wide, teasing smile that reminded her of other smiles, other times, dark and whispered moments between the sheets, of thudding hearts and entwined legs. She shook off the memories and gasped out, "Stop that!"

He lifted his brow. "Stop what?"

"Stop all this . . . taunting. I will not take it."

"Very well. Perhaps we can trade. The key for —"

"The diary."

"No. For a kiss."

"A kiss?" She was aghast. "You *must* be teasing."

"I am not. One kiss and the key is yours."

She bit her lip. It was tempting, really it was. But before she could speak, Jacobs knocked on the door and entered. "The Earl of Standwick."

"Max, let me go," Sophia muttered under her breath, all too aware of the butler's sharp gaze. Max's large, warm hand was still pressed over hers, and she could not move an inch.

"My lady, is everything well?" Jacobs said, faltering a little.

"It's nothing," Sophia said. "Please see Standwick in." As soon as the door closed, she turned to Max. "You must let me go."

"No."

"But John will see and —" The door opened and John entered, the door closing behind him.

"There you are, Sophie! I just —" John blinked. "I say, don't you two need to oh, you know, get up or take a walk or something?"

"No!" they answered as one.

John laughed. "You should see yourselves, holding hands and yet glaring at one another

488

like mortal enemies."

Sophia tossed her head. "John, he has the key to this house."

John looked at Max. "Do you?"

"The house is in my name," Max said imperturbably.

"Oh." John rubbed his chin. Finally, he said, "Soph, I think he has you there."

She stiffened. "How can you side with *him?*"

"I'm not siding with anyone. He owns the house, therefore it makes sense he must have a key."

"While I'm in it?"

He looked at Max with a narrow gaze. "Will you use it?"

"Only if she invites me."

John looked at Max a bit longer, then seemed satisfied at last by the serious expression in Max's eyes. "Sophia, he promises not to use it. And he's a man of his word, as we all know."

She flared a look at Max guaranteed to scorch his stockings, then tugged on her hand. "Blast you! Just keep the key. I shall have the locks changed in the morning."

"And I shall make use of any window with a loose latch, should I wish to visit."

"You said you'd ask first!"

"That was if I had the key," he said with a smug smile. "If I don't, then any window will do."

"Try it and you will be shot. I shall arm all of my servants."

"Balderdash," John said. He took a large plush chair near the tea tray, sitting in a full slouch and crossing his legs at the ankle. "You have said a thousand times that you don't believe in having weapons — said they cause more harm than good."

She shot him a dagger glance, wishing Max would release her hand so she could box her brother's ears. "Did anyone invite you into this conversation?"

"Actually, yes. You did when you asked me —"

"Don't make me sorry for it, then." She turned to Max. "I offered to trade you the key for the diary."

"I named my price."

"Price?" John asked.

Sophia sent him a baleful glare. "Max makes no sense. If that diary leaks out, his family name will be the topic of conversation in every salon and sitting room in town."

Max shrugged. "That will be nothing new."

"Then why did you return to England if not to get the diary?"

"I returned because you asked me to."

She looked at him, too startled to even speak for a moment. "That's all it would have taken."

"Yes."

"Oh!" She stomped her foot, tugging even harder on her hand. "I hate that!"

Max's brow lowered. "You hate what?"

"How you've made it all my fault! Not only did you leave because of me, but now, you return because of me! Maxwell, you are — you are —" She snapped her mouth together, took a deep breath, then burst out, "You are a beast!" She yanked her hand free, jumped up, and marched from the room, slamming the door behind her.

Max looked at the door in astonishment. All he'd done was tell the truth.

"Whew!" John said, sitting forward to peer into the half empty tea tray.

"Your sister is stubborn to an inch."

John picked up a tea cake and munched it thoughtfully. "Two of a kind, I'd say. You're not known for your mild manner, yourself."

Max's face flashed darkly, but then he caught himself. "I daresay you are right. Sophia and I are not known for our level temperaments, even under the best of circumstances."

"No," John said. He poked another tea cake and scrunched his nose. "Raspberry. Never could abide that."

Max glanced at John from beneath his brows. "I didn't come here to upset her."

"I know. Sophia's just a bit touchy when you're about. She has no sense, which is why

I'm worried about her chasing after that damned bracelet."

"Chasing?"

"She wants to catch the thief and clear your name."

"Bloody hell! Who asked her to do that?" Of all the impulsive, quixotic, Sophia-like things to do . . . how like her.

"No one. I think she's just trying to make reparations."

"That's not necessary."

"It is to Sophia." John sighed and rested the tips of his finger on the folded piece of paper that rested beside Sophia's abandoned teacup. He fingered the edge thoughtfully. "This is her list of suspects. I fear she could end up in a hell of a situation if she might be right and one of them did indeed steal that bracelet."

Max muttered an oath. "She's an impetuous fool."

"Indeed," John said, leaving the list to pick up a crustless sandwich hardly larger than his small finger. He eyed the morsel uncertainly, sniffing at the edge.

Max raked a hand through his hair. "Even if there is no danger, she is likely to start a new scandal while trying to put a cap on this one."

"Exactly so," John said cheerfully. He popped the sandwich in his mouth and smiled. "Plum jam!"

Max's gaze fixed on the paper that lay on the table. "I suppose I should keep an eye on her."

"Someone should." John casually picked up the paper. "Let's see . . . Lord Alberton, Lord Rowe, Mrs. Warehorse, Lady Markland, and Lady Neeley's nephew, Mr. Henry Brooks."

"Henry Brooks? But Lady Neeley had him searched at the dinner."

"Sophia seems to think that something might have been missed. I'm glad you're going to be there for m'sister, Easterly. Don't like her out there, wandering around and asking awkward questions."

Max pinned him with a sharp look. John gestured with his sandwich. "I'd do it myself, you know, but I'm very busy just now. I accepted a challenge at whist with Comte du Lac. Can't let the old gent down, so I thought I should brush up on my game in the interim. So it's whist, whist, whist for the next two weeks, at least. In fact, I should leave now." John finished his sandwich and then ran a finger over the empty plate, sighing regretfully when the last dab of jelly was removed. "Well! I suppose I must go. Nothing else to be done here." He stood and patted his stomach. "I love tea."

Max shook his head. "You're incorrigible."

"You should be glad for that."

"I am," Max said promptly. He went to the

door and held it wide. "Shall we retreat, Standwick? With this weather, Sophia should be safe here for a while. Besides, I've a feeling we'll be more welcome at White's. I'll even treat you to a nice rack of lamb, if there's one available."

John's eyes brightened. "Lamb? You don't need to ask twice." He ambled out the door, humming a happy tune.

Max followed John out the door, wishing Sophia would be as amenable. But somehow he could not see her changing her mind so easily, and only for a rack of lamb, at that. He'd have to discover what it was that she needed from him in order to open her heart once more. And once he did find that secret key, he'd never let the door close again.

Chapter 5

The Easterly drama continues. By all accounts, Lord Easterly was chasing his wife down Bond Street Saturday morning. And if that weren't cause enough for comment, Lady Easterly was dragging Mrs. Warehorse the entire way.

Although Lady Easterly and Mrs. Warehorse have not been known as close friends, the viscountess was clutching the widow's hand as if her very life depended on their reaching their destination together and in one piece.

Alas, the latter was not to be. Lady Easterly pulled Mrs. Warehorse along at such a speedy clip that the older lady lost her shoe directly in front of Prother & Co.

Perhaps the good milliners would see their way to constructing for her a matching bonnet?

Lady Whistledown's Society Papers,
3 June 1816

It took Sophia a good bit of time to arrange a chance meeting with Lord Alberton. He was at a hot air balloon launching, sitting in his curricle in a field crowded with spectators. Sophia instructed her coachman to pull up beside his carriage so that she could lean out the window and speak to him, all under the guise of watching the launch. Alberton seemed pleased for the company, expounding on his life with little prompting.

To her chagrin, Sophia soon discovered that Alberton had benefited from the same flash of good luck that had blessed Lord Rowe. "The horse's name was Cold Hearted Loser," Alberton said with a beatific smile. "As Rowe and I decided, how could it lose?"

Unable to follow this rather convoluted logic, Sophia merely nodded and smiled, all the while gritting her teeth in frustration. The conversation then turned to ballooning, and Sophia learned far more than she wished on the subject. She was inordinately glad when a companion of Lord Alberton's pulled in on the other side of him and she was spared more explanation.

Feeling a little dejected, she was still sitting in her coach, watching out the window as a particularly large balloon was being filled, when a curricle pulled up beside her. Sophia knew before she turned and looked that it was Max. It had to be — no one else had the power to make her body perk to such awareness.

She steeled herself before tossing a glance in his direction.

Max touched his hat, the brim throwing a shadow over his eyes. "Good afternoon."

Sophia nodded coolly, though her stomach tightened into a hot knot. She'd seen neither hide nor hair of the wretch since he'd held her hand imprisoned. She noted irritably that he was dressed in the peak of fashion, his multicaped greatcoat obviously cut by a master hand, his cravat showing at his throat, expertly tied and adorned with a sapphire cravat pin. It surprised her that he could wear it so well. The Max of her youth, though always impeccably neat, had never been one to bother with fashion.

But this Max, leaner and edgier, the one with the shadowed eyes and the hard smile, this Max was one she didn't seem to know at all. To cover her uncertainty, she said in as cool a tone as she could muster, "How are you?"

Max's brows rose. "How *do* you do that?"

She shot him a suspicious glance. "How do I do what?"

"Ask commonplace questions in that go-to-hell voice. Makes me feel as if I should answer, 'Fine, except for this horrid pain in my chest. Not sure I'll last the day.'"

She sniffed. "That wouldn't please me at all."

"No?"

"No. Your curricle is in the way. If something were to happen to you at this moment, I could be stuck until someone moved it."

Max sighed and looked up at the heavens. "See what I must contend with? Is it any wonder I eschewed painting people for such a length of time?"

That caught her interest. "People? When did you start doing portraits?"

He shrugged and glanced past her at the balloon that lay in the field, slowly growing in girth as it filled. "Twelve years ago."

She wanted to ask more, but couldn't think of a way to do it without appearing far more interested in his life than she should be. "I didn't know you enjoyed this sort of spectacle."

"I don't. I just came to see you. Why did *you* come?"

It was just as she'd suspected: Jacobs must have told Max where she was. Sophia would have a sharp word for her butler when she returned home. "If you must know, I came to speak with Lord Alberton."

Max looked past her to Alberton, who was engaged in an energetic conversation with the man in the coach on the other side. "A bit old for you, isn't he?"

"I didn't wish to speak with him about anything of a personal nature. I wanted to ask him —" She caught herself just in time, glancing at Max from beneath her lashes.

"Ask him what?" His voice was rich and deep, like the clover honey her father used to cultivate when she was a child.

It enticed her to relent, to confess all. She bit her lip, regarding him for a long moment. God knew she could use all of the help she could get. And wasn't she doing all of this for him? Well, partly because of him, anyway. If she was honest, there was something appealing about doing something *with* Max. Not as a couple, of course — they could never be that again. But as *partners*. Yes, that's what they would be, partners. Good, friendly partners. "I am trying to discover who took the bracelet from Lady Neeley's. It's the only way to keep her from bespoiling your good name."

Max sighed. "You can't leave well enough alone, can you?"

That wasn't the reaction she'd expected. "I am helping you."

"That is a matter of opinion," he replied ruthlessly.

"Someone has to act since you will not," she replied hotly, her hands curling into fists. He was so stubborn! "I cannot sit tamely by while others mock you."

"Why do you care?" The question hung in the air like the crack of a pistol shot.

Sophia wet her lips. "I didn't say I did."

"You must, or you wouldn't be doing this."

"I —" Her voice lodged in her throat,

wrapped around a jumble of thoughts, none coherent enough to utter aloud. Oh, blast it! Why did she get so muddled just talking to Max? It was silly. She never felt this way with anyone else — all nervous, her tongue unwieldy, her mind fuzzed with chaotic thoughts and memories, her heart thudding as if she'd been running. Not a single male of her acquaintance had this power over her, not even Thomas — She paused. She hadn't thought about Riddleton at all, not even once, since the night of the Hargreaves' Grand Ball. How strange. Of course, she'd known he'd be out of town for some time; he went to his mother's every year at this time and always stayed at least a month, sometimes more. She'd just thought that she'd miss him, since they'd been together so often in the months before he'd left.

Max eyed her with a resigned air. "Who else do you suspect, besides poor Lord Alberton? The prince, perhaps? Or Wellington?"

"Neither the prince nor Wellington were at Lady Neeley's dinner." Sophia glanced over her shoulder at Alberton, who was still deep in conversation with his other neighbor. "And it is not *poor* Lord Alberton. He and Lord Rowe just made a fortune off the races. Other than that, they were both good suspects."

Max raised his brows. "Who else is on your list?"

"Lady Markland."

"Can't be," Max said promptly. "I sat beside Lady Markland at Lady Neeley's dinner and she told me three times that her brother had just died. She inherited a rather large and bulky estate in the Americas. Seems to expect a good income from the lot."

Blast it. That left only one name on her list — Mr. Henry Brooks. Sophia bit her lip, and her brow lowered as she considered the possibility. What if Lady Neeley's first instincts were right when she'd ordered her own nephew searched at her table? He was a notorious spendthrift, and everyone knew he'd been living off his aunt's grudging bounty for years. Added to that, there was something about him that Sophia didn't trust. . . . She wasn't sure if it was his rather protuberant eyes or his weak chin. Whatever it was, he bore watching. She had to find that silly bracelet, even if she had to follow Lady Neeley's nephew to the pits of hell.

Which was, unfortunately, where he tended to reside. Brooks was a well-known figure at any number of disreputable gaming hells. She pursed her lips and glanced under her lashes at Max. She supposed that if she had to, she could find *someone* to escort her to a gambling den. Certainly John would never do so, but Max had never been as prudish as —

"I don't like that look," Max said abruptly, leaning back in his seat and crossing his arms, his silvered eyes narrow. "What trouble

501

are you brewing now, I wonder."

A normal man would have instantly offered to assist her in whatever way he could. Of course, "normal" was not a word one applied to the large, muscular behemoth beside her. Max was many, many things, but using a word as mundane as "normal" around him seemed a sacrilege of some sort. A misstatement, rather like calling a sleek, powerful lion a "rather small, fluffy kitten." She sighed. "I have only one name left on my list."

"Henry Brooks."

"Why — yes. How did you know?"

He shrugged. "Who else could it be?"

That was true. There simply were not a lot of suspects. "I must speak with him, but he is not usually found in locales I frequent. I've heard he is rather fond of gaming hells."

"Yes, he is," Max said without hesitation. "And no, I will not escort you to one."

There were definite liabilities to speaking with someone who knew one Too Well. Sophia sent Max a dagger glance. "How else am I to interview him? He goes to very few acceptable events, unless forced by his aunt."

"Maybe Lady Neeley will invite you to another dinner."

Sophia remembered her interview with Lady Neeley. "I doubt that will happen."

Max's lips twitched. "Burned your bridges, did you?"

"No, I did not. It's just that I have no wish

to associate with people who toss out accusations without the slightest bit of evidence to back their claims."

"Hm." Max gathered the reins. "Tell your coachman to go home. You are coming with me."

Her heart thudded against her third rib. "I am?"

"Brooks is expected at the Tewkesberry Musicale this evening. If we leave now, I should be able to get you home to change into a more suitable gown, and then we can go on to the musicale."

"How do you know all this?" she asked, astonished.

Max gave her a mysterious smile. "What does it matter? We have to hurry, though. The musicale is over at eight, since some of the party are going on to Lady Norton's ball."

Sophia considered this. It was too good an offer to refuse. "Why can't I have my coachman take me home? You will need to change as well."

"Yes, but I can make twice the time in the curricle. Besides, I *am* dressed." He undid the top button of his greatcoat and gave her a glimpse of his black evening coat.

Suspicion darkened her eyes. "You already knew who was on my list! Did John —"

"If you don't wish to go, then don't," Max said promptly. "Good luck finding Brooks and in locating an escort to take you to a gaming hell. A word of warning, though; do not drink the sherry. It's far inferior to what you are used to and will make you tipsy in an instant. Oh, and I would not wear many jewels, either. Gaming hells are not located in the best part of town, and there are thieves on every corner."

She regarded him with a flat stare. "And perhaps a wild boar might be residing in that part of the city. Or horrid, unwashed gypsies could come and bear me off, as well."

He considered this a moment, then shook his head. "You'd scream and they'd drop you. Gypsies do not like loud noises."

A faint quiver passed over her face, a flash of humor that she quickly suppressed. "You are incorrigible. I am certain I have John to thank for leaking my confidences within your hearing. As underhanded as it is, I will accept your offer simply because I have no choice. I must speak to Brooks."

She told her coachman of the change in plans as Max tied off the reins and lightly jumped down to open the door to her carriage. She stood and leaned forward, ducking her head to avoid the low roof. He grinned up at her, holding out his hand. "I knew you'd see reason. Your calm logic has ever been one of your strong points."

She placed her hand in his, her fingers tightening as she stepped to the edge of the doorway. "Trying to turn me up sweet, are you? Now I *am* worried —"

Max tugged on Sophia's hand. She gasped and lurched forward, falling out of the carriage to land right in his arms, her blonde hair golden against his black greatcoat.

He stood there a second, smiling down into her astonished face, achingly aware of her soft curves pressed against his chest. It took all of his control to gently set her feet on the ground and step away. A pity there were so many prying eyes about; he would have enjoyed another kiss or ten. Hell, he'd have enjoyed tumbling her to the damp grass then and there, tossing her skirts, and having his way with her, society be damned.

Tightening his control over the flood of heated lust that raged through him, he assisted her into the seat of his curricle.

"I have a feeling I'm going to regret this," she muttered, her color high.

He climbed in beside her and loosened the reins. "Indeed you might. But just think of the fun you'll have on your way to that regret." Without giving her time to mull over that remark too closely, he set the curricle in motion, and they were soon on their way.

Sophia and Max arrived at the Tewkesberry Musicale just as the performance began. Sophia was rather sorry to arrive as, for once, Max had been everything most

505

pleasant, talking at his ease of people they both knew or used to know, several times surprising a laugh from her. But beneath the quiet, friendly attention hummed a current of sensual awareness that left Sophia hot and restless.

Soon they were seated side by side in the Tewkesberrys' grand salon, listening to a pretty Italian aria performed very creditably by Lady Maria Townsbridge. Sophia barely heard a note, for sitting only two rows away from her and Max sat Brooks. He was an unimpressive man, with little to recommend him other than a decidedly weak chin.

The musical performance ended promptly at seven. Lady Tewkesberry announced that refreshments could be had in the green salon. Out of the corner of her eye, Sophia saw Lady Neeley's nephew exchange a nod with someone in the back of the room.

She leaned toward Max and whispered, "Who is he gesturing to?"

Max glanced behind her. "Lord Afton."

"Ah!" Sophia said, excitement stirring. Lord Afton was a barely accepted member of the peerage known for his eccentric hobbies, which included collecting lewdly decorated snuffboxes, raising rare birds, and designing waistcoats for fribbles. In his spare time, he was also renowned for leading well-heeled sprigs of fashion into the worst gaming hells to be found. Rumor said he was personally responsible for the ruin of Lord Chauncy Hendrickson, who blew out his brains after losing his entire fortune at the faro table a full ten days before his nineteenth birthday. If Brooks was embroiled with Afton, there was a chance he was deeply in debt, which gave him the perfect motive.

She watched as first Lord Afton and then Brooks began to ease their way toward the door. Caught by the press of people, Sophia could not move. She watched in silent frustration as her quarry slipped out the door to join Lord Afton in private speech. She fairly itched to hear the conversation. If she could just get to the hallway, perhaps —

A hand clamped about her elbow. She glanced down and sighed. She knew that elegant, masculine hand. "Max, let me go. I must get to the hallway."

"You are determined in this, aren't you? I suppose I shall have to help you."

"I don't need your help." And she didn't. Though she *did* have to ask herself why she cared so much when he obviously did not. Was it because Max's name was partly her own? Could that be it? Or was it something else? Something that had to do with the fact that standing here beside Max, his hand warm on the bare skin of her arm, was the most natural, the most right-feeling thing she'd ever experienced?

As she wondered about it, a tall, elderly

matron in an orange turban tapped Max on the shoulder with her fan. "Easterly! So you have indeed returned."

Max had to reply, and when he did, Sophia made her escape. She turned a little, tugged on her arm and was gone, threading through the crowd before Max could do more than give a startled glance her way, the matron immediately recalling his attention.

Sophia slipped out the door, but found no sign of either Brooks or Afton. On silent feet, she made her way down the hallway, stopping now and then to listen. Finally, she heard it — a faint murmur of male voices from behind a large, oak door.

She glanced right and left, assured herself that no one was nearby, then pressed her ear to the cool wooden panel. There she stood, perfectly still, straining to distinguish words while the coldness of the marble floor seeped through her slippers. She could hear the aggravating buzz of male voices, low and intriguing, but very little else.

It was maddening. She pressed her ear closer, plugging up her other ear with a finger in the hopes of increasing her hearing, but to no avail. The door was just too thick.

Something brushed against her arm and she jumped.

Max glinted down at her. "It works much better if you use a turned-over glass," he whispered. He held out a glass and positioned it on the door. "Press your ear to it and see if it works."

She whispered back, "I don't need your glass, thank you."

"Are you certain?" His silver eyes laughed down at her. "Give it a try."

She had to glance at the glass he held against the door in such an inviting fashion. It *would* work better. With a sigh of exasperation, she took the glass from him and positioned it on the door.

He grinned, leaning against the wall to one side of the door to give her better access. "I don't understand why you are going to all this trouble, though I must admit it is rather flattering."

She ignored this sally and held her ear against the cool, smooth bottom. Inside, she could hear Brooks's distinctive voice. "She would kill me if she knew," he said.

"Surely not?" Afton answered.

"After the hue and cry she raised when it went missing? Are you sane?"

Sophia blinked. He had to be talking about Lady Neeley and the bracelet.

"My aunt is like a hound with a bone once she decides she is fond of something," Brooks continued. "That's why I had to find a fake one, one that matched the original perfectly."

Sophia's heart tripped a faster beat. The fake one? Had there been two bracelets perhaps? Had Brooks meant to switch them, but something had gone awry?

Max moved closer, bending his head so that he, too, could listen.

Brooks sighed heavily, so close to the door that Sophia almost jumped. "Are you sure that box is well hidden?"

"Oh yes," Afton said, a soothing note in his voice. "On my honor, no one will ever find it. I buried it in Hyde Park, behind that copse of trees on the south end."

"And you're sure no one saw you."

"Not a soul."

"Good. If my aunt ever found out about this, she'd cut me out of the will before you could count to two. Which is something my cousin Percy would love to witness."

"Your aunt will never know. Just put the fake one in front of her and before you know it, she will think as highly of it as the other."

"If she doesn't discover the difference. I'm sorry I'm so worried — in truth, I am indebted to you, Afton. I'm not sure how I can repay you."

There it was! Sophia almost gave a little hop of joy. Brooks *did* owe money to Lord Afton! "It's hidden in Hyde Park," she whispered excitedly. "Buried behind some trees on the south end."

Max's hand gripped her elbow. "Someone is coming." He nodded down the hall. The faint slap of leather shoes sounded, coming closer. "It's Tewkesberry."

Sophia took a step away from the door just as it began to swing open. Her gaze met Max's — they were trapped. Quick as a wink, he grabbed her hand and pulled her down the hallway to a narrow doorway. He yanked open the door, revealing a closet of some sort. Without a word, he stepped in, pulled Sophia against him, and closed the door behind them.

It was dark, unlit except for the line of light under the door that outlined their shoes with gold. The space was limited and they were pressed together, hip brushing hip as Afton and Brooks paused in the hallway to talk to Tewkesberry.

"Blast it," Sophia whispered. "We'll be in here for hours."

Max glanced down, unable to make out more than the faint outline of her cheek. He'd been with Sophia for over three hours now, three hours of torture. His body was already primed, his blood simmering. And now, here they were in the dark, the faint smell of lemon lifting through the air, Sophia's hair tickling his nose. He leaned down and took a deep breath, letting the richness of her scent wash over him.

She stirred restlessly, her hip brushing his and causing him to wince. She had no idea what she did to him. None at all. It was maddening and as seductive as hell.

"Oh no," Sophia whispered into the silence. "I — I think I'm going to sneeze."

"That's just because you don't want to. Stop thinking about it."

She was silent a moment more before bursting out in an impassioned whisper, "I *know* I'm going to sneeze! We'll be caught and they'll want to know why we're here and —"

Max tipped her face to his and kissed her. It wasn't a tentative, explorative kiss like the first one, but a wild burst of passion, of wanting and needing. He molded her to him, holding her tight, the kiss exploding into something more. And Sophia, his darling beloved Sophia, responded with all the wanton passion he remembered, clutching at his coat, moaning softly. She was ruining his cravat. He was rumpling her gown. And he didn't give a damn. Deeper and deeper the kiss pulled, tugged. Further and further he went, his tongue slipping between her teeth, his hands cupping her breasts through her gown. He ran his thumbs over the tight nubs. She gasped out his name and ached against him, falling back.

Against the door. The unlocked door.

One moment they were standing in complete darkness, their senses raging, the next they were staggering into the hallway, mussed and squinting in the light.

Afton, Brooks, and Tewkesberry stood

looking at them, blinking in astonishment.

Sophia waited for a sense of embarrassment to hit her, that shrinking, pulling feel of humiliation. But for some reason, all she felt was a glorious warmth from Max's embrace.

He moved to stand in front of her, his hands already smoothing his coat, adjusting his cravat. "Gentlemen," he said smoothly, as if he hadn't just stumbled out of a broom closet. "We were looking for the lady's dressing room. My wife has torn her flounce."

Tewkesberry pointed down the hall past them.

Max bowed, took Sophia's hand and placed it in the crook of his arm, then escorted her to the dressing room, out of sight of Afton and Lady Neeley's dissolute nephew. The silence grew tenser. Sophia stole a look up at Max and was dismayed to see his stern expression. "Max, I —"

"Go inside and fix yourself."

"But —"

He placed his fingers over her lips, his fingers warm on her skin. "There's nothing to be said. You had to sneeze. I helped distract you. That was it." His hand dropped to his side. "I understand that. There is no need for further explanation."

Of course that was all it had been. How silly of her to think otherwise. Suddenly bereft, she nodded and went into the dressing room, pausing when she caught sight of herself in the mirror. Her lips were swollen, her hair half tumbled down, her gown askew. But for some reason, the sight reassured her. She looked like a woman who had been loved. And she almost had been.

She straightened herself as well as she could, then went to rejoin Max. They left shortly after that, Max handing her into his curricle and then taking the reins.

He was strangely silent, so she attempted to make conversation. "It will only take a moment for me to throw on an old gown and collect a shovel from the stable."

He lifted a brow. "You are mad if you think we're going to Hyde Park this late."

"We have to get the bracelet and —"

"Tomorrow," he said abruptly. "I will pick you up at eleven."

"Eleven? That's so late! How about eight?"

"I am not getting up at eight just so I can dig a hole in the ground." He slanted a hard look down at her. "And you, madam, are not to go without me."

"But if we go so late, there will be scads of people about!"

"Not in that copse of trees. And even if there were, what difference would it make? We will tell them we are gardening or some such nonsense."

She sniffed her disappointment. He was taking all of the romance out of the affair, which was a great pity. They soon reached the house and Max walked her to the door. Sophia held out her hand. "Thank you for your assistance."

He held her fingers lightly. "Thank you for allowing me to accompany you."

Sophia searched for the words to set him back at ease, to regain the warm companion he'd been before the musicale, but none came to mind. The door opened, and bright lamplight spilled over them. "Well. Tomorrow then. At eight."

"Eleven." Max bowed, then stepped back, making his way to his curricle. He jumped in without pause and gathered the reins.

"How about nine?" she called.

"Eleven," came the ringing answer as he hawed the horses into motion. All too soon, the curricle clattered down the cobble street and disappeared around the corner.

On arriving home, Max found that he couldn't sleep. His blood was still heated, his mind alive with the sensations of holding Sophia, his body still tight with need. Worse than the lust that poured through his veins was the realization that, had the door not fallen open when it had, he would have made love to his wife right there in a stifling closet. A wife who had attempted to lure him home with a threat of blackmail only to ask for an annulment.

The more Max was with Sophia, the more

he wanted her. He sighed as he went to his room, realizing that there would be no sleeping tonight. So he did what he always did when sleep evaded him; he painted. He lost himself in the images that appeared on the canvas, on the colors and the shadows and lights, on the wind stirring a leaf, or the curve of a blade of grass. He worked feverishly, so caught up in his work that the sun was cresting over the city before he realized it. Suddenly exhausted, he staggered to bed, his mind awash with the memory and taste of Sophia.

Max awoke some time later, stretching in the darkness of his room, the heavy curtains blocking out all but the smallest slice of light. Sighing, he looked at the clock on the mantel — and bolted straight upright. It was ten minutes past eleven. God knew what Sophia was into. He threw back the covers, calling for his valet. He washed and dressed in a matter of moments and dashed down the steps, buttoning his waistcoat as he went.

Max went straight to the park, finding Sophia's carriage beside the small copse of trees on the south side. He hopped down, tossed the reins to his groom, then made his way into the trimmed brush. He found Sophia not far away, already digging a hole. She was facing away from the road and was dressed in an older gown and sensible shoes. Her hands were encased in leather riding

516

gloves, and holding a long-handled shovel. A brilliant smile burst from her on seeing him. "There you are!"

He refused to acknowledge the flicker of warmth that touched his heart at her unchecked greeting. "I overslept."

"Oh, I had only one shovel, so it wouldn't have mattered if you were here or not."

He reached for the shovel, but she didn't move. She merely looked at his hand and raised her brows.

He had to smile. "I suppose you are telling me you are Mistress of the Shovel."

"I do think I should be allowed to dig, since I am the one who found the clue as to where the bracelet was hidden."

"I see. If you get to dig, what do I get to do?"

She leaned against the shovel and considered this. "You can be lookout."

"Lookout? What a paltry position that is, to be sure. What am I on the lookout for?"

"For Brooks or Afton."

"You think they might return to get the bracelet? Now? In broad daylight?"

She scrunched her nose as if considering this. "I suppose you are right."

Max crossed his arms and leaned against the tree. "I feel as if I should do something. Perhaps I should direct you."

She paused and pushed her hair from her face, leaving a smear of dirt on one cheek.

"Direct me? I hardly think I need it."

Max hid a smile and said in his best head groom's voice, "Hey there, dig lively now!"

"Oh that's lovely," she said, sending him a scathing look, though there was laughter hidden behind her grimace. "I do hope I'm digging in the right location. It was the only place with freshly overturned dirt."

"That must be it then —"

"Hello there!" came a voice from the other side of the brush. John stepped into the small clearing. He was dressed for riding, a fashionable hat set jauntily on his head, his nose a little red from the sun. "I thought that was the two of you."

"You can see us from the path?" Max asked.

"You can from a horse. I thought you might be having a picnic or something." John looked around. "I could have sworn I smelled lemon custard."

"You and food," Sophia said disgustedly. "We're not having a picnic. We are digging for Lady Neeley's bracelet."

"Actually," Max said apologetically, "your sister is digging. I'm directing." He pointed to the hole. "Watch what you're about, Sophia. Your hole is no longer round, but oval, so have a care —"

Thunk. A shovelful of dirt hit the ground dangerously near his feet.

"Oh ho!" John said, holding up his hands

and backing away. "I think I'll continue my ride. Take care of m'sister, Easterly. Can't have her tossing dirt on the prince or someone important." With a wink, John left.

"He is such a bother," Sophia said. She dug the shovel into the ground once again, and a comfortable silence reined for several minutes as she continued. Suddenly a loud scrape filled the air. Sophia blinked at Max, eyes wide with excitement.

Max pushed himself from the tree and leaned forward to peer into the hole. The edge of a small wooden box was visible. "It isn't buried very deeply, is it?"

"No." She tossed aside the shovel and bent to scrape dirt away. As soon as the entire box was exposed, she grasped it with both hands and pulled it out. Whatever was inside, it slid to one side. Sophia frowned as she stood. "That doesn't sound like a bracelet."

"Maybe it's wrapped in something. Open it and see."

She fumbled a little with the latch.

"My God!" The cry rang through the air.

Max whirled around and found Brooks standing before him. The man was ludicrously dressed in a riding coat of blue velvet with large brass buttons.

Sophia wrapped her arms around the box and backed away. "We know about the box, Brooks. And we know that Afton assisted you."

Brooks's face went as pale as it had been red. "Blast it all! It's my cousin, Percy, isn't it? He put you up to this." The man's shoulders slumped. "Damn, I knew — I told Afton to be sure — and he said he had, but — oh damn it all!" He wiped a hand over his face. "I suppose you are going straight to my aunt?"

"We have to," Sophia said. "We must clear Easterly's name."

Brooks blinked. "Easterly?" He looked at Max, his confusion plain. "What do you have to do with my aunt's parrot?"

There was a moment of stunned silence.

"Parrot?" Sophia said.

"Well, yes." Brooks frowned. "What did you think —" His brow suddenly cleared. "The bracelet! You thought Aunt Theodora's silly bracelet was in there!"

Sophia looked at Max, confused beyond comprehension. He stepped forward. "If the bracelet is not what you were hiding, then what is in the box?"

Sophia suddenly paled and slowly held the box before her at arm's length. "Do not tell me Lady Neeley's parrot —"

"Lord, no!" Brooks said. "That *would* be a gruesome find, wouldn't it?"

Max reached over and took the box from Sophia's unresisting hands, then laid it on the ground. "Brooks, you had better explain yourself."

"I rather think I should. Aunt Theodora's bird had a horrible trick of sleeping in the cushions on the settee. M'aunt was forever warning me to plump the pillows. One day, I forgot and I sat on the blasted thing. That bird raised such a fuss! He swooped at me and tried to pluck my hair." Brooks shuddered. "I ran for my life. Out of the room and out the front door. The problem is, the bird went with me."

Max frowned. "With you?"

"Yes. Followed me nigh on a mile, screeching and pecking at my head. It's a wonder I didn't lose an eye."

"So the parrot escaped."

"Gone forever. I looked and looked, but there was no finding it." Brooks sighed. "Meanwhile, m'aunt found out her precious pet was gone and put up a huge fuss. No one knew the blasted animal had followed me out the door and I deuced well wasn't going to tell anyone, especially not m'cousin Percy."

"Who would have informed Lady Neeley," Sophia said.

"He would have, but I outfoxed him." Brooks straightened, obviously proud of himself. "I couldn't find the real bird, though I looked for days on end. So I got another one from Afton. He has a slew of them, and this one looked just like m'aunt's old one. Then I took the bird to m'aunt's house and left it inside an open window. She thinks it flew back on its own."

"A perfect plan," Max said.

"Well. No," Brooks said uneasily. "There was one rub. See, the new bird is a bit of a crackpot, too. Didn't like anything that belonged to the old bird, not the stand, the toys, even hated the silver bell m'aunt had bought for the stupid thing."

Sophia's toe came out to rest on the box. "So that's what's in here?"

"All the bird's toys, his bedding, everything. Didn't dare dispose of it near m'aunt's house. Feel free to look if you wish."

Sophia undid the latch and opened the box. "Heavens," she said looking at the jumble of items.

"Sad what she spends on that thing," Brooks said with a regretful shake of his head. "What was worse was that I had to purchase the same exact things for the new bird, which was a pain, let me tell you."

Sophia closed the box, her arms suddenly tired. "I suppose we should rebury this."

Brooks looked relieved. "Would you mind? Percy is a dastardly man and will do what he can to cut me out of the will."

"Of course," Sophia said, realizing that Brooks was her last suspect. She had failed Max once again. The realization closed her throat. She picked up the box and went to place it in the hole.

But as she did so, Max's warm hand closed over her arm. "Let me," he said. And he took the box and replaced it, then began steadily shoveling the dirt back into the hole.

Brooks meanwhile droned on and on about his troubles and the quirks of the new parrot and how it had fallen in love with Lady Neeley's companion, and how it now refused to eat tea crackers, though the old bird had loved the stale things. Sophia barely listened. Sighing, she turned so that she could see the pathway and all the people riding by. She thought she caught a glimpse of her cousin, Charlotte, looking pink-cheeked and refined. Sophia brightened. Perhaps she should invite Charlotte over for dinner one night. Perhaps if she stayed very busy and kept people about her, she wouldn't think of Max quite so often and thus could break the spell he seemed able to cast over her without even the slightest effort. For some reason, the more she saw Max, the stronger that spell seemed to be, and it was beginning to frighten her just the tiniest bit.

Max put the final shovelful of dirt on the mound. "There. Good as new."

"Thank you," Brooks said. "And ah . . . do you mind not noising this around?"

"Of course." Max took Sophia's elbow and, with a final nod to Brooks, escorted her back to her carriage. Max handed the shovel to the footman and assisted Sophia into her seat, then stood beside the open window, his gaze questioning.

She couldn't begin to explain how miserable she felt. "I should go home and wash up." She splayed her hand over her skirts. "I fear I've ruined —" She meant to say "my gown." But the words stuck in her throat.

Max gave an impatient sigh. "Sophia, don't look so defeated. It doesn't matter about Lady Neeley's bracelet —"

"It matters to me. It was my one chance to prove that I am not what I once was, that I —" She stopped, suddenly realizing what she'd almost said.

"What is it, Sophia?" he asked quietly, his voice intent.

But her pride would not allow her to say the painful words. Words that left her bare, exposed, vulnerable in some way; an object of pity. Years of being alone had taught her one thing — if she wished to avoid pity, then she could not admit to weakness.

Gulping air, she steeled herself to meet his gaze evenly. "It's not about anything, Max. You seem to forget that you are not the only one bearing the Easterly name. It is my name that I am protecting."

Max's face hardened. "You still want the annulment."

The hurt inside of her pressed forward, moving her lips, forcing a brittle laugh. "Of course I still want it! It's all I've ever wanted.

And as soon as you give it to me, I'm going to begin again, living life and finding love."

White lines appeared on either side of his mouth. "I thought we were beginning anew. Starting to know one another again —"

"I want the annulment," she repeated.

To her utter disappointment, he stepped away from her carriage. "Then that is what you shall have." He nodded curtly to her, then turned on his heel and walked away.

Sophia watched him go, her heart already shedding the tears her eyes could not. With eyes painfully dry, she motioned to the coachman to take her home.

Chapter 6

It is difficult to credit, but Lady East-erly was seen in Hyde Park yesterday morning with a shovel. Stranger still, she was using the rather rustic tool to dig a hole behind a rather large bit of shrubbery on the south side of the park.

And if that weren't enough for com-ment, Lord Easterly was there as well, but he was merely laughing and directing the poor woman in her la-bors.

This Author hasn't a clue what they were looking for, or indeed, if they found it.

Lady Whistledown's Society Papers,
12 June 1816

By the next morning, Sophia found herself in even more dismal spirits. She stayed home and paced the length of her sitting room, hands clasped behind her back. She should have been thinking of the bracelet, for she was once again back at point nonplus. But instead, she was thinking of Max.

What was it about him that made her forget herself? She was torn, torn between throwing caution to the wind and the need to protect herself from more hurt. What she needed was a promise. No, not a promise — hadn't Max once promised never to leave her, only to walk away a few months later? She needed something stronger than a promise.

She hugged herself, aware of the tears that threatened. She wanted to love him the way she once had — freely, openly, without an underlying feeling of doubt and dread. But how could she? Whatever her feelings for Max, they were dangerous to her peace of mind. Being with him stripped her bare, made her vulnerable in a way she hadn't allowed herself to be since . . . well, since the first time she'd loved him.

Never again. Perhaps if she only saw him when there were people about. Of course, the Tewkesberrys' house had been filled with people and that hadn't seemed to change things. She sighed. She needed to stop thinking about Max so much. Perhaps she *should* invite her cousin Charlotte to visit this weekend. Yes, that was exactly what she would do.

Sophia had just turned toward her escritoire to pen a note when a soft knock preceded Jacobs. "My lady, Mr. Riddleton to see you."

Thomas! Good Lord, but she'd almost forgotten he was due back. She supposed it was telling that it had taken so little time to remove him from her mind. Still, it would be nice to see a friend. "Show him in."

Moments later, Jacobs escorted Thomas into the room and then closed the door.

Thomas came forward. He was tall and handsome, with thick brown hair and a sincere expression. He took her hand and pressed his lips to her fingers, a genuine smile in his eyes. "Sophia. You look lovely."

"Thank you." She pulled her hand free, slightly embarrassed by the gesture. Why couldn't she have fallen in love with a man like Thomas? Life simply was not fair. She gestured to a chair. "Won't you be seated?"

Thomas took it, watching with a complacent air as she took the chair opposite his.

"How was your visit with your mother?"

"Fine. Though it would have passed more quickly had you written more often."

"More often?" she exclaimed. "But I didn't write at all."

"My point exactly," he said in a dry voice.

She managed a smile. "I warned you that I was not a very enthusiastic correspondent."

"Yes, you did. I suppose I just thought . . ." His smile dimmed a little, his gaze became searching. "Sophia, I know that Easterly has returned."

For some reason, her cheeks heated. "Yes, he has."

"I see. I had hoped he would not have to return in person . . . but that is neither here nor there. I trust you have already talked to him about the annulment?"

Oh yes, they had "talked." They had "talked" and kissed and come darn close to doing Other Things, as well. "We haven't quite agreed on . . . things."

Thomas's brow lowered. "Perhaps I should send my solicitor around to see him, just to expedite —"

"I beg your pardon?" Sophia blinked. "Are you suggesting I cannot handle my own affairs?"

He regarded her with surprise for a moment, then suddenly relaxed, smiling a little. "I see what it is. You are overset. And it's no wonder. Your emotions are in disarray since Easterly's return, and that is only natural."

Really? She wondered what was the correct amount of emotional disarray caused by a passionate kiss while hiding in a dark closet? "I'm sorry, Thomas, but my disarray is perhaps a bit more —"

He held up a hand. "Please. In this instance, I believe I know you better than you know yourself."

Sophia's mouth opened, then closed. When

had Thomas gotten so *arrogant?* Surely he hadn't always been that way. She shifted in her seat, a little uncomfortable at how matters were turning. "Excuse me, but I am perfectly able to interpret my own feelings and thoughts. There is no reason for you to think you need to do so for me."

She had meant it as a gentle rebuke and hoped he would not take it amiss.

He chuckled. "Sophia, I believe we are beyond the point of pretending that we do not know one another far better than that. Now come, tell me all about Easterly's return. I vow, but I did not think he would come back to England himself, but I suppose my letter left him feeling —"

"*Your* letter?"

"Why, yes. I took the liberty of sending him a missive describing how his efforts on behalf of your request would be to his benefit."

Sophia could not believe what she was hearing. "You sent my husband a letter about my personal efforts —"

"Yes, well —" Thomas straightened in his seat a little. "I didn't think you'd mind."

"If you didn't think I'd mind, why didn't you ask my permission?"

His face reddened. "Now see here, Sophia, I have a stake in this too."

"You? What makes you think that?"

"What? Come now. You cannot pretend

that we have not been much in each other's company of the last several months."

"I don't pretend anything. We have become very good friends, or so I thought." She began to wonder if he spoke about her like this when he was with his friends at White's. Perhaps that was the reason so many people were whispering about the two of them. "Friends and that is all," she stated firmly.

"Sh! I will not hear another word." He smiled kindly, as if to alleviate the words of their pomposity. "I am a patient man, Sophia. I will wait until the annulment is done and Easterly leaves once again."

Max leave . . . Sophia had to swallow to unlock her throat. Surely he wouldn't. Not now that she . . . *Not now that she what?* she asked herself. But her cowardly heart did not answer.

Thomas crossed one booted foot over the other, his gaze never leaving her face. "I have heard about the incident with the bracelet. An unseemly affair, though I supposed one should not be surprised, considering everything."

That blasted bracelet. "I don't know what you heard, but I assure you the real case is much different than the rumors being bandied about."

"It is a pity that Easterly has once again allowed his reputation to be so damaged."

Sophia could not take another moment of

it. In the past, she had rather enjoyed Thomas's air of certainty. But now she found it supremely annoying. Had he changed? she wondered. Or had she?

Thomas shrugged, his broad shoulders moving easily beneath the fine cut of his coat. "It doesn't really matter if he took the bracelet or not. All the incident does is stress that the sooner he proceeds with the annulment and returns to Italy, the better it will be for you." He smiled. "For us both."

"Wait." Sophia stood. "Thomas, I'm afraid you've made an error. We are friends and no more."

His smile faltered a little. "Sophia! Don't we get along well?"

"Usually, yes."

"And don't we enjoy the same things — the theater, riding, and more?"

"Yes."

"Well then . . ." His eyes softened. "Why not? I know your heart is still tender from Max's thoughtlessness, but I can promise you this: I will never leave you."

He meant it, she could see that he did. But it didn't matter. "Thomas, I don't feel for you what I should. And I can never marry without feeling love, real love. You and I . . . we can never be more than friends."

She gave his hand a gentle squeeze, then released it. "I cannot accept anything less than what I had with Max when we first met.

I want all of that and more."

"I don't understand."

"You don't need to. I'm afraid I can no longer see you. I'm sorry, but . . . This is better for us both. Good-bye." Without waiting for more protestations, she turned on her heel and left, feeling as if a weight had been removed from her shoulders.

The next few days were a quandary of emotion. First of all, the man she'd asked to leave her, would not. Thomas called every day. He sent letters. Poems. Flowers. Even a remarkably pretty ring. Sophia returned them all with a kind, but clearly worded note.

What was worse than Thomas's refusal to heed her requests was that the man she *wanted* to visit her, made no appearance at all. It was maddening. After two days, she enlisted the help of her brother. "You must," she insisted.

John looked up from where he sprawled in the best chair in the sitting room, cracking nuts from a dish at his elbow. "No, I don't," he said bluntly. "Besides, it's a deuced stupid idea, driving over there and knocking on the door to see if he's well. He's a grown man, for heaven's sake. He'll think I've taken leave of my senses."

"But no one has seen him for days."

"He's probably painting," John said, cracking another nut. "You know how he gets when he does that."

"But what if he's hurt? Or if he fell? At least just go over there and just see —" John's frown made her sigh. After a moment, she brightened. "I know! Take him a gift of some sort. Then he won't think it is strange that you stopped by."

"A gift? You *have* gone soft in your head."

"No, no! It's the perfect excuse." Her gaze flew about the room, landing finally on a new bottle of port. She brightened and scooped up the bottle. "Take this! John, please do this. For me."

"No."

"I'll have Cook prepare lamb with mint sauce. *And* plum pudding."

John threw the last nut back into the bowl and then stood, giving her a disgusted look. "Give me that damn bottle. I swear, but you and Max are the biggest set of gudgeons I've ever met." And off he went. He returned a remarkably short time later with a very unsatisfactory report. Yes, he'd gone to Max's. And yes, John had seen the man, but only for a short time. "And let me tell you, a bottle of port was not the thing to take him. He was already properly shot in the neck, and loading his guns was not a good idea at all."

Sophia grabbed the back of the settee, her knees suddenly weak. "Shot?"

"No! Not like that." John pinched his nose

between his finger and thumb, then said in a voice of long suffering. "Sophia, Max was drunk."

"Drunk?"

"Ripped. Soaked. Bedeviled."

"But he *never* drinks!"

"Drew me up short, too," John said. He shook his head. "Better leave him alone. He'll come out when he's good and ready."

Sophia was forced to be content with that. She thought of visiting Max, but the idea of facing him in his own lodgings while he was tipsy did not seem to be a very logical thing to do. So she instead planned a huge, very busy day that would keep her mind occupied.

To her satisfaction, she found herself crawling into bed that night completely exhausted. A good sleep followed by a nice long visit from her cousin Charlotte would shake her doldrums. But though she could barely keep her eyes open, Sophia did not sleep well. Every time sleep teased her mind, an image of Max would rudely shove its way into her thoughts, where it would linger, dancing on her lids and taunting her in the most annoying manner. Sometimes it was a memory from when they'd first met and their passions had run hot. Sometimes it wasn't a memory, but a new, yet-to-happen moment, as sensual as her most fervid reminiscences.

Sophia struggled to stem the flow and tried her best to fall asleep. She grew more and more annoyed until she finally sat up, gathered her plumpest pillow, and spent a vigorous ten minutes pretending it was the entirety of her life with Max as she pounded the stuffing from it. Feathers flew, yet still she pounded until, finally exhausted, she fell back in bed.

She brushed away the down and pressed her fingers over her eyes. Heavens, they had almost made love, right there in a closet. What was wrong with her that she couldn't seem to remember that she was angry with him, that he'd all but abandoned her?

She sighed and dropped her hands from her eyes. Somehow, over the years, she'd forgotten the strength of the physical pull between herself and Max and remembered only the pain of being left behind. But there was something else she'd forgotten — how much she'd enjoyed those moments of raw passion, of damp skin and hot mouths, the feel of his bared shoulder pressed to her cheek as he thrust inside her. . . . She moaned, then kicked off the blankets. No more, her mind shouted.

Sophia took a deep breath and began counting backwards from a thousand. She might have to count all night, but she didn't care. Anything to keep from thinking about Max. It took her an hour and several counts of a thousand and more, but finally Sophia managed to drift off into a deep, dreamless sleep.

The sun rose, and with it, Sophia's eyelids. It was horrid to be awake so early, but there was nothing for it. So she climbed from bed, bathed, dressed, and made plans for the day. She'd shop. And perhaps she'd make some calls, as well. She owed Lady Sefton a visit. Surely she could stay busy until Charlotte arrived.

Hours later, Sophia returned home just in time to greet her cousin. Charlotte looked pretty as a picture in a blue visiting gown and hat with matching ribbons. Sophia barely waited until the footman had taken Charlotte's things before she swept her into a hug. "I'm so glad you could come! I am in dire need of good, logical, feminine conversation. Are you hungry yet? I ordered a light dinner to be served at seven."

"That's fine," Charlotte said. "I just had tea and couldn't eat another bite."

"Excellent. I'll have it brought to my room. I've been so looking forward to seeing you, but I must tell you that I have set a rule for this visit."

Charlotte's brows rose, and she looked at Sophia inquiringly. "A rule?"

She had really grown into a beautiful woman, Sophia decided, hugging her cousin impulsively. "Yes, a rule. We can discuss clothes, hats, gloves, hemlines, jewelry, shoes, carriages, horses, balls, food of all sorts, women we like or don't like, and which of the latest dances we most enjoy, but we are not going to say one word about men."

Charlotte appeared relieved. "I think I can do that."

"Perfect!" Sophia took Charlotte's arm. "Come and see the new gown I just purchased. It is blue with Russian trim, and it's just the loveliest thing. Oh, and I have a pale pink silk gown with delightful red rosettes that I think would be just the thing for you."

"For me? I couldn't —"

"You can and will. I purchased it on a whim last month, but it is just not for me, and I so hate to waste things." Still chatting, Sophia took Charlotte to her room to look at the gowns.

That was the beginning. They spent several delightful hours discussing fashions, what they liked and couldn't abide among the latest trends, and who among their acquaintance had the worst taste. They were both shocked when the housekeeper came to announce that supper was being brought up, as it was almost seven.

A half hour later, Sophia sighed contentedly as she poured tea into the cups, their finished plates still on the table before the fireplace. It truly was lovely not to have to talk about, wonder about, or in any way bother herself with thoughts of Max, rude, vain, foolish man that he was. Really, it was galling to think of how he'd allowed his pride to ruin their relationship. She could almost find it in herself to pity the man. She opened her mouth to say as much to Charlotte, but then she remembered their rule.

Charlotte must have caught her expression, for she paused in taking a sip of tea. "Yes?"

"Nothing. I was just — it was nothing."

Charlotte looked as if she might disagree but thought better of it. She continued to sip her tea. The silence grew. Sophia decided that not having to think about Max was doing her a world of good. Heaven knew the man had occupied far too much of her thoughts of late, especially after her battle with all the memories she'd somehow saved over the years.

It really was amazing how vivid her memories were. But only of certain things. For example, she couldn't remember the color of the flowers she'd held at the wedding or what he'd said when he'd first asked her to marry him, but if she closed her eyes, she could clearly see the burnished brown of his hair as he bent to say something to her while riding through the park. She could remember the exact curve of his lips when he grinned up at her after lifting her to sit on a rock during one of their many forays into the countryside.

Sophia sighed and opened her eyes, her gaze focusing slowly on Charlotte, who sat staring blankly into her own teacup, a rather wistful look on her face.

Sophia replaced her cup in her saucer with an audible clink. "What are you thinking about so seriously?"

Charlotte's gaze jerked to Sophia, a faint color staining her cheeks. "I was thinking of —" She bit her lip. "Nothing really. I was just daydreaming."

"Your parents are at it again, aren't they? Trying to wheedle you into marrying. I vow, I would shake my Aunt Vivian until her teeth rattle."

"Oh, she means well, but —"

"They all mean well, but that doesn't mean they are right. Perhaps I should speak with Aunt Vivian and Uncle Edward about the dangers of being wed too soon. Do they not see my sad state of affairs as a warning? That every woman should wait until she is at least twenty-five to make such a decision?"

Charlotte blinked. "Twenty-five?"

"Or older."

"Older? Than twenty-five? But that would be six years! Surely — I mean, if you met the right person, that is, if you *thought* you'd met the right person, there would be no reason to wait."

Sophia digested this. Something about Charlotte seemed . . . different. Older, somehow. "No, I don't suppose there would be any reason to wait if you'd met the right person. The problem is that there are no guarantees. I married for love, you know. Sometimes even that is not easy." It didn't seem as if that was strong enough to warn of the pain she'd suffered. "Perhaps we should suspend our rule and speak frankly about — a man, a particular man, just to give an example."

"No names, though. You know how my mother hates me gossiping."

Sophia instantly felt sorry for her young cousin. The poor girl was tethered in words as well as action. It was a wonder Charlotte hadn't exploded into a welter of rebellion, for Sophia was certain she would have. Still, there was much to be said in not naming names. Max would make an excellent lesson for all young women of the world, and by not having to say his name aloud, she wouldn't have to deal with that annoying little jump her heart did whenever the word rolled off her lips. No names it would be, then. "Agreed."

Charlotte grabbed Sophia's hands and smiled almost mistily. "How nice to be able to speak frankly!"

"So it is! I believe that is why men manage to dupe us poor women so often; we do not share our feelings about them in an honest and frank manner." Sophia met Charlotte's gaze with a meaningful look. "But you know what I mean when I say that *men* are prideful, difficult creatures."

"Yes, yes, they are."

"All of them," Sophia agreed. Max was the absolute worst. He wore his pride like a mantle. He was even proud that he was proud, the cur. "And stubborn men are the worst."

Charlotte nodded enthusiastically. "Especially those who refuse to listen to reason, even when they have to know you've been completely logical."

It was amazing how much Charlotte understood Max. "You are so right!"

"I also believe that some men enjoy causing disruptions simply so they can charge in to set things right again. Or think they can," Charlotte added, as if warming to the topic.

"That is certainly true." It was horrible the way Max had returned, and not to assist her by offering an annulment. No, he'd come to upset her peace. Now look at her — she couldn't even sleep without thinking of him. Why was that? she wondered. Surely it wasn't possible that she . . . that she cared for him still. That she loved him? No. It was simply a physical attraction and nothing more. "I also hate the way some men are forever trying to get us to —" She caught Charlotte's wide gaze. Sophia's cheeks heated. "I'm sorry. Perhaps —"

"No, you're right." Charlotte's cheeks glowed to match Sophia's, but she continued nonetheless. "They are always stealing kisses.

And in the most inappropriate places, too. And all you have is their word that it means anything at all."

A desolate feeling pressed against Sophia's chest, and she stood in an effort to shake off the moribund sentiment. "I'd rather have Lady Neeley's horrid parrot than any man I know."

"Or that monkey Liza Pemberley is forever carting about. I heard that it bites."

"Does it?" Sophia asked, momentarily diverted.

"I've never seen it do so, but it would be lovely if it did," Charlotte said musingly. "I can think of at least one person I'd like that monkey to bite."

Sophia looked at her younger cousin with surprise. For all her composed ways, Charlotte had far more wit than Sophia had realized. "It would be quite handy to have a trained attack monkey at one's command."

"Better than a dog, because no one would see it coming."

Very true. Why, Sophia could just imagine Max's face if, the next time he tried to seduce her, her seemingly tame monkey jumped on his shoulders and ripped off a piece of his ear.

Charlotte sighed. "I daresay the monkey doesn't even really bite. It always seemed quite a docile creature to me."

"Yes, but one never knows with monkeys. Or men."

"So I've noticed," Charlotte said, her brow lowered as if deep in thought. "I've often thought that . . . *men* . . . always seem to think they know best."

"Pride. They are swollen with it, like the Thames after a rain." It was so nice to be able to say such things about Max to someone without being taken to task for being unreasonable, or being looked at with pity.

Plink!

Sophia glanced at the window. Must be a tree branch. She turned back to Charlotte. "I also hate it when certain men refuse to admit when they are wrong. I —"

Plink! Plink!

Charlotte frowned. "Is it raining? What *is* that?"

Plink! It came again, only this time it was louder. More insistent. "That is not rain. It sounds more like a fool standing outside my window, throwing rocks."

"Ah, it must be Mr. Riddleton. He's quite infatuated with you, isn't he?"

"I don't believe he is as infatuated with me as you might think." But even as she said the words, another shower of pebbles rained against the glass.

"Goodness!" Charlotte exclaimed, frowning at the window. "He sounds a bit determined. I think he is using larger pebbles."

Sophia sighed. "Perhaps I should see what

he wants, before the window —"

Crack! Glass shards rained against the curtain and tinkled to the floor, followed by the thud of a rock. It hit the rug and rolled to Sophia's feet.

"Blast it!" Sophia snatched up the rock and made her way through the broken glass, careful not to step on any of the shimmering pieces. She reached the window, tossed back the curtains, and undid the latch. "I cannot believe Thomas —" She leaned out, then stopped, her fingers still curled around the rock.

"What is it?" Charlotte asked.

Sophia opened her mouth to say, but then couldn't seem to get the words out. Standing in the road below, another rock in his hand, stood Max. He was hatless, the wind ruffling his hair, his cravat hastily tied, his chin unshaven. She leaned out. "What in the name of Hades do you think you're doing?"

He looked strangely relieved to see her. "There you are." Then, as if he hadn't just broken one of her bedroom windows, he dropped the rock into the street and dusted his hand on his coat, wavering unsteadily as he did so.

"You are drunk."

"No, I am good and drunk." He grinned, his teeth white in his tanned face. "That's even better."

She made an exasperated noise. "You just

broke my window!"

"I noticed. Some of the glass fell this way. It's a wonder I didn't get cut."

Astonishment warred with anger. Anger won. "Look, you! I don't know who you think you are, but —"

"I'm your husband. And I came to talk to you, but that blasted butler of yours would not let me in."

"That is because it is late and I am entertaining someone."

His face hardened. "In your bedroom?"

"My cousin, Charlotte." Sophia heard Charlotte give an encouraging flounce on the bed. "Not that it's any of your business."

"It is my business. Everything about you is my business."

"Not when you come here like a ruffian and throw rocks at my windows."

He shrugged dismissively. "You really should get better quality glass."

Blast it, she did not want to hear that she had an inferior grade of glass in her windows. What she wanted to hear was . . . she frowned, aware of a hollow ache in the region of her heart. What *did* she want to hear? Soft words? Pleas of undying passion?

At one time, she'd have denied she wanted anything like that. But now, looking down at Max, thinking of how he'd spent the last few days with her, searching for that blasted bracelet, she had to admit that something had changed in that time. Something . . . important. She noted the circles under his eyes, the disarray with which he had come to her house. . . . The kernel of anger that was lodged deep in her heart loosened just the tiniest bit more. He looked so forlorn in a way, so very . . . dear, standing in the street beneath her window, his head uncovered, his eyes dark and serious. "Max," she said softly, shaking her head. "I cannot believe you."

"And I cannot believe you," he returned promptly. "Sophia, I want to apologize for my flippancy the other day." He paused, his jaw tightening. "It's difficult, coming back and —" He broke off as a man walked by, a common laborer from the looks of his clothing, craning his neck. The man's gaze widened appreciatively when he saw Sophia leaning out the window.

Max flexed his shoulders, his gaze narrowed as he faced the intruder. "What are you looking at?" he snapped.

The man paused, suddenly uncertain. "Nothin', guvnor! I was jus' walkin' —" Max took a threatening step forward, and the man threw up his hands. "But I'm gone now, see?"

"You'd better!" Max glared until the man was out of earshot before sending Sophia a burning look. "Damn it, this is no good. Tell your butler to open the bloody door."

Sophia glanced over her shoulder, but

Charlotte was no longer listening. Instead, she was lost in a brown study, her gaze fixed on the silk gown Sophia had given her, her fingers absently twirling one of the rosettes. Sophia leaned back out the window and said in a lowered tone, "Max, you know what happens when we 'talk.' It will be just like the broom closet."

He beamed affably. "I know 'zactly what happens. And that's good."

"No, it's not."

"It's not?" He blinked repeatedly, and then a smile lit his face. "You are wrong," he said as if that solved everything. "Before, I was wrong. And now, you are wrong."

"I am not wrong. No more talking for us. At least not unless there are other people present."

"It's cold out here," he said in a plaintive voice. "I should come inside."

"It is June and it is not cold. Besides, you have a coat."

"It might rain and I forgot my hat."

"Then you'd better talk quickly before you catch the ague."

He sighed in frustration. "Why must you be so stubborn?"

"I was just going to ask you the same thing."

They stood there, staring at each other for a long moment. The breeze danced across Sophia's face, cooling it even as her body heated from his intense gaze. He looked so masculine, standing there all mussed, his brown throat exposed from the loose knotting of his cravat, his eyes silver hot. He had always affected her this way, his raw masculinity tumbling her defenses and overpowering her good sense.

The truth was that she loved him. She had never stopped. But she had loved him before and trusted him with her heart, only to be dismissed for one ill-thought mistake. She would not hurt like that again. Never.

Her fingers tightened over the edge of the sill. "Max, please go. I will not talk to you today." Maybe tomorrow, or next week — whenever her traitorous body had rebuilt the walls she'd been so carefully erecting all this time. When she could talk to him without betraying herself worse than she already had.

From where he stood on the street, Max thrust his hands into his pockets and tried to get his numbed brain to think. Damn it, all he wanted to do was talk to her, *really* talk this time, though he wouldn't be averse to anything more, if it happened.

Which it would. She was right about that. Every time they talked, they ended up in a passionate embrace. Somehow, he couldn't dredge up the least regret. After all, that was a sign that there was something left to their relationship. A sign that perhaps they shouldn't quit. Not yet. "Sophia, I will speak with you, if not inside, then here."

"I am sending out one of my footmen to see you home."

Max fisted his hands. "Send him out."

"Oh! For the love of — Max, you are drunk!"

"I may be drunk, but I still know what I want. And I want you. To talk to you, I mean," he amended hastily.

Her gaze narrowed. "You are causing a scene."

"I don't care. I'll stay here all day if I have to."

"Max, no! I don't want you to —" Her gaze flickered past him, a faint smile suddenly touching her lips.

He turned to see what she was looking at, but her voice drew his attention back to the window above him. "I wish you would go away," she said. "Please?"

"No." He drew himself up. "Open the door, Sophia. Now." There, that sounded forceful, even to his numbed ears.

"What are you going to do?" she asked, a tantalizing smile on her lips — lips that had haunted Max's dreams every night for the last twelve years. "Throw another rock?"

"No. I won't throw any more rocks. Sophia, I just —"

"Good, because I doubt you could hit another window." Her gaze traveled over him in what seemed a disparaging manner. "Not today, anyway."

That stung. He drew himself upright and said in a reasonably lofty manner, "Drunk or not, I can hit every window here, and you know it."

"The lower ones, perhaps."

Her taunting voice fanned his irritation into something more. He reached down and grabbed a rock. "Move aside."

"Very well. If you're certain." And with that, she disappeared from sight.

Max looked at the window nearest hers — it was probably to her dressing room, if she had indeed been in her own chamber. Squinting at his target, he pulled back his arm and —

Rough hands grabbed his arms and hauled them behind his back. " 'Ere now! Whot ye doin', throwin' rocks at a lady's winder?"

Three men surrounded him. Max blinked at their uniforms; it was the watch. "I was just —"

"Oh, thank you, Officer!" called a cheery voice from above Max's head.

He looked up and caught Sophia's merry gaze, Charlotte peeking over her shoulder. It took just a moment for Max to realize the meaning of Sophia's sparkling gaze. "You tricked me, you —"

" 'Ere now, guvnor! Not in front o' the ladies. Come along. It's to gaol wit' ye."

"Do you know who I am?"

"I don't care who ye are. I daresay I've

locked up higher gentleman than ye." The man nodded to his companions. "Take him along now. And if he fights, nick his blinkers, the both of 'em."

Max glared up at Sophia only to catch the full impact of her wide grin, of the way the wind had loosened tendrils of her hair and blew them now across her face, of the sparkle in her eyes. In that moment, the lunacy of the situation hit him, as did something else. *B'God we are perfectly suited.* She was just as stubborn, just as cheeky, just as unconventional as he.

He wondered what would happen if they ever met toe to toe over something. Would either give? Or would they stand there, refusing to budge until they both died of malnourishment? Hadn't they, in a way, done that very thing to their own marriage?

The thought caused him to grin in return. He planted his feet so that his captors were forced to halt their tugging. "I concede my defeat," he shouted up to the window. "You have won this battle, m'dear. But not the war."

She chuckled, the sound clear in the night air. "One battle at a time, then."

"And to the victor?"

Her eyes sparkled down at him. "Everything."

His heart thudded an extra beat. "You vow it?"

She paused, the wind blowing a strand of honey-colored hair over her chin. Finally, she gave a sharp nod. "Everything." And then with that, she shut the shattered window and yanked the curtain back into place.

For the first time in weeks, hope surged through Max. Grinning foolishly, he allowed the watch to haul him off to gaol. B'God, he wasn't through yet.

Chapter 7

Both Lord Easterly and Mr. Riddleton continue to woo Lady Easterly with flowers and gifts, but one would have to think that the former enjoys a certain advantage. Despite his rakish good looks, he does, after all, share the same last name as the lady in question.

Lady Whistledown's Society Papers,
17 June 1816

"You've done some silly things before, but this takes the cake," John declared. "It's a deuced good thing Max has some address or those fools would have locked him away for good."

"Be quiet and eat your lamb."

"He is serious in his feelings. The entire foyer is full of flowers and cards and —"

"Some of those are from Riddleton."

John glared. "Those don't count."

Sophia put down her fork, the tines ringing on the edge of the plate. "John, it's not that simple. I — I want to trust Max, to believe in him again, but . . ." She paused, and he saw with alarm that tears threatened. Finally, she burst out, "I just don't know if I can!"

John's gaze fell on his plate. His throat was too tight to eat another bite. He sighed and replaced his knife and fork on the table. "I'm sorry. I've said too much."

"No, no," she said, sniffing a little. "I refuse to allow myself to care the way I once did." Her lips quivered.

"There, there," John said hurriedly. Bloody hell, he was just making things worse. Still, someone had to talk to Sophia. Someone who knew Max. "He's sent as many cards and flowers as that silly oaf Riddleton, and has come to see you every day, if you would but receive him. On top of that, he must have delivered twenty letters, and he almost haunts the foyer. What more can he do?"

"I don't know. Maybe nothing." She stood and crossed to the tea table, where she picked up a small packet. "Do you . . . do you think you could give this to Max for me? It is something that belongs to him."

"Of course." John tucked the packet into his coat pocket. He sighed. "I suppose we should go. We're to meet the Jerseys near the Grand Pavilion." Vauxhall's anniversary celebration was supposed to be quite the event, and John never missed fireworks unless forced.

"Of course," she said, visibly gathering herself. "I just need to collect my shawl. It won't take a moment."

"I'll wait on you in the foyer." He winked to reassure her and made his way down to the front hall.

A knock sounded on the door as John reached his destination. Jacobs appeared and opened the door.

It was Max. He held up a hand when Jacobs began to speak. "I know your mistress is not receiving guests. She never is when I come. But I've come to see Standwick. I saw his carriage outside, so he must be here."

Jacobs flickered a glance at John.

Max followed his gaze. "There you are! Do you have time for a glass of port?"

John glanced up the stairs. "If it's a short one. Jacobs, if m'sister comes down, tell her I'm checking on the horses."

The butler nodded primly and opened the door to the library.

Max led the way inside, waiting until the door shut before saying, "I'm deuced glad you were here."

"As am I." John hesitated, wondering how much he should say. Finally, he sighed. "I'm in your corner, you know. I have been all along."

"Yes, you have. The day I received Sophia's missive asking for the annulment, I received two other letters. One from Riddleton and one from —"

"Riddleton wrote as well? That pompous ass!" John paused, then smiled faintly. "Since I have no business meddling in Sophia's affairs either, I suppose that makes me a pompous ass, as well."

"Oh, not a pompous one," Max said, a twitch of humor relieving the strained look on his face.

"Thank you," John said with a wry grin. "I just couldn't let things continue without you knowing that since you'd gone, Sophia has been living in a sort of frozen wasteland. Alone in a way I cannot explain."

Max winced. His damnable temper. "When I left, I told myself that it was to protect her, but now . . . I am not sure that my motives were as pure as they should have been."

"Put the blame where it belongs, with Richard. It is difficult to admit that your own brother was a —" John clamped his mouth closed, lines of white to either side. "I had to do what I could to fix things. Life is passing Sophia by and she is just standing there, allowing it."

Max's chest ached. He straightened and said in a resolute tone, "But I have returned now, and whether Her Royal Loveliness knows it or not, I'm here for the rest of her life. If I have to wait a year, ten years, forever — it doesn't matter. I will never give up, never stop hoping. I can't."

"You love her."

"I always have. At first, I was angry, and then I feared that she . . ." Max sighed, raking a hand through his hair. "I feared that she didn't love me the way I wished her to."

"She did and does." John reached into his coat. "By the way, she asked me to give this to you."

Max took the packet and opened it. He knew what it was the second the paper fell off, exposing a thin booklet with gold lettering. "My uncle's diary."

"I don't think she ever meant to use it."

No, she wouldn't. That had never been Sophia's way. "She was bluffing."

John nodded thoughtfully. "She has gotten so used to bluffing that I sometimes wonder if she knows who or what she is anymore."

Max tucked the slim volume into his pocket. "Thank you, John. I have to find a way to regain her trust. And I will, no matter what it takes."

John let go of an explosive breath. "Damn, but I envy you."

"Envy me? Are you mad? I've made a mull of my life."

"So many people look for love. You not only found it, but you have the strength to win it." Outside the room came the soft murmur of Sophia's voice. John turned his head and listened a moment, and then his gaze found Max's. "I must go, but I believe you wanted something more than conversation?"

Max quirked a smile. "Am I so transparent?"

"No. I just know that you hate port. Nothing short of a scheme of some sort would have induced you to make such an offer."

Max laughed. "You are right; I need a favor. It's a rather large one. And I'm afraid it has to do with tricking your sister."

"So much the better! Tell me what you need and it's yours."

Vauxhall was crammed with people. The anniversary celebration had been lauded far and wide with the result that members of every walk of society found their way within the gated walls. Milliners and bakers strolled the lawns and pathways near dukes and duchesses. The mix was intoxicating.

Sophia sat with the Jerseys in their private box. The sky glowed above, the night air rippling across her face, cooling her, though it did little to ease her heart.

"Sophia?"

She looked up to find John standing beside her chair. He glanced at Lady Jersey, who was regaling Sophia with the latest gossip from Almack's.

John swept a bow. "Lady Jersey! I didn't

recognize you in this uncertain light." He took the older woman's hand and planted a passionate kiss on the back of it. "I vow but you look stunning in blue. You should never wear another color."

Sally raised her brows, her eyes twinkling. An inveterate flirt, she had a soft spot for young men with address. Especially handsome young earls who knew how to turn a phrase. "Fie on you, Standwick! I'm old enough to be your . . . aunt."

"Never say it," John declared, evidently scandalized. "My sister, perhaps, but never my aunt!"

Sophia had to hide a smile when Lady Jersey's delighted laughter ended with a snort. Many people did not enjoy Sally Jersey's earthiness, but Sophia was not one of them.

John caught her eye. "Soph, I'm sorry to steal you from such entertaining company, but I thought you might take a turn with me."

"Now? But the fireworks —"

"Oh, we'll be back before then."

Sophia shrugged, picking up her wineglass. "Of course. Lady Jersey, if you'll excuse me."

"Go, m'dear. I've no wish to wander the dark pathways at my age."

John took a glass of wine off a nearby tray and held out his other arm to Sophia.

Lady Jersey nodded her approval. "Off with you, my children! Standwick, I do hope you are carrying a short sword. She has so many suitors nowadays that you are likely to be challenged."

John laughed, pulling Sophia away from the Jerseys' party and down a path.

As soon as they were out of earshot, Sophia looked up at him. "Well?"

"Well what?" he asked, looking over her head, as if searching for someone.

"You would never waste a lovely walk on your sister unless something was wrong."

"Nothing is wrong. I was just restless. Besides," he gestured with his wineglass, "I would rather walk this pathway with you than anyone."

"Even Miss Moreland? She is stunning."

"Well, except for Miss Moreland, you would be my first choice." He turned down a rather dim pathway, picking up his pace.

Sophia followed along easily. They made several more turns, the night air lovely and cool. She was enjoying the quiet, sipping her wine and listening to the murmur of voices. The path became more narrow, the hedgerows taller. She glanced up at John. "You seem very conversant with these pathways."

He wagged his brows in a rakish fashion. "So I am." They turned another corner and John stopped. They had found a small alcove with a smooth, curved bench and a small fountain sporting a Grecian statue in the center. "Ah," John said. "Here we are."

"How lovely!" Sophia said.

"Yes, it is," John replied, looking around as if he'd mislaid something. "Do you know what we need? Refreshments."

"We have wine. I still have half a glass and you have a full one."

"But nothing of substance." He took her hand and seated her on the bench. "Wait here and I shall fetch something for our rumbling stomachs."

"My stomach is not rumbling."

"Well, mine is." He set his glass beside her and smiled in a beguiling fashion. "I'll be right back. And if Miss Moreland should wander in, ask her to stay, would you? I have a special, non-sister path for her to enjoy."

Before Sophia could answer, he was gone. She stared at the black opening he'd disappeared through. What was that all about?

She shook her head, leaning back on the bench and sipping her wine. It was actually quite nice to be alone. She enjoyed the silence. Well, the almost-silence. The longer she sat, the more aware she became of hushed voices. Lovers' voices, murmuring and whispering. Feeling a little uncomfortable, she stood, wondering where John could be.

The minutes ticked on and still John did not come. Sophia sipped her wine nervously. Twice she had gone to the opening of the alcove, only to stare down the dark pathways, wondering if she could find her way back to the Jerseys' pavilion. Blast it, where was John? As many drunken rogues as were wandering about in the dark, she didn't dare walk on her own.

Sophia finished her wine and picked up John's. It would serve him right if she drank all of his wine, as well. She would have a good deal to say to her brother when he returned. No doubt he had been diverted by the buffet table and had forgotten all about her. "Wretch," she said aloud.

"That isn't the greeting I was hoping for, but it will do."

The voice melted through her, hot and sudden. Sophia whirled to find Max standing in the opening, looking darkly handsome. "What are you doing here?"

He came further into the alcove, filling up the space, warming the air. "I suppose I could say that I am here to rescue you. That I knew, by some unimaginable manner, that you were in need of me."

"But that would be a lie. John told you where I was."

"More than that. He left you here, right where I asked him to."

That was bold indeed. Sophia tentatively waited to see if she was angry. She was surprised to find that she was only a little irritated, and mainly at John. She finished his wine and placed the empty glass on the bench. "This is indeed a day of surprises."

"Sophia, we must talk."

The wine made her bold. "Talk. I've had enough talk in my life."

His face darkened. "I do not lie. Nor do I break my word. Never again."

"Max, I don't —"

From down the pathway came a loud giggle, followed by a drunken admonition to shush. The voices grew closer, and Max gave a fervent curse. "It appears we are about to be invaded." He held out his arm. "We'll have to find another place."

She looked at his arm, drawn to it. After a moment's hesitation, she took it and allowed him to lead her down the path. They walked some way, turning here and there. At one point, they found themselves in a small alcove much like the one they'd just left. This time, Max came to a sudden halt, causing Sophia to run into his back. He made a soft "oof" sound, then quickly guided Sophia away. As she turned, she caught a glimpse past Max's shoulder and saw a couple in a passionate embrace. Strange, the woman had on a gown that was just like the one she had given her cousin Charlotte. Surely not —

Max turned another corner and came to yet another abrupt halt. He murmured an apology, then turned and left. Sophia hung back and caught a glimpse of Lord Roxbury embracing a slender waif of a woman. Good heavens! Was everyone at Vauxhall locked in a passionate embrace? Everyone except her? Suddenly, that seemed a very unfair thing.

On they walked, running into three more couples and two more dead ends. Max turned this way and that and before long, she began to wonder if they were lost. After several more moments, she pulled to a halt. "Max, do you know where we are?"

"Of course I do," he growled. They made another turn and found themselves facing a wall of hedgerow, another dead end.

Sophia sighed. "We will have to ask someone for directions out of this blasted maze."

His chin jutted stubbornly. "No. I can find it. I know where I am."

"You do not. We're lost. Just admit it."

"I will not admit any such thing." He took her hand and pulled her down another pathway. "I'm certain that if we keep walking, we'll find a place to talk and we can —" They were suddenly standing outside the hedgerow in a large field. People milled around, laughing and talking. "Bloody hell," Max said.

Sophia hid a laugh behind a cough. "I don't think we'll have much privacy here."

"No, we won't. We can't speak here at all. The only thing I know to do is —" He looked down at her, a question in his eyes.

She didn't know if it was Max's closeness,

the bite to the night air, the murmur of passion all around, or the sight of so many
people deeply in love, but she felt giddy, as if
she'd drunk too much wine. Perhaps she had,
though she found it hard to care. Instead,
she leaned forward, brushing against him as
she asked, "What?"

"We could go back to my lodgings."

Sophia found that she couldn't swallow.
Her heart, which had been racing since Max
had found her in the alcove, began to thump
loudly. Inside, she struggled, part of her
leaning toward him, part of her pulling away.
She clenched her hands together, forcing her
thoughts to quiet. And then, somehow, somewhere, she heard herself reply, "Yes."

The trip to his lodgings went in a blur.
When they arrived, Max helped her out of
the curricle, folding the carriage blanket he'd
tucked over her lap and handing it to his
footman. And then they were inside. Max
helped her take off her shawl. "Shall we go
to the sitting room?"

"First, I want to see your paintings."

He hesitated. "I paint in my bedchamber.
The light is better there than anywhere else
in the house."

She should leave. Really, she should. But
she wasn't going to. Every step took her another foot closer to Max. Closer to what she
wanted. And if tonight ended in nothing but
disappointment, wasn't that better than emp-

tiness? "I don't mind going to your bed-chamber. I've been there before."

He took one look at her face and quietly led her up the stairs, past the sitting room, past the large clock that stood at the head of the stairs. He paused before a wide oak door and looked down at her.

The false sense of bravado held her in thrall, and she put her hand on the door-knob, opened the door, and walked in. Max followed.

It was a large room, half bedroom, half work room. One wall was almost entirely windows, curtained now, but they would let in untold light by day. Everywhere she looked, there was color. From the jewel red coverlet on the bed to the rich green of the draperies that covered the finished paintings, to the deep blue of the rug beneath her feet, the entire room swirled with texture and light. "I can see why you paint in here."

"You should see it when the afternoon sun comes in the windows." He quietly began lighting the lanterns that sat here and there. Sophia walked slowly around the room, running her fingers over the silk counterpane on the bed, along the smooth marble top of a large table holding an assortment of new brushes, and across the rough surface of a bare canvas.

By the window sat a painting of a summer field awash in afternoon sun. It loomed over the room, filling it with soft colors and a sort of diaphanous light. "That's beautiful," Sophia said. "Your work is different. Deeper."

"No one stays the same." His gaze caught hers, a silent question in their depths. "That is one of life's gifts."

She didn't know what to say, so she turned to examine the other paintings. They were all covered with draperies, not an inch of painted canvas showing.

Sophia reached for the edge of a drapery to lift it.

His hand closed over her wrist. "No."

"Why not?" she asked, looking up, directly into his eyes.

"They aren't finished."

She gently disengaged her wrist, rubbing where his fingers had been. She walked to first one draped painting, and then the next. "I've never seen you work on so many paintings at the same time."

He shrugged, his gaze never leaving her. "Some paintings are never finished. There is always a little more texture to add, a little more depth, a shadow here, a touch of light there. Those are the paintings that have their own life."

"I want to see them."

"Some day. Perhaps."

A soft knock sounded on the door and a servant brought in a tray. A bottle of wine with two sparkling glasses sat to one side. A plate of cakes were placed beside a small dish of raspberries and crème. The servant set the tray on the table, moving the paint brushes aside, then bowed and left.

Max waited for the door to close before he poured the wine. "Shall we?"

Though she knew he was talking about the wine, her mind went elsewhere. She wanted to touch him, to draw him closer. She wanted him to assure her, to make her heart believe all the things her head wouldn't allow. She wanted the impossible. Sophia took the wineglass and sipped.

He poured himself one, watching her all the while. "I think you've had enough wine this evening."

"And perhaps I haven't had near enough," she retorted, meeting his gaze over the rim of her glass.

It was then that it happened. A moment when his mind and hers fell together, touched. A moment of translucent thought. She knew then he wanted her. That he ached with it just as she did. She could feel the tightness of his chest, the way his heart thundered. She could even taste his uncertainty, his fear that she would, at any moment, turn and leave.

But she wasn't leaving. Not yet, anyway. Without looking away, she set down the wineglass. Then she reached up and slowly pulled the pins from her hair. Each move took her closer. Closer to his touch. Closer to him.

He watched, his eyes darkening until they were the deep gray of a stormy sea. As the last pin came out, her hair tumbled to her shoulders.

Max sucked in his breath. "Sophia."

It was a question. In answer, she stood and slowly pushed her gown from her shoulders. It fell to the floor and pooled at her feet, a puddle of pink silk and white lace.

Max's gaze devoured her, touching without touching, caressing every curve, every shadow. He reached over to slide his finger down her chemise ribbon. "May I?" he asked, his voice husky with the same fire that burned inside her.

She nodded and he slowly, ever so slowly, pulled the ribbon free. Her chemise loosened and he dropped the ribbon to push the thin material off her shoulder, past her breasts, down to her hips and on to the floor. He moved quietly, stopping every time a new portion of her skin was revealed. Yet still he didn't touch her.

Sophia thought she would explode with need. Her entire body yearned for him. Her breasts peaked, her stomach quivered, and her thighs grew damp. He moved closer, standing with but an inch between them. An inch of thick heated air that washed across her like a summer wind. "Lay down," he whispered.

Her breath faltering, Sophia found the bed and lay across the silk red coverlet.

Max stood looking down at her, his eyes flowing silver, his black hair touched with gold by the lamplight. "I have dreamed of this day for so long that I —" He stopped and turned back to the table. He reached down and picked up a brush. Sophia watched, shifting restlessly on the coverlet. The brush tip was thick, the end heavy with silky bristles. Max took the bowl of raspberries and crème and brought them to the bed. He slid to his knees and dipped the tip of the brush into the crème.

Sophia's breath suspended as she watched Max hold the brush over her left breast. His gaze met hers, a languorous heat simmering in the depths of his eyes.

With exquisite slowness, he lowered the thick silky brush and traced a line over her breast, circling the areola with a cold, creamy stroke. Her nipple beaded instantly, her breath catching in her throat as her body quivered, awash in contrast of heated lust and chilled crème.

He looked at the perfectly coated nipple and then bent and fastened his mouth over the peak. The heat of his tongue was almost more than Sophia could handle. She arched with pleasure, a deep moan ripping from her throat.

Max intensified his ministrations, laving her

nipple with his warm tongue. Just as she thought she could stand no more, he stopped and dipped the brush back into the crème. This time, he drew a line between her breasts, down her stomach, ending where her hair curled between her thighs. She shifted beneath the magic touch of the brush, groaning when he followed the crème trail over her stomach with his mouth. Her hands found his hair, and she slid her fingers through it.

"Beautiful," he said, kissing her stomach, her hip, her breast. "So beautiful." He dipped the brush back in the crème and this time he moved lower. She gasped as he touched the brush to the inside of one of her knees. With slow, flickering strokes, frequently augmented with more raspberry and crème, he drew a line up her thigh.

Sophia's body tensed and tightened with each tortuously exquisite stroke of the brush. He touched the brush to her upper thigh, perilously close to her womanhood. His gaze locked with hers. "I've dreamed of doing this, my love. Dreamed of seeing your eyes as they are now, shining with excitement. Of seeing your peach skin, flushed with passion." He dipped the brush in the crème once more, lifting the dripping end so that she could see. "And I've dreamed of this."

Before she could utter a word, he drew the cream-soaked brush between her thighs, across her swollen womanhood, the coolness of the liquid and the silky texture of the brushing producing an exquisite sensation. She caught her breath and arched in a heart-rending spasm of pleasure. "Max!" she gasped, so filled with wanting, with needing. He was driving her mad, mad with pleasure, mad with desire. She had to have him. "Please, Max —"

"Please, what? You want more?" He stroked her again, only this time, he allowed the soft tip of the brush to linger, swirling it with an expert twist of his finger and thumb.

Sophia grabbed the sheets on either side of her, her feet planted firmly, her hips lifting. "God, Max, please! I want —" Dear God, could she say it? Dared she? What if — Another expert flick of the brush forced a cry from her throat. Her whole body burned, yearned. And not for the brush but for the man. She wanted Max to fill her, to bring her to the passion that had been theirs. She met his gaze, her eyes wet with tears. "You," she whispered brokenly. "I want you."

The words were no sooner spoken than Max stood, disrobing with a quickness that spoke of his own need. Soon, he was naked, standing beside the bed. Her gaze roamed over him, admiring the breadth of his chest, the narrowness of his waist, and his muscular thighs. But it was his manhood that drew her gaze the longest. Thick and proud, it rose before her. She squirmed in anticipation. "Now."

Then he was there, surrounding her, over her, pushing her legs apart as he tasted her neck, her cheek, her lips. His hands roamed over her, cupping her breast, smoothing the crème into her skin, and then . . . he was inside her, stretching her, filling her, thrusting hotly.

Sophia's world narrowed and collapsed onto that one moment. She lifted herself to meet him, her body aching for more even as she shuddered in pleasure. The more of him she had, the more she wanted. It was exquisite torture.

Just as she thought she'd go mad with longing, passion rose and swelled, and then exploded in a powerful thrust that left her clinging to him, crying his name into the dimness of the room.

He held her tightly, waiting patiently for the passion to subside, and then he kissed her, softly at first, then with more pressure, moving inside her once again. This time, his strokes were longer, more even, his body rigid with the desire to control himself. She lifted her legs and locked them about his waist, holding him closer, tighter, whispering his name and a thousand sweet endearments that she didn't realize she knew. Her own passion began to grow, her body softening once again.

His movements grew more frantic, more

frenzied, his excitement piquing her own. Her excitement swirled to meet his, and when he arched, shouting her name, she went with him, clutching him frantically as passion stole her away once again.

Afterwards, they subsided, limp and damp from their exertions. Sophia lay perfectly still, quivers of pleasure shivering through her. How long had it been since she'd felt anything like that, she wondered dazedly. *Twelve years,* came the answer. *The night before Max left.* Through the delicate web of after-passion that encased her like a cocoon came a wave of sadness. They had so much, yet . . . could she? She closed her eyes, listening to her heart only to hear . . . nothing. Even after such exquisite passion, she was still filled with all the feelings and doubts she had before. A sudden spate of tears threatened, and she threw her arm over her face as she fought for control.

Max's breath was warm on her temple. "Sophia? Are you well?"

She swallowed the lump of emotion and removed her arm, managing a faint smile. "I am stunned. Overwhelmed. Too boneless from exertion to do more than lay here like a lump and fight the desire to stand naked in your window and proclaim to the world how incredible that was."

His smile broke through, that peculiarly sweet, sexy smile that was all Max. "You, my love," he said, punctuating his words with a shiver-inducing kiss on her neck, "are hardly a lump. In bed, you are all silken skin and insatiable movement. A palette of delight, a canvas of rich color. Sophia, we belong together."

She brushed his hair from his forehead with a tentative stroke, sadness welling inside. "Making love was never our problem. Being in love was."

"We can fix that. I know we can."

Sophia closed her eyes. Fix their marriage? Like a broken wheel on a carriage? Or a torn flounce on one of her gowns? No, she didn't think so. They could talk away their anger and bitterness and perhaps learn to accept each other's faults. But fix her heart? That, she feared, would never mend. Even here, even now, the taste of sadness held her back, separated her from him.

He sighed, drawing her head to his shoulder. "Rest, Sophia. We will talk when you aren't so tired."

She was too sleepy to argue, the wine she'd drunk seeping through her veins, her emotions too raw and too near the surface. Tomorrow, she'd think about the painful things. But not now. She snuggled down deeper into the sheets, her cheek pressed to his chest. He stroked her hair, his warmth lulling her to a dreamless sleep.

Max lay for a long time, savoring the feel

of Sophia against him. She moved in her sleep, settling even more cozily, her hip against his hip. It was so natural, having her with him. Like blinking his eyes. Or breathing. He did it without thinking, but if he ever stopped, his entire world would fall apart.

He tightened his grip, resting his chin on her silken curls. "Never again," he murmured into her hair. "This, my love, is forever. I will find a way back into that heart of yours. Wait and see if I don't." The words comforted him, and it was with a satisfied smile that he finally fell into a deep, deep sleep.

Chapter 8

In the matter of Lord Easterly vs. Mr. Riddleton (on the question of Lady Easterly), it appears that the victory must go to the viscount.

The Easterlys disappeared quite suddenly at last night's reenactment, and no one has seen hide nor hair of them since.

Lady Whistledown's Society Papers, 19 June 1816

Sophia awoke slowly, a delicious warmth spreading throughout her body. Max lay beside her, his naked leg thrown over hers. She smiled against the pillow and closed her eyes, savoring the feel of that masculine leg, enjoying the sound of his deep, even breathing. His scent lingered on the sheets and she breathed deeply, capturing every essence of the moment.

How she'd missed this, waking to something other than an empty room. She snuggled deeper into the bed, wiggling a little as she did so. Though still asleep, Max shifted immediately, removing his leg only to draw her into his arms. Sophia held still, her back pressed to his warm body. She felt so . . . loved.

She caught her breath. That was exactly what she felt — loved. Cherished, even. But she had felt this before, only to lose it all in a single moment, ripped away as if it had meant nothing. Sophia took a slow breath, then, moving very carefully, she freed herself from Max's embrace. She slid to the edge of the bed and climbed out, careful not to awaken him.

Max frowned in his sleep, then rolled over, gathering the pillow as if to replace her. Sophia looked down at his profile, outlined so sweetly against the crisp linens. His jaw was already stubbled with morning growth, his thick black lashes making crescents over the hard angle of his cheeks. He was so beautiful, sleeping the sleep of the content. Her heart warmed at the sight. What was it about him that affected her so? With a bitter-sweet rush of feeling, she wished with all her heart that things had been different, that *they* had been different.

But that was wasted thinking, wasted time. They were what they were and that was not going to change. Sophia gathered her clothes, then washed at the small stand beside the bed. She had just fastened her gown when she spied her hair ribbon lying on the floor beside one of Max's paintings.

She bent to retrieve the ribbon, when the bottom edge of the painting caught her eye. The drapery covered the entire picture except this one small corner. It was of a woman's slipper, a delicately turned ankle rising from a silk shoe.

Sophia's hand froze over the ribbon, her gaze locked on the edge of the painting. Max never painted people. She used to tease him to put a person in one of his paintings — a wood nymph or a knight in shining armor — but he'd always laughed and said he hadn't the talent. Yet at some time, he had apparently found the talent. And a willing model by the look of it, she thought with a touch of sudden resentment.

Who was the woman who had so inspired Max to stretch his talent? Some lurid, red-lipped Italian countess? A laughing French beauty with black eyes and white skin?

Whoever it was, Sophia didn't want to know. She straightened, threading the ribbon through her fingers with short, jerky movements. Actually, it wasn't that she didn't want to know, it was that she didn't care. Not even a little. Her gaze still locked on the corner of the portrait, she wondered if the woman was pretty? Young?

Of course she was, Sophia told herself angrily. As if Max would settle for anything less than the most beautiful of women. She slapped the ribbon into her hair, yanking it into a semblance of a bow, and then jammed her feet into her own slippers.

Yet even as she did so, her gaze was drawn back to the covered portrait. Her mind raced furiously. Blast it, who was it? She glanced at the bed. Max lay sleeping. She suddenly wished he was awake to answer her questions, explain his actions.

Yes, she wanted him awake. But . . . her gaze flickered to the draped portrait. If he woke up, then she'd have to ask him to show her the portraits and he might say no.

What a quandary. She turned to the bed and eyed Max's sleeping form with a speculative gaze. She should at least attempt to wake him up.

She sniffed loudly, but he didn't move. Well. That didn't work. She cleared her throat softly, then said, "Max." She didn't raise her voice, or strain the word. She merely spoke it.

He didn't move at all, and Sophia breathed a silent sigh of relief. At least she could say she'd tried. Of course, he'd accuse her of whispering or some such nonsense. But she hadn't. Not at all. In fact . . . she pursed her lips. She had to be fair. Had to at least honestly say she'd *tried* to wake him up.

She bent over and took off one slipper, then held it at arm's length and dropped it on the floor. The resultant bang made Max jerk in his sleep, but no more.

Satisfied, Sophia stuck her foot back in the fallen shoe. There. No matter what, she could say she'd tried to wake him but he hadn't roused. Tiptoeing eagerly, she went to the first painting and lifted the drapery a tiny bit.

The folds of the skirt of a graceful white dress filled the bottom of the canvas, each stroke of the brush drawing her eye, raising her gaze up the painting. Sophia pushed the drapery up, off the portrait, until it fell to the floor.

It was her. Max had painted a portrait of her.

Only in the portrait, she was fat. Fat!

The drapery was yanked back in place. "What are you doing?" Max's voice, gruff with sleep, made her start guiltily.

"I-I was just —"

"Looking where you had no permission to look." He crossed his arms over his bared chest, his feet wide.

She lifted her chin, mainly to keep from ogling him. It was difficult to discuss anything with Max when he was naked and rumpled. "I asked if you minded, but you didn't reply."

"I was asleep."

"I tried my best to wake you. It's not my fault you're a deep sleeper. Besides," she plopped her hands on her hips, outrage beginning to build, "what right do *you* have to paint me like that?"

He frowned. "Like what?"

"Fat. You painted me fat."

"*What?*" His brows snapped down. "I did no such thing."

"I saw it." Her gaze narrowed. "Have you been selling your paintings?"

He glanced from her to the painting. Suddenly, his eyes crinkled at the corners. "Yes. I've been selling a lot of them." He rocked back on his heels, looking irritatingly smug. "In fact, the prince just bought one last week."

The prince! Good God! "Is that your idea of vengeance? To sell fat paintings of me for all the world to see?"

His gaze slid over her, lingering on her breasts. "Oh no. If I was to declare vengeance, I'd take it in a far more personal form. Face to face, as it were."

Despite herself, she blushed. "Enough of that. Just what do you mean by painting me in such a manner?"

"You didn't see what you thought you did."

"What did I see then?"

He looked at the painting again, then shrugged. "I suppose it won't hurt if you see this portion of my work. But I must tell you that this is my own private collection. Mine and no one else's."

He lifted the covering once again. Sophia had to force herself to look at it, beginning with the face. She realized that in the portrait, she was somewhat younger than she was now, and there was a dewy look to her face, a secretly pleased sort of smile. At least he hadn't painted her without teeth, or added a few inches to her nose, or something equally galling.

Gritting her teeth, she allowed her gaze to drop lower. The woman in the portrait had fuller breasts, and a much rounder . . . Sophia stopped. Blinked. Gasped. "You — I — you made me pregnant!"

He lifted his brows. "After last night, I certainly hope that is not true."

She stamped her foot. "In the portrait! You made me pregnant."

He stepped back as if to admire the painting. "It's the way I thought you'd look if I had stayed and we'd been together. Beautiful, aren't you?" His gaze moved from the painting to her. "You have always been the most beautiful woman in the world to me, Sophia. You always will be."

Her shock melted into nothingness. How could he say such things and make them sound so rich with meaning? So true?

Her gaze went back to the painting. She'd been wrong; it wasn't a work of vengeance. It was a work of an emotion of far greater power.

Sophia cleared her throat and gestured to the other paintings. "And these? May I . . . may I look at them?"

He was silent a moment, and then he nodded. "I suppose so." He stepped back and allowed her to walk to the next portrait.

In the next one, he had painted her as he'd last seen her, at age nineteen, her eyes shining with happiness and excitement. There was something unformed about her expression, as if all she'd known was happiness, which was primarily true, she decided with a grimace.

She glanced at herself in the mirror over the mantel, comparing herself to the picture. There was a tentativeness to the Sophia in the picture, a sort of wistful wondering. But the eyes that met hers in the mirror were sure, unhesitant, her head held high.

She smiled. She liked the new Sophia better than the old, but did Max? She stole a glance at him, but his expression revealed nothing.

Shaking off a sinking feeling, she moved to the next portrait and removed the drape. She caught her breath, staring in amazement. Once again, it was of her, only this time, she was older. Not quite the age she was now, but close. She was sitting in a field of flowers, sunlight in her hair.

Tears sprang to her eyes, and she reached out and rested her fingertips on the painting.

When had he done these? And why?

She slowly dropped her hand and looked at the next portrait, reaching over and tugging the drapery free. It was fresh, this one, the paint still damp. Her own face stared back, just as it was now, only she was standing before a fireplace in a room she recognized. . . . She tilted her head to one side, noting the placement of a chair, the edge of a bird cage — she straightened suddenly. He had painted her as he'd seen her at Lady Neeley's, the first time they'd met after their separation.

Tears clogged her throat, wonder blooming in her heart. It was with hands that shook that she went around the room and uncovered all of the other portraits, tossing back drapery after drapery. . . . They were all of her. All of the ways he imagined her — sometimes sitting, sometimes standing, once leaning over a fence and trailing a strand of flowers in a still pond. In some she was younger, much as she'd been when they'd first met. In others she was her own age or older. Every picture had its own warmth, its own magic.

Its own love.

Something in her heart began to melt. Her fingers grazed the last drapery. This one was larger than the others, and something about it made her pause. With shaking hands, she pulled the drapery free and then stood in be-